THIS WIDOWED LAND

KATHLEEN O'NEAL GEAR

THIS
WIDOWED
LAND

A TOM DOHERTY ASSOCIATES BOOK

NEW YORK

THIS WIDOWED LAND

This book is printed on acid-free paper.

Designed by Beth Tondreau Design

Map by Ellisa Mitchell

A Tor Book
Published by Tom Doherty Associates, Inc.
175 Fifth Avenue
New York, N.Y. 10010

Tor® is a registered trademark of Tom Doherty Associates, Inc.

Library of Congress Cataloguing-in-Publication Data

Gear, Kathleen O'Neil.
    This widowed land / Kathleen O'Neal Gear.
        p.   cm.
    "A Tom Doherty Associates book."
    ISBN 0-312-85464-1
    1. Canada—History—To 1763 (New France)—Fiction.   2. Jesuits–
–Missions—Québec (Province)—History—Fiction.   3. Wyandot Indians–
–Fiction.   I. Title.
PS3557.E18T47   1993
813'.53—dc20   92-43654
                                                                    CIP

First edition: March 1993
Printed in the United States of America

0 9 8 7 6 5 4 3 2 1

TO KAREN, RICHARD, JENNIFER AND ADAM JONES

. . . for inviting me to Wyoming, sharing their home,
and their hearts

ACKNOWLEDGMENTS

I owe deep debts of gratitude to several scholars. Joseph P. Donnelly, S.J., and Francis Xavier Talbot, S.J., have written superb biographies of Father Jean de Brebeuf. Bruce G. Trigger's book, *The Children of Aataentsic*; Cornelius J. Jaenen's *Friend and Foe: Aspects of French-Amerindian Cultural Contact in the Sixteenth and Seventeenth Centuries*; Olive Dickason's *The Myth of the Savage and the Beginnings of French Colonialism in the Americas*; and Kenneth Morrison's *The Embattled Northeast*—each of these fine books is indispensable to the serious student of Native American history.

I owe special thanks to Ken Morrison for forcing me to study historiography when I was at U.C.L.A. and far more interested in Native American religions.

Father William Barnaby Faherty, S.J., and Nancy Merz, archivists at the Jesuit Provincial Headquarters in Saint Louis, kindly helped with research.

Any errors here are, of course, my own.

Harriet McDougal read three versions of the manuscript, written over a period of four years, and gave each version a careful and insightful critique—which I know must have been grueling, Harriet. *Thank you*.

Last, W. Michael Gear, my best friend, shared with me intense discussions about the seventeenth-century fur trade, tribal warfare and the historical impact of apocalyptical expectations. He left his own books idle to help me translate three-hundred-year-old Latin texts. I owe him more than I can tell him.

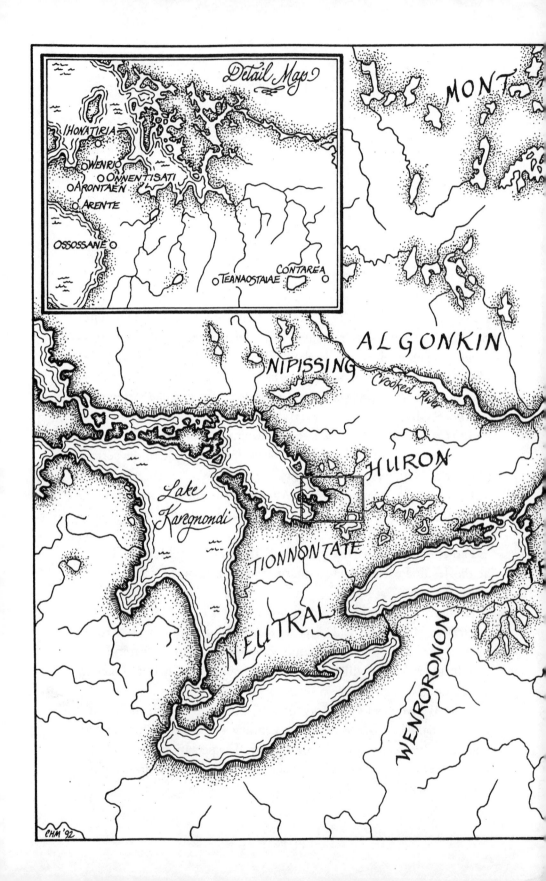

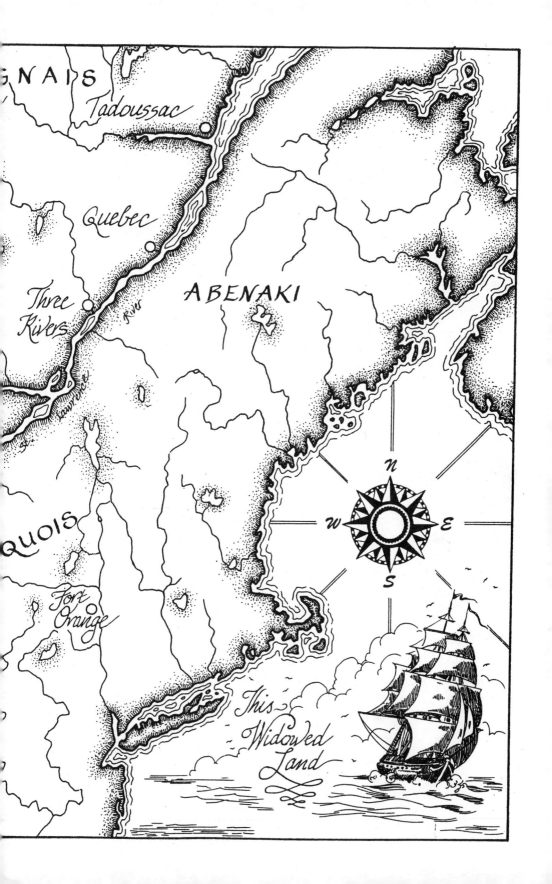

HISTORICAL PROLOGUE

O ne of the least-known elements of the Age of Discovery is its visionary passion. Christopher Columbus, and the missionaries who flooded to the Americas behind him, believed that the discovery of the New World signaled the imminent End of the World.

It was widely held during the sixteenth and seventeenth centuries that the ten Lost Tribes of Israel, who had vanished after their exile in Assyria, had found a way back to Eden. But the seventh chapter of Revelation proclaimed that they would reappear on Judgment Day. Catholic eschatological views, heavily influenced by the prophecies of the Calabrian abbot, Joachim of Fiore, expected that the Jews would be converted as the End of the World neared. Joachim prophesied that history would be divided into three ages. He predicted that during the last age, the Third Age of the Holy Spirit, human beings would have angelic natures—that they would be as innocent as Man before the Fall.

The first reports sent back by Columbus seemed to fulfill these prophecies. Columbus identified the Orinoco River, in South America, with one of the four rivers flowing out of the Garden of Eden. He wrote of the natives, "They are the best people in the world, and beyond all the mildest . . . these people have no spears or darts . . . they are as naked as the day their mothers gave them birth . . . it is impossible to believe that anyone has seen a people with such kind hearts and so ready to give."

The news electrified Europeans. For if Columbus had found Eden, and people as pure and innocent as Adam and Eve before the Fall, he might have discovered the fabled Lost Tribes.

Joachim of Fiore had prophesied that a new order of monks would ring in the Third Age by preaching the gospel "throughout the world." The Jesuits, Franciscans and Augustinian friars each claimed the honor. They flocked to the New World, willingly braving death in pursuit of the millennial kingdom.

Geronimo De Mendieta, O.F.M., wrote in 1554, "Who knows whether we are not so close to the end of the world that the conversion of the Indians is fulfilling the prophecies for which we pray that the Jews may be converted in our time? Because if the Indians descend from the Jews, then the prophecy is fulfilled."

Father Paul Lejeune, Jesuit Superior in Quebec in 1635, said: ". . . it seems as if God shed the dew of his grace much more abundantly upon this New France than upon the old, and that the internal consolations and Divine infusions are much stronger here, and hearts more on fire. The Lord knoweth who are his."

That was the hope and the source of these missionaries' extraordinary perseverance and patience. They sincerely believed that they were laboring in the "eleventh hour," and that if they could convert the native tribes, they would found the New Israel, trigger the return of Christ . . . and bring about the End of the World.

CHAPTER

I

Our hope is in God and Our Lord Jesus Christ who shed His blood
for the salvation of the Hurons as well as for the rest of the world.
It is through His support, and not our own efforts, that we hope
one day to see here a flourishing of Christianity. . . . All we have to
fear is our own sins and imperfections, and I more than all. Indeed,
I judge myself most unworthy of this employment. Send to us
those who are saintly . . .

> *Very humble and obedient servant in Our Lord,*
> JEAN DE BREBEUF, S.J.

The last crimson rays of sunset slanted through the *Soleil*'s
rigging and threw a bronze spiderweb across the weathered
deck at Marc Dupre's feet. He studied the design as he
walked toward the railing. His mind roiled with excitement, worry,
and the bittersweet sense that he was saying farewell to home and
country. He'd left his two charges, Father Luc Penchant and Brother
Phillipe Raimont, to finish unpacking while he came up to watch the
final preparations before they set sail. He wanted to remember each
detail of his journey to the New World, to tuck these scenes into the
corners of his soul, where he kept all precious memories.

High above him, the radiant light burned a golden halo around the
furled sails and gleamed off the polished hardwood spars. A grand,
three-masted sailing vessel, the *Soleil* rocked gently, creaking with the
motion of the water. Sailors rushed by Marc, cursing, calling
commands while they cast off the lines that tethered the *Soleil* to the
water-worn quay of Dieppe. The musky sea breeze brought exotic

aromas of saffron, cinnamon and cloves drifting from the white stone walls of the quayside warehouses.

Marc stopped for a moment. In the distance, the waning July sunlight shimmered on the green, rolling hills of France and flashed from the wings of a nightingale that dove over the city. His eyes tightened with longing. A tall man of twenty-six, he had blond hair and deep-set blue eyes that always seemed a little wistful. His straight nose and full lips were framed by a beard and mustache.

I'll never leave you. . . . The words echoed around in his mind, sounding more forlorn than the day he'd spoken them. Images of Marie's face rose. Crystal clear. As though they had been carved into the bones of his soul. She smiled at him, her eyes twinkling. Marc bowed his head and absently listened to the lapping of the waves against the barnacled hull. He had never been more than a few miles from her grave. How would he feel when this ship sailed out into the vast ocean? *This is something I must do, Marie. Forgive me. . . .*

When he reached the railing, he braced his hands on the moist wood. Cabbage leaves, bottles, bits of moldy bread, and other refuse bobbed in the current below—denizens of harbors everywhere.

"Ho! Marleaux!" a man dressed in tattered brown livery shouted as he stamped down the deck. Greasy straggles of dark hair draped his bearded face. "Get that rigging stowed or Mongrave'll be heaving you overboard!"

"*Sacré*, Jameson!" a lanky and sun-blackened sailor responded as he tackled a pile of cordage. "René said he'd be doing—"

"I'll not hear any excuses. Just do it!" Jameson pointed a stern finger and swaggered off, shouting at others.

Men hustled to obey, climbing up the shrouds to balance precariously on the yards, rushing to ready the sails. Voices rose and fell as rowboats moved into position to tow the *Soleil* out to sea.

The crew intrigued Marc. A curious blend of French, Dutch, Irish, and Englishmen, they mixed phrases from each language as though unaware that a difference existed. And they seemed to have developed an extensive profane vocabulary all their own. The Jesuit provincial, Etienne Binet, made a point of selecting men for the New World who had a talent for languages—Marc spoke four, including a few words of Huron—but certainly Binet had not expected this sort of training ground.

On shore, men watched as the *Soleil* was towed out of the inner basin of Dieppe, past the long jetties and breakwaters, beginning its two-month voyage. A stooped old woman who had been fishing in one of the shallow inlets waved. Marc hastily lifted a hand in return.

A man with a booming voice stood up in the crow's nest and sang a bawdy song that compared the swells of the ocean to a woman's breasts. Raucous laughter sounded. A little man standing atop the forecastle, which the sailors called the foc'sle, broke into a happy jig.

The rowboats hauled them out into the depths and cast loose. Sailors shouted crude farewells as the small craft edged out of the way and headed back to shore. Marc's gaze caressed the coastline. It rose like a blue-green fortress wall. Faint sounds carried from Dieppe: A horse whinnied, a lonesome bell tolled the hour, a blacksmith's hammer clanged.

As the sailors hoisted the sails, the *Soleil* took hold of the wind and proudly rode out on the retreating tide. Marc sank against the railing, unable to pull his eyes away from the land. He didn't know how long he stood there, lost in memories of a country he would never see again, but eventually France blurred and became a pale blue apparition that haunted the horizon. When home finally faded to nothingness, he awoke from his reverie to find that night had draped the sea. Constellations gleamed dimly in the indigo sky. The crew had lit and hung lanterns around the deck. *Oh, Marie . . . .*

A hollow thudding of boots approached from Marc's right. He turned. Against the golden background of swaying lanterns, a huge man stood. Marc guessed his age to be about forty. Black hair whipped around his shoulders to tangle in his bushy beard. He wore a plain white blouse, loosely laced at the throat, and black pants that were tucked into the tops of his knee-high boots. His bent nose appeared to have weathered one too many brawls.

"Good God Almighty," the man said in English, casually taking God's name in vain. "Ease me mind, will you? Tell me you're not Father Marc Dupre."

"Sorry." Marc straightened, shifting his mind from French to English. "I am."

"But you're so young! Too young to be leading a group of holier-than-thous into the wilderness of New France."

"Excuse me. Do I know you, sir?"

The man propped his hands on his hips and squinted one eye. "I'm Pierre Mongrave, owner and master of this vessel. . . . Perhaps I should have said the *empty-headed* owner of this vessel. Only a man lacking wits would agree to transport Jesuits. Once you get to New France, you'll see what I'm speaking of. I've been trying to figure out what sort of shenanigans I'll be put to if Pryor, the commandant of Quebec, won't let you set foot in the New World."

"Why wouldn't he? We were authorized to come by the viceroy, by Monsieur Samuel de Champlain and the directors—"

"Aye, but Pryor'll be considering such facts trifling irritations when the subject is *Catholics*. He's a Huguenot, in case you don't know. From La Rochelle." Mongrave uttered the words like a challenge to a duel.

"Is he?" Marc held Mongrave's fierce gaze. "Then I can understand his hatred. I was at the siege of La Rochelle, Monsieur."

La Rochelle had been a great victory for political and Catholic officials. It had taken fourteen months for Richelieu, King Louis XIII's brilliant chief minister, to overwhelm the population of the Protestant stronghold. He had done it by constructing a great jetty to seal off La Rochelle's harbor from the sea. Hundreds of "heretics" had been trapped and slaughtered in the streets. Scenes of the battle struggled to rise up from the burial ground in Marc's soul. He forced them away.

Mongrave looked Marc over from head to toe as though reluctantly reassessing his original opinion. "Before or after you took these robes? Whose side were you fighting on?"

"Mine."

Mongrave lifted his brows. "Since you didn't wed yourself to the papist pigs, I take it that you've not always been a Catholic?"

"No. I'm a convert."

"Well, if La Rochelle could turn you Catholic, you sure were not much of a Protestant. I'd—"

"I assume you're a Calvinist, Monsieur, since you seem to share Commandant Pryor's sentiments about Catholicism," Marc said, wondering at the man's open hostility. When he'd been in Paris, he'd been briefed on the history of the Soleil New World Trading Company and Monsieur Mongrave—a colorful character, to say the least. The trader had been run out of half a dozen countries for ethical misconduct, delivering tainted goods, cheating clients, but he apparently kept quiet on all political and religious issues, and guaranteed the safety of those he chose to transport. In these dangerous times, such a guarantee was rare, and the reason he continued to have paying passengers aboard. "Monsieur, if you hate Catholics so much, why did you agree to take us to New France and then on to the Huron village where Father Brebeuf is preaching?"

Mongrave's white teeth glinted suddenly. "I'd be selling me own soul if the devil offered as pretty a sum as you Jesuits did. But let's get an understanding here at the start. I've business to tend in Three Rivers. I'll not be taking you the entire way. A friend of mine, Huron and *a woman*," he whispered insidiously, as if it should bother Marc, "will escort you. You'll be spending time with a tame family of Montagnais Indians. I'll be rejoining you a few days before you strike the crossroads that lead to Brebeuf's village."

The ocean had grown rougher. The *Soleil* soared up on dark, glassy crests before plunging down into foamy valleys. Marc clutched the railing and bent his knees. "That will be fine, Monsieur."

"Aye, of course it will, cause that's the way 'tis going to be."

Marc cocked his head, curious. "Monsieur, do you hate all priests, or just Jesuits?"

"At this particular moment?" Mongrave appeared to be pondering the question. "I'm of a mind to hate just the Jesuits. But if you'd asked me a few years ago, I'd have cited the Recollets. 'Tis not priests, so much, you understand. I hate any high-handed evangelist heading to the New World to spout Jesus-this and Jesus-that."

"We are warriors in our Lord's battle for the salvation of souls, Monsieur. The End of the World is rapidly approaching. The seventh chapter of the Book of Revelation says that in the last days, the lost tribes of Israel will reappear. When Christopher Columbus discovered the New World and found—"

"Oh, Lord." Mongrave massaged his forehead. "You're not thinking that the Indians of the New World are the lost tribes, are you? That's pure hogwash, Dupre. The Jews have a written language, the

Indians don't. Circumcision is unknown in the New World. The Indians—"

"The Indians may have lost all memory of their Jewish origins, Monsieur, but that doesn't mean they aren't the lost tribes."

The finest scholars in Europe had proven that ten of the twelve tribes of Israel had not returned from their exile in Assyria. God had promised them much affliction as punishment for their sins, and it was widely held that IV Kings 17:6 meant that the tribes had been driven into Asia, and from there crossed a "bridge" that led into the New World. Catholicism was still largely divided over whether or not the Indians were in fact the lost tribes, but few doubted that if they were, and could be converted, it would bring about the End of the World.

Marc said, "Chapter sixteen of the Book of Mark directs us to 'go out all over the world and preach the gospel to all creation.' The Jews will be the last to be converted, Monsieur. But when that's accomplished, Judgment Day will come."

"Well, you'll be waiting a mighty long time, Dupre, because you won't convert the Indians. The Huron don't care in the slightest for your brand of salvation. They've got their own religion, which serves them plenty well. They hold themselves to be the children of a goddess named Aataentsic." Mongrave grinned. "I bet you'll be taking a shine to her. She's the spitting image of your Old Testament God—kills men and brings them disease."

Annoyed, Marc said, "No man can enter the Kingdom of Heaven unless he is cleansed by the blood of the Lamb, Mongrave. I can see that you're hell-bent, but please don't deny the savages their chance for salvation."

Mongrave's eyes widened in mock amazement. "Well, what have we here? You're a different sort, aren't you, Father? Blunt at least." The trader caressed his beard thoughtfully. Behind him, spray glimmered from the decks like a wintry sheet of ice. "Tell me something. How is it you've lasted so long in a wallow of men who wouldn't say boo to a rock?"

"I don't think you know Jesuits very well, Monsieur. My fellows and I are certainly much—"

"No, you are not alike, Dupre. And if you don't know it yet, I'm sorry for you. Getting back to the Huron. 'Tis a foul weight on them to be thinking of your notion of heaven. They dream of going to the Village of Souls, where there's good hunting, playing, and *fornicating* to a man's content."

"I studied the Huron at the College of Rouen, Monsieur. I know some of what they believe. Father Brebeuf's reports have taught us much about—"

"*Brebeuf*!" Mongrave uttered the name like a profanity. "God save us. Well, if you've taken to believing Jean's reports like the gospel itself, you're sure to be getting killed the first year. Which"—he nodded approvingly—"all considered, would be a fine thing."

"Do you know Father Brebeuf?"

"Aye."

"You don't like him?"

Mongrave lounged back against the railing, and black hair danced wildly around his face. "You did not hear me say I wasn't fond of the rogue. 'Tis just a fact that Brebeuf is a scourge in New France, and what he's doing to the Huron and Montagnais should be a hanging offense."

"And just what is he doing?"

"Christianizing them! And that's the same as killing their souls. But one of your ilk would not grasp what I'm saying."

Marc folded his arms abruptly. "No, I wouldn't. Father Brebeuf is the reason I'm on your ship, Monsieur. He called for help to save the souls in the New World, and since he is a very great and holy man—"

"Oh, is he now?" Mongrave chuckled. "Well, you're in for a good sight more than you know, Dupre. About Jean, I mean."

Marc shifted uncomfortably, offended, wondering just what that meant. The silence stretched. The wood beneath Marc's boots groaned and creaked. The shrouds twanged in the rising wind. The scents of wet hemp, tar and turpentine competed with the salty flavor that clung at the back of his throat.

Mongrave shook his head and sighed as he gazed up at the few stars that frosted the heavens. "The reason I came out here, Dupre, was not to talk theology, but to speak to you about one of your charges—the little fat one. He's been driving me to distraction."

Marc turned suddenly. "Brother Phillipe Raimont?"

"Aye, that's the one. Me crew wasted half the afternoon chasing him away from the galley. He's been robbing from the hardtack to feed the birds that scavenge 'round the ship. I watched him all day, giggling to himself like one of the mindless, tossing bits of bread into the air and watching the gulls dive for them."

"He's just a simple soul, Monsieur. He loves animals and everything and everyone. I'll talk to him. I'm sure he didn't mean to take the hardtack."

"I'd not argue about that, Dupre. Raimont doesn't seem to have enough of a mind to know what he's doing from one instant to the next. I'll never understand the way the Catholics think. Why would the Jesuit provincial be selecting a man such as him for a mission to the New World? Etienne Binet must know the horrors and privations of the wilderness. I'd be much surprised if Brebeuf hadn't been moaning on it for years."

A crescent moon had edged over the waves. It cast a gleaming silver shawl across the water. Marc felt anxious and uneasy over discussing Phillipe with a man like Mongrave. Phillipe was *special*. The records in Marc's baggage detailed the times that Phillipe had been graced with *stigmata*, and his hands and side still bore healing scars from a recent episode. How could anyone be so pure and sinless that God would grant him the wounds of Christ?

"Monsieur Mongrave, I assure you, Brother Raimont is suitable for ministering to the savages of the New World. Please, let me worry about my brothers. Is there anything else I can—"

"Let me be giving you a bit of advice, then." Mongrave leaned forward threateningly, and his black eyes glinted. "That arrogant fool, Penchant, is annoying enough, but me crew will be viewing Raimont as a target. They'll take out every frustration over the work or the weather, or any other trifle, on him. You'd be doing yourself a favor if you kept Raimont away from me men."

"I'll try."

"Good. I'll be holding you to that." Mongrave turned and swaggered off down the moonlit deck. When he reached the mainmast, he cupped a hand to his mouth and yelled, "Ho! Georges! Are you sleeping up there?"

A distant voice responded from the crow's nest, "Aye, sure, and with the loveliest mermaid you've ever laid eyes on."

Mongrave laughed and trotted up the stairs that led to the cabins, his boots thudding audibly long after he'd vanished.

Marc walked along toward the taffrail, thinking. They had been on the ship for only one day and already problems had begun to mount: Mongrave hated Catholics; Phillipe was stealing hardtack; and when they reached the New World, Pryor might stop them from entering New France. He'd not expected something so bold from the Protestant officials. What could he say to persuade the commandant to allow three Catholics to enter? What if nothing he said persuaded the man? Would Pryor simply order them back to France? A knot of anxiety formed in Marc's belly. Father Brebeuf was expecting them. He needed them. They couldn't just turn around and go home.

Marc passed the mizzenmast, where a huddle of men stood around a swinging lamp. They talked about the joy of being at sea again, about wonders seen and dreamed. One old man wearing a tweed cap pulled tight over his ears sat with his back against a crate. He worked at splicing rope while he spoke of ghost ships that still sailed the seas engulfed in flames, their yards swarming with screaming crew who could never escape. He warned about the golden-skinned serpents that would rise out of stormy water and swallow a ship whole, or coil around the masts and drag the vessel to the bottom of the ocean to keep as a treasure trove.

Marc silently slipped by them and headed for the steps that led above-deck to the two levels of cabins. On top of the cabins sat the wheel, exposed to the night and weather. When Marc opened the door to the hall, light struck his eyes. A single lamp hung from the ceiling, casting a muddy yellow glow in the narrow corridor. Cabin doors lined both walls. He made his way toward the last door, listening to the yards groan their grievances at the yanking sails.

When he reached his cabin, he quietly lifted the latch and eased the door open to peer inside. The small room held three cots and a tiny writing table. Moonlight was streaming through the porthole. Marc started to step into the cabin but stopped, frowning, when he saw Luc Penchant. The tall, willowy man lay with his wool blanket clutched tightly around his throat, his fearful gaze riveted on Phillipe.

The little Brother knelt by his own bed with his hands clasped in prayer. Phillipe's wide eyes stared unblinking at the dark ceiling while his lips moved in a barely audible song. It sounded familiar, like a child's lullaby Marc had heard as a boy.

"Luc? Is everything all right?" Marc whispered as he stepped inside and gently closed the door.

"No," Luc responded tersely. "Look at him. He's at it again. He's been singing to himself for over an hour."

"Everyone has his own way of praying."

"I've been a priest longer than you, Dupre, and I've never seen anyone pray like he does. It's not . . . natural."

"God seems to understand him. That's all that matters, isn't it?"

Luc said something under his breath and tossed to his side, turning his back to Phillipe. Marc let out a sigh. He had been with Luc and Phillipe for two weeks now, ever since they had met in Paris, and he still hadn't found anything amicable about Luc. *Time. You need more time to make these men your friends.*

Marc took off his heavy boots and began undressing. He draped his robe carefully over the foot of the bed, then slipped his white nightgown on. He said a quick prayer, pulled his blankets down and stretched out on his cot. Moonlight sheathed the cabin in liquid silver. Marc absently watched the shadows of the waves play on the walls while he thought about France, always so green at this time of year. He could still hear the beautiful songs of the nightingales. Did the New World have nightingales? Probably not. *No more nightingales. No more thatched roofs. No more glorious Masses in magnificent cathedrals.*

"Father Marc?" a soft voice called.

He shifted to look across the room. "Yes, Phillipe?"

"Don't be worried. God told me you were worried. But everything is going to be fine. God says there will be hundreds of Indians to greet us when we get to Quebec, and Monsieur Pryor won't make us go home. Don't worry."

Marc's mouth went dry. He started to ask how Phillipe knew, but hesitated. "Thank you, Phillipe . . . for telling me. Get some rest now. It's going to be a long voyage."

*　*　*

MIST ROSE FROM the shining surface of Lake Karegnondi and crept into the Huron village of Ihonatiria, where it twined through the central plaza and clung like a veil of silver moss to the fifteen bark longhouses. The houses ranged from twenty to one hundred feet in length and had high, rounded roofs, and narrow doors in the end walls. Children played outside, chasing each other or throwing sticks for their dogs. They barely looked up when Tehoren sprinted by, heading for the council house.

At the age of twenty-five winters, Tehoren was small and thin, with a pug nose. He wore his long black hair coiled at the base of his skull. Streaks of black and white paint covered his oval face: black for Aataentsic, the moon, and Mother of the People, and white for Iouskeha, the sun, and First Man. His brown tradecloth pants and shirt were decorated with bands of green and blue glass beads, a sign of the powerful shaman he had once been. People used to pay well for his abilities to cure illness and bring rain . . . but that was before the coming of the sorcerer, Jean de Brebeuf. *He's not a man. He's an evil spirit that fell from the Christians' heaven. He came to destroy the Huron.*

The Black Robe's wicked powers had already begun to put out the eyes of Tehoren's people, so that they could no longer see the truth. Last winter, twenty-eight had been converted by Brebeuf's malevolent powers. The fools! How could they abandon the generations of their families who lived in the Village of Souls to go live with Frenchmen in heaven?

And now what was this summons all about? Why was Jatoya so frantic? Tehoren ducked beneath the leather door-hanging of the council house. Copper pots and wooden bowls hung on the walls over the benches that lined each side of the house. People sat on the benches during the day and slept on them at night. Blankets lay neatly rolled beneath the rough-hewn planks. Weapons stood everywhere: tomahawks, bows and arrows, knives and war clubs. Last week the Iroquois had attacked and burned two Huron villages. The Huron men had been killed outright; the women and children had been taken for slaves. No one fell asleep these days without one hand on his weapons.

A fire gleamed at the far end of the longhouse, throwing the wavering shadows of two seated council members across the ceiling like dancing ghosts. The dwarf shaman, Tonner, poked a stick into the fire. He wore his hair in short gray braids and had a blue-and-white trade blanket wrapped around his shoulders. Beside him, Andiora sat with her knees drawn up. She looked beautiful, and worried. Black hair hung in a glossy wealth over her shoulders. Her heart-shaped face had been dyed orange by the light of the flames, but the tint didn't hide the pallor of her flesh. Was she still weak from her recent illness? He'd heard the old women whisper that Andiora had lost a great deal of blood when she'd lost her child.

"What's wrong?" Tehoren asked as he hurried toward them. "Jatoya wouldn't tell me. She said only that I should come quickly." He walked to the left around the circle, as was proper, and sat down beside Tonner.

Sparks swirled toward the smoke hole in the roof as the dwarf tossed his stick into the fire. His malformed arms looked like twisted tree limbs in the flickering light. He said, "Andiora's Spirit Helper, Cougar, brought her a Dream."

"What Dream?"

Andiora let out a long breath and looked up at Tehoren through worried eyes. "A sickness is coming, Tehoren. It will begin among the Montagnais and Neutral, then run through all of the Huron villages. I saw people dying, spitting up blood. Not even the Nipissing or Wenroronon could get away from the sickness. It left us all so weak that we could not fight when the Iroquois attacked."

"The Iroquois are coming . . . here? To Ihonatiria?" Tehoren clenched a fist. "*When?*"

"Cougar didn't tell me, but it was winter. Snow was on the trees."

Tonner pulled his blue-and-white blanket more tightly around his hunched shoulders and asked, "How did the Dream end?"

"A face and two upraised hands drifted through the forest." Andiora lifted her arms into the smoky air. "The fingers were white, very white." She extended her own fingers and put down the last two so that they almost touched her palm, but left her thumb and first two fingers extended. "He held them like this."

"Who did the face belong to? Did you know him?" Tehoren asked.

"No. He had golden hair. That's all I saw before Cougar growled and crept away into the shadows, taking the Dream with him."

"So," Tonner said. He sat still for a long time, staring at the flames, then dropped his hands to the beaded medicine bag tied around his waist. It contained the precious items—odd stones and dried flowers, strange seashells from the Village of Souls—given to him by the Spirits that wandered the forests. His mouth pressed into a tight brown line. "More sorcery," he whispered. "Are the Black Robes to blame?"

"We have no blond Black Robes in Huron territory," Tehoren pointed out.

"No," Andiora agreed. "But I'm leaving in a week's time for Quebec to bring three new priests to join Brebeuf. I promised Pierre I would go."

At the mention of Mongrave's name, Andiora's hands shook. She lowered them to her lap and tucked them into the folds of her blue dress to hide them. Tehoren looked away. Had the big trader even known that Andiora had been filled with his child when he'd left for France? *Mongrave wouldn't have cared.* The knowledge angered Tehoren. How could a man be so indifferent to the woman who loved him?

Tonner got to his feet and grimly looked down at Andiora. "Maybe you shouldn't go to Quebec. I think I'll speak to Taretande and the other leaders, call a village meeting. That way we can all discuss it and decide what to do." He hobbled toward the doorway. The flickering firelight wavered over his twisted body as he ducked outside into the fog.

A brief square of bright light flashed through the council house, and Tehoren caught the look of anguish on Andiora's face. She said, "What will I do, Tehoren, if I go to Quebec and find a blond Black Robe waiting for me?"

Tehoren pulled his iron knife from its sheath on his belt and handed it across the fire to her. The blade glinted as though molten. "Here. Keep it. You must kill him quickly. Before it's too late."

Hesitantly, she took the knife. "And if Taretande won't let me go to Quebec? What then?"

"You must go," Tehoren said. "Only you will know the blond's face. If you can kill him before he gets to our villages, perhaps we can stop the sickness. I will speak for you at the meeting."

CHAPTER

2

Marc Dupre tossed and turned in his sleep. Hours ago, his gray blanket had slipped to the floor in a heap. His dreams smelled of old battles, the tang of gunpowder and the sweet earthiness of blood. Leaving France had opened doors in his soul that he had fought for years to lock and bar. . . .

He ran down Fleur Street in La Rochelle, his musket clutched to his chest. His green homespun shirt stuck in tatters to his sweaty body. All around him, ruined buildings loomed like jagged teeth, their walls leaning precariously out over the streets. He could see the ocean glimmering darkly in the distance beyond the town's rolling hills. Naval ships dotted the water.

Marie eased up beside him, holding her pistol in both hands. Her beautiful face bore streaks of soot from their hastily made morning fire. They'd had nothing to eat, but at least they'd been warm. She had braided her long brown hair into a single plait that draped over her shoulder. Her torn flowered dress clung to the curves of her sixteen-year-old body.

"Hurry!" she whispered. "They're coming."

She darted ahead, staying to the cool shadows of the buildings, moving with catlike stealth.

He slid along behind, keeping his back to the stone wall.

Spirals of smoke still curled into the clear sky. Somewhere a baby wailed before its mother suddenly silenced the cries.

Richelieu had intensified his efforts to quell the Protestant rebellion that raged in the south of France. In 1598, Henry IV had decreed that Protestants had the right to practice their religion, except in Paris

† 26 †

and other episcopal and archepiscopal cities. Of the two hundred towns where Huguenots were free, the Protestants had garrisoned and fortified over a hundred. But when Richelieu came to power in 1624, he proclaimed that his *raison d'état*, reason of state, was the "ruin" of the Huguenots. He had started his siege of La Rochelle in 1627, and it had been holding for a year . . . a year of blood and starvation.

Marie stopped beneath a ragged yellow canopy and peered around the corner to the street beyond. When she turned back, she shook her head. "It's clear. But, Marc, let's wait. I *feel* something there."

"Let me look."

He'd edged around her, taking a moment to kiss her dirty cheek and press his body close against hers in a hug. They had met in an orphanage, and over five long years of relying on each other for everything, they had fallen in love. He'd been fifteen, she fourteen, when they'd started loving each other like a man and a woman. For a blessed year, time had held its breath, as if God had granted them a reprieve between storms. They'd talked and laughed—and loved—in the fragrant meadows beyond the orphanage. Every moment of that year was etched in Marc's memories as though frozen in amber.

Then Richelieu had attacked La Rochelle. Their orphanage had been blasted to rubble by cannon fire from the harbor, and they had been cast on the streets with only each other.

Marc lightly caressed her throat before he cocked his musket, slipped around the corner and gazed down the road. The cobblestones gleamed with a pearlescent hue in the milky light of predawn. Smashed carts and horse dung littered the way. A few bodies sprawled near the carts, drawing a glittering cloud of flies.

Marc saw nothing in the street, but Marie's uncanny ability to sense danger had saved his life more than once in the past year. He eased back around and gazed at her. Against the smoke-blackened walls, she looked frail and white, her brown eyes huge.

"Did you see anyone?" she asked.

"No, but let's go back and find another route. I'd feel better, too."

She dropped her head against his shoulder and nodded her relief. "I think we can avoid the soldiers if we go down Masse Avenue. It's so narrow and dark, they almost never chance it."

"All right, but let me go first."

Even as Marc eased in front of her, he sensed some wrongness. He took two steps, and the roar of cannon fire shredded the morning. Puffs of smoke arose from the ships in the harbor, and the ruined buildings beside Marc exploded in a spray of stone and wood. He shoved Marie as hard as he could and saw her hit the ground on her stomach and crawl frantically to get away.

The next blast sent Marc toppling backward to the road. He rolled, shielding his musket with his chest, as an avalanche of thatched roof, stone and dirt cascaded over him. He struggled to free himself, pushing with his toes while he clawed the ground with both hands. In desperation, he carefully slid his musket forward and used the stock as a shovel to scoop away the wall of dirt. Panic fired his efforts. *Marie? Are you all right? Did you get caught in this?* When light streamed down from above, he scrambled toward it. Screams, vague at first, penetrated the debris. They grew louder, more urgent, as Marc used his shoulder to heave a section of thatch out of his path.

He broke out into the pale wash of dawn scrambling to his knees. Down the street, two men in tattered uniforms were dragging Marie around the corner. Marc jerked up his musket, but they vanished before he could aim.

Marie screamed again, high, breathless. Male laughter drifted on the wind. *No, God, please. Not Marie.* Marc lurched to his feet and ran with all his might, his heart pounding sickeningly.

"*Marc!*" Marie shouted. "Marc, oh God. Help! Someone help me!" Then, "No, for the sake of God, I've done nothing!"

A rough voice responded, "You're Protestant and carrying a gun. That's enough."

A shot erupted, then another.

Marc rounded the corner and ran headlong into the two soldiers. He glimpsed Marie lying on the ground in a tumbled mass of flowered dress . . . and in that instant, all the color and wonder drained from the world. A ragged cry was torn from his throat. He leaped on the closest man, bashing him in the face with the butt of his musket, then whirled and fired at the other. The man staggered, clutching at the gaping wound in his chest before he crumpled to the road. The first soldier writhed, blindly patting the ground for his weapon, but it lay five feet away in the shadow of a former bakery. Marc dropped on the man and slammed his musket down over his throat, pressing as hard as he could. The man groped for Marc's face, then gripped the musket and tried to shove it away. Marc kept pressing until the soldier stopped struggling and his body went limp.

The sun rose over the horizon like a great crimson ball, and a gaudy wash of light reddened the streets.

Marc threw down his gun and crawled to Marie. The bullets had taken her in the stomach. Blood covered her dress. She stared up at him, her eyes drowsy with death. "Marc . . . go. More of them . . . coming."

"No, I'll never leave you."

"Go!" Feebly, she shoved his shoulder, then sank back to the ground.

"Oh, Marie . . . don't. Hold on. I'll find help." He gathered her in his arms and lifted her.

For an hour, he ran down one street and another, cutting across parks to avoid cannon fire, hiding in shadowed doorways as enemy soldiers passed. Marie's arms flopped limply, but he kept running, hunting for a refuge.

When he saw the Catholic church, he faltered, but only for an instant. He staggered up the steps and kicked the door. A man in a long black robe cracked the portal and peered out cautiously, but when he saw Marc and Marie, he flung the door wide.

"Hurry, my son. Before they see you."

"She needs help, Father. We need . . . a physician . . . she's wounded and I . . . I don't know what to do."

The priest, a tall man with dark hair and a pointed nose, quickly closed the church door and came to check Marie's wrist for a pulse. He glanced up at Marc, his eyes tight.

"I'm Father Burel. Let me take her, my son." He extended his arms.

Marc twisted away. "No, no, she needs me. I—"

"I'll be gentle with her. I promise." The priest slipped his arms beneath Marie and easily lifted her from Marc's trembling grasp. Burel's black robe flowed around him like sculpted marble when he knelt to lay Marie before the raised altar.

Marc's legs froze. The priest crossed himself and murmured a prayer. Marie lay there, her eyes wide, her mouth open. The blood on her dress had started to dry into sticky folds . . . .

MARC JERKED AWAKE, panting. For a moment, he didn't know where he was. He stared wildly at the oak walls of the cabin, at his two sleeping brothers. Moonlight streamed through the porthole, illuminating his black robe where it lay neatly over the foot of his bed. His blanket had fallen to the floor.

You're not in France. You're all right.

But his body didn't seem to hear. His trembling grew worse. He had never been away from Marie's grave for more than a few weeks at a time. Even when he'd studied philosophy and theology at the College of Rouen, he'd returned frequently . . . just to sit in the shade of the trees and talk to her.

Marc extended a hand to touch his robe. It felt cool and soft beneath his hot fingers. Until the moment of her death, the only future Marc had even imagined had been one with Marie at his side. But Father Burel taught him something else. The Jesuits had taken him in that day eight years ago at great risk to their own safety, for Richelieu hated Jesuits more than he did Huguenots. For two terrible months, Father Burel had fed, and sheltered, and *taught*. He'd kept Marc sane. They'd spent hours discussing Marie, the battle, the Book of Revelation, and the prophecies of the Calabrian Abbot, Joachim of Fiore.

Burel had been convinced that the discovery of the New World signaled that the End of the World was rapidly approaching. Joachim had divided history into three ages and said that the Third Age, the millennial Kingdom of the Apocalypse, would be inaugurated by a Supreme Teacher, the *novus dux*, who would come from Spain and found a monastic order. Ignatius of Loyola, the founder of the Jesuit Order, had been born in Spain in 1491, the very year that Columbus was preparing to undertake his New World voyage. Father Burel believed that the blessed Ignatius had indeed been Joachim's prophesied Supreme Teacher and that the Society of Jesus was destined to convert the world. Marc had been so fascinated that he'd buried himself—and his grief—in the study of Joachim of Fiore. Then he had turned to Jose de Acosta, Geronimo de Mendieta, Bernardino de Sahugun, and other missionaries who had actually seen the New World and its native inhabitants.

When the siege of La Rochelle ended, Burel had given Marc clothing and sent him on his way.

Marc began to grope on the floor for his blanket.

"Dupre?" Luc whispered. "What's the matter with you?"

"Oh, nothing, Brother. Just a bad dream. About war. I'm sorry I woke you."

"*War?*" Luc sat up in bed. In the dimness, his thin face and beaked nose appeared predatory. There was something about Luc, some eerie quality, that disturbed Marc. "What about war?"

"It's just a dream I've had before. Nothing to worry about."

"Oh, but it is, Dupre." Luc's gray eyes glowed like an owl's in the night. "I've been dreaming of war, too. I think everyone in the world is. And you know why? It's the First Horseman. *He's begun his ride!*"

Marc ran a hand through his damp blond hair. "The First Horseman of the Apocalypse? I didn't expect the signs to begin until we'd converted the Indians and established the New Jerusalem in the New World. And—"

"Oh, I think Joachim's prophecies are rubbish . . . but the End of the World has certainly begun. And we are all to be witnesses, martyrs who die for the Word of God." Luc eased back down onto his bed.

Marc sucked in a steadying breath. "Perhaps, Brother."

Something passed through the wash of moonlight beyond the porthole and cast a winged image on the wall. The shadow fluttered, as if to alight. Luc gasped and bolted to his feet, his blanket clutched to his chest. In a trembling voice, he whispered, "What is it?"

The image vanished, to be replaced by a silver sheath of moonlight.

Marc sat up and stared out the porthole. Only the vast ocean moved outside. "There's nothing there, Luc. It was probably just a gull."

"*Probably?* It might just as well have been the Holy Spirit, trying to tell us something."

"What?"

"How should I know? The ways of God are mysterious!" It was several moments before Luc crawled back into bed and covered his head with his pillow. "Good night, Dupre."

"Good night, Luc." Marc glanced for a final time out the porthole and dragged his blanket up from the floor, thinking about the twists and turns of his life.

Father Burel had sent him on his way. But he'd come back.

Marc's friends from the orphanage had laughed at him. James had taunted, "A priest? Have you lost your senses? We just fought a war! If you're going to get fervent, worship the devil. At least you've seen him face to face." Margaret had added, "You're just lost because of Marie, Marc. Stop and think about this. You're not cut of the right sackcloth for holiness."

But he'd known it was the right choice. The Order had become his family, the church his spouse. And he prayed to God it would always be so.

As the sun sank into the sea, a pink halo swelled over the western horizon. White gulls floated around the masts, squawking at each other. Below, a school of dolphins moved through the water. In the tarnished light, they seemed to leave curving trails of pale silver flame in their wake. Marc braced his elbows against the railing between Phillipe and Luc, dipped his quill in his ink bottle, and continued writing in his diary.

> *We've been at sea almost a week now, and I think I understand the awe sailors feel about the ocean. She's the ultimate enemy, capable of dashing your boat to pieces, and—at the same time—the mother who rocks you to sleep at night. Such a paradox, and so beautiful.*

Phillipe let out a cry of delight when an oddly colored dove, gray with a pale violet sheen to its feathers, fluttered down to sit on the railing about two feet away. Marc frowned. "Where in the world did a dove come from?"

"That's Roah," Phillipe said. "He's a good bird."

"Roah? You named it?"

Phillipe looked confused. "No. He told me his name." While he dug in his pocket for a piece of bread, he added, "Animals can talk, if people just listen. Sometimes I hear them calling my name and I don't even know them. But they know me. I guess God tells them people's names."

Luc grunted in disbelief and turned away, scowling at the sailors going about their duties on deck. In profile, his hooked nose was even more prominent. He had straight brown hair that lay flat against his head, accentuating the thinness of his face.

Marc eyed Roah curiously. The bird seemed to be watching him, evaluating him. "I've never seen such a bird before. Where—"

"Oh, he's from the New World," Phillipe answered excitedly. "Monsieur Tristan Marleaux told me the story. About a year ago, one of the sailors stole a handful of eggs from a dove's nest before he came on board. As a joke, he put the eggs into the gull's nest on the mainmast. Roah hatched and was raised by a gull mother. Tristan says that Roah thinks he's a gull."

Phillipe smiled, cooed to the dove and stretched out his hand, offering the crumbs in his palm. Cautiously, the bird edged forward, then lunged and gobbled them down. Phillipe giggled with childish joy. He even looked like a child. Barely five feet tall, he was pudgy and had a round, cherublike face, with large green eyes.

"Well," Luc said, deliberately changing the subject, "now that we're well on our way, tell me what you expect to find in the New World."

Luc had looked to Marc for an answer, and frowned when Phillipe piped up, "I expect to find lots of new animals. Moose and elk, and smaller things like porcupines. Father Uriah used to bring me books from the Notre Dame library. I've seen their pictures." An expression of rapture came over his face. "And the people will be good—as pure and innocent as Adam before the Fall of Man. Admiral Columbus said—"

"That was bilge!" Luc retorted. "Columbus knew nothing about the Indians. Why, he barely got off the boat! And when he did, it was only to steal gold."

Phillipe blinked as though stunned by the very idea. "I . . . I didn't know that."

"Well, now you do," Luc informed him. "You can't believe a word the man said. The Indians are filthy barbarians. Take my word for it. I've read all of Acosta's works."

Marc gave Luc a sideways glance. Jose de Acosta, Jesuit missionary and scholar, had been one of the first to minister to the Indians of the New World. Though Acosta acknowledged that mankind was living in the eleventh hour, he did not believe that the Indians were the lost tribes of Israel. Marc said, "I could be mistaken, Luc, but I believe that other scholars have disputed Acosta's conclusions. In his *Historia Eclesiastica*, Mendieta said that the Indians were of such simplicity and purity of soul that they didn't know how to sin."

Luc's mouth gaped. "Good heavens, Dupre. Mendieta was a *Franciscan*! You can't believe anything he said either."

Marc sighed. "I see," he said, and lifted his quill to write in his diary again.

> *My two charges are very different. Phillipe is odd, as Father Binet told me in Paris. He's so innocent, I feel like I'm in the presence of an angel—and someone I must protect at all costs.*
>
> *On the other hand, I'm having problems with Luc. I seem unable to have a true dialogue with him, though I've tried repeatedly. Perhaps it's our upbringing. He comes from a very wealthy family in Paris, and I from the lowest of the peasantry. Luc has only two ways of relating to others; either he bosses them, as if they were servants, or he ignores them. He refuses to discuss any personal matters, particularly his own hopes and dreams. He seems content to criticize without—*

"Oh, the Indians need Christianizing badly, I'll grant you that, Dupre," Luc was saying, "but because they're brutes, not because they're pure and innocent. Think of it! They run around naked. In squalor!"

"Squalor?" Phillipe inquired meekly. "Really?"

Marc shrugged. "I suspect that squalor is in the eyes of the beholder. You spent most of your life working in the poor districts of Paris, Phillipe. Compared to that, the New World will probably seem a garden."

"Does the New World have rats?" Phillipe grimaced.

"I'll bet they talk to you, too, don't they, Raimont?" Luc taunted, and his eyes narrowed. "When you were baptizing the sick in Paris, did they crawl right up on your lap and beg forgiveness for chewing the fingers off dying babies?"

Phillipe shook his head. "No. Mostly they asked for food. They were very hungry."

Luc slumped against the railing and massaged his temples. Phillipe blinked as though he sensed he'd done something wrong, but wasn't certain what. He looked helplessly from Marc to Luc.

Marc took the pouch from his belt and shook sand on his writing before closing his diary and stoppering his ink bottle. "I'm sure the rats were hungry, Phillipe. Everybody else was."

"What's the matter with you, Dupre?" Luc blurted. "You're always defending the ignorant and the debauched."

"I so often find myself among their ranks that it's hard not to."

Luc straightened indignantly. "Well, *give it to God*. You may not be able to overcome such failings, but He can." Luc turned and strode away down the deck, his black hem flapping in the salt-scented wind.

Marc watched him go and shook his head. Nothing pleased Luc. He saw evil in everything. Even in Phillipe . . . .

"Marc?" Phillipe's voice was pained. He nervously smoothed his fingers over the railing. "Luc doesn't like animals, does he? I like animals. I used to have a dog. His name was Henri." Tears welled up in his eyes, as though the animal's death still wounded his soul.

Marc had heard the story before. Phillipe had been dropped on the steps of Notre Dame as a baby and raised by the church. When he turned ten, he found a scrawny puppy shivering in the shadows of the walls, half covered with snow. He begged Father Uriah to let him keep it. For twenty years, Phillipe had loved that dog. Sometimes, late at night, he woke Marc by calling Henri's name while he patted the floor at his bedside, still searching for the friend he had relied on for most of his life.

Marc put a hand on Phillipe's narrow shoulder. "I don't think we can judge Luc's love of animals yet," he answered. "But I love them. Did you know there's a nest on the bowsprit, Phillipe? I think I'll go look at it. There might be some interesting eggs in there. Do you want to come?"

Phillipe beamed up at him. "Oh, yes, I'd like that."

"GO AWAY, ANDIORA! We can take camp down by ourselves," Klami said. A small woman with a flat nose and short black hair, she could have fierce eyes when she wanted to. She glared at Andiora, then stooped to remove the rocks that held down the edge of the bark lodge covering.

"But, aunt, I can help," Andiora insisted. "I just needed some rest. I feel much better now."

"You're not better. Look how pale you are. You'll kill yourself if you don't get more rest. Now go away and sit down somewhere. Dyto and I will finish this."

Dyto trotted around the lodge and began rolling up the bark from the opposite side, revealing the stick frame beneath.

"Go!" Klami said with a wave of her hand.

Andiora reluctantly turned and walked away through the forest. Shadows dappled the leaf-strewn path that led down to the Crooked River. Klami was right. She wasn't well. But it hurt to be reminded of it every day. Her womb still ached, sometimes so badly that it kept her awake at night. She bled almost every day. It forced her to stop frequently to strip the soft inner bark of a cottonwood for an absorbent.

Aataentsic, what's wrong with me?

Angry, she picked up a stone and threw it at the water. Frogs leaped off the bank and dove into the shallows, watching her with only their eyes showing. One boldly croaked, then disappeared into a series of colliding silver rings.

Andiora sighed. What a beautiful day. The brilliant glare of Iouskeha's face painted the tree-covered hills with patches of gold, while Wind Girl gently ran her fingers through the tawny autumn grass. For three days they'd been canoeing toward Quebec, and the closer they came, the weaker Andiora felt—as though just the thought of seeing Pierre drained her of her strength. *No, don't think about the baby. Not yet. You'll have to soon enough . . . when you tell Pierre.* Despair settled in her chest. Somberly, she sat down in the cool grass that lined the bank of the river and watched a glittering cloud of insects swarming above the water.

Her Montagnais family yelled back and forth to each other as they struck camp and reloaded the canoes. The Huron traced their clan lineage through the mother, but a child also belonged to her father's people. Since Andiora's mother was Huron, Andiora was from the

Bear Clan, but she was claimed as a Big Badger child by her Montagnais father's clan.

Her uncle Atti, forty summers old, stood with one foot in the lead canoe and one foot on the land, picking up and packing the bundles of jerky, bags of corn and other items that Dyto's husband, Nanco, placed on the ground beside him. Tall and muscular, Atti wore his hair in a warrior's cut: shaved on the sides, leaving a bristly crest of black hair down the center of his head. A long blue tradecloth shirt was belted over his deerhide pants. Her real father had been killed shortly after Andiora's birth. Atti was the only father she had ever known. He had disciplined her, taught her right from wrong, loved her. Andiora smiled at him and he lifted a hand to wave, then went back to loading their supplies. Onrea, her young cousin, frolicked through the woods, playing with her dog and laughing.

Andiora inclined her head, and a wealth of blue-black hair cascaded over one shoulder. It sparkled in the sunlight that reflected from the water. She picked up a twig and brushed it over the hem of her red dress, feeling lonely and disoriented. *Oh, Pierre, I miss you so much.*

When she was younger, she had driven him crazy, stealing out of her longhouse to run to his camp, so she could spend the whole day with him. He would carry on trading conversations with her sitting at his side, his fingers twined with hers. Many of the men Pierre dealt with did not like Andiora. They considered her a nuisance and went out of their way to be unkind to her. More than once she'd endured shouts and name-calling. But she didn't care. When night came, she and Pierre would lie in each other's arms, listening to the wind buffeting his canvas tent while they talked of faraway places like France and England . . . and loved long into the night. Often she would sing for him, softly, so as not to wake the men sleeping in nearby tents. And sometimes—rarely—he would sing for her. Songs like nothing she'd ever imagined. Christian songs mostly, about God and sin and grace. She loved to hear him sing.

Andiora locked her arms around her drawn-up knees. Memory of those times hurt. The world was changing too fast for her. Five summers ago Pierre had been one of the few traders who ventured deep into Huron country. But every summer more traders came, seeking furs, offering dried peas, iron axes, brightly colored trade-cloth, kettles and other goods in exchange.

Beaver was in great demand. Europeans liked hats made from the pelt. She'd seen many such hats in Quebec and at Three Rivers, oddly shaped things with broad brims and high tops. But traders rarely bought green pelts. They insisted that the Huron trap the beaver in the depths of winter, when the furs were the thickest, then wear the pelts with the fur next to the body, for eighteen moons. Then, when the long guard hairs dropped out and only the fine underhair remained, the traders wanted the furs.

Sealing, walrus hunting and whaling also brought large numbers of Europeans to the blue waters of the Seagull River—the St. Lawrence, the French called it. Black Robes frequently traveled with them, preaching, and healing with the strange Spirit plants they'd brought from Europe. Few liked the Black Robes, but many converted to the religion because the French government paid higher prices for furs brought in by Christian Hurons.

Huron shamans, men like Tehoren and Tonner, watched with growing alarm. They warned that conversion would tear the people apart. What if the Huron ever went to war against the Christians? Whose side would the converts fight on? It would shred the clans . . . or so Tehoren said. Andiora did not know what to think. So far, only a few of the converts had refused to carry out their clan duties, saying that ceremonials to Iouskeha and Ataentsic were evil, but who knew about the future?

The voice of her Spirit Helper, Cougar, echoed from her memories, deep, ominous. *Sickness and death are coming. They walk with the Black Robes. . . .*

Andiora turned her head as a gust of wind swept into the forest and red leaves cascaded from the trees. They tangled in her hair and tumbled into the river, where the current washed them downstream. She picked a leaf from her hair and studied the pale green veins that striped it. Softly, she murmured, "The world is changing, Cougar."

CHAPTER

4

L uc sat on the edge of his cot with a bucket between his feet and his breviary in his hands. He read his daily Offices halfheartedly. They'd sailed through a storm last night, and each time the ship had heaved, so had Luc's stomach. Despicable thing, sailing. The man who'd invented boats deserved to be shot. That wasn't Noah, was it? Well, no matter . . . . Sunlight gleamed like honey from the polished oak walls of the cabin, reminding him of the deep warmth of summer evenings in Paris. The thought made him feel worse.

He cast a hostile glance at Dupre and Raimont. Each slept soundly despite the fact that dawn had brightened into day. But then Dupre had been gone most of the night, out on deck talking to one of the vermin boys who'd run away from home to become a sailor and now regretted the decision. Before he'd retired, Luc had overheard part of Dupre's conversation. Apparently the boy was homesick. In Luc's opinion, the brat deserved the pain for having abandoned his family.

Finishing his Offices, he laid his breviary aside and reached for the bag at the foot of his bed. He drew out his writing box, which contained his quill, a bottle of ink, a vial of sand, and a few precious sheets of paper. Gingerly, he rose—testing the fortitude of his stomach—and took the box to the tiny table by the door. He needed to write home, though he knew that this letter would not reach his mother for another three months. Quietly, he pulled out the chair and arranged the paper so that it caught the light.

Cher Mama,

We are nearly a month into our journey to New France. I wanted you to know that I am well, though the voyage is unbearable. I've felt myself soiled by constant contact with the unholy sailors, who curse and brandish knives at the slightest provocation. Yesterday one threatened to "slit my gullet" for accidentally kicking over a lamp he'd been reading by. I am endeavoring to isolate myself from the aura of their wickedness and have succeeded to some extent.

We've heard many stories of the Indians. It seems that the New World is as I expected, filled with naked barbarians worshiping demons. I am badly needed. Unfortunately, my two confreres are less than adequate. As you discovered in your research, Raimont is a blithering idiot, and Dupre is clearly the son of a harlot. His demeanor reeks of the lower classes. He is forever defending the unvirtuous, to my constant annoyance, and whereas I shield my eyes from the depraved acts of the sailors aboard, Dupre stares openly. I don't know why Father Binet selected Dupre to be in charge of this venture—especially after I told him about the vision I had when I was so ill with smallpox. You remember the one? I was being pursued by an army of demons when God fluttered down in the form of a dove and put a flaming sword in my hand.

Dupre is incompetent. I've been praying to God to grant me patience and forbearance until I reach the sanctuary of Father Brebeuf's presence. I know that his dignity and holiness will shelter me.

I will write you more before I post this letter in Quebec.
Be comforted that I am enduring for the greater glory of God.
Your devoted son,
Luc Penchant, S.J.

Luc poured sand on his letter and shook it, then gathered up his quill and ink and replaced them in his box. He went back to his bag and bent to tuck his writing box into its place, but froze when Phillipe gasped and sat bolt upright in his bed. The ugly little Brother stared wide-eyed at the wall, then, in a flurry of blankets, lunged out of bed, threw on a brown robe and dashed from the cabin without so much as a "Good Morning."

Luc stared after him for a moment, then shoved his box down beside his wool socks and buttoned his bag. "He's as demented as a rabid dog," he muttered to himself.

After combing his hair and straightening his robe, he headed for the deck.

When he emerged into the cool morning air, Mongrave trotted up the steps toward him, his brown cloak flapping around him like wings in the brisk wind. "Good morning, Monsieur," Luc said amiably.

Mongrave threw him a glance of distaste and passed without a word, hurrying toward the wheel on the poop deck.

Luc turned around to watch him. Not only were these sailors depraved, they were rude. He descended the stairs two at a time and wandered along, gazing upward at the flock of gulls that soared around the masts. Two sailors sat talking by the railing while they refilled the lamps with oil. Several more men had gathered near the prow, where they were mending long lengths of canvas.

When Luc neared the mainmast, he spotted Raimont. The little brother knelt at the feet of Tristan Marleaux, who was leaning against the mast. Marleaux was one of the worst of the sailors, boastful, nasty all the time, without a good word for anyone. Yet Raimont looked as rapt as if he were praying before a statue of one of the saints. Luc eased forward to stand half-hidden behind a row of wooden crates. He cocked his head, listening.

Raimont was saying, "I know, Monsieur Tristan. But God told me to come and find you. He told me to get out of bed and hurry to you."

"And what was the Lord thinking you should be asking me, Brother?" Marleaux inquired. He had a lean face like a weasel's, with a long nose, and eyes the color of slate.

"Have you ever been in a shipwreck, Monsieur Tristan? God wanted me to find out."

"Well, aye, I'd have to be admitting to that," Marleaux answered. "'Twas when I was new to the sea. But the telling of the tale's hardly something for the ears of a Religious."

Raimont twisted his hands before him. "Oh, but I need to hear it. God says so. Please tell me."

"Wouldn't you rather be watching the birds play? This time of morning, they're always—"

"No. Please, I . . . I need to hear the story."

"Why do you suppose the Lord would be caring about shipwreck stories?"

"I don't know. But He told me that someday I'd need to remember it. *Please.*"

Marleaux's face tightened before he relented. "Well, if God's insisting and you won't be minding the sinful details, I'll—"

"I won't mind," Raimont assured him.

Marleaux settled his lanky body down cross-legged next to Raimont. His grease-splotched red pants and tan blouse contrasted oddly with Raimont's simple clean robe. "Well," Marleaux began, "it happened 'long about fifteen years ago. 'Twas a fine, bright day, with birds singing in the trees . . ." Raimont's face shone at the mention of the animals, and Marleaux reached out to pat his shoulder affectionately. "I was caulking one of the shallops, working hard, for it was me first trip to New France and I'd felt the ocean come into me soul on the voyage. 'Tis a hard thing for a man not born to the sea to get, but the waves and wind, they crawl inside you so powerful that sometimes you'll be thinking they're God—not intending to be blasphemous, you know. 'Tis just a fact."

Marleaux braced his elbows on his knees, and his eyes took on a haunted look. "Pierre'd been gone to see one of the chiefs in a village of the Montagnais. You've got to see that it would've never happened if he'd been close at hand. He'd never have allowed it. But he wasn't at hand, and the men, they took it on themselves to go out and grab one of the fairest of the Huron maidens in Tadoussac. Beautiful, she was, with long black hair hanging down to her knees and the biggest brown eyes you've ever seen." He stopped and glanced seriously at Raimont, judging his response so far. Raimont sat absolutely still, staring at Marleaux through eyes that seemed fixed on some point far away.

"You must understand, Brother Raimont, that men are men, and they've got needs, though God knows, sometimes they're not too smart about the ways they take to fill 'em. Anyway, four of me crewmates brought the maiden on board and decided to cast lots to see who would have her first . . . are you understanding me meaning?"

Horror darkened Raimont's face. "Did you . . . cast?"

"Me? Lord, no! I'm a God-fearing Catholic."

"I know." Raimont beamed up at him.

"Well, anyway, the poor Indian girl—she couldn't have been more than fourteen—she knew what was coming. She screamed and carried on something fierce. You see, to the savages, a woman can lie with as many men as she wants, but it's her right to choose who and when. If a man takes her against her mind, he's mighty lucky if he survives with his—" Marleaux grimaced at Raimont's naive face. "—well, with his *vitals* intact."

"Go on," Raimont responded.

"The men, they lashed her to the mast and we sailed out to sea. But 'long about nighttime, they came to gather like a hungry pack of dogs around her and undid her hands. They played with her for a while before the man who'd won the lot stepped forward to claim her first, as was his right—I mean, Brother, his right in the sinful eyes of the crew—on account of him winning. His name was Harn. A big man, with cruel eyes. He dragged the girl toward the railing and threw her on the deck, and I swear, Brother, when he started to unlace his pants, why, that little red-skinned girl turned as white as snow. Before anybody could grab onto her, she let out a cry that would curl your hair and flung herself overboard. I remember the word she screamed to this day. It was *teouastato*, which means 'I can't stand this', or 'I don't wish it', or some such."

Tears came to Raimont's eyes. He put a trembling hand over his mouth.

"Every man there hung over the railing, trying to see her. But there wasn't nothing in those black waters, not a bubble, not a hint of flailing arms. Well, we all thought that was that.

"Along about four nights later, we were well out to sea, and the trade wind had been breathing so much life into the sails that we all felt we could fly if we just spread our arms a bit. I'd the first watch and was sitting like a bird up in the nest, gazing at the stars that roofed me head, when I heard a scream from below and saw big Harn stumbling wild across the deck.

"'What're you carrying on like a banshee for?' I shouted down at him, and I thought he'd faint. When he looked up at me, I could see the fear of the devil on his face. 'There's a woman,' he shrieked and pointed to the wheelhouse. 'She's standing at the wheel! It's her, Marleaux! The one that jumped ship. Seaweed's hanging all over her!'

"Well, I scrambled out of that nest, you can well guess, and ran to look. But the house was empty, the wheel spinning with the force of the waves. I told that lazy Harn to get back to tending the wheel or I'd kick him overboard meself and he could find his place in hell with that little girl he'd killed.

"Later on that same eve, up came one of the men out of the hold, clawing at his throat and screaming, 'She's down there! Oh, Merciful God, I saw her! Dripping wet, with seaweed knotted all over her!'

"Well, we talked him down for least an hour, 'til the bell tolled the next watch. Then we all got to our duties whether they needed doing right then or not. Tired and scared as rats at a bonfire we was.

"The next night, I was in me bunk when I heard such a commotion up top that me soul nearly left me body. The ship was tossing around and spinning like a whirlpool had risen up and taken hold of her, and I needn't tell you what terror went through me. I ran stark naked down to the deck and met men running from the stern, their faces gone gray as a corpse's. I demanded to know what was going on with them. 'She's there!' one of them shrieked. 'There at the wheel. Oh, God save us! She came and drove us all out, screaming at us!'

"I started to go forward, but I heard the yards over me head groan, and I looked up to see the sails listing. Then a mighty crack like the fist of God split the air—and the sails, they toppled into the sea like snowy angels' wings.

"Me and me friends that had nothing to do with the girl's death, we grabbed onto any bit of wood we could find and threw ourselves overboard."

Marleaux paused and let out a long breath. His lean face had pinched until the crow's feet around his eyes looked as deep as gullies.

Luc clutched his crucifix and offered a fervent prayer: *God give me the strength to endure these brutes.*

Marleaux continued, "I'm telling you the truth, Brother. I don't know much about the ways of God, but none of them other fellows came out of the wreck alive. And I been thinking since then that the Lord must have given that poor lot of men what they deserved for killing that little girl." He shook his head forlornly. "Well, that's the story God wanted you to be hearing . . . though I've not the faintest idea why He'd put you through it."

Raimont swallowed and whispered, "Sometimes God needs me to know things. I don't know why." Tenderly, he reached out and made the sign of the cross over Marleaux's chest, then crossed himself and said a soft prayer, begging God to forgive Marleaux for having laid eyes on such a thing at all.

Luc sniffed disdainfully. Instead of asking forgiveness, Raimont should have been hoping that God would punish Marleaux for not having stepped up and tried to put a stop to the gruesome event. Anyone could see that Marleaux had been an accomplice in the girl's death.

"Well," Marleaux said, "now that we've gotten that done, let's go forward to the foc'sle and watch the birds." A smile touched his lips. "See here what I saved from me breakfast this morn." He drew a piece of hardtack from his pants pocket and handed it to Raimont.

Raimont took the bread and held it to his chest like a sacred relic. "Oh, thank you. I saved some from dinner last night. Maybe, if we break them into enough crumbs, we can feed a little to each of the birds who are hungry."

Marleaux stood and helped Raimont to his feet. "I'll not be guaranteeing such a thing, Brother. I think there's more gulls that calls this old boat home than there are bits of bread in the whole world—but we'll be trying, we will."

Locking his arm in Raimont's, Marleaux started off down the deck toward the prow.

Luc dropped onto the closest crate and shook his head. God couldn't have wanted Raimont to hear such a grisly tale. It was satanic. Probably some demon had appeared in Raimont's dreams and . . . Luc's eyes widened. Suspiciously, he leaned forward and peered around the crates after Raimont. Marleaux had led him to the railing and was crushing hardtack with the handle of his knife. Raimont's childish laughter carried in the wind.

Maybe all those ridiculous songs Raimont sings when he's supposed to be praying aren't in praise of God at all. No one who loves God sings while he prays. Its . . . disrespectful. Prayer is a solemn, sublime activity.

Luc lifted a brow. He would have to keep an eye on Raimont; the little man might be more than he seemed.

IN SEARCH OF pumpkins, Andiora knelt and pushed away a brown shroud of autumn vines. As she worked, she uncovered two pumpkins, resting on their sides, glowing orange in the patchwork of sunlight that fell through the trees. She picked up the closest one, twisted it and broke the stem with a loud pop. She smiled when a mockingbird jerked in surprise on a pine branch over her head. The bird, curious, peered through the needles to eye her, then opened its beak and cawed like an annoyed raven.

"Oh, that's very good, Grandfather. Try this one." She inhaled a deep breath and let out a sparrow call that sounded like tinkling icicles, *tseet teedle-eet, teedle eet.* The mockingbird ruffled its feathers, shrilled and took wing, flying away through the forest. Andiora laughed and twisted the other pumpkin until it broke loose.

Back in camp, Onrea chattered as the rest of her family labored to set up lodges and start the evening cook fires. Suma barked in excited accompaniment.

Andiora gathered her pumpkins and rose. Above the treetops, threads of cloud gleamed golden, as though they'd been dipped in the finest lichen dye. Brittle autumn scents rode the breeze, the fragrance of molding leaves and wood smoke mixing pungently.

Her moccasins crackled in the vines as she stepped out of the pumpkin patch, skirted the edge of a small pond and headed back to camp along a well-worn trail. When she reached the clearing, she saw Onrea throw a stick for Suma. The black-and-white dog barked and bounded into the forest after it. Klami and Dyto had finished setting up the lodge. It stood like a round beast at the edge of the trees, its bark roof a patchwork of shadows. Atti and Nanco lounged on their sides before the fire, smoking and talking about trading, while their wives hunched over a copper pot filled with fish stew. Klami was throwing wild rice into the pot.

"Andiora," Atti said as she entered the clearing. His long nose made the ridge of hair on his otherwise shaved head look longer, like the fur rising on an angry wolf's back. He'd put on a deerhide shirt painted with the image of Iouskeha, the sun. He braced himself on one elbow. "We were talking about Quebec and how much noise the Frenchmen make. Have you ever noticed?"

"Yes, uncle. I've noticed," she answered and squatted to put her pumpkins into the coals of the fire. Every summer, the racket grew worse, and not just in Quebec. Everywhere the French went, they brought clanging pots, musket blasts, and the shrieks of the drunken traders who reeled along the forest paths. "They are noisy."

"How do you think Bobcat is making a living with their constant howling? Or Weasel? These Frenchmen act like their lives are the only ones that count."

"I talked to Pierre about it once." Andiora rose. Just saying his name out loud gave her pain. "He told me that Christians believe the world is dead—that only men have souls. He said the Christian god put animals and plants here just for men to kill."

Atti's mouth pursed in disgust. "Then I hope Iouskeha strikes them dead before they kill the whole world, and us with it."

Andiora sat near the pumpkins, on the side of the fire where the smoke would keep away the insects, and tucked the hem of her red tradecloth dress about her ankles. Fringes fell from the sleeves, and a ring of red glass beads encircled the collar. As the sunlight waned, a chill entered the breeze and made her shiver. "They want the world to die, Uncle."

"*What*! Why?"

Nanco, a short man with long black hair and a heavily tattooed face, blurted, "That's ridiculous. How could anyone *want* the world to die?"

Klami stopped stirring the stew pot and looked up. Her tan and green dress had flecks of dirt down the front. "Don't they know that if the world dies, *they* die?" she asked.

"Oh, yes, they know that."

Atti smoked his pipe contemplatively, his brow furrowed, while he waited for Andiora to finish.

She shrugged. "I don't really understand it, but Pierre says it has to do with the Christian god, Jehovah. He has to destroy the world before the Christians can go to their Village of Souls. They call it 'heaven'."

"And how will their god destroy the world?"

Andiora extended her hands to the crackling flames, letting the glow warm them. Her family stared at her intently. In the background, the green drained from the forest as the sun set, leaving dark spears of trees standing watch. "That's why the Black Robes come. They think that if they can force our people to believe in their god, then he will reward them by killing the world."

"Some reward!" Klami remarked.

"It sounds more like punishment—for us—for believing in their god," Nanco said. "Maybe it isn't Jehovah who destroys the world at all. Maybe Iouskeha gets angry because we convert and then burns all of us to cinders."

Klami nodded. "We would deserve it."

Andiora took the pumpkins by their stems and turned them so they'd cook on the other side. Juices bubbled on the skins, smelling rich and sweet. No matter how many times she'd talked to Pierre about Christianity, she'd never grasped this part. How could Jehovah murder the animals, trees and land just so men could go to heaven? Other creatures, apparently, went nowhere. *What happens to their souls? Do they get lost in the darkness after the world is dead?*

Andiora frowned. "Their Village of Souls is very different from ours. It has streets covered with gold and thousands of stone longhouses. Men never have to work. Jehovah gives them food and clothes and places to live. Christians want the world to die so they can move to their heaven forever. They look forward to it and think we should, too."

Atti's brows drew down over his long nose. He smoked his pipe for a few moments, then asked, "But why do we have to go with them? Why can't they just leave us alone?"

"I don't know, Uncle," Andiora sighed. "Pierre said once that Jehovah is a jealous god and demands that everybody believe in him."

Atti blew out a long streamer of gray smoke, watching it drift upward through the branches of a crimson-leafed maple. "So, if we never believe in Jehovah, the world will live?"

"Yes. At least I think so."

As dusk deepened, the animals of the night began to rouse. An owl's eyes glinted as it sailed low over the ground, as silent as a shadow, listening for mice scurrying beneath the bed of leaves on the forest floor. Near the edge of the pond, back toward the pumpkin patch, a doe and a fawn dipped their heads to drink. Their fur glittered with a silver cast in the dim light.

Klami reached down and picked up six wooden bowls. "Onrea?" she called. "We're eating. If you want some, you'd better come in."

Thrashing sounded in the underbrush and Suma bounded out into the clearing, Onrea at his heels. They both looked disheveled, with grass and old leaves tangled in their hair. Only thirteen summers, Onrea was not yet a woman, but she would be soon. Her breasts and hips had started to fill out, and now they stretched the green fabric of her dress. Suma had his pointed ears pricked. Onrea grinned as she ran up to the fire. "I'm sorry, Cousin," she explained. "Suma was sniffing out a rabbit. I was hoping we could find its burrow and bring it back to throw into the stew pot."

"Too late now," Klami replied. "Here, I need you to help me." She ladled out the stew and Onrea carefully carried the steaming bowls to the adults sitting around the fire.

Atti blew on his stew, then tilted the bowl to his lips and drank. When he lowered it, he said, "Then we must make sure that no one converts."

"To do that," Nanco replied, "we'd have to drive all the Black Robes from our country."

"There aren't very many. It wouldn't take long," Klami noted.

"No," Atti said through a long exhalation, "but if we drive them out, there will be no more copper pots, iron ax heads, sugar, or other trade goods."

"I don't need any of those things," Klami insisted. She filled her own bowl and went around the fire to sit at Atti's left side. "I want the world to live."

Atti's gaze slid to Andiora, who was silently turning the pumpkins again. They sizzled and spat, sending up a swirling veil of steam. "And you, Andiora? What do you think we should do?"

She glanced up to meet his serious eyes. "Drive them out, Uncle. That way, we never have to worry about the blond Black Robe who's bringing the sickness."

CHAPTER

5

. . . For these Spiritual Exercises (of Saint Ignatius) we have so
much the more need, since the sublimity of our labors requires so
much the more a union with God, and since we are forced to live in
continual turmoil. This makes us frequently realize that those who
come here must bring a rich fund of virtue with them.
> JEAN DE BREBEUF, S.J.
> *Ihonatiria, 1635*

Jean de Brebeuf mumbled incoherently, staring around the
common room through fever-brilliant eyes. Outside, the night
wind gusted like a raging lion. He could hear the tree branches
creaking and cracking as though a mad beast ran through them at
full speed. He'd been ill for three days, his body alternately freezing
and burning up. *Influenza . . . it killed hundreds of villagers last summer.*
He blinked at the red glow on the longhouse's ridgepole. The fire in
the center of the common room had faded to glowing coals, giving a
crimson hue to the darkness.

"What is it, Lord?" he asked softly, trying not to wake Antoine
Daniel and Ambrose Davost, whose cots stood next to his.

The presence of God filled the room so strongly that his skin
prickled. He tugged his blanket up around his throat and shivered.
Cold, so cold. He had only one blanket and a ratty deerhide with
patches of fur missing. Hides had grown very expensive over the past
nine years, ever since the greedy trading companies had flocked to
New France. The Huron had been hunting and trapping so exhaus-

tively that in a few years, he feared, they wouldn't have enough hides for their own use, let alone as items of trade.

Faint wavering images of screaming Iroquois lingered in his mind. He had been having terrible dreams of famine, plagues and war. Restlessly, he tossed to his left side and curled into a fetal position. He was so tall, six feet two inches, that his knees stuck out over the edge of his bed. Sweat drenched his black beard and mustache. Every time a breath of wind seeped through the bark walls, fanning the hearth coals to scarlet, he shuddered until his teeth chattered.

Is that it . . . Lord? The Iroquois are finally going to attack?

He closed his eyes and prayed, *Show me the way, Lord. What can I do to stop them?* He thought he heard a voice, murmuring through the gusts of wind, calling him. Jean breathed deeply, and his body seemed to float high above his bed, as though his soul had been freed from the cage of his body. He tried to follow the voice, letting it lead him . . .

He found himself up and dressed, pacing the longhouse, which stretched thirty feet in length and eighteen feet in width. It was divided into three sections. A small chapel with an altar and a crucifix filled the northern chamber. The central portion, the common room where they slept, was eighteen feet in length and lined on both sides with shelves which held the mission's precious books and a few personal items. A stone-lined hearth dented the middle of the floor. Their beds stood side-by-side against the northern wall that divided the common room from the chapel. The southern room was smaller than the others and served as an antechamber and a closet for tools and muskets, wood, food and other provisions.

A chill ran up Jean's spine. God called to him so powerfully that he almost couldn't bear it. At times like this, he felt as if God had poured too much Spirit into him for the frail vessel of his body to hold. Quietly, he walked into the antechamber and pulled his broad-brimmed black hat off the hook by the door, then went outside into the frigid wind.

Around the central plaza of the village, longhouses sat in rows, silent and dark, their snowy roofs awash in silver starlight. Log barricades, three feet high, which served as shooting boxes, lined the perimeters of the village. He walked around one and headed out into the forest.

A light dusting of snow glistened in the shadows, but autumn leaves still clung to the maples and oaks that stood among the evergreens. The branches wove a black filigree against the star-studded indigo sky. The rich, damp smells of Lake Karegnondi—as the Indians called Lake Huron—scented the wind.

Jean took an icy path that led up the wooded hill east of Ihonatiria. Gusts of wind mixed hauntingly with the distant howls of wolves. The deeper Jean went into the forest, the more unbearably the voice of God swelled within him. Now he could almost make out his words, but not quite, not clearly enough to understand them.

The trail crested the hill and plunged down the other side toward a heart-shaped pond rippling with a leaden brilliance. Midway down the hill, he halted. His legs seemed to have developed a consciousness of their own. They would not take him farther.

His eyes searched the trees and brush, as though some hidden danger lurked just beyond . . .

Something white moved on the pond below. A silver-crested wave spread as a woman's head emerged from the water. She rose like a dandelion seed borne on morning breezes and drifted over the pond toward him, calling, "*Echon. Echon,*" the name the Huron called him because they could not pronounce "Jean." Beautiful and terrible she was; long black hair hung wetly over her drenched ivory gown.

Jean's throat constricted. He scrambled back up the slippery trail so quickly that he fell and slid backward, tumbling and clawing at the patches of snow to stop himself. "No!"

"*Come,*" she called. A horrifying smile curled her lips as she floated closer, now only five feet from him. "*Come to me, Echon. I must teach you about the Way and the Truth and the Life, or the Huron will die.*"

"What?" he whispered. The parody of Christ's words entranced him with fear. "Who . . . who are you? What do you want?"

She formed the fingers of her right hand into the Teaching Hand and hovered directly over him. Water from her soaked gown dripped on him like cold rain. "*You are bringing great evil into this world. You must make straight the Way.*"

"What evil?"

The creature extended her arms as though to grab him by the shoulders, and he rolled away, shouting, "Jesus, help me! *Lord, I beg you!*"

In a burst of light, she vanished.

"*Father Jean* . . ." A voice, as though from some great distance, penetrated his terror.

Jean lay panting, his wide eyes searching the trees and sky. He lifted a shaking hand and crossed himself. Despite the wind, mist coalesced on the pond below. Shapes moved, visages, forming and disappearing. In the midst of them, a red spot appeared and wavered. A rearing horse formed and pawed the mist. Jean cried out as the red ran down like blood to pool on the surface of the pond.

He scrambled back up the icy trail, grabbing onto brush and tree limbs to keep from falling, while he repeated over and over, "I believe in God, the Father Almighty, creator of heaven and earth. I believe in Jesus Christ, His only Son, our Lord—"

"Father Jean? . . . Jean?"

He felt a hand shaking his shoulder, gently, and a cool cloth being laid on his forehead. When he opened his eyes, he saw Fathers Daniel and Davost leaning over him. Each young and dark-haired, their eyes were brimming with concern.

"Are you all right, Father?" Antoine Daniel asked. "You cried out in your sleep."

Jean let out a shuddering breath and nodded weakly. "I . . . I'm all right." The room felt agonizingly cold. He shivered and tugged at the coarse wool of his blanket. "Antoine, please . . . a little tea . . . something hot."

As Antoine threw kindling onto the coals to coax the fire to life, Ambrose Davost wrung out another wet cloth and wiped Jean's face. Jean closed his eyes. His mind wavered in and out of sleep, sometimes seeing the common room, sometimes walking the path through the forest. The ghostly woman formed in his memories, her white dress dripping water, and then blood. *You are bringing great evil into this world . . . the Huron will die.*

Jean tried to answer but his throat had gone dry. The woman reached for him with wet arms, and he screamed and crawled away, crying, "I believe in God, the Father Almighty—"

"He's delirious," Ambrose's deep voice echoed around him, as though borne on the glacial wind. "Hurry, Antoine. Get your blanket and mine. We'll cover him and build up the fire . . ."

BY THE TIME they entered the Gulf of St. Lawrence, night had fallen. Excitement fired Marc's veins as he paced along the railing beside Luc, thinking, praying. Autumn had touched the New World, splashing the rolling hills with russet and gold. For four days, the wind had whispered out of the south, forcing the *Soleil* to zigzag toward Tadoussac. The crew had cursed as they'd heaved to tack, shifting the sails to catch the meager breeze.

A crowd of savages had gathered along the shore. The children ran up and down, waving, calling greetings, while the women stood by, cooking and watching. Strips of fur or feathers adorned their hair-styles. The men at the front of the group had tattooed their faces in red, blue, black and white geometric designs. They moved with the controlled strength of wolves on a blood trail.

"Now that you see the savages in the flesh, do you still believe that rubbish about their purity?" Luc asked with a tilt of his head.

"It's difficult to tell from this distance, don't you think, Luc?"

"Only if you're blind." As the night deepened, fires flickered among the trees and along the shore. They heard the faint music of flutes and drums. Luc gestured toward a woman who sat at the edge of the water, suckling a baby at her bare breast. "Look at that. Brazen. She's worse than our courtesans."

"Why? Because she's not ashamed of her nudity? I call that 'innocence'."

"What is it about you, Dupre?" Luc demanded as he turned to glare. Locks of brown hair fell into his gray eyes when the ship turned to the north again, catching the new breeze that blew out from the land. "Have you *no* moral standards?"

The closer they came to Quebec, the more surly and difficult Luc became. Was he frightened of the New World? Perhaps he was nervous about completing his mission here? Or homesick? *Be chari-table—it could be lots of things.* Marc tipped his chin to study the sails. "Oh, I have a few standards, Brother. Thou shalt not kill; thou shalt not commit adultery; thou shalt not steal; thou shalt not bear false witness against thy neighbor; thou—"

"Are you trying to avoid my question?"

"Uh . . . no."

"Well, answer me!"

"You don't consider the Commandments to be moral standards, Luc?"

"Oh, they're a start. But hardly adequate. What do you think of Peter Abelard's work, 'Ethics, or Know Thyself'?"

Marc frowned and glanced speculatively at Luc. "I've read it, but a very long time ago. I don't remember much about it. Sorry."

"Well, you should remember. Abelard says that sin is contempt for the Creator. That to sin is to despise God; that is, not to do for Him what we know we should do; not to renounce what must be renounced for His sake. That *must* be the basis of all ethics."

"I suppose I agree with that." Marc responded.

"Correct actions spring from correct intentions. Incorrect actions spring from incorrect intentions."

"I'm not sure that the eye of the heart can see clearly enough to constantly guard itself from such error, Luc. We're all frail human beings."

Luc grimaced. "Really, Dupre. God plants in each of us the ability to know the difference. Including these savages. Surely you—"

Phillipe's bright laughter made them turn. Marleaux had pounded a piece of hardtack into crumbs, and Phillipe was tossing them as high as he could into the air. He stamped his feet in joy when the gulls dove to catch them. A huge flock had gathered around him. As more and more birds swooped down from the sky, the Indians on shore began to point and whisper behind their hands, casting uncertain looks at Phillipe.

Luc lifted a brow and said, "We should have left Raimont in France. Look at him. He's already got the natives believing he's a demon from hell."

"How can you say that? He's just feeding the birds. You know how he loves animals."

"Yes, just like these satanic Indians do. They have animal familiars, you know."

"That's silly, Luc. You can't believe—"

From the crow's nest, the lookout shouted, "Ho! Pointes Aux Alouettes ahead!"

The *Soleil* rounded a tree-shrouded bend, and a bank of sand appeared in the black water. Moments later, a rocky promontory emerged from the forests and thrust its blunt nose into the slate-gray sky.

Phillipe gripped the railing suddenly. "Look! Indians! They're coming!"

Marc and Luc ran to join Phillipe. Two copper-skinned men were paddling a bark canoe out to intersect the path of the *Soleil*. They shouted in deep, guttural tones, and Mongrave, standing in the forecastle, responded in the same language, then laughed.

"Oh, Marc," Phillipe said softly, his eyes shining. "They're beautiful. Just like Adam before the serpent entered the Garden."

Luc threw up his hands in exasperation. "I can't stand this! I'm going to our cabin to prepare Mass."

"Thank you, Luc," Marc said. "We'll be along shortly."

Luc left, and Marc and Phillipe gazed out at the Indians. The darkness had grown so thick that they could discern only dark shapes moving before the fires on shore. Marc could hear laughter. The Indians lived so simply. Hunt. Fish. Cook dinner. Sleep. Surely this was the way God had intended man to live.

Marc put a hand on Phillipe's arm. "I'd better go help Luc. Stay for a while longer if you want."

Phillipe shook his head and reluctantly straightened up. "No, I'll help, too."

After Mass, Marc and Luc offered each other their confessions, and Marc heard Phillipe's. Then they restlessly climbed into their cots and tried to sleep.

Nightmares tormented Marc, filling him with doubts and fears so strong that he kept waking himself. He repeatedly lived through a scene wherein Pryor refused them entry to Quebec. Finally, when he couldn't stand it anymore, he put on his robe, took his blanket and went down to the deck.

He strolled along beside the railing, watching the gulls that perched there, deep in sleep. In the starlight, their feathers flashed like polished ivory.

When Marc found a coil of rope, he sat down, braced his shoulders against it, and spread his blanket over himself. Out here, with the cool wind on his face, he could think more clearly. He had fulfilled his promise to God, had left his home and loved ones. What would happen now? Would Pryor order them out of New France before they'd even had a chance to begin their work? Were the Indians truly the lost tribes of Israel? Would his efforts to convert them bring about Christ's triumphant return?

Above him, the spars glowed eerily. A sailor sat curled against the mainmast, his cap pulled down over his eyes. The lamp beside him had burned low, the wick no more than a thin crescent of gold.

Marc grasped the crucifix that lay over his chest. Christopher Columbus—a deep believer in Joachim's prophecies—had written in 1502 that only one hundred and fifty-five years remained before the fulfillment of all biblical prophecies and the End of the World. That set Judgment Day in the year 1652, only sixteen years away. Was that enough time to convert all of the Indians? How many of them were there in the New World?

The lapping of the waves, sounding soft and frail, called to Marc. He closed his eyes and drifted, his thoughts rambling. Sleep crept through his tired body like a sultry wind, easing itself into his soul, stirring memories of Marie and of his mother.

He'd been ten when he'd last seen his mother, and he'd barely recognized her. She had lost so much weight that she looked like a skeleton. "I'm going away, Marc. I have to put you in an orphanage. It'll be all right. You just be good and do what they tell you to. You understand? Don't be any trouble to anybody. I love you, Marc." Then she'd broken into sobs.

She hadn't told him she was dying. Perhaps she couldn't have borne his fears. He didn't know, but he wished—

Marc jerked awake when a heavy boot kicked his bare foot. He opened one eye and saw Mongrave looming over him, his brown cape billowing in the breeze, a paper in his right hand.

"Monsieur," Marc yawned, "can I be of assistance?"

"What, may I ask, are you doing out on deck at this hour?"

"Sleeping." Marc squinted up at the pale blue glow on the eastern horizon. It would be dawn soon. "What are you doing?"

Mongrave waved his paper. "Checking the dates of the eclipses that will occur in New France over the next months. 'Tis a good thing to know. The Indians take them as divine signs." He hesitated, studying Marc curiously. "I could see that you were sleeping, Father. Why *here*? Did your cot grow splinters suddenly?"

Marc sat up. The scents of the ocean, of kelp and fish, pervaded the air most strongly at dawn. Already the gulls had begun circling the masts, screeching raucously and diving in search of food. "No, Monsieur, I wanted to look at the stars and feel the mist on my face."

Mongrave gazed out across the dark water. "Didn't I tell you that you were different from your dour brothers in the Society of Jesus?" A gleam lit the trader's eyes. "Well, sorry to have bothered you, Father. I'll get back to me duties. Be aware that we'll start readying the barque after breakfast. I'll expect you and your charges to be packed for the trip to Quebec by noon."

"We will be, Monsieur."

"Then good night to you, Father." Mongrave swaggered away toward the stern.

Marc leaned back against the rope again. Just for a while longer, he wanted to watch the fading stars and listen to the water caressing the hull. At moments like this, he felt the certainty of miracles rousing deep in his soul. *They are the lost tribes. They must be . . .*

CHAPTER

6

ive days later, Marc and Phillipe sat on deck with their backs propped against the mizzenmast of a different ship, smaller, more streamlined, named the *Cruz*. Phillipe had learned a great deal about barques from Tristan Marleaux, and he bubbled over with the need to share it, though Marc was anxious and preoccupied, barely listening. A smudge of gray smoke smeared the sky in the distance, trailing over a rocky cliff. Quebec. Pryor would be waiting for them, he was sure of it.

"See, Marc?" Phillipe pointed to the sail billowing over their heads. "Barques are rigged for a fore-and-aft sail instead of a square sail."

"Hmm. Oh . . . really?"

"Yes. It takes fewer men to sail a ship when you have a fore-and-aft sail—because you can move it around to catch the wind. That's why . . ."

Marc was absorbing every scent and sound, marveling at the majesty of the countryside. Despite his anxiety, he could sense the divine in the rocky cliffs and in the deer and moose that grazed at the water's edge. Even the thousands of insects that tormented him seemed part of the holy symphony of the wilderness.

Luc stood at the railing, his back to them as he gazed over the wake of the ship. He had barely spoken to either Marc or Phillipe today, apparently determined to keep everyone and everything in the New World at a distance. With such an attitude, how could he effectively minister to the Indians?

"Look!" Phillipe shouted and pointed. He shoved to his feet and ran to the railing.

In the distance, a huge brown bear waded into the river and slapped at the water until it scooped a fish into the air. Catching it in its mouth, it trotted back toward the forest.

Phillipe grinned up at Luc. "Did you see the bear, Father Luc? God gave him a fish!"

Luc scowled. "What makes you think it was God and not Satan? The devil is everywhere in this wasteland."

Phillipe's face reflected his dismay. Thoughtfully, he gazed around, taking in the magnificent autumn colors, the crystal-blue sky, the languid water. "I haven't seen him."

"You're not looking very hard. I see him in every Indian face."

Marc shook his head. "But I haven't seen Satan either. Perhaps you shouldn't look so hard, Luc."

"And perhaps you should look harder, Dupre. The End of the World is near. Divine revelation should guide us all—regardless of which of us perceives it."

"So you think the devil reveals himself just to you? Why would you imagine that is?"

Their staring contest quickly turned into a glowering struggle of wills. Luc's nostrils flared.

Phillipe bit his lip uncomfortably. "I . . . I saw Roah . . . this morning," he said, clearly attempting to defuse the tension. "He was up sitting on the bow. Would . . . would you like to go look for him?"

Luc scoffed, "I have more important things to do. I need to read my Bible. How long has it been since you read your Bible, *Father* Dupre?"

A heated retort came to Marc's lips, but he suppressed it. "I think that's a good idea, Luc. Why don't you go read the Book of Matthew?"

Obliviously, Phillipe smiled and recited, "'Thou shalt love the Lord thy God with all thy heart, with all thy soul, and with all thy mind. . . . Thou shalt love thy neighbor as thyself.'"

Luc stiffened as though he had been physically struck.

Phillipe's head swiveled around to watch Luc as he stamped away across the deck. Phillipe asked, "Marc, why doesn't Father Luc see God here?"

"Because he's so caught up with himself that—" He cut off the rest and fought to muster patience. "I'm sure he'll be fine once we get to Ihonatiria. It's probably just hostility from being cooped up on shipboard for two months."

Phillipe nodded sagaciously. "When we get to Father Brebeuf, we'll all be all right. It won't be very long now." Abruptly, he turned and squinted at the masts, where thirty birds dove and soared. "There's Roah! Do you see him?"

Marc shielded his eyes, seeking Roah's characteristic shape and lavender color. "No. Are you sure you see him?"

"Oh, yes. He's up there. I can hear him calling me. He's saying, *'Phillipe! Phillipe!'*" He laughed and clapped his hands.

"Roah followed us? From the *Soleil*?"

"Yes. He said he needs to be close to me."

"Why?"

"I don't know." Phillipe's brow furrowed. "Except that it has to do with the little girl who died in the shipwreck. She went down in that cold, cold water, and no one was there to help her." Phillipe's lips moved as if he were silently reciting a word or a phrase.

Almost unconsciously, Marc reached up to grasp his silver crucifix. The mention of the death of a girl stirred dark memories of his own. Guilt and grief made his heart pound. *She's been dead for eight years. It wasn't your fault* . . . "What shipwreck, Phillipe?"

"The seaweed . . . it tangled around her hands and feet. It dragged her down into the dark . . . so dark . . ."

From the prow, Mongrave's voice carried. "Jameson? Have 'em take in the sails! I'll ready the passengers."

"Aye, Pierre." Jameson began shouting orders.

The sudden noise snapped Phillipe from his thoughts. He turned and squinted at the men who climbed the shrouds. "They look like spiders!" He laughed. "See them, Marc?"

"Yes," Marc replied softly, his eyes on Phillipe's childlike face. The little Brother seemed to have forgotten all about their shipwreck conversation.

Four rowboats left shore and glided out to meet them. Sailors waved their caps, calling greetings as the *Cruz* swayed toward a cluster of squat log houses that lined the water's edge. Blue smoke rose from the chimneys and billowed along the towering bluff behind the city. The whinnying of horses carried. Several hundred people had gathered by the water, most of them Indians, but in the front about a dozen Europeans stood. Marc's stomach muscles clenched. The men in white-ruffled collars and shiny boots had an air of authority about them. Government officials?

Mongrave, heading toward Marc, shouldered through the men who rushed around the deck. He wore a clean yellow blouse with brown pants and had his coarse hair pulled back and tied with a length of cord.

Phillipe pressed close at Marc's side and patted his arm. "Look at all the Indians who came to meet us. Just like God said." His voice had a touch of wonder.

Mongrave gave Marc a cavalier grin. "Good afternoon to you, Father Dupre. If you'll take a good look out there, you'll see a man in a red coat."

Marc nodded. "Pryor?"

"Aye. I've never known him to be waiting when a ship came in. He must've had lookouts watching for us, which means he's been expecting you, Father. Let me give you some advice. Beneath those fancy boots of his are cloven hooves. If you've composed any speeches for this moment, best brush up on them now. *And stand your ground, Dupre.* In the New World, the weak die and nobody cares."

"How long do we have?"

"About an hour. It'll take some time to load the rowboats. Marleaux will see that your belongings are stowed, but if there's anything you need at hand, like your entry papers, now's the time to fetch it."

"ANDIORA! ANDIORA, THEY'RE here!" Onrea yelled as she rushed up the trail with her black hair flying.

"Here?" Andiora rose from where she'd been helping Klami and Dyto weave a fishing net out of the reeds that grew so thickly along the river's edge. The half-finished net lay limply on the dry grass. She wiped her hands on her clean doeskin dress. She had bathed and washed her hair that morning—in preparation. She didn't know whether to feel excited that Pierre was home, or terrified that he might have brought the man in her Dream with him.

Klami and Dyto straightened up, and Klami anxiously peered through the forest toward the gray wall of rock that loomed into the blue sky above Quebec. Only a small slice of the river could be seen from their camp, but they had a clear view of the mob of people on the shore. There had to be two, maybe three hundred.

Klami stepped forward. "Onrea? Where are Atti and Nanco?"

"Down at the harbor. They sent me for you." By the river a huge flock of gulls had gathered, diving and screeching over the heads of the crowd.

Klami turned to face Andiora. "You'd better go. You have your knife?"

Andiora nodded. There was a giddy feeling in her chest, like crawling worms. "It's in my moccasin."

"Then hurry. We'll follow you as soon as we grab our war clubs."

"Yes . . . all right. I . . ." Andiora backed away, then sprinted down the trail.

She raced along the perimeter of a marsh and almost lost her footing in the slimy weeds. Out in the river, the *Cruz* rocked. Her sails had been furled, giving the spars a skeletal appearance.

Oh, Pierre, you didn't bring the blond Black Robe, did you?

She could sense Power building around her, like a bubble swelling to the bursting point. The hair at the nape of her neck prickled. *Cougar? Where are you? I feel you here . . .*

When she reached the edge of the crowd, she saw Atti and Nanco standing near the front, just behind the Frenchmen from the government. She recognized Guillaume Pryor, who paced at the edge of the water with his arms crossed, watching the boats that rowed in from the *Cruz*. A short man, he had a bulbous nose and bulging blue eyes. Locks of red hair fell from beneath the brim of his beaver hat. The golden threads in his red coat blazed as though set aflame by the afternoon sunlight.

Two members of the crew jumped into the waist-deep water and pulled the lead rowboat up on land. Pierre stepped out of the boat, and Andiora pushed forward and broke into a run—until she saw the blond Black Robe. Her legs went weak. Two other Black Robes stepped out of the boat behind him and followed him to stand before Pryor. Andiora worked her way to Atti and Nanco. Atti had painted two white circles around his eyes. Daubs of purple and black adorned his cheeks and chin. He proudly wore a European waistcoat made of fine leather, given him by Pierre.

"The blond. Is it him?" Atti whispered.

"I don't know. I need to see him more closely."

Atti nodded, but his eyes slitted, studying every movement the man made. The Black Robe was tall and handsome, with an oval face half covered by a blond beard and mustache.

Pryor lifted his chin. "Father Dupre, I assume?"

"Yes, Monsieur." The blond bowed respectfully. "May I introduce Brother Phillipe Raimont and Father Luc Penchant?"

Pryor ignored them and extended his hand to Dupre. "Where are your letters of introduction and your letters patent from France giving you permission to land in Quebec?"

Dupre extended several pieces of paper. Pryor unfolded the first one, then another, and another. Pierre strode forward to loom over Dupre's shoulder like a dark giant. His black beard had grown more bushy, his hair longer. Andiora's heart pounded. *Pierre, I've needed you . . .* He kept giving Pryor unflattering looks.

"As you can see," Dupre said, "our entry to New France was authorized by the viceroy, and Samuel—"

"I can read quite well, *Father*," Pryor remarked.

Dupre gave Pierre a questioning glance, then continued, "We come in the name of Lord Jesus to minister to the savage populations of your country. Our destination is the Huron village of Ihonatiria, where Father Jean de Brebeuf lives. We'll be needing supplies. Could you direct me to an honest trader?"

"I don't think there's one in the whole country, Father." Pryor's lips quirked. "So you're going to Ihonatiria? That's very far. Do you have an escort? We do not allow inexperienced fledglings to venture out alone into the wilderness. If you have no escort—"

Pierre growled, "They've an escort, Guillaume."

"You, I presume?" Pryor examined him sourly.

"Me and me Huron and Montagnais friends. They'll be in good enough hands."

"Well, if they trust you, they're welcome to you, Mongrave," Pryor said. "Since we have a new governor, *a Jesuit lover*, there's not a good deal I can do to stop them." He haphazardly refolded the papers and shoved them at Dupre.

Dupre took them. "Who is the new governor, Monsieur?"

"Charles Huault de Montmagny, Chevalier of the Order of St. John of Jerusalem. I believe you're familiar with them, Father?"

Marc nodded. It was difficult to hide his relief. "I am. And with Montmagny's reputation." Indeed!

"Well, then, I hope you survive your journey, Father," Pryor said and glowered at Pierre before tramping away across the sand, waving and shouting to make the Indians move back. His entourage followed in single file.

Mongrave put his hands on his hips and asked, "And who is Montmagny?"

"A pious Catholic," Dupre answered. "He was educated by Jesuits and is very well disposed toward us."

Pierre grunted disapprovingly.

People from a variety of tribes rushed forward, speaking to the Black Robes, asking them why they had come and what they wanted here, touching their clothing. To Andiora, it was obvious that the Black Robes understood none of it. They smiled and nodded awkwardly. Strange. She herself spoke five languages—Mohawk, Montagnais, Huron, French and English—but the Europeans seemed to know only their own. Were their countries so large that they didn't need to talk to each other? An elderly Abenaki man took Pierre aside to speak to him privately, showing him a necklace of polished stones.

Nanco leaned down. "I don't like the looks of that brown-haired Black Robe. He keeps that book clutched to his chest like it's a weapon."

The skinny man had his teeth gritted so hard that his jaw stuck out. *Penchant*, Dupre called him. The man's eyes darted fearfully; his fingers dimpled the brown fabric covering his book.

"Maybe it *is* a weapon," Nanco whispered. "I want to see, before I take him in my canoe." He lunged forward, raced over the sand and ripped the book from Penchant's hands.

Penchant let out a shriek and dodged behind Dupre, shouting, "Thieves! They're all thieves. I told you! You wouldn't believe me!"

Another brave, Montagnais but Andiora didn't know him, tore the book from Nanco's hands, feathered through the white pages, then threw the book on the sand. Penchant quickly scuttled over to pick it up. Nanco stalked back to Andiora and Atti. "Empty," he said. "Just paper."

"Andiora!" Pierre cried. He ran forward, grabbed her in his arms and swung her around, half crushing her ribs while she laughed. "Oh, darlin', I missed you so that I thought I'd die."

"I missed you, too, Pierre."

Their lips met in a desperate kiss, but Andiora tore her mouth away when the blond Black Robe walked up behind Pierre. She examined the priest breathlessly. The knife in her tall moccasin beckoned. His face was different, the nose straighter, the eyes larger. He was not the same one as in her Dream. At least she didn't think so . . . but she wasn't certain. She hugged Pierre and whispered, "I must see this Black Robe more closely. I had a Dream, Pierre."

"A Dream?" His bushy eyebrows knitted. "What Dream?"

"I saw a blond Black Robe bring disease and death to the Huron."

Pierre's face hardened. He glanced at the Black Robe. "His name is Marc Dupre. I'll wait here, Andiora. Do what you must."

Cautiously she walked forward and took Dupre's bearded face between her hands, examining it in detail. Dupre looked uncomfortably at Pierre. In English, he asked, "What does she want, Mongrave? Is there something I can do for her?"

"Aye," Pierre responded gruffly. "Stand still."

Dupre blinked as Andiora turned his face first to the left, then to the right. When she had finished, he met her eyes squarely.

"I'm Father Dupre," he said. "You're Andiora?"

She let her hands fall, worried that she might be wrong. "Why do you come to our country?"

He seemed surprised that she spoke French. He smiled. "We come in the name of our Lord Jesus to offer salvation to your people. To all the people of the New World. A great prophet named Joachim said that—"

"And if we don't want to be saved by you?"

Dupre seemed taken aback. He straightened. Behind him, Penchant muttered something unpleasant that sounded like it was in Latin, though Andiora knew only a few words of that odd language. Dupre ignored Penchant. "Please, give us time to show you. Just a few months."

Something in his eyes touched her. A kindness, a strength. "You'll be traveling with me and my family. Tomorrow morning at dawn, we will leave and go to the place we have hidden our canoes."

Pierre came forward and put his heavy arm over her shoulders. He scrutinized Dupre. In Huron, he said, "Is he the one in your Dream?"

She shook her head, but uncertainly. "I don't think so."

"Are you sure you want to risk taking him to Ihonatiria?"

Andiora slipped her arm around Pierre's waist and hugged him. "You're getting paid for this, yes?"

"Aye, but 'tis not worth—"

"It will be all right. We can always kill him on the trail if it turns out he's the one."

Pierre scratched his beard thoughtfully. "Aye, that's true enough." He grinned amiably at Dupre and leaned forward to clap him on the shoulder. "You'd best be going into town to get the supplies you need for the trip, Father. The shops will be closing soon. Marleaux will bring your bags up to the Indian camp, on the top of the hill—" he pointed "—and I'll see you in the morning."

"But I thought you'd . . ."

Pierre tightened his hold on Andiora, and Dupre hesitated, apparently understanding that Pierre wanted to be alone with her. Dupre inclined his head obligingly. "Thank you, Monsieur. We'll see you then."

Pierre turned around and guided Andiora up the dirt trail that led into the trees. "I've not been able to get you out of me mind for months. I'd started to think you were just an angel conjured in me imagination. Is everything all right here?"

"Yes, Pierre," she answered. Her heart ached at his touch. Perhaps

later, after they'd had time to be alone, she would tell him about the
baby . . . if she could.

MUSKET CRACKS SPLIT the air, followed by crude laughter.

"Why do they keep shooting off their guns?" Luc asked.

"Probably because the boat's in. I suspect it's a big event around
here," Dupre responded.

A blue pall of wood smoke hung low over the rough-hewn buildings
of Quebec. The stale scents of urine and whiskey filled the air. Luc
held his black sleeve over his nose as he walked, frowning at the
coarse men who lounged along the streets. They looked like criminals,
every one. Demonic gleams lit their eyes, and grease and soot streaked
their hide clothing. In the past half-hour, he'd heard curses in
English, Portuguese, Italian, Spanish and, of course, French.

"A den of iniquity," Luc said.

"It is . . . interesting." Dupre smiled.

"You find this place amusing?"

"Entertaining would be a better word."

Raimont clung to Dupre's left sleeve, his green eyes wide, as
though fascinated by everything. He smiled inanely at the horses that
clip-clopped by, then frowned at the shattered pieces of crockery and
glass that littered the ground, glittering in the sun.

They passed a building where quarters of meat hung from the
porch rafters. Crawling black flies coated them. The purveyor, an
ugly man with only one eye, yelled, "Ho! Wait up there, Fathers.
You're new here, aren't you? How about trying some of the delicacies
of the New World?" He pounded the closest quarter with a fist, and
the flies burst into flight, whining angrily around his head. "Take a
look at this fellow. Caribou! The finest eating this side of—"

Luc replied, "We're not interested in rotting meat."

"You just scrape off the maggots, Father. They won't hurt you."

"No!"

"Pretty high and mighty, aren't you?" the man shouted after Luc,
who was hurrying down the street. "In a few months, you'll be
begging me for meat. After you've been eating corn three times a
day!"

Luc gritted his teeth and turned to Dupre. "What did he mean by that—three times a day?"

Raimont piped up, "Oh, the Indians love corn! It's their favorite food. I read about it in Father Brebeuf's letters."

"So did I," Luc informed him. "But Brebeuf never said it was their *sole* source of sustenance. I hate corn. It gives me a stomachache."

Raimont blinked owlishly. "Oh, I'm sure they must have berries and roots, too."

"The New World is a garden," Dupre said. "You'll have plenty, Luc."

Ahead, another man stood dipping whiskey from an open-topped barrel and guzzling it like he was dying of thirst. It ran down his chin and splotched his shirt. Three Indian women lay stretched out on bear hides beside him. As Luc passed, they smiled coyly and lifted their skirts to show long, bronze legs.

Luc's mouth gaped. "Harlots!"

"Aye!" the guzzler yelled as he hung his dipper on the side of the barrel. He shook filthy brown hair from his eyes and bared yellow teeth. "You've an eye for women, I see, Father. Come right over! I'll make you a special deal."

"How dare you!" Luc snapped.

"Now, don't be worried, Father. We can be discreet. Why, we handle all sorts here, Brown Robes, Gray Robes and Black Robes. Not to mention a Protestant or two. But," the man hastily added, "you needn't be concerned about that. Me girls bathe twice a week."

Revulsion gurgled in Luc's throat. He stepped backward into a puddle that shone a sickly green—and realized that it was horse urine.

Dupre took him by the arm and dragged him away. "It'll wash off, Luc. Come on. I think we'd better find a shop, buy our supplies and get out of here."

Luc trudged on morosely. Scrawny cats slunk through the shadows, their ribs sticking out. Everywhere he looked, brutes chuckled and pointed at him, some calling coarse remarks. *Now I see why You sent me here, Lord. Satan has taken this New World as his own.*

Almost unconsciously, Luc reached into his pocket to touch his breviary. His mother had given it to him on the day he had decided to enter the priesthood. He'd been ill, sick unto death with smallpox, and God had sent him a vision. Angels had flown into his room, covered him with their blindingly white wings and sung "Hosanna" for days—until he was well again. Then they'd shoved a flaming sword into his hand and whispered, "Be sober, be vigiliant, because your adversary, the devil, like a roaring lion, walketh about, seeking whom he may devour. Fight him, fight him . . ."

"I'm going to be a priest, Mother," he'd announced the very next day.

"A . . . priest?"

"Yes. God has called me to do battle with Satan."

"I'd always imagined you'd go into mercantilism with your brother Francois or . . ." She paused. A plump wren of a woman, she invariably dressed in silk brocades and satins. She'd smoothed a hand down her pink sleeve. "But that might not be such a bad idea. I could benefit—politically—from having a son in the church. Well, let's think about it for a while. You—"

"No, Mother. I know what I must do. I'm going to join the Jesuits and—"

"Oh, Luc! Really. You've never been practical. Cardinal Richelieu hates the Society of Jesus. Why don't you become a Dominican, or even a Franciscan, God forbid—but anything's better than the Jesuits."

"But, Mother, it's my life! I want—"

"Stop sniveling, Luc. You *always* snivel."

"Here," Dupre said, breaking Luc from his memories. "This shop should do."

He had stopped before a lean-to shack marked "Dry Goods." A rocky trail led around the building to an outhouse in the back. The odor of human excrement carried powerfully. They entered through a rickety door that Luc felt certain would fall off its hinges the instant he closed it.

"*Bonjour!*" the proprietor called. He came across the floor drying his hands on a dirty white apron. Of medium height, he had fat jowls and gray hair. "I was just washing my counter. I'm La Salle. What may I get for you?"

Dupre scrutinized the sacks of dried peas and wheat, the bottles of wine, horseshoes, fish hooks and other items that filled the shelves. "We're heading to Ihonatiria. We'll—"

"Ah, to join Father Brebeuf!" La Salle said. His face glowed suddenly. "The last time he was in, he said he had new priests coming. It's good you're here. He needs help. Converting the savages isn't an easy job. Brebeuf works too hard."

Dupre smiled. "He's a very holy man."

"*Oui*. And a good friend." La Salle nodded fondly. "Well, if you'll be traveling for a month, you'll need things for the trip, and for Mass. Bags of wheat, bottles of wine. Maybe some candles?"

"Yes. Thank you. I see you've filled orders for Father Brebeuf before."

"Oh, many times." La Salle waved a hand and hurried across the room. "I know just what you'll need. Come over here and let me show you."

Dupre and Raimont followed, but Luc stared out the grimy window. Across the street, two dogs fought over a bone. The battle grew vicious, and then a man on a gray horse charged them, laughing when they yipped and scampered away. The instant the man dismounted the harlots were all over him. They came out of nowhere, pressing their bodies against him, stroking his hair, calling teasingly. The man laughed and kissed them.

A dungeon of demons, Luc's eyes narrowed. *Don't worry, Lord. I've come to do Your work.*

CHAPTER

Ghostly fingers of smoke spiraled up from the morning camp fires as Marc shook out his dew-soaked blanket. The camp covered the entire hilltop above him. The traders had pitched their canvas tents on the east slope, to catch the morning sun; no one there had awakened yet. But throughout the Indian camp, people moved, talking in low voices while they readied themselves for the long journey to Ihonatiria. The wet scents of pine duff and river rose strongly. The St. Lawrence cut a gleaming silver swath across the land.

They'd come in so late last night that Marc had decided they should make their beds at the very northern edge of the camp, so as not to disturb anyone. But he'd barely slept. Owls haunted the forests here, hooting constantly through the night, and the yips of lonesome wolves had echoed eerily. The land excited him, as new sights and sounds always did, warming the cold, civilized part of his soul.

Marc had been wide awake when Phillipe had gasped and suddenly sat up in his blanket to stare out across the moonlit river below. Marc had tried to talk to him, but he didn't answer. From the position of the stars, it had to be around midnight. Phillipe hadn't moved since. He was still sitting beneath the spreading limbs of the oak, his blanket coiled around his waist and his hands steepled in prayer—staring at nothing. In the dim light, his round face shone as though from inner fire.

Luc knelt ten feet away, almost invisible in his black robe and black cape. He brusquely shoved sugar, bottles of wine and sacks of wheat into his pack while he glanced suspiciously at Phillipe. "I think he's possessed," he said as he rearranged a sack. "Look at his eyes. They're empty, as if his soul has been drained away by some malignant demon."

"I think he's talking to God."

"Have you ever seen a holy man go blank the way he does?"

"Yes. Once."

Marc finished rolling up his blanket and tied it to the top of his pack, which sat propped against the trunk of a fir tree. He'd asked dozens of questions about the vegetation when he'd been in Quebec yesterday, and felt fairly confident that he could identify the main trees and bushes. A cool breeze permeated the forest, rustling the needles and leaves, and stirring the blond hair over his forehead.

"Well?" Luc sounded hostile. "When?"

"Just before his death in sixteen twenty-nine, I had the privilege of praying in the company of Father Pierre de Berulle. I sat next to him for over four hours while he stared at the crucifix in the Cathedral of Notre Dame. His eyes were just as full of God as Phillipe's are."

Luc's jaw moved with his grinding teeth, then his mouth pursed. Gruffly, he went back to shoving things into his pack; wool socks, gloves, a copy of *The Last Temptation of Christ*. He looked as if he wanted to shout at someone but couldn't find a good enough excuse.

Marc turned back to his own pack. He placed his breviary atop his sacred vestments and carefully folded the edges of his white surplice around it. Pierre de Berulle was above question, even by Luc. Berulle had founded the French Oratory, a group of priests with no binding vows who promoted education, established new seminaries, attacked Cardinal de Richelieu's insane political policies, and in general enhanced the image of the French clergy. He was a very holy man.

"Why is it," Luc asked, "that we're always arguing about Raimont?"

"I wasn't arguing, Luc."

"You disagreed with me!"

"If my disagreement sounded like argument, it was unintentional."

Marc cinched the ropes around his pack, rose and quietly walked around Phillipe. He picked up Phillipe's pack and leaned it against the fir beside his own, then began filling it with the lightweight medicinal supplies they had purchased in Quebec: prunes, bags of raisins, lemon peel, senna leaves and wild purslane. Phillipe was so small, he wouldn't be able to carry heavy things like iron pans or sacks of wheat. At least, not for very long. And Marc had no way of knowing how far upriver Andiora and her family had cached the canoes. He would carry Phillipe's share of those things—it would be easier on everyone concerned.

"Luc," he asked gently, "why is it you won't let either Phillipe or myself get close to you? We're going to be very alone here in the New World. All we have is each other. We want to be your friend."

"Friendship isn't the issue, Dupre," Luc responded curtly. "Raimont's nature is. Is he holy? Or demonic? That's the question."

Marc sat back on his heels and stared at Luc. "I don't understand you. What evil can you possibly find in someone as innocent—"

A soft whisper came from Phillipe, almost inaudible. Luc whirled to glare at him. "What did you say?"

"Did you see him?" Phillipe asked a little louder. He sat so still, he didn't even seem to be breathing, but his arm had lifted to point. His face had a serene, unearthly expression.

"See what?" Luc demanded.

"That *big* cougar. He's been moving through the forests since late last night."

Luc frowned at Marc. "What's a 'cougar'?"

"It's a New World lion," Marc explained. "Though it doesn't have a mane like our—"

"A . . . a *lion?*"

"Yes."

Marc's gaze searched the dense woods beyond camp. Firelight shot eerie shadows through the smoke-colored trunks. Leaves quaked in the breeze. Birds hopped from branch to branch, twittering and singing. But nothing else moved. What had Phillipe seen? One of the dogs that skulked around Quebec? *Yes, it must have been a dog.* Marc let out the breath he'd unwittingly been holding.

A short distance away, Mongrave and Andiora crawled through the flap of the canvas tent where they'd spent the night together. She looked beautiful. Her long braid and the beads on her hide dress glinted in the flickers of firelight. Mongrave's dark hair looked wild and unkempt. He hadn't laced up his yellow blouse, leaving a thick mat of dark chest hair visible. He stood and stretched his arms over his head while he yawned. Marc lowered his eyes and turned back to Luc.

"Let's finish packing, Luc. Andiora will want to be leaving as soon as the sun rises."

Luc walked over and stood in front of Phillipe, looking down warily. "Mark my words, Dupre. That's not God in those eyes. You'll see. Just wait." Then he grabbed his blanket, shook out the beads of dew and proceeded to roll it up.

"Perhaps if you kept company with God more often, you'd learn to recognize Him better, Luc."

Luc stood up, his back so straight that he looked like he'd swallowed a ramrod. He slung his pack over his shoulders and announced, "I'll be waiting on the trail at the top of the hill."

Marc listened to his retreating steps and silently berated himself. *You didn't have to say that. Why did you? You don't need an enemy here.*

Mongrave and Andiora had dropped their tent. Their voices carried as they folded the canvas into a neat square, then tied ropes around it. They kept on giving each other warm glances. On the eastern slope, the traders had risen, and raucous laughter and curses laced the still morning air. The Indians stopped for a moment to listen, then shook their heads and continued with their breakfast.

Brusquely, Marc tied three copper pots to the outside of his pack. Their flat bottoms glowed like liquid gold in the rays of sun that lanced up over the St. Lawrence River, puncturing the indigo sky. Only a few of the brightest stars continued to twinkle low on the western horizon. From Quebec, the familiar crow of a rooster rose to greet the dawn. Marc closed his eyes for a moment, letting the sound seep down into his soul. The farms that covered the hills around La Rochelle had wakened with a roosters' symphony every morning. When he'd first arrived at the orphanage, frightened and lonely, the sounds of the animals outside had been his greatest joy. *No more crowing roosters. . . .*

Very softly, Phillipe started singing.

Marc opened his eyes. Phillipe braced a hand on the ground and grunted as he rose to his feet. He gazed around, as though seeing the New World for the first time, and a beneficent smile brightened his face.

"Good morning, Marc. We'd better hurry. It's very late, and God's waiting for us."

"Waiting?"

"Oh, yes. He's been waiting for a very long time. He needed us to come to the New World. To help Jesus, you know." Phillipe smoothed down his wrinkled brown robe and marched to where his pack leaned against the fir.

Marc hoisted his own pack onto his back and slung his newly purchased musket over his left shoulder while he watched Phillipe struggle with his pack. Finally, Phillipe dropped it to take a deep breath. His face and bald head had gone pink from effort. Marc stepped forward.

"May I help you, Brother?"

"Oh, yes, Marc. *Merci*."

Marc lifted the pack, and Phillipe slipped his pudgy arms through the loops and adjusted the weight. "How does that feel, Phillipe?"

"It's fine. Not too heavy."

"Good. Our Montagnais guides have put on their packs, too. We'd better let them know we're ready."

As they worked their way up the hill, Marc noticed that the Indian men wore deerhide cloaks or beaver robes, but their shoulders were almost unladen. They carried only their snowshoes and weapons of the hunt. The women, however, were loaded like oxen, with packs twice the size of Marc's. The one child, a wraith of a girl, bore a pack about the size of Phillipe's. She stood off to the side of the camp, swinging a long stick at the pine boughs, gently knocking off the pearls of dew that sparkled on the needles. When they showered her, she laughed and her dog barked.

Mongrave rose as they neared. "So you're ready, Father? Fine. The Indians hate to be kept waiting."

"Monsieur," Marc said. He extended his hand . . . and halted when Andiora leaned forward to peer intently at his palms. Marc's brows lowered, but he continued, "Thank you for your help so far. We look forward to meeting you again outside of Ihonatiria."

Mongrave took his hand and shook it hard. "Aye, Father, I'll be there in about three weeks. Hopefully, you will too."

Marc's smile faded. "Why wouldn't we be?"

"Oh, I think you will. You're with the best guides in the country. But 'tis a hard thing to judge. I knew me a Recollet priest years back. Mighty fervent one. Went away to preach the ears off the Iroquois on the east side of Lake Ontario."

"What happened to him?"

Mongrave shook his head. "They ate him. But that's the way of things. You be careful. You're not in Iroquois country, but they've been raiding far to the west. There's no saying where you might run up on 'em."

"We'll be careful, Monsieur. Thank you."

"You'd best be going. Your party's waiting on you."

Andiora embraced Mongrave tightly, then backed away and put on her small pack. Odd, Marc thought; he couldn't figure out why some women carried more than others. Andiora's pack looked even lighter than the little girl's. Did Andiora have a special status that made her above such things?

As she walked toward her relatives, Marc and Phillipe fell in line behind her. Before they even reached the group, the Indians began moving at a trot, taking the worn trail past Luc and down into the depths of the forest. Quebec quickly vanished from view. The women and the little girl ran well considering their heavy burdens, but quickly fell to the end of the line with Andiora. In no time, Phillipe had joined them, but Marc and Luc panted to keep up with the men, who raced through the trees as silently as hunting wolves.

For hours they paralleled the St. Lawrence, running and stopping, running and stopping, seemingly at the whim of Atti, the tall warrior who led them, but by midday they had reached the canoes, which had been cached in a grove of birch and hickory trees. A small pine, three feet high, had sprouted at the base of the largest birch; its deep green needles contrasted sharply with the white bark behind it. Deadfall, mounded six feet high in places, scalloped the edges of the grove.

The women peeled away a pile of branches, revealing two boats, each about fifteen feet long. The inside of the bark was the outside of the hull. Designs had been scraped into the bark rind, then painted with white circles, red wavy lines and blue diamonds. Phillipe smiled delightedly, but Luc wandered away, sulking.

Andiora had gone to sit on the edge of the St. Lawrence. With her long braid draped down her back, she gazed across the rippling blue water, where gulls dove and screeched. She used her forearm to wipe her smooth brow, then dropped her head in her hand. Was she ill? It had been a hard run, granted, but not even little Phillipe looked so exhausted.

Marc dropped his pack to the ground and propped his musket atop it. After he'd combed his fingers through his tangled, sweat-matted blond hair and brushed the dust from his beard, he cautiously walked toward her. She spun around when she heard his steps nearing. Fear lined her face, pulling her mouth tight. He could see her legs trembling beneath her hide dress.

Marc smiled. Awkwardly, he asked, "Why do you cache the canoes? Why not just row them into Quebec?"

"You don't know the ways of the Iroquois, Marc Dupre. Only two months ago they attacked a party of Montagnais traders in Quebec. They stole five canoes and three women."

"So the Iroquois are as wild as Monsieur Mongrave implied?"

"Wild?" she asked contemplatively, as though uncertain about the way he was using the French word. "No. They are not 'wild,' Dupre. They are vicious beasts. If you live in our land long enough, you will see. Though I pray to Aataentsic that you won't have to."

"Thank you—for your prayers. Sometime I would like to talk to you about Aataentsic and your other . . . gods."

"Sometime I will let you." She stood up too quickly and swayed on her feet. Instinctively, he grabbed her arm. She glanced at his hand, using the moment to steady herself, then lifted her gaze to meet his. Vulnerability and indecision lit her eyes, as though she were unsure of what to make of him. It affected him oddly. *A man could get lost in those black eyes. No wonder Mongrave . . .*

He released her arm and stepped back, uneasy with his own responses. "I'll look forward to that talk."

"Yes, we'll have many chances," she said as she strode by him.

"But now we must get in the canoes. We have a very long way to go, and Iouskeha will be breathing winter over the land soon."

"Who is Iouskeha?" he asked, running to catch up with her.

"The Bringer of Light." She pointed to the sun. "He created the rivers and lakes, and holds the storms in his hands."

Marc nodded in delight. *So they have a Creator. That's a starting point.* He wondered why he didn't recall reading about that in Father Brebeuf's reports.

While Atti and Nanco shoved the canoes into the water, Marc, Phillipe and Luc took their packs and waited to be told where to put them. Atti waved to Marc, calling him to the lead canoe. When Phillipe and Luc started to follow, Atti shouted something that sounded unpleasant, and pointed to the other canoe.

Andiora translated. "You two will go in Nanco's canoe." Then she turned to Marc and reached for his pack. "Here. Let me take it."

"It's very heavy," he said. "Tell me where you want it."

"Down there, in the middle for balance."

Marc stepped into the canoe and dropped his pack in the place she'd indicated, but he kept his musket with him, holding it in a tight grip. If what she and Mongrave said about the Iroquois were true, he might need his gun at any moment.

"You'll sit up front, opposite me," Andiora said and handed him a beautifully carved paddle. Vines, a moose and three rifle-bearing braves covered the blade and grip.

Andiora made her way to the bow, where she dropped to her knees on the right side and Marc took the left, placing his musket within easy reach. Atti and Klami stepped in, chattering as they took up their places in the rear. Andiora called something over her shoulder and Atti answered, waving his hand. She used her paddle to shove the canoe away from shore and out into the slow-moving water. They drifted, letting the current take hold and tug them out into the main channel before they started rowing.

Marc swiveled around to watch Phillipe's canoe; he and Luc had been split up. Phillipe knelt in the front with a broad smile on his face, next to Nanco, while Luc sat in the rear beside Dyto. Onrea and her dog had stretched out in the center of the canoe, watching an eagle that circled high overhead.

For hours, they rowed in silence, listening to the insects that buzzed around the boats. Blazing gold sunlight reflected blindingly from the river, but thunderheads were piling up on the western horizon. Lightning occasionally flashed, gilding the hearts of the clouds, and Marc thought he could smell the earthiness of rain on the wind. Atti and Andiora kept the canoe skimming close to the western shore, just beyond the grasp of the snags and willows that lined the bank. Fish jumped in the green waters, leaving widening rings expanding outward to touch the wake of Marc's rowing.

He grinned. Ahead, only the wide river gleamed, while on either side, trees bearded the hills. He saw no houses, no roads. In Europe, a man was almost never out of sight of a church steeple. There farmers had cleared and tilled the soil, leaving only tiny stands of trees near their homes. But here the land still dominated man. A power pervaded these rich forests, as though the Holy Spirit thrived in this New World.

When sunset came at last, they pulled the canoes out onto the shore, and the hunters vanished into the forest looking for prey. Onrea gathered wood for fires, while the women set up two bark lodges. Soft talk echoed through the stillness.

Marc dropped his pack and sank wearily against the trunk of a pine. Phillipe eased down beside him, panting, obviously tired to his bones. Only Luc continued standing. Sweat coated his thin face, beading on his hooked nose and matting his brown hair to his head. He propped his pack against a rock, opened it, and reverently began removing his vestments—white surplice, biretta.

"Dupre," he announced, without looking at Marc, "while you and Raimont set up camp and start dinner, I'll ready the Mass."

"It's my night to prepare the Mass, Luc."

"I've already begun, Dupre. You don't have to," Luc responded as he pulled out the silver communion chalice and dug deeper into his pack, producing a bottle of wine. "It'll be dark soon. I wouldn't dally if I were you."

Marc glanced tiredly at Phillipe and they both rose. "Why don't you roll out our blankets, Phillipe? I'll make the fire and cook dinner."

"All right." Phillipe walked to Marc's pack to untie his blanket first.

Marc gathered wood and used a sharp-edged stone to scrape out a hearth in the thick leafbed of the forest. But his thoughts were on Luc. They'd been taking turns with religious duties such as Mass, as Father Brebeuf's letter had instructed all prospective New World missionaries. Marc did not like this new change. And not just because preparing Mass brought him joy, while setting up camp was drudgery. The sparkling gold bullion on the vestments, the odd Latin words, the solemn ritual—all these fascinated the Indians. Father Brebeuf had written that the Indians ascribed a magical character to the Mass, and he had told the missionaries that they must share responsibilities for it, or the Indians would believe one of them greater than the other. Luc had apparently decided that this first night among the Indians would be his chance to make an impression.

Marc collected kindling, got the fire going, then took a copper pot down to the river and filled it with water. By the time he returned, Luc had slipped his white surplice over his black robe and the Indians had begun to stare. They spoke quietly to each other, absently unrolling the bark coverings over the lodge frames as they studied Luc. He put on quite a show, lifting his hands and praying loudly while he finished dressing.

Marc threw some of the dried meat and peas they'd purchased in Quebec into his pot, added a dash of flour to thicken it, and hung the pot on an iron tripod over the fire. Flames licked up around the bottom. As soon as he had unrolled their blankets, Phillipe wandered around, talking to himself and petting the trees. Then he carried two large rocks over and set them near Luc, in preparation for communion. His brown robe spread around his ankles when he sat down and gazed beatifically at Luc, as though in the presence of God Himself. Marc put the lid on their dinner and came to sit beside Phillipe. Against the dark trees, Luc seemed taller, larger than life, in his magnificent vestments.

Andiora walked close to study their actions. She leaned against a maple, her braid falling over her shoulder, her beautiful face glowing orange in the light of the flames. As dusk faded into night, her large eyes looked like glistening black diamonds. She seemed to listen carefully as Luc said the Latin words of consecration that caused the transubstantiation of simple bread and wine into the real body and blood of Christ. Luc gave it a special twist tonight, repeatedly waving his hands over the chalice as if to make a rabbit spring out of a hat. Irritated, Marc thought he looked like one of the charlatans who infested the lower side of Paris, those who dragged passersby to their tables, promising that, for a fee, they had a potion that would cure every ailment known to man.

Andiora frowned disdainfully, and Marc bowed his head, praying that Andiora's contempt rose because she had seen a Mass before and despised Luc's arrogance. Perhaps she'd witnessed one of Father Brebeuf's Masses in Ihonatiria. Did she know that in the Eucharist, Christ gave Himself to the faithful as nourishment for their souls? That He was the living bread that gave life to men through His flesh? It comforted him to think that perhaps she did. But what if she didn't?

Marc promised himself that he would talk to her about it as soon as they finished Mass, perhaps invite her to take dinner with them. But when Luc held the chalice to Marc's lips, saying, "The blood of Christ," she turned and went back to her own fire, where noisy conversation broke out, Klami and Atti asking several questions at once. *Oh, Lord, they've never seen a Mass before . . .*

Marc dourly accepted the bread from Luc's hand and let it melt on his tongue. Andiora had launched into a long explanation of some sort. What was she saying? Atti threw back his head and laughed. Marc's shoulder muscles clenched tight. He strained his ears and thought he caught the words "clown" and "fools."

His anger with Luc festered through dinner, flaring every time Luc gave him a smug smile. Phillipe babbled on about the birds and animals he'd seen: "That redheaded bird was a woodpecker, and the duck with the green patch on its head was a New World widgeon. I saw them both in a book once. Have—have you ever seen those books, Father Luc? They're in the Notre Dame library." When Luc didn't respond, he hastily turned to Marc. "Have you ever seen them, Marc?"

"No, Phillipe."

Phillipe sank into a silence, pushing his stew around in his bowl with his spoon for several minutes before he murmured, "I think maybe I'll say my prayers and go to bed."

"That's a good idea, Phillipe. We'll be starting out very early tomorrow. Before dawn, I'll wager." Marc gave him an encouraging smile.

Phillipe lowered his eyes, put down his bowl and walked away. Marc saw him kneel beside his blanket, his body no more than a black spot against the dark forest.

Luc gulped down the last of his dinner as though uncomfortable at being alone with Marc. He tossed his dirty bowl and spoon atop Phillipe's and rose to his full height of almost six feet. "It's your night to wash dishes, Dupre. I'll see you in the morning." His mouth quirked with self-satisfaction before he turned and strode away.

Marc's stomach roiled. He dumped the remainder of his stew back into the pot, gathered up the dirty dishes and went to wash them. Starlight coated the dead grass as he walked down to the river. Pungent scents of pine and mud filled the air. He inhaled deeply, hoping the fragrance would soothe his anger. But nothing seemed to work. He knelt at the side of the river and roughly scooped each bowl in the sand, scouring them out before rinsing them in the cold water. *This isn't like me, Lord. You know it's not. Why does Luc bring out the worst in me?*

Eyes glinted in the trees, blinking slowly while they scanned the woods. Owls. There were so many of them in the New World. He caught sight of black wings swooping over the shore in the distance. When the wings suddenly dropped into a clump of brush, a squeak erupted, then died. A chorus of hoots began, coming from nowhere, from everywhere at once. Eerie. They reverberated over the water.

Marc finished the washing and headed back up the bank. Dry leaves crunched beneath his boots, startling the closest crickets into silence. When he crested the slope, he saw the Indians sitting around their fire, laughing, talking, shaking gourd rattles. Andiora sat near the flames with a blanket around her shoulders, watching Atti, who gestured with one arm while he spoke. Monstrous shadows swept the forest behind him. Marc hurried to his own camp.

Tucking the bowls and spoons into his pack, he kicked dirt over the fire, then tiptoed to his blanket and rolled up in it. Phillipe, who lay between him and Luc, was snoring softly. Marc tried to force himself to relax by counting Phillipe's snores the same way he would count sheep jumping a fence. *One. Two. Threefour . . . five . . . Luc's*

*an idiot . . . six . . . seven . . . how did he ever gain approval for ordination?
. . . eight . . . somebody must like him . . . nine . . .*

Klami interrupted his tally by shaking her rattle and laughing. Did the Indians tell stories every night? He wished he could understand more of what they were saying. Wind teased the branches over his head. As they swayed through the starlight, they wove a glittering tapestry of light and shadow across the ground. The persistent buzzing of mosquitoes began. At first he gently waved at them, then he slapped them and scratched at their bites. Finally he surrendered and tucked his head beneath his blanket.

"How can Raimont sleep with that unholy racket going on?" Luc whispered.

Marc answered, "Probably because he has a clear conscience."

"What's that supposed to mean?"

He rolled to his right side and pulled down his blanket to stare at Luc. A shaft of starlight glinted in his eyes. "It's not supposed to mean anything."

"What's that tone in your voice?"

"What tone?"

"You sound angry, Dupre. Are you?"

"No."

"Yes, you are. Be honest," Luc chided, and his teeth shone in the starlight. "You're angry because I'm better at Mass than you are."

Marc propped himself on one elbow. "I didn't realize that it was a competition, Luc."

"Yes, you did. You've been trying to outdo me ever since we boarded the *Soleil*. Your holier-than-thou charade—"

"I don't think I'm holier than you. But I do wonder why you put on such a show tonight."

"The Indians enjoyed it."

"You profaned it."

Luc sat up, fuming. His blanket fell down around his waist, revealing his silver crucifix. "Well, you'd know far more about the profane side of the world than I would, Dupre. After all, you've lived it most of your . . ."

*   *   *

PHILLIPE BIT HIS lip, pretending to be asleep. Luc's loud voice had awakened him often in the past two months, but tonight it sounded so harsh that it made Phillipe feel like he had to throw up. He'd been in the middle of a beautiful dream. It was winter. Feathers were falling . . . falling all around him . . . they'd formed at the edges of a white cloud and fluttered down so thickly that at first he'd thought they were snow. Luc had been there. He'd been shouting, "The End has come! The End has come!"

"You're a peasant, Dupre. That's what's the matter with you. You've no sense of glory or majesty. That's why you can't appreciate me or my ways."

"Does being born rich make one majestic, Luc? I believe our Savior said that it was easier for a camel to go through the eye of a needle than for a rich man to enter heaven."

"Don't preach at me, Dupre! If you had any sense of God . . ."

Phillipe curled into a ball and buried his face in his sleeve to cry. Marc and Father Luc had been arguing more and more. Marc tried not to, but it seemed that he couldn't talk at all without Father Luc making some cutting remark. Tears trickled down Phillipe's face. Rage frightened him. It always had. When he was a child and someone shouted at him, he would run away through the long halls of the cathedral to find Henri. Holding Henri, petting his soft fur, feeling that rough tongue on his face, had always consoled Phillipe. He sniffed, missing Henri again, even after all these years.

Marc paused for a long time before saying, "We're both tired, Luc. It was a long day. Good night."

"That's another thing you're not good at, Dupre. Discussion."

Marc did not respond, and Phillipe held his breath. Was it over? Finally?

He felt a hand, large and gentle, grope in the darkness for his shoulder. Marc patted him and said, "Good night to you, too, Phillipe."

Phillipe quickly reached up to pat his hand back. "Good night, Marc."

8

Michael Jameson dragged himself into a tangled brier of dead raspberry vines, gasping, trying to keep one hand on the arrow wound in his side while the other hand rested on the hilt of his sword. Musket blasts shredded the sunlit morning around him. Jagged screams died suddenly, but their echoes filtered through the autumn forests like the wails of ghosts. The Iroquois, howling and shrieking, had attacked them while they still slept; their tents had gone up in flames. When they'd rushed out of the blazing infernos into the predawn glow, they had been shot down like dogs.

He held his breath. *What was that?* It sounded like . . . moccasins moving stealthily through the grass. Slowly, he lowered his head and peered through the vines. Two Iroquois warriors stood thirty feet away, using sign language to talk to each other. They were in war paint. Red and black dots covered the closest one's ugly face. The man farther back had a purple band across his forehead. Both wore breechclouts and carried tomahawks. They'd slung their bows over their shoulders.

Michael pressed on his wound, trying to quell the flow of blood, but it throbbed hotly under his fingers, as if the arrow had sliced an artery. *No, God, please . . .*

The lead warrior stepped closer and sniffed the wind, scenting for blood.

Dear God Almighty, let them pass me by!

Michael frantically searched the hills for Pierre or any of the other members of the trading party. The creek bottom below showed movement, but he couldn't make out who or what it was. White or Indian? He dared not call out.

Gingerly, he slipped his bloody hand from the wound to his sword in its belt scabbard. He'd lost so much blood that he doubted he could swing it more than a time or two—*but maybe that will be enough.*

The second brave scowled and trotted back a hundred feet, walking in circles to cut for tracks. So many people had run in this direction that the trail would be churned up, but Michael had been dropping a lot of blood.

The warrior smiled and waved his tomahawk to his friend, who stood no more than ten feet from Michael, then ran back, laughing. Together, they began tiptoeing through the frosty leaves, taking their time as they worked their way toward the brier.

Michael closed his eyes briefly, begging God to take his soul even though it was filled with sins of all kinds. When he opened his eyes, the warriors stood directly over him, peering down through the vines. He gathered his strength.

The lead warrior let out a bloodcurdling war whoop and Michael rose like the wrath of God, shoving away the vines to draw his sword. The warrior dove at him, his tomahawk raised, and Michael swung. The sword sliced through the brave's midsection, disemboweling him. His insides spilled on the ground before he staggered and toppled over. Michael stumbled sideways, trying to heft his bloody sword again, but the second brave lunged with lightning quickness. His knife went deep into Michael's stomach, ripped up through his chest and into his lungs. The sword fell from Michael's hand. He stood for a moment longer, staring at the warrior, before his legs went weak and he crumpled to the ground.

Through the blades of grass he saw Pierre and Tristan scrambling up the hill, screaming, guns aimed. The Iroquois spun and tried to make a run for it.

Two muskets boomed.

Michael couldn't see whether the brave dropped or not. A gray haze had swallowed the edges of his vision, leaving only a pinpoint of the sky visible. Through it, he watched the clouds swirl and melt. *Tired. So tired.*

"Oh, Michael, for the sake of God," Pierre whispered.

Michael felt an arm slip beneath his head, lifting him so he could breathe more easily through his torn lungs. Blood had begun to well warmly into his throat, choking him. He coughed and managed to wheeze, "Andiora?"

Pierre's swarthy face went pale. "I don't know. I pray they've made it through."

Michael blinked and found it difficult to raise his lids again. If anything happened to that little girl, it would kill Pierre. Forcing his eyes to focus, he counted the men who leaned over him. Six. Six of eight. He smiled. They'd taught the damned Iroquois, by God! Why, that war party had consisted of at least twenty men, and . . .

The clouds kept swirling above him. Swirling and swirling, turning as black as storm clouds.

SNOW BEGAN FALLING that afternoon. Huge, wet flakes tumbled out of a gray sky. When it grew so thick that they could no longer see to keep the canoes away from snags and rocks, Atti ordered them to make camp.

Marc, Phillipe and Luc crouched around their fire with their blankets over their shoulders, sipping cups of hot tea. Snow coated Marc's beard, making him look older than his twenty-six years. He lifted his cup and took a long drink. The Indians had erected a single bark lodge in the lee of a hill, surrounded by pines, out of the wind. They would be dry tonight.

Marc frowned down into the crackling flames. Father Brebeuf had instructed that they obey every command of the Indians but keep themselves separate, making their own camp, cooking their own meals—*"Don't be burdens to them."* But in the snow? The Indian lodge looked big enough to hold all nine of them. Should he ask? He was worried about Phillipe. The little Brother had been shivering nonstop for over an hour, though he never complained.

A cheer rose from the Indians. Marc looked up. Atti and Nanco had returned from hunting carrying five beaver strung on a pole between them. The women praised them and clapped, while Onrea and her dog danced happily around the bonfire they'd built.

Luc grimaced. "They have fresh meat. All we have left is a few dried peas. One of us will have to hunt tomorrow."

"I'll do it," Marc offered. "I'm good with a musket."

They had been coldly polite to each other since the first night of the journey, barely meeting each other's eyes for fear of starting something unpleasant.

Phillipe's teeth chattered when he said, "I—I want to h-help you. We could hunt r-rabbits. I watched a man snare—"

"Birds would be easier," Luc remarked. "We've passed hundreds of ponds, and every one of them was filled with ducks and geese."

Phillipe's green eyes went wide. "Oh, but . . . birds? I c-couldn't kill—" At Luc's glare, he hugged his knees to his chest and breathed down the front of his blanket in silence.

Marc threw another branch on the fire. Sparks rose and sizzled into nothingness in the falling snow. A few stars twinkled above. Perhaps the storm would break soon. "On second thought," he said, "I think we should try fishing before we waste our musket ammunition. Luc's right about the ponds, and we bought those iron fishhooks in Quebec. We may as well try them."

Phillipe closed his eyes in gratitude. "I like fish."

"So do I, and I think—"

Marc stopped. Andiora had come silently to stand before their small blaze. She wore a thick fox coat with the hood up, but her long hair danced around her face, teased by the wind. Her gaze landed first on Phillipe, then on Luc, and finally came to rest on Marc. The light of the flames flickered in her dark eyes.

"Iouskeha watched us today. He saw that we were cold and hungry." Reverently, she lifted her arms to the sky. "He talked to Brother Beaver, and Beaver told his children to give themselves to us for food. I don't know what your customs are, but if you can, we want you to come eat with us."

Marc smiled. "We'd like that very much."

She bowed slightly and backed away.

They followed her across camp and sat in the spaces made for them between Andiora and young Onrea. Phillipe claimed the place beside the girl because she had her dog lying next to her. The black-and-white animal looked ghostly in the orange light. It had pointed ears and a wolfish face, and black spots speckled its legs. It wagged its tail when Phillipe petted it. Onrea pointed to the dog and said, "Suma." Phillipe smiled and repeated "Suma." Luc dropped to his knees beside Phillipe, eying the beavers ravenously, and Marc sat cross-legged next to Andiora.

She didn't look at him. She was watching Atti and Nanco pick up the beaver pole and carry it toward the fire. The beavers' tails swung in unison. A chant began, low, like a hymn. Klami shook her gourd rattle in time with the careful, rhythmic steps of Atti and Nanco. They entered the firelight and knelt. Dyto hurried forward to set a copper pot beneath the beaver on the far right, then pulled out her knife. She made a tiny puncture in the hide between the forepaws and carefully slit down around the procreative organs, making certain that every drop of blood landed in the pot. The chant rose to echo from the trees.

Andiora leaned toward Marc as though to speak, but apparently thought better of it and straightened. Marc boldly inquired, "Does Iouskeha demand that the animals be treated in this way?"

"Not Iouskeha. Our mother, Aataentsic. In the beginning of the world, Aataentsic was attacked by Bear. Beaver fought to save her, but he wasn't as strong as Bear. Bear killed him. Aataentsic got to Beaver before Bear could eat him and sucked all of Beaver's blood from the earth. Then she breathed it back into his body so he could live again." Andiora glanced at Marc, gauging his reaction. "We cannot let Beaver's blood touch the earth, because he would consider it an insult and his children would not let us kill them for food."

Marc nodded solemnly. "Thank you for telling me."

Dyto finished slitting open the last beaver. With great care, she took the animal's entrails and placed them in a pile away from the camp, then returned and began the skinning process. As she finished each animal, she cut it into fourths and handed the quarters to the people. Marc took his quarter and watched the way Andiora skewered hers on a stick and braced it over the flames to roast. He did the same and gestured for Phillipe and Luc to follow his lead. The sweet scent of meat filled the air as people came to sit around the fire. Klami and Dyto observed the priests with great curiosity, keeping track of each movement they made.

When Marc bit into his quarter, juice squirted out and drenched his blond beard. Onrea squealed and pointed. Laughter spread through the gathering. Marc raised his arms in a gesture of helplessness and laughed, too. The meat had a sweet, delicate flavor, unlike anything he'd eaten in France. He gobbled it hungrily. By the time he'd finished, a layer of shiny fat coated his hands. He noticed that the natives wiped their hands on their hair or on the dog whenever it happened to pass by. Luc gathered pine needles for cleaning his fingers, but Marc waited for Suma to pass and did as the others had.

The Indians nodded approvingly. Atti nudged Andiora and said something.

She turned to Marc. "Atti wants to know why you Black Robes have nothing to do with women."

"Please tell Atti that we take a vow of chastity, so that we can concentrate all of our attention on God."

Andiora relayed the words, and Atti shrugged. He waved his hands when he gave his response to Andiora. Turning to Marc, she said, "Atti says it is your business, but it's unnatural. Doesn't your holy book say that 'man should be fruitful and multiply'?"

"Atti knows our holy book?" Marc asked in surprise. He saw Luc stiffen at his side, as though there were something vaguely sacrilegious about the fact.

"Some of it, yes," Andiora replied. She took another bite of her beaver and slowly chewed it. "Father Davost came to preach to the Montagnais last year. Atti talked to him a great deal about your religion."

"Well . . . that's wonderful."

Atti asked another question, and Andiora frowned. "Atti wants you to tell him about your God. He says Davost tried to explain the three faces of God to him, but he has never understood it."

"The Trinity?" Marc's face fell. "Of all the questions Atti could ask, that is perhaps the most difficult to answer." Andiora translated and Marc continued. "The dogma of the Trinity says that there are three persons in God—Father, Son, and Holy Spirit. They are One in essence, but each person is distinct from the others. The Trinity is really beyond human understanding. It's one of the mysteries of God."

Atti frowned, then said something in response. Andiora told Marc, "Atti understands the part about the Father and the Son, but he wants to know more about this Holy Spirit."

Marc leaned forward and began, "God is everywhere, but He doesn't dwell in everyone. The Holy Spirit is the aspect of God that lives in us. But, again, God the Father and God the Son aren't really separate from the Holy Spirit. It's very difficult to explain."

Andiora shrugged. "We believe something like that. Spirit is everywhere, in the rocks, trees, land, and people, but only certain beings can use Power to affect others. We call them *oki*."

"Affect others how?" Luc demanded. His gray eyes had narrowed, making his hooked nose seem more prominent. He'd pulled his gray blanket up to his chin and knotted it there. The snow had stopped. As the sky cleared, cold breathed from every inch of the earth.

"To bring good or bad fortune. Many *oki* are witches who use Power for bad things."

"Well, is Power bad or good?" Luc questioned.

"Neither. It just is. You can use it for bad or good."

Phillipe listened with his mouth open while he stroked Suma's side. The dog had stretched out across his feet, and Marc noticed that Phillipe had stopped shivering. Onrea had curled up next to the fire in front of Suma and was sound asleep, though the dog kept kicking her in the back. Perhaps, when they were settled at Ihonatiria, Father Brebeuf would let Phillipe have a dog.

Klami, Dyto and Nanco whispered back and forth among themselves, as though uninterested in the conversation Marc was having with Atti.

Atti asked something else, and again Andiora translated. "Atti says that maybe he does understand about God now—because there are some things that can be seen only with the eyes of the soul."

Marc smiled. "Yes. Yes, that's true. You believe in a soul?"

Andiora clasped her fingers in her lap. Long hair fell from the frame of her hood to rest on her chest. Each strand shone as though it had been individually polished. "We believe we have two souls. At death, the first soul separates from the body and stays in the village of the living. It comes into the longhouses and eats what is left in the cook pots, and sometimes it talks to people. The other soul stays with the bones until the Feast of the Dead. Then it is properly cared for and prayed to the Village of Souls."

"And where is the Village of Souls?"

She pointed to the west. "It is where Aataentsic and Iouskeha live. The souls have to follow the path of stars in the sky to get there." Her hand swept up toward the thick band of the Milky Way.

Marc stared at her, fascinated. "Do all souls go to the Village of Souls?"

"No. People who kill themselves cannot go there. They are not allowed in. And people who die violently are kept out, too, because they are dangerous. Warriors who die in battle form their own band and live by themselves in another land."

"Tell me about Aataentsic. Who was she and how did she 'fall'?" *The Fall of man from Grace? Adam being cast out of the Garden?*

Andiora smiled at his interest. Then she glanced at Phillipe and Luc and sighed deeply. Phillipe was whispering in Suma's pointed ear, while Luc read his breviary. Marc shook his head. How could they *not* be intrigued by the strong similarities between Judaism and the Indian beliefs? Here was *proof* that the Indians stemmed from the lost tribes!

Andiora said, "Aataentsic fell from heaven because of her husband. He was very hungry and told her to climb a tree and get him some fruit. But when Aataentsic climbed the tree, she fell and went through a hole in the sky. Sometimes Aataentsic comes to our ceremonials to make certain we are being good. She usually comes as an old woman, but she has the ability to turn herself into a beautiful young girl when she wants to teach a spiritual lesson."

"Who created men?"

"Aataentsic's son, Iouskeha."

"The *Son* created." Marc's chest tingled as the opening to the Book of John ran through his mind: "In the beginning was the Word . . . He was in the world, and the world was made by him . . ." "How many children did Aataentsic have?"

"Two. When Aataentsic fell, she was pregnant. She gave birth to twin sons, Iouskeha, Guardian of the Sky, and Tawiscaron. When the boys grew up, they fought, and Iouskeha severely wounded Tawiscaron. Tawiscaron ran away, and his drops of blood turned to stone. Our people still use that flint to make arrow and lance points . . . because Tawiscaron's Spirit lives in the rock."

The Cain and Abel story. Different . . . but close.

"And what does Iouskeha do now?"

Andiora laughed at Marc. A gay sound, it made him smile in return. "You are very interested in our religion. I'm surprised. Most Black Robes do not care. They want to teach us their ways, but they will not listen to ours."

"I want to know your ways. Very much. Teach me about Iouskeha."

"He protects humans. He loves us and is very good to us. He brought men fire and taught them how to grow corn. Whenever Aataentsic judges that we have been wicked and need to be punished, Iouskeha pleads against it and tries to protect us."

Marc was captivated. Stretching out on his side and propping his head on one hand, he continued asking Andiora questions and listening so intently to her responses that he barely noticed Luc, Phillipe, Atti and the others begin to drift away from the fire. He felt wide awake, as though he could talk all night. Finally only he and Andiora remained to watch the beaver bones charring in the coals. The fire had dwindled, and in the embers' light, the season's last insects flitted, their membranous wings glinting as silver as the stars that crowded the sky overhead. Only a few shreds of cloud remained, drifting lazily westward.

Marc surreptitiously studied the way the firelight accentuated the smooth curve of Andiora's jaw. She was a beautiful woman, indeed. Her eyes were downcast, watching the fire, and her long lashes threw dark crescents over her cheeks.

"Your stories are wonderful," Marc said sincerely. "So many of your beliefs are similar to ours. Many Christians think that your people knew God long before our own did, that you originally came from a part of the world called Israel. I believe it."

"I don't know anything about this Israel, but Spirit has always lived in my people's hearts. Especially my mother's people, the Huron."

"You're half Montagnais and half Huron?" Marc asked.

"Yes. My father was Montagnais. My mother was a very great shaman among the Bear Clan of the Huron. She sent her Guardian Spirit to me after her death."

"The Huron believe in guardian spirits?" The thought delighted him. "We do, too. We call them guardian angels."

Andiora eyed him speculatively. "You have found your guardian 'angel'?"

"I've never seen him, but I know he's there. Sometimes I can feel his presence."

"But he never shows himself to you? You never Dream of him? Maybe you did not fast long enough, or perhaps your sweat was not true and you were not pure when you started seeking the Spirit. You should try again."

Marc grasped the part about fasting, but he didn't understand her comments about sweat at all. He nodded politely. "Does your guardian spirit show himself to you?"

Her eyes tightened. As she looked up at the shimmering bowl of stars, her fur hood fell back, revealing the wealth of her hair. "Sometimes."

"What is he like? What kinds of things does he tell you?"

"Mostly, he brings me warnings about evil things entering our land." She tucked her fingers beneath her arms, hugging herself. She seemed to be considering what she could and could not say to him. Softly, half-afraid, she said, "My Guardian Spirit told my mother that you whites would come. He told her that you would destroy our land and kill our people."

The words left Marc groping for a response. He picked up a stick to prod the fire with. A cloud of sparks spiraled into the dark branches overhead. The snow had stopped completely, though a few flakes shook loose from the treetops and fluttered around them when the wind blew. "I can't speak for the traders or the politicians who are here seeking the wealth of the New World, but we Catholics, we seek only to open the door for you to God's love and grace."

He felt as if Andiora's stare were probing his soul. What was it about her eyes? Flashes of gold sparkled in their black depths. Something there reminded him of Marie. After several seconds, a smile touched her lips. He smiled back, but when a tingle grew in his chest and spread through his limbs in a warm rush, he looked away. She stirred feelings in him that he hadn't experienced in years.

"Andiora, I should go to bed. I—"

"Before you leave, I want to show you something. Maybe you can tell me what it means." She lifted her hand and put her last two fingers down and left her first two fingers and thumb extended.

Marc smiled broadly. "That's very good. Did Father Brebeuf teach you that?"

"You know this sign?"

His smile faded. "Well . . . yes. It's the Teaching Hand of our Lord. Jesus used it when He was teaching about heaven, or the salvation of the soul, and sometimes when He was healing."

"Healing?"

Marc nodded. "Yes, our Lord performed many miracles. He healed the blind and the crippled, and even raised the dead."

Andiora's hand trembled. She tucked it into the folds of her dress. "I don't understand. Maybe he comes to heal—"

Something thrashed through the forest to Marc's left. It sounded huge, angry, running at full speed toward them. He jerked around and caught sight of a dark shape flicking through the trees.

"What—" Andiora got to her knees, preparing to run, but the thrashing stopped.

Marc searched the forest for movement. Sticks cracked as the creature stalked closer. A low growl rose. Marc slowly stood up. At the very edge of the forest, yellow eyes gleamed. A wolf? *Your musket is thirty yards away.* Could he make a run for it? He turned toward his own camp. Phillipe and Luc, rolled in their blankets around the dying fire, hadn't moved. The red coals cast a crimson veil over their faces.

Marc took a cautious step backward, then another. The growl exploded into a high-pitched shriek that turned his blood to ice. He froze, his heart pounding. Not a wolf. He'd never heard such a cry in his life . . . *almost human.* Frantically, he searched the area for any kind of weapon, and grabbed a rock.

"No, Marc," Andiora said. She shivered as though a deep cold had penetrated her. "He wants me. Stay here."

"What? What are you talking about?"

She rose. "Don't follow me, Marc."

"Wait! *Who* wants you?" Marc called as she disappeared into the dark forest. "Andiora?" He took three running steps.

"*Don't!*" she shouted.

His steps faltered, remembering Brebeuf's instructions to obey everything the Indians told them: "Your lives may depend upon it. They know this world far better than you ever will."

A huge black shadow moved across the face of the trees, lithe, catlike. Andiora's face gleamed for an instant, then she was gone.

Motionless, Marc stood staring into the woods . . . until the cold drove him to his blankets.

9

. . . Certainly, here are many silly things: and I am afraid things
darker and more occult. . . . There is therefore some foundation for
the belief that the devil sometimes guides their hands, and reveals
himself to them for some temporal profit and for their eternal
damnation.

> JEAN DE BREBEUF, S.J.
> *Ihonatiria, 1636*

The dark silhouettes of maples and poplars lightened into
autumn brilliance as the sun edged over the horizon. Snow
frosted the hills with a glimmering blanket of white. The
temperature had dropped dramatically since yesterday and was now
well below freezing. Not even the birds had the courage to sing this
morning. With their feathers fluffed out, they sat morosely on the
branches, peering inquisitively at the activities in the human camp
below.

"But you had to hear it," Marc said as he kicked dirt over their
morning fire. His breath condensed into a cloud before him. "It
sounded . . . I don't know . . . like a woman's scream." He'd thrown
his black cape over his robe and put on his broad-brimmed hat, as
had Phillipe and Luc. Any shield against the damp bite of the wind
was welcome.

Luc looked up from tying his blanket to his pack. His brown hair
stuck out at odd angles from beneath his hat brim. In the background,
Andiora and her family went about cleaning up their camp. Atti and

Nanco had already trudged down to the canoes with the first load. Luc said, "I didn't hear any screeching. Did you, Raimont?"

Phillipe shook his head. His round face was flushed pink from the cold. "No, but I heard an owl go *hoo-hoo-hoooo*."

"The animal couldn't have been more than fifty yards away!" Marc insisted, his eyes on Andiora. She spoke quietly to Klami as they packed copper pots. How could she be so calm after last night? *What happened out there in the forest? What was that creature?*

Luc slung his pack over his shoulders. "You must have been dreaming, Dupre."

"I was wide awake!" Marc growled.

Luc's gray eyes glinted. "Then maybe I'm not the only one Satan has decided to reveal himself to."

Blood surged in Marc's ears. He wanted to shout the idea down, but . . . could it have been? No, Andiora was a good woman, though good people had sometimes fallen to the Prince of Evil's wiles, too. He propped his hands on his hips and glared up at the sky, where clouds sailed through the lavender veil of dawn. The wind had picked up, showering their camp with a flood of gold and red leaves. To change the subject, Marc asked, "Do you think we have another storm coming in?"

"Yes," Phillipe answered. "I was cold all night."

Luc started down toward the river, his boots crunching in the snow. "Then we'd better stop dallying, or we'll get trapped in this godforsaken wilderness until spring."

FOR EIGHT DAYS, the snow fell.

Andiora rowed steadily, trying to keep warm, but her toes and fingers ached miserably. Snow-clad pines lined both sides of the river, rising like white spears to lance the scudding clouds. Each time the wind gusted, more snow shook from those limbs and showered their canoes. Andiora had the hood of her foxhide coat pulled up, but the snow still sifted down her collar, chilling her to the bone. Every day seemed worse than the one before. Slabs of ice lined the river banks now. They couldn't land unless they took their oars and slammed them into the ice to break it up, or found a section of ice thick enough that it would support them while they crawled over it, dragging their canoes behind them in freezing misery.

And she hadn't been feeling well. The pain in her womb had grown worse, draining her strength until she felt as weak as a newborn. Klami had been making rose-hip tea for her every night, but it hadn't helped.

Andiora glanced across the bow of the canoe at Marc. His blond beard and mustache had grown a mantle of ice. They had barely spoken during the last week, and never about Cougar's visit. An odd night. Cougar had been reluctant, wary. She'd stayed in the forest for a long time, until she'd fallen asleep against a tree—and only then had Cougar come out of the shadows to warn her that the storm was coming.

But she and Marc hadn't had much time to talk. When they stopped at night, everyone wanted only to set up the lodge, eat and go to sleep. Bitter cold drained so much strength from the body that no one had the energy for conversation. Atti had invited the Black Robes into their lodge; everyone stayed warmer that way. Marc and the little Black Robe, Phillipe, seemed happy about the change. But Penchant tossed and turned like a homeless ghost, complaining about everything: "Suma's lying on my feet again. Get him off!" "Who is that? Is that Onrea talking in her sleep? Someone wake her up." "Raimont, stop that snoring!"

After a solid week of such complainings, no one liked Penchant very much. Atti had threatened to slit his throat and leave him for the wolves, and Klami took every opportunity to torment him, calling him names in Montagnais, accusing him of having no semen in his body. Fortunately, Penchant never asked Andiora to translate those taunts, but he seemed to understand them just the same. He kept as far away from Klami as he could.

Andiora had been thinking about Pierre. *Why couldn't you tell him about the baby? What were you afraid of? That he would leave you? Any man who would leave you after what you've been through* . . . The other side of her soul challenged, *Pierre wouldn't do that to you. Stop thinking it! He loves you . . . loves you . . . Then why is he always gone? He's never there when you need him . . . never has been . . .*

They paddled around a turn in the river, and Atti exclaimed, "*Haee! Haee!*"

Andiora groaned, "Oh, no."

A tangled mass of rotting logs and ice choked the stream. They would have to portage. But how could they? The wind had blown the snow into twenty-hand-tall drifts on the forest trails, and trying to shoulder the canoes along the water's edge would be suicidal. A fall into the freezing water could mean death.

Everyone turned their oars to slow the boats.

"Andiora?" Marc said. She turned to see him looking at the mounds of snow that covered the ice leading to the shore. "There's no way of telling how thick the ice is here. Shouldn't we go back downstream and find a better place?" His black hat provided scant warmth for his ears. They shone red through the mat of blond hair.

Andiora turned toward Atti, who sat in the rear of the canoe, across from Klami. Both of them wore heavy moosehide coats with the hoods pulled up. She called, "Should we go back? This looks very bad for stopping."

"It's like this for half a day's journey," Atti responded. "We'll have to try it."

Andiora nodded, but swallowed hard. Whoever went out on the ice would have a sixty-hand journey to the shore. "I'll go," she volunteered.

"No," Klami said. "You're not well! If something happens, you won't have the strength to pull yourself out of the water."

"I'm the lightest," Andiora said. "It will be safer for me to test the ice. Unless we want to send Onrea?"

Klami sat back, looking miserable, knowing that Onrea would have less chance than Andiora if she fell. "Be careful," Klami said.

They paddled up to the edge of the crust, and Andiora peered at the surface. In places, she could see through the snow to the ice. Water rushed beneath.

"Move downstream another ten hands," she instructed. Atti and Marc carefully did as she asked.

Andiora took her paddle, scraped away the snow and started over the edge of the boat, but when Marc realized that she was getting out, he grabbed her arm.

"What are you doing?" he asked. His blue eyes had gone tight with concern.

"I'm going to find a way to shore."

"Let me do it. I can—"

"You're too heavy, Marc."

She shook off his hand and cautiously put one foot out onto the ice. With her paddle, she pounded the slab, testing its strength, then climbed out of the canoe. A cold, white expanse spread before her. She could hear the water gurgling beneath it. Marc's face tensed as she dropped down and crawled forward. He crossed himself, and his mouth moved with silent words. Asking his God to keep her safe? She uttered a prayer of her own to Aataentsic.

Andiora moved around a thin spot filled with bubbles, then proceeded forward. A low ridge of frozen snow blocked her path ahead; three hands tall, it thrust up like the gnawed spine of a long-dead water animal.

"How are you?" Atti called. He had risen to his knees in the canoe. His hood had fallen back, revealing his tuft of black hair. Snowflakes had already begun to turn it gray.

"Fine! Not much farther," she answered. She had made it halfway to the shore now and felt more confident. Any of the people could follow the path she'd taken, though in some places the heaviest might have to cross on their stomachs.

Marc crouched in the bow, watching her pensively. Frigid gusts of wind whipped his blond hair around his face.

Andiora eased forward to the ridge of snow and peered over the edge, scrutinizing the ice warily. She prodded it with her paddle, then pounded it hard. It felt sturdy.

She put one hand across it, then the other, and finally brought over a knee. In that instant the ice groaned like a dying elk, and she knew she had made a mistake. The frozen surface gave way in a stunning splash of frigid water that made her cry out as she fell in headfirst.

Water gushed into her mouth and nostrils before she had the sense to hold her breath. The current latched onto her and ruthlessly dragged her under, bashing her on upthrust rocks and limbs. She caught blurred images of frozen mud and grass.

Andiora clawed at the ice, trying to keep herself from being carried farther from her entry point. But the river had smoothed the ice to the gloss of trader's silk, and she had nothing to hold on to. The current swept her downstream like cattail down in the wind.

The bitter cold of the water numbed her. In only moments, her muscles cramped and her arms would not obey her commands.

Hope blinded her when she realized that she was being pulled toward the center of the river, where the water was unfrozen. *Atti will see me!*

But with a violent jerk, she stopped moving, though the current still yanked at her arms and legs. Her foxhide coat had snagged on something. Her lungs burned as though on fire. In terror, she looked up through the ice and saw a blurred face. It swam in her vision as though unreal. *Who . . .* Without thinking, she tried to take a breath. Bubbles spurted up around her and frigid water flowed into her lungs. *Oh, Aataentsic, no!*

A burst of light.

Hands, warm hands, dipped into the water, pulling her up. She couldn't feel her body, only those blessed hands. She thought she heard shouts. Wind gusted over her as she lay on the ice.

Someone rolled her onto her side, and water trickled from her lips. Marc's deep, familiar voice penetrated the terror.

"Andiora? Breathe . . . breathe!"

Aren't I breathing? She'd begun to feel warm, as though she floated in a hot pool . . . blessedly warm.

Marc shoved her onto her stomach, straddled her and began pushing on her back. Water gushed from her mouth, freezing almost instantly on the ice. She gasped and began to cough agonizingly, while Marc continued to press on her back.

Finally he said, "We have to get off of this ice."

Strong fingers twined in her dripping coat and pulled her a hand's length at a time, until she felt powdery snow beneath her. For an eternity longer, he dragged her through the snow, at last halting beneath an ash tree. Through the boughs, she could see the gray sky. Clouds tumbled. Snowflakes swayed and spun as they fell.

Marc bent over her and gently brushed away the dark web of hair covering her face. His blond hair and black robe hung wetly. His hat was gone. Had he fallen in, too? When?

He shivered. "I'm going to build a fire. I'll be very close if you need me. Just call out." Then he sprinted away.

Her lungs ached. She coughed and coughed.

When Marc returned, he lifted her effortlessly and carried her into a clearing where he'd piled the snow into a sheltering wall and built a small fire on the lee side. He laid her down on her back. The blaze warmed her face like the touch of a lover. If she could have, she would have embraced the flames and tried to draw them into her very soul.

She was still coughing violently. She couldn't seem to catch her breath. Each time she inhaled, something pushed the air back out. She choked and gasped. "*Marc!*" Struggling with her wet foxhide coat, she fought to sit up, but couldn't. Wildly, she flailed her arms, trying to turn over.

"Andiora?" He grabbed her, pulled her to a sitting position and clutched her against him. She rested her head on his broad shoulder. Between the bouts of coughing, she was able to breathe deeply.

"They'll be coming soon," he comforted. "Atti was going to go downstream to find a new way across."

She nodded. Weakly, she touched his drenched black sleeve. "You . . . fell in?"

"Yes, when I saw you go under, I jumped out of the boat and tried to follow the path you'd taken. I must have lost it. I broke through the crust, but I pulled myself right back out. I slithered the rest of the way on my stomach, until I saw you beneath the ice."

"Thank you . . ."

"Thank God. For saving both of us."

He stroked her shoulder comfortingly, and she braced her forehead in the crook of his neck and closed her eyes. Sleep overtook her almost immediately.

Marc held her in his arms while she slept. Occasionally he reached out and fed nearby branches to the fire. He hoped the warmth from his body would keep her warm, even though he was shivering himself. *Even though his heart pounded so hard it threatened to burst through his ribs.* He found her closeness soothing—and it made him almost ill. He hadn't held a woman in his arms since . . . since Marie, eight years ago. He smoothed his fingers over the silken tangles of Andiora's hair—and stopped.

His crucifix gleamed like a silver beacon through the dark strands. Guilt swept him. *Don't be a fool. You're not betraying your vows. God wouldn't want you to let her freeze to death.*

He pulled Andiora closer and crossed himself. *Oh, my God, I love You above all things, with my whole heart and soul . . .*

A stick cracked and Marc looked out to the wintry forest. A lone moose stood watching him through the weave of trees. Snow coated the animal's broad back and head. The moose took a step closer and lifted its chin to scent the wind. As though satisfied, it grunted and trotted away into the haze of snow.

JEAN DE BREBEUF and Antoine Daniel walked through the charred remains of a Neutral village far south of Ihonatiria. Wind howled over the rolling hills, swirling snow through the remains of burned longhouses. Everywhere, bodies and belongings lay strewn. Musket-blasted copper pots and hide bags of corn tumbled in the storm.

"How long ago?" Daniel asked. He was a medium-sized man, with wavy black hair and pale green eyes. His mustache was frosted with ice. Over his black robe, he wore a heavy caribou coat.

Jean shook his head. "Maybe two days."

Around the village, maples and oaks clustered, their stark branches blackened by the fires that had destroyed these people.

They'd passed three abandoned villages today, and each had set Jean's heart to pounding. The Neutral people believed they had many souls, and one clung to the village where it had lived out its life. He half believed it, for he could feel the ghosts of the dead rustling in the smoke-blackened chaos. Every time the trees creaked, he heard voices. They sounded soft and pitiful, as if those killed continued to live in a nightmare world, where the attack still raged, where the fires still roared and they were running, running, never to escape.

He kicked over a large iron kettle and winced. Human bones spilled out across the snow.

Antoine crossed himself and looked away.

"They do it to gain the courage of the person killed," Jean explained. "Generally they pull the victim's heart from his living body and eat it raw. Then they cook the rest of the corpse and divide it among their best warriors."

"Why are the Iroquois suddenly so bold?"

"Perhaps because they know that illness has struck these people. Many of the Neutral warriors are too sick to fight back."

"The illness is bad enough," Antoine said passionately. "Already thirty of those we've baptized have died. These people can't bear war on top of this epidemic. They can't even hunt, they're so weak. The Iroquois rob their food stores. They'll starve to death!"

Jean batted snow from his black gloves and stared at the trees. They'd received word a week ago of the first pox victims among the northern Montagnais. Father Davost had gone to them. Adept with a lancet, Davost knew which veins to puncture and how much blood to let to reduce fever. Then a half-starved Neutral had run into Ihonatiria raving that demons had possessed his people, that red rashes had covered their bodies and they were spitting up blood. Jean and Antoine had taken the trails south . . .

And now this.

"There's nothing more we can do here, Antoine. Let's try to make the next village by nightfall."

Antoine nodded. But they stood for a time longer, gazing about in silence. Death had possessed the land. No birds drifted in the skies. No animals crept through the hills. Not even squirrels chittered in the forest. The eyeless bodies of the dead watched them silently.

"Jean, I—I know this sounds foolish, but first the war starts in Europe, then civil strife tears the tribes of the New World apart. And now an epidemic, and the probability of famine." Antoine fixed Jean with glowing eyes. On the horizon behind him, black clouds roiled as though alive. "Do you think the Horsemen have begun their rides?"

Jean gripped Antoine by the arm and led him forward, out of the devastation. In his mind, a red horse formed out of mist, reared on its hind legs, then melted into a pool of blood.

"Perhaps, Antoine. If so, our Lord has chosen the Iroquois as His handmaidens."

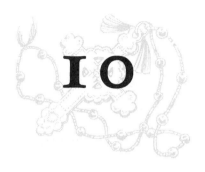

IO

It took an hour before Atti reached Marc's fire. Phillipe ran close on his heels, his short legs pumping, his cheeks crimson from the cold and exertion. He glanced somberly at Andiora, then took off his coat and draped it over Marc's broad shoulders.

"Marc," Phillipe said, "you have to get out of your wet robe. Luc is bringing your pack."

Luc arrived, trailing the women and Onrea, his own pack on one shoulder and Marc's on the other. Together, the packs had to weigh a hundred and fifty pounds. Gratitude stirred in Marc's breast. Luc dropped both packs against the trunk of an oak and dug through Marc's to find his extra robe. He pulled it out and strode forward.

Luc eyed Andiora suspiciously, then said, "Get up, Dupre. Before you freeze to death." He threw the robe at Marc.

Marc caught it. "Thank you, Luc."

Klami and Dyto knelt on either side of Marc, speaking rapidly to each other while they gently pulled Andiora from his arms. He took his robe into the forest to dress.

He'd started to shiver so badly that he had trouble unbuttoning his wet robe. His fingers felt like sticks of wood, but his heart raced. The world seemed so *alive*! He'd felt like this once before—during the siege of La Rochelle, when he had feared for his own life, and Marie's.

He peeled off his robe and undergarments and draped them on a pine bough. A rush of exultation overwhelmed him as he stood naked beneath the magnificent canopy of the forest. Scents of river and mountain rode the storm's shoulders like powerful pagan gods. He

watched the clouds soaring over the tops of the trees, and all the pain
and fear of the day drained out of him. Like sacramental wine on a
high holy day, the wind that whistled through the branches seemed
to breathe its wild spirit into his veins. He felt dizzy with the glory
of it.

"Thank you, Lord, for letting me see this land."

Once he was dressed, his fresh robe felt warm and soft. He
gathered his wet garments and Phillipe's coat and batted the ice from
his beard before weaving back through the trees toward the voices in
the distance.

Atti and Nanco were standing before a rock outcropping where the
snow had swirled into a drift twelve feet high and twenty feet long.
Andiora lay sleeping beneath the sheltering branches of a fir about
thirty feet away. Everyone else had gone into the forest, collecting
wood, hunting for game, gathering roots. He could see them moving
through the trees.

"Atti?" Marc called. He pointed to himself and said the Montagnais
word for work.

Atti reached down and picked up a broad piece of bark. He
gestured for Marc to find another.

Marc went away to search. When he had pulled a sturdy section of
bark from a tangle of deadfall, he walked back and saw Atti and Nanco
shoveling out the center of the drift. He pitched into the effort, careful
to leave the same thickness of snow for a roof that they were. Scary.
He kept glancing at the overhang, expecting it to crash down and bury
him at any moment. When they had hollowed out a space ten feet
long and six feet high, Atti ordered them to pack the snow while he
cut pine saplings. Marc and Nanco tamped down the snow hard; then
they and Atti used Atti's saplings to build a three-sided structure
within the hollowed-out drift. On the fourth side they erected four
poles and tied the bark coverings they used for lodges to them.

While Marc dragged in everyone's packs and stacked them in the
southern corner, Klami and Onrea gathered evergreen needles and
covered the compacted snow floor with a thick carpeting. Atti set a
large iron plate in the center of the floor and built a fire in it.

Dyto came back with six fish and a hide bag full of frozen acorns.
She threw all of the fish and nuts into a copper pot filled with snow

and hung it on a stick tripod to cook over the fire. Atti carried Andiora in. He laid her down beside the fire and spoke gently to her. She smiled up at him and laughed.

The sound of her voice relieved Marc. He walked across the pine needles and knelt beside her. Andiora's face seemed to brighten. Klami had dressed her in a dry leather dress and braided her wet hair into a long plait, but her bronze skin was still pale.

"How are you?" Marc asked.

"My Spirit has tied to my body again. I'll be able to travel tomorrow. How are you?"

"Better now that I see you awake and talking." He smiled at her and was rewarded when her dark eyes sparkled.

Noise erupted near the door. Marc turned to see Luc and Phillipe duck beneath the dark door-hanging. Phillipe held a live rabbit in his plump arms. His eyes landed on Marc and he blurted, "I snared it!" He hurried forward. "Here, Marc. You—you, take care of it. So we can add it to the stew." He handed the squirming animal to Marc and patted it gently. Then, on wobbly legs, he sat down next to Andiora.

Marc headed for the door. Luc glowered at him as he passed.

"I offered to do the beast in," Luc said sharply. "He wouldn't let me. He said *you* knew how to do it correctly. What did Raimont mean by that?"

"I always pray for them. It makes Phillipe feel better."

Luc expelled a disgruntled breath. "I'm sure there's something heretical about that, but I'm too hungry to care. Get it over with so we can eat and get some rest." He stalked across the room and pulled his breviary from his pack. Sitting cross-legged in the corner, he shut out the world to read.

After they'd eaten, they wrapped themselves in their blankets and lay down to sleep, pressed closely together and glad of the warmth of the others. All except Luc. Marc gazed at the firelight dancing over the bark walls. The tangy pine needles beneath him smelled as fine as the incense at an Easter Mass.

Luc grunted and rolled onto his side to face Marc. "The smoke in here and the smell of these savages is almost too much to bear."

"Would you rather be outside?" Marc whispered.

"I would rather be in Ihonatiria."

"Andiora told me this morning that we should meet Mongrave in another four or five days. After that, it may take a week to get to the village."

"The sooner, the better. I've been thinking about a few things."

"What?"

Luc's eyes glinted. "A few nights ago, when you heard the ghostly animal shriek? I'd been praying to God to protect us from evil. Today, just before Andiora fell into the water, I was doing the same thing."

"So?"

"Are you blind?" Firelight fluttered over his thin face and matted brown hair like translucent amber wings. "Can't you see that God answered my prayers? He's taken a hand in driving out the wickedness that besets these barbaric savages."

"I don't understand."

Luc raised up on one elbow and leaned forward to whisper, "Just after you leaped out of the canoe to save Andiora, Atti opened that little bag he always has tied around his waist. He took out a green pebble, a strand of moose hair and the tooth of some animal, then proceeded to sing over them in a low voice, as though consulting the demons in them for advice. Everyone started moaning and carrying on. Atti jumped around as if possessed! He twisted his body into dreadful contortions on the floor of the canoe. Then Klami started screeching like a frightened owl, while Nanco howled like a wolf." He crossed himself fervently. "I swear, I thought I was in the presence of the Prince of Evil himself."

"I wish you'd stop seeing demons in their lightest utterances, Luc. Their ways are different from ours."

Luc's mouth pursed. "It's Andiora. She's the source of it. I heard Klami talking about it. That was a cougar you heard; it comes to her call! The beast is her demon familiar! God drove the demon away that night you heard it scream, and today God tried to kill her to cleanse the evil—"

"Oh, Luc!" Marc whispered in exasperation. "If that was so, why would God let me save her? Hmm? That doesn't make any sense at all!"

Luc flopped onto his back and closed his eyes. "I *have* been wondering about that. Maybe it wasn't God who gave you the strength to save her. Maybe you're being tempted. Did you think of that? When I saw you holding Andiora like a . . ."

Marc sat bolt upright, breathing like he'd just finished a hard race. Several other people in the house roused and turned to stare. Marc forced himself to lie down again.

Silently, he turned his back to Luc.

THE SNOW WHIRLED out of the October sky as Pierre dragged another log to the top of the hill and dropped it beside his fire. Snow puffed up in a silver haze. Tristan, who sat at the edge of the fire sipping tea, squinted and batted the fluff from his coat sleeves.

"That God of yours hasn't the wits of a groundhog, Tristan. Why, with Him sending winter so early, there's no saying what malady He'll be calling down on us next."

Tristan nodded. "Aye, 'tisn't."

Pierre crouched next to him and poured himself a cup of tea from the sooty copper pot resting in the coals. Tristan's weasel face had a perpetual frown these days. And for good reason, too. Not even their heavy hide coats and beaver hats could protect them from the bite of winter. Their canvas tents looked like mounds of snow, so much had collected on them.

"For a good twenty years I've been stumbling around this unholy land and have never witnessed winter setting in so early. Have you?" Pierre asked.

"No. Not me."

Over two weeks had passed since the Iroquois attack that had killed Jameson. They'd seen no more war parties, but Andiora was five days late, and Pierre was so worried that he'd taken to snapping the head off of anybody who so much as smiled at him.

As a result, the other four members of his trading party had made camp thirty yards away. He could see them down the slope, cooking breakfast and talking. He kicked the log he'd just hauled in, forcing the dry end into the fire. The flames crackled and spit in response. From this high vantage, he had a good view of the surrounding forested hills and the white slash of trail below. The pines were iced in silver, their branches drooping mournfully. Not a spot of dirt showed anywhere. Only snow, and more snow.

Tristan gave him a sideways look and went back to sipping his tea.

"What's the matter with you, Tristan?"

"Not one thing, Pierre."

"Well, you're sure not much of a conversationalist!"

"Pierre." Tristan looked pained. He set down his tea near his boot and folded his arms to keep them warm. "I wish you'd try to see the straight of things. You're making all the men daffy with your ways."

"They've always been daffy."

"Well . . . more so recently."

Pierre clenched a fist and propped it on his knee. "I've not been meself, I'll grant you that."

"Aye. I've fretted about it." Tristan looked up, and his pointed nose caught ten flakes of snow at once. "There's not one thing you could have done to save Michael. Since then, you've been blaming yourself for Andiora when you don't even know whether something's gone wrong. So they've not come in yet. That's not to say they've run aground of trouble. 'Tis just this storm. It's slowed 'em. That's all."

Pierre grunted. He'd been unable to get Andiora's Dream out of his mind. She had told him about the sickness and the blond man's face drifting through the trees. He had told her not to worry about it, that he'd lived with Dupre for two months and found him to be decent enough—for a priest. But now Pierre had begun to wonder.

He threw his cup down against the hearthstones and got to his feet again, unable to sit still. Half of his tea had spilled onto the stones, where it sizzled. "'Tis just that . . . Tristan, I can't bear to think of Andiora lying out there somewhere. You know she'd have been up that trail long ago if she'd been able. Something's amiss. I can *feel* it." He pounded his chest.

Tristan refilled his cup, retrieved Pierre's and sloshed more tea into it as well, then handed it up to Pierre, who took it silently. "Well, Pierre, I'm not the man to be saying it, but since you haven't many good friends of late, it seems I've got the burden on me. Would you be doing all your crew a favor and ask that little girl to marry you?

It'd be a great weight off me and would keep your men above keelhauling each other . . . if you'll be seeing me point."

Pierre stood for a moment longer, then crouched before the fire and stared into the flames. "Aye, Tristan, I see it plain enough. I just . . . I don't know."

"You been chewing them same words for five years. Andiora's gone from a pert maid in the eyes of her tribe to being an old spinster. She's past twenty-one, Pierre. I don't think she'll be waiting much longer."

"Aye, I know, but . . . me life's less than what she needs. You can see that. I'm certain to be off to sea half the year, trading in England and France. I'm not—"

"Why can't you let her decide that? More than one time I have witnessed her good sense going a league or so farther than your own. You've got to be standing up or stepping aside, Pierre. Which'll it be?"

Pierre knew the truth when he heard it, but his mind couldn't seem to get set on it. It wasn't that he didn't love Andiora, for he did. But he was thirty-nine years old and had so much of the wild sea in his blood that like the waves themselves, he feared breakwaters and jetties—feared them worse than most men feared the fires of hell.

Still, his eyes returned to the white slash of trail that lined the hills below, and he had to fight with himself not to throw everything in his pack and rush out to hunt for her.

Tristan must have heard his thoughts. He said, "Don't be getting foolhardy, Pierre. The Iroquois don't like you to begin with. Give her two more days. Then we'll all be going if she's not come up that trail."

CHAPTER

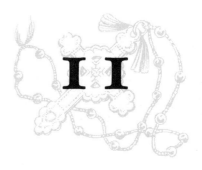

II

They turn to the earth, to the rivers, to the lakes, to dangerous rocks, but above all, to the sky, believing that these things are animate. . . . There are some indications that they formerly had some more than natural knowledge of the true God, as may be seen in some details of their fables.

JEAN DE BREBEUF, S.J.
Ihonatiria, 1628

Marc and Andiora brought up the rear as the group walked down the icy forest trail. Ahead of them, people laughed and joked in the morning stillness. Marc marveled at the change in the weather. He'd awakened just after dawn to find a brilliant flood of golden light streaming around the bark door-hanging. Dark clouds piled up on the northern horizon, but the wind that swept the hills blew redolent with the autumn scents of fish and moss.

Andiora smiled up at him, and a warmth grew in Marc's chest. She wore a fringed leather dress beneath her foxhide coat. One long braid hung down over her pack. Her cough had almost gone. He thanked God that she had healed at last. For three days she had fallen into agonizing coughing fits, and he'd feared that the bitter river water might have permanently damaged her lungs. But today she seemed to be much better.

The trail wound through a copse of maples and cottonwoods whose bare branches cast a lattice of shadows over the snowy ground. Marc studied the patterns like a child who'd never seen such things before.

They looked as delicate and frail as a spider's web. "The weather changes very quickly here," he said.

"Yes. Sometimes Iouskeha plays with us. If he sees that we've been lazy and don't have all of our food dried or our wood gathered, he will Dance winter into the world early. He laughs at us when we run around trying to get everything done at once. But when he sees that we are working hard again, he will Dance the clouds away." She tipped her beautiful face up to the sun and smiled. "Iouskeha loves us. He teaches us how to live better lives."

Marc looked up at the bright sky. "Does he live in the sun?"

"Iouskeha is the sun," she explained. "He created the lakes and rivers and released the animals from the great cave where they had hidden from men since the beginning of the world."

"But I thought Iouskeha was a man?"

"He is—when he wants to be."

Light. Creator. Sun. And Son—of Aataentsic. *In Him was life; and the life was the light of men. . . .*

Marc nodded to himself. The Huron knew *Him*, and yet they didn't. Somehow, they had confused the story. But the similarities would make the process of conversion so much easier. If only they were at Ihonatiria and he could discuss this with Father Brebeuf, he would know better how to proceed. Until then, he would continue to learn all that he could of Huron beliefs to prepare himself for the fateful day when he could open his whole heart to these people.

When they rounded a bend in the trail, Marc could see Phillipe waddling alongside Onrea and Suma. Phillipe had hold of the white dog's bushy tail, letting the animal tug him up the slight incline. Suma didn't seem to mind; he trotted on contentedly. Farther ahead, beyond the women, Luc strode alone, his chin lifted high, seemingly so he could look down on everything. Luc had grown even more withdrawn since the night they had discussed Andiora, and Marc had to admit that he preferred the silence. They spoke now only when conducting Mass or offering each other their nightly confessions.

"Marc?" Andiora said. "I've been wondering about something."

"What is it?"

"At Quebec, you spoke about a man I had never heard of before: Joachim. Who was he?"

"He was a prophet. He lived in a country called Italy. It's very far—"

"Is it near France?"

Marc nodded. "Yes. Do you know where France is?"

"Yes. It's near England. Pierre goes there for many months each year, to do trading." A disheartened expression crossed her face. Then her eyes tightened against it.

Marc politely shifted his gaze to the wisps of cloud that sailed through the azure sky. "Is there . . . do you want to talk about Monsieur Mongrave? I'm a priest. My obligations—"

"No. Pierre is my friend. I wouldn't say anything to you that I didn't say to him first." She touched Marc's shoulder in gratitude, and he nodded his understanding.

"Anyway," he continued, "Joachim was a Catholic, like me, and he lived in the mountains, where he received visions from God."

"Visions?"

"Yes. Sometimes God sends people images of the future."

She stopped walking. Her dark eyes gleamed when she studied Marc's face. "Your God gives you Dreams, the way our Spirit Helpers do?"

Marc shrugged awkwardly. "They're like dreams, except that visions are real. Through the power and majesty of God, we are allowed to see things that—"

"What did Joachim Dream?"

"He had visions that told him history was divided into three ages, each of which was presided over by one of the Persons of the Trinity. The First Age was the Age of Law. God the Father ruled over it. The Second Age was the Age of the Gospel. The Son, our Lord Jesus Christ, led it. The Third Age was to be the Age of the Spirit, presided over by the Holy Spirit. Joachim prophesied that the Third Age would be as broad daylight compared to the starlight of the First Age and the dawn of the Second. He said that it would be a time when God's truths would be revealed directly to the hearts of men."

"And what does his vision have to do with my people?"

"God told Joachim that a new religious order would be needed to preach all over the world to usher in the Third Age of the Holy Ghost.

"Order? Like Jesuits?"

"Yes." He nodded humbly. Of course, the Franciscans and Dominicans had claimed the honor as well, but he didn't think he should confuse her by telling her that. "Joachim said that if we worked hard enough, we could establish a new church that had the purity of the original Church of the Apostles. That was Jesus's church."

"I've heard Brebeuf talk of Jesus. He is like Iouskeha?"

"Yes. Something like Iouskeha. All things were made by Him. He is the Light that shines in the Darkness. He is the Son of God and protector of men. He intercedes on our behalf when God is angry with us."

Andiora lifted her graceful brows. "Then he is very much like Iouskeha, except that Iouskeha did not create all things. Just men, the rivers and the lakes. Tortoise and the creatures of the sea created the earth. When Aataentsic fell from the sky, only the oceans were below. Tortoise saw her falling and ordered all the other water animals to dive very deep and bring up dirt and pile it on his back. They did this, and when Aataentsic landed, she landed softly."

Marc smiled in sheer delight. "That's a beautiful story."

Andiora inclined her head. "And I like your story about Joachim. If he lived here, now, my people would consider him a great shaman."

Andiora gazed at him, and Marc's breathing went shallow for no reason, except that she gazed at him so intently. He caught himself noticing the way the moss-scented wind tugged at her hair, and the way the light reflecting from the icy trail danced in her beautiful eyes.

Phillipe's shout shattered the spell. *"Marc! Look! Look, it's Roah!"*

Ahead, Phillipe was standing in a patch of blue shadows, pointing up at a pine. A flock of gulls sailed over the tops of the trees, but one bird had perched on a lower limb. It cooed melodiously at Phillipe . . . just as Roah had done aboard the *Soleil*.

Marc carefully moved up the trail. He could hear the soft padding of Andiora's moccasins behind him.

Phillips waddled closer to the pine and reached into his cape pocket to draw out a sliver of the roast rabbit they had consumed for breakfast. He always did that—saved food to feed the creatures they saw daily on the trail. His whole clean heart shone on his face when he offered the meat in his hand. The dove hopped to a still lower limb and cocked its head inquisitively.

Marc glanced at Atti and the Montagnais. They had gone very quiet, their eyes darting from the dove to Phillipe. No one moved except Luc, who spun and trudged up the trail alone. The hem of his black cape flapped beneath his pack.

"Roah?" Phillipe called lovingly. "It's all right. These people like birds. You can come and eat."

Andiora eased up behind Marc and translated for her relatives. Their eyes widened as the dove fluttered down from the pine to alight on Phillipe's wrist; it snatched the meat and quickly burst into flight, swooping into the sky with the flock of gulls in hot pursuit.

Phillipe laughed and clapped his hands. His green eyes were luminous when he looked at Marc. "See?" he said. "I told you it was Roah. He needs to be with me."

"He followed us all the way from Quebec?" Marc asked, dubious.

"Oh, yes. God must have guided him. He's a good bird." Phillipe put up a hand to shield his eyes from the sun while he watched the flock wheeling through the azure sky.

Marc shielded his eyes, too, then pointed. "Andiora? Is that smoke?"

She scrutinized the thin wisps of gray that he indicated and nodded gravely. "Let us pray to both our gods that that is Pierre and not an Iroquois war party."

AS THE SUN edged below the horizon, purple mist rose from the melting snowfields and curled in the branches of the trees. Pierre sat on a damp log beside Andiora, watching Tristan, Dupre, Raimont and Penchant pull their own logs around the fire. They had left their packs down the hill in a copse of pines but had brought their tin cups for the night's conversations.

Tristan chattered about their journey and the weather. Only Andiora was silent. It made Pierre ache. What had happened? The warmth of her body, so close, penetrated his hide sleeve. Yet her mind seemed far away. Above, the sky flamed as the sunset shot bars of yellow and orange through the clouds.

The Montagnais had pitched their camp a hundred yards down the slope, in the trees at the base of the hill. Their fires sparkled like amber jewels. His trading party had moved down near the Montagnais camp. And would, no doubt, be enjoying themselves by now, for the Montagnais considered it good hospitality to share their wives with friends. He could hear faint laughter coming up the hill on the wind.

Pierre sipped his tea and looked at Andiora. Her face was rosy with cold; it made her even more alluring. She'd unbraided her long hair and it hung in a rippling black mass over her shoulders. Against the pale foxhide coat, it shimmered like polished ebony.

"Here, Father," Tristan said to Marc as he pulled his sleeve down over one hand and used it to tug the steaming copper teapot out of the coals. The leather bore a crust of soot, built up over the weeks since they'd left the *Cruz*. "Let me pour you something hot. Then you can tell your stories of the journey."

"Thank you," Dupre responded and extended his cup. Tristan filled it, then poured tea for the others before turning to his own cup. "We had an exciting trip."

"No Iroquois, I hope.'

"No. Just harrowing adventures on the river. Andiora fell in, and I—"

"You fell in?" Pierre asked, turning to her suddenly, scrutinizing her from head to toe.

"Yes. I wasn't under for very long. Marc pulled me out."

Pierre glanced at Dupre. He sat awkwardly, his blond hair shining beaneath the brim of his black hat. His beard had grown long enough to touch the middle of his chest when he bowed his head. On Dupre's left, Raimont was looking up at him as though he were a god, and on his right, Penchant sat scowling.

Pierre reached a hand across the fire. "Let me thank you, then, Dupre."

Dupre shook his head. "It was terrifying. When she broke through the ice, she went in headfirst."

Raimont excitedly chimed in, "And then Marc jumped out of the canoe and moved across the ice on his stomach. He fell in once, too. But he pulled himself out and kept hunting until he found Andiora— he saw her down beneath the ice."

"My coat," Andiora added softly, "had snagged on something."

Pierre wrapped an arm around her shoulders and pulled her snugly against him. "Thank God—and Dupre—that you're all right."

Andiora looked at Dupre and straightened in Pierre's grasp, forcing him to release his tight hold on her. What was she doing? Putting distance between them? He looked at Dupre, too, but speculatively now.

"Well, God knows," Tristan said as he wiped his dirty sleeve beneath his pointed nose, "you had a better trip than we. We ran head-on into an Iroquois war party. They attacked us before sunrise—"

"*What?*" Andiora exclaimed. She spun to stare up into Pierre's face.

"Aye," he whispered. "We lost Jameson."

"Michael? Oh, no." Andiora closed her eyes.

As the night grew darker and stars peeked through the wispy clouds, Pierre's original joy and relief at seeing Andiora settled into a sullen tightness in his chest. She said little. So little that he began to feel that she was punishing him for something—but he hadn't the slightest idea of what.

Dupre and Tristan talked until the constellations rose high into the midnight sky. Dupre laughed and dominated the conversation in a way that Pierre had never seen while they were aboard ship. He told about Raimont and his refusal to kill the animals he caught for dinner, about Atti's views on God and the early winter . . . and about Andiora. He talked so much about Andiora that Pierre began to seethe.

Possessively he put a hand on her knee. She gave him a probing look. In her dark eyes he could see hurt, and a soft kind of pleading that puzzled him. Finally her gaze faltered. Pierre removed his hand and looked back at the flickering flames of the fire.

Tristan glanced between them, understanding more than he should have, Pierre guessed. Getting to his feet, Tristan yawned and said, "Time for bed. Good night to you all." He drifted into the darkness.

Dupre seemed suddenly lost, without an audience; he fumbled with his empty teacup. Penchant's eyes darted back and forth between Dupre and Andiora; then he raised an eyebrow, which accentuated the hook of his beaked nose. Raimont stared up at the stars as though enraptured by their shimmering beauty.

"Well," Pierre said. He splashed the remainder of his tea onto the snow. "I'll be retiring, too. We'll head up the trail early, so you'd best be getting all the rest you can."

He stood up, waiting for Andiora, but she remained sitting, gazing into her teacup as though she could read the leaves in the bottom. "Good night to you all," Pierre said and walked into his tent. He had the urge to slam his fists into something, but he merely took off his coat and tossed it into the corner, then sank down fully clothed atop his blankets. He could see Andiora's silhouette on the fire-dyed wall of his tent.

Dupre and the other men rose, each with a pleasant "good night," and vanished, leaving Andiora sitting alone before the dwindling flames. Pierre expelled a taut breath. She didn't move.

A part of him shouted that he ought to get up and go to her, but another part insisted that she ought to come to him. Scents of snow and rotting autumn leaves rode the night like ghosts. He concentrated on them, using them as a salve for the knots in his gut. But when wind jostled the canvas and he saw Andiora shiver, he reached for his coat and crawled through his tent flap.

Andiora looked up hollowly. He draped his coat over her narrow shoulders, then crouched in front of her. Firelight danced like embers through the waves of her hair.

"I don't know what I've done," he said softly, "but if you'll tell me, I'll make it right."

Her beautiful face showed signs of struggle, as if she were trying to decide what she should and should not say to him. Then she tipped her face to the dark heavens and frowned at the stars. "When you were away, in France and England, I . . . I ached for you, all the time. It felt like a wound inside me that bled my spirit away."

"But I'm here now."

In the quiet that followed, he could hear one of the priests snoring. An owl hooted down in the lowlands. The line of Andiora's jaw hardened. "Now, yes. But next week? After we get to Ihonatiria?"

He gestured futilely. "I have to get to Fort Orange. There's a trader there said to have fine fabrics . . ." His voice died in his throat at the look on her face. "Andiora, I am a trader. 'Tis what I do."

"Why won't you let me go with you? I have asked and asked."

Pierre ran a hand through his black, tangled hair. He could see breakwaters being erected around him, stone by stone, so massive that he couldn't climb high enough to see over them. "There's dangers out there that you don't know! The Iroquois are growing wilder every instant. I won't let you expose yourself—"

"That's not the reason. You just do not . . ." She laced her fingers in her lap and squeezed them so tightly that her nails went white. "Pierre," she said faintly, "I want you to tell me something. These places you go to, Paris and London, do you have another woman there? Is that why you—"

"Oh, good Lord, Andiora. No, and no again." He sat back on his haunches and wrapped his arms around his drawn-up knees. "It's not that, 'tis just that . . . I . . ." He lifted his hands and let them hover uncertainly in the air. "You're making a mountain out of this! I love you, Andiora. You're not doubting that, are you?"

She moved one of her hands to rest on her belly as though a pain throbbed there. "Sometimes that is not enough."

"What more can I be giving you than me love?" he demanded.

At his harsh tone, tears glinted in her eyes. In a bare murmur, she replied, "You."

She rose and walked away like a pale ghost, down the hill to where the priests had thrown out their blankets in the copse of pines. Pierre heard Dupre's deep voice, questioning, anxious, then Andiora's.

He picked up a branch and scattered the coals of the fire while he fought the ache that swelled in his breast. Getting to his feet, he stared up at the sky. The stars glittered with a bluish tint, like frost crystals at dawn.

He ducked back into his tent.

CHAPTER

12

J ust before sunrise, Marc woke. To the east, a turquoise band
stretched across the horizon, but the arching dome of the sky
still glittered with thousands of stars. Below, in the Montagnais
camp, a fire glowed. Soft voices carried.

Andiora lay near Marc, wrapped in his blanket. She wore a tense
expression, as though even in sleep she fought something unpleasant.
Waves of black hair spread out over the frosty ground, framing her
face. When she'd asked to share Marc's blanket the night before, he
hadn't had the heart to tell her no. Nor had he had the courage to
share. He'd given her his blanket and slipped in beside Phillipe.

*Why did she come to me? Why didn't she go down to her relatives' camp?
Don't be a fool . . . she knew you wouldn't ask her any questions about
Mongrave.*

Very gently, Marc eased away from Phillipe and put on his boots
and hat; he'd worn his black cape to bed for warmth. Quietly he
went about building a fire. His breath fogged and drifted around his
head in shimmering wreaths. When the tinder crackled to life, he
threw on two branches, then shoved in the end of a log. Rising, he
dug through his pack until he found twine and a fish hook, then
tramped down through the snow to the river. He cut a long stem of
willow for a pole, but finding bait was not so easy. After prying the
bark off of several dead logs, he'd gathered exactly six grubs.

*I hope the fish are hungry. If they don't snap these up quickly, the current
will jerk them off my hook, and we'll be stuck with cornmeal for breakfast
again.*

He sat down on an icy rock on the riverbank and fixed his pole, making sure to tie the hook securely. Twine could be replaced and his pole could be replaced, but not the iron hook. In this world, it was precious.

Darkness wrapped around him, filled with new scents of wood smoke and breakfast cooking in Atti's camp. The frigid breeze seeped through the forest and tugged at Marc's cape and hat. He stood up to cast. When his line plopped into the river, he sat back down and waited.

Within half an hour, he'd caught five fish. He strung them on a line and headed back to camp.

Phillipe and Luc had already put their packs together and sat drinking tea near the fire. Andiora had a pan out and was using a knife to slice something into it. As he approached, he could smell the sizzling concoction; it had a sweet, flowery odor. He strode into camp and lifted his string of fish high. "Breakfast!" he announced.

"Oh, good, Marc!" Phillipe cried.

Luc added, "They'll be quite a change from the rodents we've been consuming." He kept casting wary looks at Andiora's pan, as though he suspected a rat lay there right now.

Andiora reached for Marc's string of fish. "I have made *maka* to go with your fish."

"*Maka?*" He handed the catch to her and frowned when their hands briefly touched, for her skin radiated heat. But after all, she'd been working over the camp fire.

She smiled up at him, a bright glow in her dark eyes. "Yes. Come and see. We have rose hips, nuts, and *maka* leaves. You'll like it. When cooked with the fish, the *maka* has a taste like dandelion leaves. It's very good for you."

He bent down and peered into the pan while Andiora split open his fish, cleaned them and laid them in with the *maka*. A heavenly scent rose.

Phillipe's nose wiggled like a rabbit's. He leaned forward to sniff. He'd pushed his hat down on his head so hard that the brim rested on his eyebrows. To look up, he had to crane his neck way back. "That smells good, Andiora."

Luc peered suspiciously over his teacup. "What is a *maka* leaf?"

Andiora shook the pan. "I don't know the word in your language.

It's medicine. Sometimes Brebeuf gives us raisins when we are sick. *Maka* is like that. It's good for stomachaches."

"But I don't have a stomachache. Why should I eat it?"

She hesitated. "You don't have to be sick to eat *maka*. Just like raisins, yes? You can eat them even when you are well." She gazed at Marc.

"Yes," he answered. "We used to have raisins in holiday feasts in college." A soft reverie overcame him. What peaceful days those had been, sitting around with his brothers, talking philosophy and ethics and dreaming of the future.

Andiora took a spoon and turned the fish, then rearranged the *maka* leaves on top again. "And what about you, Phillipe?" she asked, ignoring Luc. "Do you have good memories about raisins?"

Phillipe smiled and clutched his teacup in both hands. "Yes. Father Uriah used to make wonderful bread puddings for me on my birthday . . . even though he wasn't sure of when I was born. We made up a day."

Marc knelt and warmed his hands over the fire. "Phillipe, may I have a cup of that tea, please? My cup is in the top of my pack, right behind you."

"Oh, yes, Marc!" Phillipe found the cup and poured it full. Carefully he gave it to Marc. "Luc put a little bit of sugar in it. It tastes very good."

Marc took a sip. "Yes, it does. Andiora, would you like some of this? I know you left your pack at Monsieur Mongrave's . . ." His voice faltered when she looked up forlornly. He hurried on, "I'd be happy to share my cup with you, if you'd like." He handed it to her.

She drank from it and handed it back. "It is good, Father Penchant. Thank you for making it so sweet."

Luc said, "I'm hungry. Is that fish done?"

Andiora prodded the fish with her spoon, then reached for their three bowls and served out three equal portions. She started to hand the first one to Luc, but Marc gently took it away. He borrowed her spoon and reapportioned their breakfast, scooping enough out of Phillipe and Luc's bowls into his to form a fourth portion. Then he handed his brothers theirs and gave Andiora his bowl. "Eat as much as you want and I'll finish the rest," he said.

She hesitated, then took the bowl from his hand. *"Merci."*

Marc studied her as she sat and ate. She didn't look well. He couldn't quite place it, but she seemed weak.

She consumed about a third of the bowl and handed it back to Marc. "You finish it," she said. "You need more than I do." She rose to her feet and took a deep breath. "And excuse me now. I must go get my pack and talk to my relatives about today's journey."

"We'll meet you on the trail at the bottom of the hill," Marc said.

She nodded and walked toward Mongrave's camp. Marc ate the *maka* contemplatively. It tasted good, a little like lemons sautéed in an earthy claret.

When Andiora was beyond hearing range, Luc looked at Marc hostilely. "Why did she come to *you* last night?"

Phillipe stopped eating in mid-chew to listen.

Marc shrugged. "I'm not certain. She knows I'm her friend. I suppose that she and Mongrave had trouble and she—"

"She could have walked straight downhill to her relatives' camp. Instead, she came here. That's curious, don't you think, *Father?*"

The emphasis Luc gave the title sounded like a threat. Worse, it implied things that Marc himself feared. He finished his breakfast and picked up his tea again. "Should I have turned her away? She was cold and . . . and I don't think she's well."

"Well," Luc scoffed, "her own people can certainly take better care of her than we can. If she's ill, it's probably because God's punishing her for unrighteousness. I—"

"I don't care to hear it!" Marc snapped. He got to his feet, scrubbed out his bowl and cup with snow, then went to shove them into his pack. When he knelt to roll up his blanket, his heart stopped. A spot of blood stained the center. His gaze involuntarily shot toward Mongrave's fire. *Probably just female . . . things.* His own embarrassment made him angry. He knew about such things, though it had been a long time since he'd had to face them. He rolled the blanket up quickly and tied it to the top of his pack.

"Marc?" Phillipe called. "Could you help me, please?"

Marc looked up to see Luc already halfway down the hillside. Phillipe stood braced against a pine, his pack tipped awkwardly to one side. He'd obviously been trying to prop it against a limb and get underneath it. Marc grabbed the pack and held it up so Phillipe could slip his arms through the straps.

"Thank you." While he adjusted the weight on his back, Phillipe stood blinking at the frosty pine needles that littered the ground. "Marc," he asked, "do you remember when our Lord was talking about the Judgment? He said, 'Depart from me, ye cursed, into everlasting fire, prepared for the devil and his angels; for I was hungry and ye gave me no food; I was thirsty and ye gave me no drink . . .' and the people he had condemned said 'Lord, when did we see thee hungry, or athirst, or a stranger, or naked, or sick . . . and not minister unto thee?' And our Lord answered, 'Verily I say unto you, inasmuch as ye did it not to one of the least of these, ye did it not to me.'" Phillipe smiled gently. "Do you remember that, Marc?"

Gratitude and love for Phillipe filled Marc. "Yes. I remember."

Phillipe patted Marc's arm. "Luc will be better when we get to Father Brebeuf. He's just lonely and afraid."

"I'm sure you're right."

Together they headed down the hill to the trail.

LUC PURPOSELY WALKED just behind Andiora and Atti, so he could keep an eye on them. The brat Onrea skipped at Andiora's side, singing a song to herself as they hiked down into a densely forested area, where trees laced into a canopy over their heads. That half-wolf dog of hers trotted at her heels, its tongue hanging out the side of its mouth, dripping saliva onto the trail.

Luc grimaced and shifted the weight of his pack higher on his shoulders. Dupre and Raimont straggled along in the rear—undoubtedly talking about him behind his back.

Mongrave led the group, tramping angrily down the trail with his coarse traders. Luc could smell them from here. *What brutes*! They looked dangerous today. Especially Mongrave, whose mouth was pursed as though ready to spit on anything that happened to get in his way.

Atti nudged Andiora with his elbow and gave her a licentious look. He said something and laughed teasingly. Luc caught only one word: *Dupre.*

Andiora waved a hand dismissively when she answered. Klami and Dyto giggled and clapped. Atti threw back his head and guffawed.

Luc ground his teeth. What were they doing? Teasing Andiora about sleeping in the camp of the priests? The very thought irked him. How could Dupre have just . . . just opened their camp to anyone? Especially to a *woman*? If such news ever reached their Jesuit superiors in France, well, no telling what sort of penance they'd be in for.

It became clearer every day that Father Binet should have selected him to lead this expedition. He . . .

"*What?*" Mongrave whirled and grabbed one of the traders behind him by the coat front. The young redhead cowered in his grip. Mongrave snarled, "Be repeating that, Dafyyd, boy!"

"I didn't mean nothing, Pierre! 'Twas just—"

Mongrave brutally shoved Dafyyd to the ground and loomed over him with his fists clenched. "Get up, damn you!"

Dafyyd scooted away through the snow, shaking his head. "I'm not of a mind to be fighting you, Pierre. I was just making a joke, that's all."

"A *joke* was it?" Mongrave reached for him. "Well, you'll not be—"

"Stop it, Pierre!" Marleaux intervened. He put his hands in the middle of Mongrave's chest and shoved him away. They both slipped several paces down the trail, clutching at each other's leather sleeves while they scrambled on the ice. "You're not thinking straight! The boy meant nothing!"

Mongrave wiped his mouth with the back of his hand, glowered at everyone, especially at Atti and Andiora, then tramped away. Marleaux ran to catch up with him, saying, "The boy was just repeating what he'd heard Atti say! 'Twas a joke!"

Luc shook his head. Two of the other crude traders grabbed Dafyyd's arms and hauled him to his feet. The lad dusted the snow from his pants and said in a low, angry voice, "'Tisn't me problem if he cannot be keeping his woman."

Luc left the path to walk around them, following behind Onrea. Andiora glanced ahead at Mongrave with hurt in her eyes, then lowered her head. *Harlot. You should be miserable, for being the cause of such a scene.*

"Blessed Lord," Luc prayed as he stepped back onto the slick path, "just let me get to Ihonatiria and I'll offer a novena to Our Lady in penance for Dupre's *idiocy*."

CHAPTER

13

The snow had melted under six days of brilliant sun, leaving murky puddles in the trail. To make matters worse, hundreds of sharp deer hooves had churned up the mud. Walking was misery. The grunts of struggling people echoed down the line.

Marc and Phillipe slogged along at the rear, their mud-encrusted hems flapping in the cool wind. They had to watch every step they took; everyone had fallen at least once. Phillipe clutched a handful of Marc's black cape, holding on tight.

"It's not much farther, Phillipe. Mongrave said that we should reach Ihonatiria tonight."

"We'll see Father Brebeuf," Phillipe responded breathlessly. His smiling cherub face looked as filthy as his brown robe. Streaks of mud ran across his forehead and down his chin. But his green eyes were bright.

"This is magnificent country, isn't it?" Marc asked.

Lake Karegnondi shimmered blue and vast on their right, stretching all the way to the western horizon. Waves crashed on miles of sandy beach. Gulls squealed and followed the sway of the water, darting forward to grab titbits when the waves retreated.

"It's hard to believe it's a lake and not an ocean," Phillipe remarked. "God must have made it so big to fool people."

"Perhaps." Marc smiled.

From every high point, they could look eastward over an infinity of rolling, forested hills, dissected by hundreds of streams and ponds.

A quarter-mile ahead lay a low, oak-covered ridge. Marc gripped

Phillipe's arm. He would concentrate on forcing his weary legs that far; then they would rest. As they neared the ridge, the sound of children's laughter carried over it, and a small boy, perhaps five years old, raced down the slope toward them, waving in excitement. *"Mongrave! Mongrave!"*

Onrea squealed, and she and Suma raced forward, slipping and sliding in the mud. The dog barked while Onrea shouted, *"Totiri!"*

"Are we there, Marc? We must be there!"

"I don't know. Let's go and see."

He helped Phillipe forward, winding through the traders and Indians to reach Andiora, Luc and Mongrave. Marc heard Mongrave say, "Andiora, you're being as bullheaded as a—"

"You *never* listen to me, Pierre," she responded in a low voice, obviously not wanting anyone else to hear.

Mongrave gave her a half-hurt, half-angry look. Marc stopped, embarrassed, and glanced at Phillipe. The little Brother bit his lower lip and studied the trail.

When Andiora saw Marc, she walked back. "Ihonatiria is just over that ridge," she told him.

"Thank God," he sighed. "I was beginning to think we'd never make it."

"Tonight we will feast. And you will meet Brebeuf."

"At last."

"I must go ahead and talk to Taretande, the chief of our village. But I will see you soon." She touched his arm briefly before striding up the ridge and out of sight.

As the rest of the party topped the ridge, Ihonatiria came into view, on the hilltop. Marc counted fifteen longhouses arranged in a rough square, with a central plaza in the middle. Unlike the tiny bark houses of the Montagnais, the Huron houses were enormous. Thirty feet wide, they had to be eighty to a hundred feet long. The rounded roofs rose fourteen or fifteen feet high. He couldn't tell for certain, but the walls seemed to be composed of bark. They had no windows, and the only doors were low, narrow entries in the end walls, covered by hide flaps. They reminded Marc of the shaggy, thatch-roofed barns that dotted the French countryside.

When they reached the edge of the village, he saw that twenty or thirty small log structures—square, about three feet tall, with no roofs—surrounded the perimeter. Fortifications? They looked like it. He'd dug plenty of musket pits into the sides of the hills around La Rochelle. If these didn't have the same defensive purpose, they could easily be adapted for it.

Phillipe clung to Marc's arm, grinning in delight.

People filled the plaza. Women stood with hafted stone tools in their hands, half-scraped rabbit hides stretched on wooden frames before them. Infants, swaddled in furs and tied to cradleboards, had been propped against the longhouses. Blue smoke from wood fires clung to the rooftops, and the aroma of cooking rabbit filled the air.

Children rushed from the buildings, barking dogs at their heels, to cluster around Mongrave. The youngsters laughed and shoved each other as Mongrave waded into their midst and knelt down, patting some children, embracing others. He spoke to them in Huron, his usually gruff voice gentle.

Most of the women wore their black hair greased and twisted into chignons or braids, while the men wore the same tufts of hair as Atti, with the rest of the head shaved. Was it the mark of a warrior? The eyes that met Marc's held curiosity, but no malice. He nodded to them.

Marleaux and the other traders dropped their packs in a pile near the closest longhouse. Then they filtered through the crowd toward the women around the cook fires.

Marc pressed forward toward Mongrave, ruffling the hair of the children crowding around. Overhead, the clouds had gone from pink to blue as afternoon shaded into evening. Darkness grew up around the edges of the village, turning the towering oaks that loomed over the longhouses into gaunt black giants.

"Monsieur?" Marc called. "Where would we find Father Brebeuf?"

Mongrave disentangled himself from the arms of a tiny girl and stood. "Last I knew, he was living in Maconta's longhouse. But Andiora said he'd built a new—" He stopped and looked at something behind Marc.

A very little man hobbled toward them, using a stick to support himself. He had a gnarled face and hunched back, and beaver fur had been woven into his short gray braids. The crowd faded back, leaving a broad path for him.

Mongrave leaned sideways to whisper, "Stand up straight, Dupre. You're about to be honored by the most powerful shaman in the Huron confederacy."

"Who is he?"

"His name's Tonner. He lives in Onnentisati, but he visits here when he's needed."

"He's a Religious, then?"

"Aye, Dupre." Mongrave folded his arms. "Tonner claims he's the incarnation of a powerful Spirit that penetrated into a woman's womb. But I'd not repeat that to Penchant."

"Why not?"

Mongrave gave him a speculative glance. "On second thought, go right ahead. The sooner he kills himself, the better off we'll all be."

Tonner hobbled forward and extended a twisted hand to Marc. "*Bonjour*," he said. He had eyes as black and wary as a wolf's.

Marc took the hand and bowed reverentially. "*Bonjour*, Monsieur."

Mongrave said something in Huron, and Tonner made a lengthy reply, so lengthy that Marc began to wonder what the topic of discussion was. Finally Tonner bowed to Marc and hobbled away across the plaza.

"What was that about?" Marc inquired.

Mongrave stroked his bushy beard. "Tonner gave you new priests a grand welcome. Says he looks forward to talking with you about your God. If you're surviving."

"Surviving?"

"Aye. Tonner says that before the month's half done, Ihonatiria will be attacked by the Iroquois." Mongrave's eyes narrowed as he surveyed the village. "Were I you, Dupre, I'd be sleeping with me musket."

The dwarf greeted Andiora as she came out of one of the longhouses. She talked with him briefly, then hurried across the crowded plaza toward Marc, her foxhide coat rippling beneath the caress of the wind. She raised her voice to yell, "Taretande says that Brebeuf, Daniel and Davost are gone."

"Oh, no." Marc's face fell.

Andiora slapped him teasingly on the shoulder. "It won't be for long. Brebeuf will be back tomorrow night. Come. I'll show you where his new mission is."

She cut a swath through the chattering children. Marc waved to Phillipe and Luc and trotted after her. He caught up with her as they approached a smaller longhouse, perhaps thirty feet in length. It sat on the south side of the village, the last house in a row of seven. Tall trees curved around two sides. It had windows, and a European-style door. A white cross jutted proudly from the roof.

Andiora pushed on the door, but it would not open. She leaned into it but was quickly out of breath and trembling. She stepped aside, then gestured to Marc. "You try."

He shoved the door open with little effort. Scents of dried corn and damp leather met his nostrils. He smiled at Andiora and made a sweeping motion for her to enter first. She stepped inside, into the darkness.

Marc, Phillipe and Luc followed, going through the first room, where whole cobs of corn hung from the ridgepole and wood lay stacked in the corners, and then into the central chamber, clearly the common room. Six narrow cots lined the northern wall. Along the eastern and western walls, shelves held a few books. Paintings of the saints hung here and there. The room was a large square of about eighteen feet, with a small fire pit in the middle of the dirt floor. A smoke hole pierced the roof. Through it, Marc could see the sunset sky gleaming purple. He took his pack and set it against the wall. Phillipe and Luc did the same.

Andiora eased down onto one of the cots and waved a hand helplessly. "It was a long walk," she explained. "Go look, and tell me what's in the front room."

Marc's eyes examined her carefully.

"Go," she said.

"Are you all right?"

"Yes, yes, I just need to sit down for a moment. Go on."

Marc hesitantly walked on, into the small chapel. An altar stood on a raised platform before two wooden benches. One step led up the left side of the platform. A beautifully painted tabernacle sat on the altar. On the wall a crucifix hung, and on either side of it, pictures of Mary and Jesus stared down on him. Marc looked into the face of the Blessed Savior, and elation swept him. He dropped to his knees and crossed himself. Luc and Phillipe knelt behind him. Together, they chanted the *Benedictus*.

When Marc rose, he felt as though he walked on air. "Let's prepare Mass, Brothers."

He went back to speak to Andiora, but found her asleep. She lay on her back, breathing deeply. Her long braid had fallen over the edge of the cot and snaked across the dirt floor. Despite the gloom, he noticed the fevered glow of her heart-shaped face, the pinched look around her button nose. She'd folded her arms over her chest as though against the cold. Marc picked up a blanket from one of the other cots and spread it over her. She made a soft sound. Tenderly, he pulled the blanket up and gathered it warmly around her throat. Then he knelt by her bedside and said a soft prayer.

Metal clattered in the chapel as Luc pulled the monstrance from the tabernacle on the altar. Marc rose and quietly went about making a fire in the hearth. Phillipe searched through the storage room and came back with candles. By the time they were ready to celebrate Mass, a warm amber glow suffused the mission.

The outer door opened, and a rush of cold wind swept the common room. The chapel candle flames wavered violently.

"Dupre? It's Mongrave. May I come in?"

"Please do, Monsieur. You're always welcome here."

The door closed and Mongrave stepped into the central room, his shoulder-length black hair awry from the wind. His eyes landed on Andiora and he hurried across to bend over her. The light of the fire threw his burly shadow on the wall above her head. His swarthy face tightened, vulnerability glinting briefly in his hard eyes. "If you won't be objecting, Dupre, I'll borrow your blanket long enough to carry Andiora to her own longhouse. She'll be happier there."

"Of course. Monsieur . . . is she all right? She seems—"

"She's ill. I don't know the malady, but she's home now. There's plenty of people to care for her. She'll be well soon enough." He tucked the blanket around Andiora, then slipped his arms beneath her shoulders and knees and lifted her.

She woke and struggled weakly until Mongrave gently murmured, "'Tis just me, Andiora. I am carrying you home. You don't mind, I hope?"

She sank back in his arms. "No, Pierre. No."

CHAPTER

14

The lavender glow of evening filtered through the two windows in the common room of the mission. Marc lay propped on his pillow, reading from his breviary. It had been a leisurely day. They'd unpacked, then washed their clothes and hung them from the ridgepole in the storage room to dry. Marc had heated a pot of water for a warm bath, and his hair and beard felt truly clean for the first time in a month.

Luc had been wandering the mission aimlessly, thumping the shelves that lined the walls, leafing through the missals, patting the chairs that sat around the table beside the hearth. He'd fiddled with the grinding mill that rested in the west corner, then investigated the carpentry tools in the east corner. Now he was toying with the clock, turning the hand so that it bonged the hour even though it wasn't close to seven.

Phillipe knelt in the chapel. He'd been there for over three hours, his green eyes far away, though focused on the crucifix. It made Marc feel good to know that Phillipe talked to God.

Firelight flickered over Luc's thin face when he peered into the pot that hung from the tripod over the hearth. "Are we *really* expected to eat this?"

Marc turned the page of his breviary. Without looking up, he responded, "Andiora says that cornmeal soup mixed with dried meat and nuts is good. You might like it."

Luc cocked his head, looking for all the world like a gawky bird. His nose lifted. "I doubt it."

"What did you expect to eat in New France? Beef in burgundy sauce?"

"I didn't expect to have to grub for roots and bark like savages—as we did on the journey."

"I was never hungry, Brother. The Lord provided well."

Luc paced around the hearth with his arms folded. "You're interesting, did you know that, Dupre? I'd like to get to know you better. Tell me something about yourself. Do you like music?"

"I don't know very much about it. What I've heard, I like."

"Well." Luc seemed to be casting about. "Have you ever heard Monteverdi's opera, *Arianna?* Or seen the paintings of El Greco? Have you ever tasted roasted nightingale tongues?"

Marc's brows drew together. "No. I've never heard *Arianna* or seen the paintings of El Greco, and as for nightingale tongues, I wouldn't eat them if they were offered to me."

"For heaven's sake, why not? It takes four hundred to make a decent meal. And they're delicious!"

"Four *hundred?*" As a boy, he had sat for hours listening to the sweet, lilting songs of the nightingales. Even on the worst of evenings, when his mother would not let him in the house because she had a "guest," at least the birds had kept him company. "And what of their songs, Luc? How could you take such beauty from the world to fill a hunger that bread would satisfy? I could not bear to think that their songs had been silenced for my stomach."

Luc walked near the fire, and his shadow moved like an amorphous monster over the far wall. He smiled disdainfully. "Songs? Who cares about *birdsongs?* You revere nothing worthy of reverence, Dupre. I almost think—"

"God."

"What?"

"*God.*"

Luc waved a hand. "Oh, well, of course, but I mean things of this world. Didn't you ever learn to overcome the peasant tastes of your upbringing? Were your parents as . . . drab as you?"

"I never knew them very well. My mother died when I was ten. She put me in an orphanage in La Rochelle, for which I'll always love her." Sweet flashes of Marie's face rose in his mind, making his heart ache.

"And what did your father do?"

"I haven't the slightest idea."

"Oh, you must. How did your mother feed herself—and you?"

Luc's smug tone set Marc on edge. He closed his breviary. Mostly, he remembered his mother's beauty, her golden hair piled high on her head—and the love and the shame in her eyes when she had tried to explain things to him that he'd been too young to understand. "We are all equal in the eyes of God, aren't we, Brother?"

"Yes, of course."

"Then, pray tell, what does it matter?"

Luc set his jaw. "It matters because I—"

Phillipe ambled out of the chapel. His face gleamed with sweat, as though he'd been laboring in a searing desert rather than praying in a cold chapel. Tan dirt clung to the knees of his brown robe. He walked unsteadily, but his eyes were radiant.

Marc rose to take Phillipe's arm and guide him to the table. "Are you hungry, Brother? I think dinner is ready."

Phillipe nodded vaguely and lowered himself into a chair.

Marc knelt beside the cook pot to stir the cornmeal soup.

Phillipe said, "Marc?"

"What is it, Brother?"

"We have to watch Onrea, Marc. We can't let her leave the village alone. She's the little girl on Tristan's ship. We have to keep her safe or . . . or . . ." Tears leaked from his eyes and traced silver lines down his pudgy cheeks.

"I don't understand, Phillipe," Marc said gently. "What do you mean?"

Phillipe lifted his hands and spread his fingers to the firelight. He gazed at them as though he'd never seen them before. "And Suma. We must watch Suma, too. They eat dogs, Marc. Did you know that?"

"No, Phillipe. I didn't."

Marc glanced at Luc. He was peering at Phillipe through half-closed eyes. Marc removed the spoon and hung it on the side of the kettle. As he rose, shouts and shrieks erupted outside.

"Oh, good Lord," Luc cried. "What now? Iroquois?" He bounded through the storage room and flung open the door.

The pandemonium rose to a shrill uproar, but above all the other voices, Mongrave shouted, "*Kill him!*"

Marc shoved Luc aside to run out into the chill night.

Fires blazed in the plaza, but no one tended them. The people had gathered before Andiora's longhouse. They were pushing and shoving each other, laughing. Through the tangle of observers, Marc glimpsed flailing arms and legs.

Mongrave stood in the foreground with his hands on his hips. He had a blue-and-red trade blanket knotted around his burly shoulders. "You've gotten too fat, Brebeuf!" Mongrave shouted.

Brebeuf! Marc shouldered through the crowd to get a better look. A very tall man, with a heavy, graying black beard and dressed in a black robe, was in a contest of strength with a young Huron warrior. Each man was obviously trying to throw the other. Their struggling loomed large on the firelit bark walls of the longhouse.

When the man in black saw Marc, he smiled broadly. "You must . . . be Marc Dupre," Brebeuf gritted between clenched teeth as he grabbed the warrior's hide jacket and whirled him around. Straining against the younger man's countermove, Brebeuf stumbled backward into the crowd. With a raucous cheer, people surged forward, whooping and laughing.

"My dear God," Luc whispered. "*That's* Father Brebeuf?"

Marc looked over his shoulder. Luc's pale face was only inches from his. "Apparently."

Suddenly the warrior released Brebeuf, and the two men circled each other, their faces shining with perspiration.

Marc edged toward Mongrave. "That *is* Father Brebeuf, isn't it?"

"As the Lord is me witness."

"I'm . . . surprised."

Mongrave's face twitched as he watched the battle. "Aye, me too. I'm accustomed to him making a better showing for himself."

"Does he do this often?"

"Not near often enough. Just look at him embarrassing himself out there! And me with an ivory-handled knife bet on him."

The warrior lunged, reaching for Brebeuf's arm, but Brebeuf jumped aside, gripping the young man's shoulder and shoving hard. The warrior tripped Brebeuf and sent him sprawling face first to the ground. Screams of appreciation filled the air. The villagers rushed to help Brebeuf to his feet. He brushed dirt from his black robe and spoke to them in Huron, nodding and laughing.

Mongrave took a fine knife from his belt and slapped it into the hand of a grinning warrior, who whooped and raced away. Then Mongrave grimaced at Marc. "Go and meet your hero. He's sure to be needing friends. Half the village is poorer tonight on account of him."

Marc went forward through the dispersing crowd. Brebeuf saw him coming and smiled. He had an oval, patrician face, with a straight nose and warm brown eyes. His white teeth shone through his graying mustache and beard. He was still slapping dirt from his sleeves when Marc stopped before him.

"Father Superior," Marc said and started to drop to his knees.

But Brebeuf stepped forward and embraced him so hard it drove the air from Marc's lungs. "Welcome to Ihonatiria, Marc. I'm delighted to see you. We have a lot of work to do here. How was your trip?"

"It went very well."

Brebeuf released him and put a hand on his shoulder, guiding him toward the mission. Indians filtered around them, occasionally speaking to Brebeuf, some of them slapping him on the back amiably. When they got to the edge of the crowd, Luc appeared.

"Father Superior," Marc said, "this is Father Luc Penchant."

Luc's face still mirrored his shock. He pointed to the location of the match. "*What* was that all about?"

Brebeuf squinted at Luc's horrified tone. "You mean the fight?"

"Of course I mean the fight. What do you—"

"He challenged me."

Luc swallowed hard. "I see. I'm pleased to meet you, Father."

"And I to meet you. You made good time, considering the poor weather we've been having."

Marc shoved his cold hands into the pockets of his robe. "Yes, Andiora and Monsieur Mongrave are good guides."

Brebeuf glanced over at Mongrave, surrounded by a small group of Huron fifteen feet away. He raised his voice. "Pierre is a bestial taskmaster and direct kin to the demons in hell." Then he swung back to Marc. "Did he call you a papist pig?"

"Uh . . . not that I recall."

"Didn't he tell you that he hates priests?"

"He said he didn't hate all of them. Just Jesuits."

Brebeuf scrutinized Mongrave, who straightened warily. "I hear you're getting broad-minded, Pierre."

"Depends. What subject are we speaking of?"

"Father Dupre tells me you've decided you don't hate all priests."

"Aye, well," Mongrave admitted reluctantly. "'Twas a moment of weakness on me part. Dupre looked so like he'd be sick when I told him about Pryor that I hadn't the heart to give him me full opinion on priests."

Brebeuf turned to Marc. "Did you have problems entering Quebec?"

"No, Father. Everything went well."

"I'm relieved. Let's get out of this cold and back to the mission. I've a great deal I need to discuss with the two of you. And with you, too, Pierre . . . if you're not obligated elsewhere."

Mongrave shook his head. "No. And I'm so starved for news that I'll even endure your company, Jean. By the way, I did not see Daniel or Davost dragging in behind you. They're not still out and about are they?"

Brebeuf strode for the mission, with Mongrave, Marc and Luc trailing behind. Over his shoulder, he said, "Ambrose is in the north with the Montagnais, and I left Antoine to minister to the sick in the south. The Montagnais and Neutral have been struck by an epidemic. I'm fairly certain it's smallpox, though the symptoms are different from those I witnessed in France. The chiefs are saying that the first to fall ill were two warriors who visited Quebec a month ago. Their families brought them home lying prostrate in their canoes."

Mongrave's steps faltered. Marc slowed to wait for him. The trader's face slackened as though he had just heard his own eulogy uttered. He glanced back at Andiora's longhouse. "The Montagnais and Neutral?"

"Yes."

Marc trotted to catch up with Brebeuf. "A month ago? When we were in Quebec? We saw no one who was ill."

Brebeuf shrugged uneasily. "We've much to discuss, Marc. I hope the records you carried have arrived intact?"

"Yes, Father."

Brebeuf opened the door to the longhouse and they entered. Candlelight coated the bark ceiling and walls like a translucent amber resin. Brebeuf walked halfway across the common room before he noticed Phillipe sitting at the table—and stopped suddenly. Phillipe's bald head was cocked as though listening. His wide eyes stared absently.

"Father," Marc said as he went to put his hands on the back of Phillipe's chair. "This is Brother Phillipe Raimont. He—"

"Yes," Brebeuf whispered. He stood as though rooted to the floor, examining every detail of Phillipe's round face. "I—I've been wondering what he'd be like."

Brebeuf eased into a chair across from Phillipe and gestured vaguely at the pot boiling over the fire. "Is that dinner, Marc? I'm starved."

"Oh, yes. Forgive me."

As Marc and Luc began filling bowls, Mongrave dropped into a chair beside Brebeuf, saying something about the "Dutch at Fort Orange" and "that fat woman on the throne in England."

Marc set bowls of soup and spoons in front of Brebeuf and Mongrave, then went back for two more. He put one before Phillipe, though the little Brother didn't notice, and one at Luc's place beside Mongrave. Luc brought the last bowl. When they'd all taken their places, Father Brebeuf offered a long and beautiful prayer thanking God for bringing them safely to New France.

Marc found the corn soup delicious, just as Andiora had said. The dried venison added a hearty tang to the sweetness of the corn and nuts. Luc didn't seem to relish it nearly as much; his mouth had puckered into a pout.

Mongrave finished his soup and unknotted the red-and-blue blanket from around his shoulders, then draped it over the back of his chair. His leather shirt bore beautiful beadwork designs of green and white chevrons. He fixed Brebeuf with a hard eye. "You're not thinking of sending your fledgling boys to the outlying villages, are you? I don't care how many of the sick need baptism—"

"No." Brebeuf shook his head. "Maybe in six months, after they've learned more about Indian ways." He ate contemplatively, stealing glances at Phillipe. The candle in the center of the table reflected brilliantly in Phillipe's unblinking eyes.

"Good. I suspect that Dupre might survive," Mongrave said straightforwardly. "But the others would not be lasting a day. You know it as well as I."

Brebeuf sat back and smoothed his beard, his evaluative gaze on Marc. "Why do you say that? About Marc, I mean?"

Mongrave shrugged. "Well, I don't like to say it in front of him, but he's not your average priest. He's got a good sight more iron in his soul. I've heard he hunted better than Atti on the inland journey."

"Indeed?" Brebeuf said. "I take it that means you're good with a musket, Marc?"

"Yes, Father, I am," Marc answered.

Brebeuf braced his elbows on the table. "First, you must call me 'Jean.' Second, if you don't object, I'd like to assign you the duty of hunting for the mission."

"I'd be honored . . . Jean." Marc felt Luc shift uncomfortably beside him. When he looked over, he saw Luc's jaw vibrating with resentment.

"Let me tell you another thing, Jean," Mongrave began. "If you're going to—"

"Father Superior," Luc interrupted. His nostrils looked huge when he lifted his nose. "Could I beg your indulgence? It was a long day for us. I'd like to get some rest."

"Yes, Luc. We'll talk more tomorrow. Good night." Brebeuf smiled. Luc left the table to go and pull his nightshirt from beneath his pillow.

Brebeuf pushed back his chair. Phillipe didn't move. Quietly, Brebeuf suggested, "Why don't we retire to the chapel to finish our discussion?"

Pierre retrieved his blanket and followed Jean into the sanctuary. Marc brought up the rear. A candelabra with seven candles blazed beneath the crucifix. Mongrave paused just inside the chapel while Marc and Brebeuf knelt and crossed themselves.

Brebeuf rose and walked down the length of the chapel to the end of the benches, as far from the door as he could get. Marc and Mongrave followed him. Mongrave sank onto the bench beside Brebeuf, lounged back against the wall, and propped a black boot on the bench in front of him.

"Marc," Brebeuf said seriously, "everything you hear tonight should be kept in confidence. I want you to hear it, because if anything should happen to me, you will be in charge of the mission here. You understand?"

"Yes, Jean."

"Good. All right, Pierre. Go on."

Mongrave stroked his bushy beard. He kept his voice low. "They're an odd lot, Jean."

Brebeuf nodded. His brows had drawn together, and Marc marveled at how seriously he and Mongrave looked at each other. "Tell me about them, Pierre. Files never give accurate pictures of men, just lists of events and likes and dislikes."

"You'll be having problems with Penchant. He is born of aristocracy and can't stand mixing with those beneath him. The Huron are no exception. I've been told that his mother travels the high roads in France—which is sure part of his problem, if not the whole of it. Until he settles in, you'd best limit his contact with the Huron or you're going to wake some fine morning and find your little boy's throat gaping."

"I think I can teach him how to understand and appreciate these people, Pierre. And if I can't, I'll recommend that he be sent home. I don't have time to pamper people out here."

"You wouldn't do it anyway."

"Well, I might if I—"

"A day or two wouldn't make a difference either way, Jean. And as for Raimont, keep an eye on him. He forgets where he's at before he gets there. But he'll be your best champion here." Mongrave inclined his head apologetically to Marc. "You know how the Huron view the demented or the deformed. They see them as having a special link to Power. But I'm warning you, I've spoken long and hard with Tristan Marleaux, who you'll be remembering from—"

"I remember Marleaux very well. He's one of the few devout Catholics in New France."

"Aye, that's right. You've heard his confessions more than a time or two, if I'm recalling right."

"You are."

"Anyway, Marleaux was telling me that Raimont goes into these . . ." He shrugged helplessly. "I don't know what to call them . . . these 'spells,' where his mind shuts off—"

"Excuse me, Father . . . *Jean*," Marc said, "but these 'spells' are genuine visions. He comes out of them talking about things I don't understand, but sometimes they're clearly prophetic."

"For example?" Brebeuf asked.

"He told me on board the *Soleil* that we'd be met in Quebec by hundreds of Indians and that Pryor would not even try to stop us. And . . . there have been other things." Marc couldn't bring himself to discuss in front of Mongrave Phillipe's statements about Onrea and the little girl on Tristan's ship.

Brebeuf nodded. "We'll talk about them later."

Mongrave didn't seem offended. He continued, "The Huron shamans will see Raimont as a powerful holy man. You'd best be pondering that. If you don't manage it right, you'll find yourself the brunt of Huron suspicion, and I don't have to tell you what that means."

Brebeuf massaged his forehead. "No, you don't. Last summer Tehoren accused me of witchcraft. I—"

Marc abruptly sat forward, and Brebeuf stopped. "I'm sorry, Jean. But how could anyone accuse *you* of witchcraft?"

Mongrave grunted.

Brebeuf gave him a sideways look and said, "It's a long story. We were in the midst of a drought. Tehoren, who is one of the Hurons' most powerful shamans, had begged his Spirit Helpers for rain, but no rain came. He said it was because Thunderbird was afraid of the red cross that hung outside the mission. I painted the cross white, but rain still did not come. I told the Huron it was because Tehoren was a false shaman. Then I prayed to God, begging Him for rain."

"And?" Fascinating! A battle between shaman and priest! He wondered how he'd handle that.

"The Lord sent us rain the same afternoon. Six people converted that night."

Marc crossed himself and thanked God.

Mongrave glanced between Marc and Jean. "Your new charges aren't the only thing you've to think about, Jean. The damned Dutch at Fort Orange are stirring up so much trouble that I fear we're going to be embroiled in a war the likes of which we've never seen. The Dutch are inciting the Iroquois, promising them that if they wipe out the Huron—our trading partners—and take over this country, they'll be rich beyond their dreams. Raiding parties are sneaking through every forest in Huron territory. People are scared witless. Don't let your fledglings beyond shouting distance of Ihonatiria."

Brebeuf nodded. "I won't. They'll go out for hunting or wood gathering, but little else. Thank you, Pierre. I appreciate hearing your thoughts. Is there anything else you want to discuss with me?"

The chill in the chapel had deepened. Mongrave adjusted the blanket over his shoulders. "Aye. How are you? You're looking thinner."

"It was a hard summer, Pierre," Brebeuf admitted. "I was sick for two weeks, as was Ambrose." He ran a hand through the thin gray hair on top of his head. "With the Iroquois raids and the epidemic, no one has been quite sane. Perhaps myself least of all. I have a mound of inquiries to answer. I've been putting them off for over a month."

"Inquiries? Regarding what?"

Brebeuf shook his head dismissively. "Oh, the usual. The Inquisition wants information on demonism; the Franciscans have lodged another protest about our methods in New France—they want us to use the military to 'encourage' conversions, as they're doing in New Spain; Reverend Father Binet demands that we tone down our appeals for money."

"Tell Binet that a body can't live on cornmeal alone, or on the Hurons' generosity, either. They like you, Jean, but—"

"Well, even if we could expect their generosity to go on forever, there are things we must have from home. Medicines, books, wine and wheat for Mass. Next year I'll plant a vineyard, but until then—"

"I'll do what I can for you, but I've me limits, too, you know."

"Yes, I know. We're very grateful for the help you've already given us, Pierre." Brebeuf slapped Mongrave's knee genially. "Let's talk about you. How are you? How is Andiora? I didn't see her tonight when I came in."

Mongrave tilted his head and let out a breath. "She's . . . she's not well, Jean. Maybe 'tis just a touch of rheumatism mixed with being tired. I don't know. But me gut aches over it."

Brebeuf sat very still, searching Pierre's face. "I'll go to her tomorrow—first thing."

"No, get some rest. With the epidemic among the Montagnais and Neutral, there's no telling what you've in store for you here. It could strike Ihonatiria any day. Besides, I plan on sitting on Andiora, if I have to, to keep her in bed tomorrow."

Brebeuf nodded. "How long will you be here?"

"Another day. Then I have to be off to Fort Orange."

"I understand. I'll watch over Andiora for you while you're gone."

There was softness in Mongrave's voice when he responded. "I'd be appreciating that, Jean. So would she." He got to his feet and loomed over them. The blanket over his shoulders fell open, and in the candlelight, the beadwork on his leather shirt glimmered like emeralds and diamonds. "I'd best be going. Good night to you both."

"Good night, Pierre."

Mongrave walked out of the chapel, and Brebeuf looked at Marc. He waited until he heard the storeroom door close to say, "Marc, I can't tell you how joyous I am to have you here. Thank you for establishing yourself as a good hunter among the Indians. You'll find that's one of the greatest gifts you've ever given God. When the Huron respect you, they listen to you. You've already made our work here a great deal easier. Now, please tell me your thoughts on what Pierre had to say. Do you agree with him about Luc and Phillipe?"

Marc laced his fingers over the knees of his robe. "Yes. Especially . . ." he hesitated.

"Please go on. You mustn't keep things from me. I need to know what to expect. You've had problems with Father Penchant, too?"

"Yes. Though it could just be that Luc and I are so different. But he seems disappointed by everything. I don't know what he expected to find here, but nothing satisfies him. Phillipe and I were hoping that Luc's disposition would improve once we arrived at Ihonatiria."

"Well, let me find out what sort of a man he is, and I'll see what I can do to make him happier. I'll talk with him in the morning. And Brother Raimont?"

"Oh, Jean . . . he's difficult to explain. Pure. Loving. Phillipe is an Innocent. Just being in his presence is a sacrament. Forgive me for the comparison, but whenever I'm near Phillipe, I feel the way I do after holy communion . . . cleansed, full of God."

Brebeuf studied Marc intently. "How often does God call him?"

Marc studied the floor as he shrugged uncertainly. Phillipe's knee prints still dented the dirt before the altar. "I don't know. He seems to drift off frequently during the day, but these deep conversations happen only occasionally. In the past three months, I've noticed five of them. Tonight he . . . he came out of chapel in a daze and spoke in riddles I didn't understand."

"Parables?"

"No. They're more like incoherent connections of bits and pieces of information. Tonight he talked about how Onrea—do you know her?"

"Yes. Andiora's young cousin."

"Phillipe said that Onrea was the little girl on Tristan Marleaux's ship. I can't fathom what that meant, but Phillipe seemed deeply disturbed by it."

Brebeuf folded his arms and shivered. Tendrils of cold seeped up from the dirt floor. "You've read the confidential files. Do you remember any recent illness among your brothers? Or your own?"

"Luc was very ill with smallpox five years ago. But he's been fine since. In fact, he spent most of his last months before the voyage ministering to smallpox victims in Paris. I don't think Phillipe has ever been sick. At least there's no documentation of it. As for me, I'm as healthy as an ox. I haven't even suffered from a cold in years. Why do you ask?"

Brebeuf frowned. "Just rumors—probably unfounded. Is there anything else I should know? Anything major?"

"Yes. About Phillipe. I'll bring you all the records before I retire, so you can look at them for yourself, but sometimes when God comes over him very strongly, he manifests *stigmata*."

Brebeuf nodded. "Father Binet wrote me of that. Have you witnessed it?"

"No. But when we first met in Paris, I saw the healing scars in his palms. I asked him about them . . . because, Father, I wanted to touch them with my own hands. I guess I—"

"I understand, Marc. Please go on. What did Brother Raimont do when you asked about the scars?"

"He bit his lip and acted as though he expected me to shout at him if he answered. I don't know, perhaps someone has done just that in the past. When I begged him to tell me, he said . . . and I remember his words exactly: 'Our Lord's passion is everywhere, Marc, in the air and the earth and the animals and people. But I only feel it in me sometimes. That's because I'm not a very good person.'"

Brebeuf's eyes went to the crucifix, and the lines around his mouth pulled tight. Marc followed his gaze. The carved body of Jesus seemed to have changed while they'd been talking: The face twisted more agonizingly than before, the muscles in His arms and legs had grown tense. And His eyes—those deeply carved eyes—had caught the candlelight, and now they gleamed like pits of molten gold.

A tingle climbed Marc's spine.

He almost jumped out of his skin when a huge shadow moved across the wall like a disembodied ghost. Marc spun. Phillipe stood in the doorway, sobbing silently. Tears ran down his cheeks. Marc started to rise, but Brebeuf was on his feet and across the floor before Marc moved.

"Oh, my son." Brebeuf had to stoop to take little Phillipe in his arms. "I'm Father Jean de Brebeuf. I've been looking forward—"

Phillipe looked up miserably. "Bless me, Father," he whispered, "for I have sinned."

Marc rose and headed for the door, leaving Phillipe alone to offer his confession to Father Brebeuf.

PIERRE DUCKED BENEATH the hide door-curtain and entered the longhouse. Firelight cast a burnished-gold aura over the rounded roof and shone from the faces of the people who lay rolled in blankets on the benches that lined both sides of the hundred-foot-long structure.

During the day, the benches were used for sitting. People stowed their possessions beneath the benches, or hung them on the walls. Copper and iron pots, strings of wampum beads, elaborately carved religious masks, and children's toys adorned the walls. It was easy to tell where the men slept. The walls over their spaces were nearly bare; a bow hung here or there, but most men kept their weapons beside them on the bench while they slept. Men owned little else. Everything, including the fields, belonged to the women in Huron society. Because of that, each longhouse had a clan designation. This one belonged to Maconta, elder of the Bear Clan. Eighteen people lived here, including Andiora.

Pierre let the door-hanging drop and stepped into the golden warmth. Andiora's place stood next to this door, on the left side of the house. Oak boxes were stashed beneath her bench. He'd brought her those, to keep her special things safe from the damp and the field mice. The wall above her displayed a patchwork quilt. He had found it in a village nestled in the darkest forests of northern England. Made of coarsely woven cotton, it had been cheap but Andiora cherished it. She'd said the blue and green stars on the white quilt had Power, and that Cougar had told her never to use the quilt. So she'd tacked it up on the bark wall and kept it there—even in the coldest part of winter, when she could have used another blanket.

Pierre looked down at her. She was curled into a ball beneath a thick moosehide. Such hides were rare these days. Each longhouse was lucky to have one, and it was used only on grim occasions, like illness. The fur side had been turned against Andiora's skin. Her long hair fell over the finely tanned leather in a blue-black wealth. She slept restlessly, her eyelids jumping. Occasional mournful sounds, like half-voiced groans, escaped her lips.

Pierre took the blanket from his shoulders and spread it out over the moosehide, then sank down on the dirt floor at her side.

"How are you, Andiora?" he murmured, knowing that she couldn't hear him. "I'm here. I know I've not been in a long time, but I am now. Sleep easy, darlin'."

Firelight shadowed the hollows of her face, making her eyes appear sunken, her cheeks hollow. Fever had flushed her smooth skin until it seemed to blaze as ruby red as the coals at the edge of the fire.

Careful not to wake her, Pierre propped one elbow on the bench above her head and lifted a strand of her hair. It felt as soft as eiderdown. He brushed it over his forehead and closed his eyes.

"I've been feeling anxious, darlin'," he whispered. "Like there's some great evil looming over me shoulder. Why are you being so unkind to me? What have I done? You've got me feeling helpless . . . half crazy."

He would never have been able to admit such things to her had she been awake. Perhaps because he was a coward and feared her response. She'd been harsh on the journey, and colder than he'd ever witnessed.

He ran a hand through his black tangle of hair. "Why are you trying to keep your distance from me, Andiora?"

Always before, his first days home with her had made him believe that heaven really existed. Now he missed hearing her laughter, and the sound of her beautiful voice echoing in the darkness when they would talk long into the night. He'd tell her stories about Europe, about narrow misses with pirates. She'd smooth her hand over his beard and gossip about who was going to marry who and what old Maconta had demanded as dowry.

More than anything, he missed waking with her in his arms.

Tenderly, he brushed damp hair away from her temple and kissed her. Her skin was so hot. "I love you, Andiora. Get well for me."

He laid his forehead against hers and, very softly, began to sing a song that he knew she loved: "A mighty fortress is our God . . ."

CHAPTER

Among the other qualities with which the laborer in this Mission ought to shine, gentleness and patience hold first place. This field will never bear fruit except with amiability and patience. One should never hope to force it by violence or severity. All who are here are zealously striving for perfection. It seems to me that I alone am weak, to my own great disadvantage.

> JEAN DE BREBEUF, S.J.
> *Ihonatiria, 1636*

L uc crested the hill, and the wind hit him. Irritated, he started down the other side, behind Dupre and Raimont. The dawn sky glowed through the dark branches like wet carnelian. Brebeuf led the way along the winding path.

The forest rustled softly as their feet stirred the frost-encrusted leaves. Luc clutched the collar of his black cape tightly and kept following, though he hadn't the vaguest idea why they had to go so far from the village to gather wood. He hated these woods. They creaked and whimpered like a gathering of demons.

Dupre shifted the musket slung over his left arm and smiled at Raimont. "Isn't it a beautiful day, Phillipe?"

"Oh, yes. Look at the colors of the leaves—"

"It's freezing," Luc interjected.

"You'll get used to it," Dupre said unsympathetically. "Andiora told me it takes only a few weeks to adjust."

"And you believe everything she says, don't you?"

Brebeuf turned and gave them both a look that would have silenced

God. Luc lowered his eyes. What did Dupre know of suffering? The man had been poor all his life and was used to eating rock-hard bread and sleeping in cold, drafty places.

Luc, having been born to wealth, desperately missed the pleasures it brought. Right now, this last week of October, his mother would be making plans to celebrate All Saints Day on November first. The cooks would be busy creating sugar confections, while the seamstresses would be industriously sewing elegant new clothing. Evening Masses all over Paris would shimmer with bright satin brocades and gold embroidery.

He felt so miserable that he wanted to slam his fists into something—preferably Dupre and that stoic face he always wore, the expression that practically shouted "Nothing touches me. I can stand anything." It irked Luc unbearably.

Brebeuf stopped at the top of the next hill and gazed down over the forest. He was such a big man. At the College of la Fleche, Luc had heard Brebeuf affectionately called *vrai boeuf*, a real ox. He'd never understood why until he'd seen him. He stood a head taller than Luc and had shoulders that would span an ax handle.

"Let's start here," Brebeuf said. "I assume that the Montagnais showed you how to gather wood properly?"

"Oh, yes, Reverend Father," Raimont responded and bestowed on Brebeuf that mindless look of love. He appeared even sillier today than he usually did. His black hat sat askew on his bald head, and he was so short that his cape, meant to be knee length, brushed the ground. "Atti told us to break off the dead limbs still on the trees. He said they would be drier because they'd never lain on the ground."

"Good. Let's get to work, then."

Luc trudged morosely through the thick pines and maples, cracking branches off and bundling them in the crook of his arm. Oh, for a stone fireplace and a cup of cinnamon tea. *Blessed fire. Hell might well be better than this New World.*

Raimont trotted through the forest, laughing every time he found a twig to snap. Shadows devoured the little man. Luc stayed close to Brebeuf, but Dupre stuck to Raimont's heels, watching over him like a guardian angel.

Luc sniffed in disgust. Phillipe Raimont was demented, and everyone knew it . . . at least, everyone Luc's mother had spoken to had known it. *Him and his ghost dog.* A dozen times since they'd left Paris, Luc had been awakened by Raimont calling "Henri? Henri?" in his sleep. When Luc looked over, he would see Raimont searching the floor with his hand, and when he found only emptiness, he whimpered like a little child. *They should have locked him in a Carthusian monastery, where he wouldn't be a burden to anyone.*

Dupre was nearly as bad, though he apparently knew the writings of the church fathers better than his professors at the College of Rouen. But nothing could make up for the fact that Dupre's mother had been a harlot. She had died when Dupre was ten all right, but it had been from one of those . . . diseases.

Luc glumly went on gathering wood. Sunlight had melted the frost in the treetops. It dripped down on them like rain, soaking his cape and his robe beneath.

Brebeuf turned and smiled at him. "I read your file last night, Luc. Your work at the College of la Fleche was very impressive."

"Thank you, Father."

"I'm particularly interested in the essays you wrote on moral theology. Father Binet was kind enough to include two of them for my review."

"They were very simple, Father," Luc said humbly. "I've always been drawn to concepts of right and wrong."

Brebeuf cracked another limb off and added it to the pile in his arm. "You believe moral laws bind absolutely?"

"Of course. We must take the moral teachings of the Bible at their word. I don't believe God would have allowed the writers to fall into error. We can only commit errors ourselves by trying to interpret their meanings."

"You're a rigorist, then? Interesting."

"Why do you say that?"

"Well, let me ask you this. If a madman had ten of your loved ones—all of your family and best friends—lined up and was going to shoot them with his musket, and you had a musket, would you shoot the madman?"

"No, Father. I would not. Thou shalt not kill."

"What if your parents were murderers and thieves? Thou shalt honor thy mother and thy father?"

Luc dropped his armload of wood and glared. "What are you getting at?"

"The world is full of variety and inconsistency, Luc. It's very difficult to find absolute truths. I fear that the very concept of absolute truth has caused more suffering than all the tyrants and diseases in history."

"Father, you sound as though you're in agreement with Pierre Gassendi's blasphemous work!"

"What work is that?"

"*Exercitationes Paradoxica Adversus Aristoteleos*. Gassendi asserted that knowledge of the true nature of things could never be attained."

"When was it published?"

"Sixteen twenty-four."

"Ah." Brebeuf sighed. "I was preparing to come here at that time, and I'm afraid that I didn't see it when I was in France three years ago."

"Well, it's blasphemous!"

"Is it? Why?"

Luc's mouth gaped while he stared unblinking at Brebeuf. "Surely, you're joking?"

"No." Brebeuf stretched his back muscles. Wind fluttered the wispy gray hair on top of his head. "Consider the history of the church. In the year of our Lord, six hundred and one, Pope Gregory instructed Augustine and Melletus to use accommodation in their techniques for converting the British. In India only thirteen years ago, Father Roberto de Nobili had adopted the long saffron robes of the Brahmin priests. He had scrupulously taught himself the Hindu holy language, Sanskrit, and lived and acted very much like a Hindu priest. Except that what he preached, Luc, was the word of our Lord. Nobili gained converts from every caste in India." He lifted a finger. "And think of Father Schall in China. At this very moment, he and our brother Jesuits are wearing the robes of the Chinese scholar to conduct Mass. And they're saying Mass in Chinese so that the people can understand them. They're also not telling the Chinese about the crucifixion, because the natives find such a thing abhorrent."

A dagger of flame crept into Luc's heart. He turned on Brebeuf. "Schall is in grave danger of perdition! The Dominicans and Franciscans are outraged over the 'Chinese Rites.'"

"Yes, but Schall has gained over two hundred thousand converts for our Lord."

Luc closed his mouth and clenched his teeth for a moment. "Well, I doubt he'll have time to gain very many more. I heard rumors in Paris that Schall and his rogue priests will be brought up before the Inquisition before long."

Brebeuf nodded. "Every Jesuit in the New World should fear that."

"Why?"

"Because we're using similar techniques of accommodation here. We're trying very hard to link our beliefs and morals with those of the native peoples, so that they can see that we are not their enemies, and more important, that our religions are very much alike."

"But we aren't like them! We're better than they are! We have Truth and Light. They're wallowing in a pit of satanic darkness!" Luc's blood was rising. "Father Superior, don't you believe that our Lord Jesus Christ brought Truth?"

"Oh, yes. Yes, I do. I wouldn't be here if I didn't." Brebeuf broke off another dead branch and paused. "But I'm not convinced that our Lord didn't appear to the Huron as well as to us. This is not a pit of darkness, Luc. There are glimmers of True Light all through Huron religion. I think you'll find them if you look."

Brebeuf smiled in a kindly way, ducked beneath a low limb and went to the next tree down the slope.

Luc haphazardly gathered his wood and headed away from his brethren.

Brebeuf's words were heretical. This land *was* a pit of satanic darkness.

ANDIORA SAT ON the longhouse bench, leaning forward to braid Onrea's hair. The girl had become a woman two days ago, and the

entire village was celebrating. Seven fires blazed down the length of
Maconta's longhouse, and over each there simmered a huge pot of
soup, sending up the sweet scents of corn and rabbit.

Andiora had coiled her hair on top of her head and fixed it with
two tortoiseshell combs, then bathed and put on her finest deerhide
dress for the day's festivities. Blue and purple porcupine quills banded
the chest of the garment. She'd wrapped the longhouse's thick
moosehide robe around her shoulders, but it barely held her shivers
at bay. She was still bleeding, more than at any time in the past three
months, and it seemed to have drained away all of her strength.
Today, of all days, she had barely the stamina to sit up. She'd talked
long into the night with Pierre, knowing that he had to leave early
this morning for Fort Orange. He'd delayed his journey for three
days because of her. The lack of sleep had made her fever worse. Her
vision swam every time she moved too quickly.

Onrea stood naked in front of Andiora, her long hair hanging to
her waist, half braided. While Andiora finished, Maconta, Onrea's
grandmother, had the honor of washing her for the ceremony. A very
old woman with a deeply wrinkled face, Maconta did not have a
tooth left in her mouth. Her gray hair had been greased back into a
bun. She dipped a cloth into a kettle of warm water.

Though only thirteen summers old, Onrea's breasts had begun to
bud and her hips to broaden. In the light of the fire, her skin glowed
a golden brown.

Before lifting Onrea's arm, Maconta squeezed out a cloth. "Stop
wiggling," she ordered.

"It tickles," Onrea said, and squirmed when the cloth touched her
skin.

"Do you want to go to your husband with a dirty armpit? He'll
take one whiff of you and begin searching for another wife."

Onrea gritted her teeth and squeezed her eyes shut, trying desperately not to wiggle as Maconta continued washing.

"After I'm married to the Spirit of the net," Onrea said eagerly,
"he'll catch more fish for us. And in the wintertime, we won't be so
hungry."

"Yes," Andiora said. She tied Onrea's braid with a length of red fabric. "Once you're married, the net will be so happy, he'll sneak up on lots more fish."

"And if I am a good wife—" Onrea smiled "—for the next year my family will get a special part of the catch."

"As your husband, the Net Spirit has to provide food to keep you and your family happy, or you might get mad and divorce him."

Onrea nodded seriously. "Yes. I might."

Andiora lowered her hands to her lap; they'd begun to tremble and she didn't want anyone to see. She looked at Onrea's white-doeskin wedding dress lying on the bench beside her. The beadwork sparkled magnificently. Red and green squares adorned the shoulders and chest. A thick band of blue surrounded the hem and sleeves. "This is the most beautiful wedding dress I've ever seen. It's much prettier than mine was when I married the nets."

Onrea's brown eyes sparkled in pride. "Mother worked on it day and night for four moons."

"Do you know what the colors mean?" Maconta squinted, waiting to pounce.

Onrea shifted uncertainly. "The blue is the sky, for Iouskeha. The green beads and brown leather are the earth, for Aataentsic, and the red . . ." She bit her lip.

"Well, you got the important ones right." Maconta nodded approvingly. "But the red is the first one you should have known."

"What is it?" Onrea asked sheepishly.

"It's for you. Your blood ties you to all of the Spirit Powers."

"Here," Andiora said. "Let's dress you. We're already late."

Onrea turned around and Andiora picked up the ceremonial dress from the bench and slipped it over the girl's head. "You look very beautiful. The Net Spirit will be honored to take you as his bride."

The hanging over the longhouse door opened and Jatoya ducked inside. She had hair the yellowish-white hues of ancient elk ivories and a thin, wrinkled face, with faded brown eyes.

"You're not ready yet?" she barked at Onrea.

"Almost, Mama," Onrea responded. She sat on the bench beside Andiora and slipped on her white moccasins. Their red, blue, and yellow beads winked in the firelight.

Jatoya smiled at Andiora and Maconta, then went to help Onrea with the moccasins' laces. "That young squirrel, Tehoren, is fidgeting so much, I am afraid his heart will stop."

Andiora forced a smile she didn't feel. "I wouldn't worry. He's a powerful shaman. He could get it started again."

"Bah!" Jatoya spat. "Tehoren is a fool still pretending he has Power. But it all drained out long ago."

Maconta's eyes widened. She made a quick, magical sign of protection in the air. "Better not say that too loud. Do you want him to curse your womb?"

"Do you think he would?" Jatoya asked hopefully, patting her child-heavy belly. "Maybe I ought to shout it to the skies. Ten children is enough for any woman."

"You're asking for it. He has ears like a—"

"Who cares?" Jatoya growled. "He can't make magic with his ears—or with any other part of him, for that matter."

"You don't think he has Power, cousin?" Andiora asked.

"Power? Great Bear, no." Jatoya smoothed her hands down Onrea's beautiful dress. "Have you forgotten the drought last summer? Tehoren pranced around for three weeks trying to make rain, and it never came. The corn withered in the fields. Finally Taretande had to ask Brebeuf to bring a storm."

"I remember that," Maconta said. "Brebeuf distributed corn to all the hungry families in the village, painted that cross of his white, then kissed it and nailed it back up on top of his mission. Rain poured from the sky on that very day."

Maconta turned to Onrea. "Are you ready, young woman?"

"Yes, I am!" Onrea jumped to her feet.

"Where's your gift for the Lake Spirit?" Jatoya asked.

"Oh!" Onrea raced to the back of the longhouse where the supplies were stored in copper pots and dipped out a dishful of corn. It would be consecrated by Tehoren when he began the ceremony.

Jatoya, Onrea and Maconta ducked beneath the door-hanging into the windswept plaza. Andiora braced both hands on the bench and pushed to her feet. The edges of her vision went gray, and she reached for the wall to steady herself. Her entire body ached, but for a week now, her bleeding had been turning blacker and blacker.

In her Dreams, Cougar came. Almost every night he stretched out on the floor at her bedside, his gold-and-brown fur shimmering in the darkness, and in a deep, echoing voice told her what she must do to make herself well.

But by morning she would have forgotten all his words. She remembered only that she must listen to something Marc Dupre wanted to tell her.

Andiora held on to the door frame as she ducked beneath the hanging and stepped out into the bright sunlight. Winter had retreated for today. The sun on her face was warm, but the wind still bit. People had gathered in the center of the plaza, smiling proudly at Onrea, who ducked her chin in embarrassment.

Jatoya took Onrea's hand and started down a narrow path through the forest. Everyone in the village fell into the procession, old men and women, boys and girls, even the priests. Andiora plodded along in the rear. Tree branches laced over her head, but she kept her eyes on the trail—just the trail—just watch the trail. *You can do this! Just a short time longer*.

When they reached the crest of the last hill, Lake Karegnondi spread vast and blue before them, sparkling as if strewn with crushed seashells. The fishing nets had been spread like thick spiderwebs across the sands of the shore. Tehoren paced beside them.

Andiora smiled when she saw Phillipe running up and down the shore with two children, laughing, playing games with the waves. Suma and another village dog bounded at their heels. The gulls fluttered warily above the activities, screeching at each other. Marc, Brebeuf and Penchant stood beneath a winter-bare oak. When Marc spotted Andiora, he lifted a hand in greeting and walked toward her. She eased down onto the sand beneath the overhanging branches of a willow. Cold sweat had popped out on her face. She closed her eyes for a moment to fight the shiver that ran up her spine.

She opened her eyes when Marc sat down beside her on the sand. He looked very handsome in his clean black robe. His blond hair and beard shone like cornsilk at dawn.

"How are you, Marc?"

"Very well, Andiora. How are you?" His face tensed, waiting for her answer.

She smiled at his concern. "I'm fine."

"Good." He smiled and looked away. "I'd hoped that if I sat next to you, you might explain the celebration to me."

Andiora rubbed her cold arms. Even the slightest wind chilled her to the bone. "Today Onrea will be married to the Spirit of the fishing net. It will ensure a good catch. If the Spirit has a wife, he tries harder to be a good provider."

Marc's brows lowered. "How do you know the net wants to be married?"

A breath of wind swept the lake. Andiora shivered. Marc noticed. His jaw muscles clenched as though in protest against her weakness. She answered, "How do you know when an angel wants something?"

"The angel comes and tells—"

"It's the same with the Net Spirit. He appears to a man or a woman in a Dream and says he's lonely and needs a wife."

Across the sands, Onrea walked slowly to the edge of the water and set down her offering dish so the waves could come and take the corn. Smiling happily, she walked back and knelt before the net. Tehoren sang as he wrapped the net around her shoulders.

"What's he singing about?" Marc asked.

"Oh, he's telling Onrea that a good wife takes care of her husband and loves him even when he fails. That she must help him and praise him and always be there when he needs her."

"How do you know the Net Spirit is male?"

Andiora lifted a brow. "Because he shows himself in Dreams."

Marc rubbed his bearded jaw. "I'm sorry. My questions must sound strange to you."

"No. Your ways are just different than ours."

Sudden laughter welled from the gathering. People cheered as Onrea hugged Tehoren, then Jatoya, and ran into the crowd to be embraced by everyone.

"What's happening?" Marc asked.

"The wedding is over. Now we go back to the village and feast."

Andiora braced her hands in the sand and stood. Her heart pounded. She mustered her strength, but her legs felt even weaker now than minutes ago. "Marc, I . . . I'm not . . ." She winced as pain stabbed through her womb like a white-hot lance. Reeling, she grabbed for one of the gnarled willow branches, but missed it and fell.

Someone cried out.

Just before she lost consciousness, she saw fluttering black sleeves swooping down like wings, saw Marc's hands . . . reaching . . .

One thing here, it seems to me, might give some apprehension to a
son of the Society, to see himself in the midst of a brutal and
sensual people, whose example might tarnish the lustre of the most,
as it is also the least, delicate of all virtues for him who does not
take special care of it—I mean chastity. . . . Do you remember that
plant, named "the fear of God," with which it was said in the
beginning of our Society that our Fathers charmed away the spirit
of impurity? It does not grow in the land of the Hurons.

JEAN DE BREBEUF, S.J.
The Village of Toanche, 1629

Marc kept vigil through the dark hours, kneeling by
Andiora's side, praying the rosary. The pearls on his chain
glimmered orange in the light of the fire's coals. He had
been kneeling for so long that his legs ached miserably. The wind
kept breaking his concentration; it stormed across the lake like a wild
beast, battering the bark walls of the longhouse.

Jatoya lay fast asleep on the bench at Andiora's head. She had her
red-and-black-striped blanket pulled up so that it partially covered
her withered face. Age-yellowed hair stuck out around the edges.
Jatoya had tended to Andiora, wiping her face with wet cloths,
feeding her otter broth, speaking gently to her, for thirty-six hours
straight before succumbing to sleep. Throughout the house, people
slept, their faces glowing amber in the dim light.

The sun would be rising soon. Already Marc could see the pale
blue stain of dawn through the smoke holes in the roof. But he
couldn't sleep. Not yet. He was certain that God was listening to his

pleas for Andiora. A sweet lightness had entered him, as though the mirror of his soul had been washed clean and bright. He *knew* that if he could just stay up for a few more hours, God's infinite grace would touch Andiora and heal her illness.

Andiora's fever had soared so high that Jatoya had undressed her and wrapped her naked body in a white blanket before throwing the moosehide over her. In the past hour, Andiora had shoved the hide down around her waist, leaving only the damp blanket to cover her; it clung to her body like a second skin, accentuating the curves of her breasts. She looked so frail, Marc longed to reach out and touch her, to comfort her, to let her know someone was there. Her beautiful face tilted toward him, her full lips slightly parted. The wealth of her black hair flowed over the edge of the bench.

That morning he'd heard the old women, Jatoya and Maconta, whispering about Andiora's illness, but he could only discern certain Huron words: "baby" and "dead" and "blood." Had she lost a child?

Jean and Phillipe had been kneeling beside him at the time, and he'd noticed Jean's eyes close tightly at the overheard conversation, but Marc had not had the luxury yet of discussing the matter with him. Jean had stayed for ten hours of prayer, but then he'd had to tend to others in the village who were ill. Phillipe had prayed for twenty hours straight. He'd left only because Marc had insisted, once Phillipe's stomach had started to growl like a rusty hinge.

Luc had appeared briefly, just after Jean had left. His brown hair had looked freshly washed, still half-wet. It stuck to his temples. Andiora had been tossing and turning, deliriously whimpering Mongrave's name.

"She's not better, I see," Luc had said.

"No. I think she's worse."

"'The wages of sin,'" Luc said, quoting from the Epistle to the Romans. "She's ill, Dupre, because she's unholy. God has smitten her to punish her."

"Why don't you try to find Jean, Luc? I'm sure *he* could use you. Four other people in the village fell ill this morning."

Luc had folded his arms and lifted his beak nose to flare his nostrils at the musty smell of the longhouse. "Raimont went to help him. He doesn't need me."

Marc had tilted his head to peer up at Luc. "Do you ever plan on helping the people here?"

"I'm bringing them Truth, Dupre. The Word of—"

"So you think you can just preach sermons and leave the rest to God? Our Lord tended the sick, touched lepers—"

"He also cast out demons. And that's what this woman needs. Exorcism."

Andiora had roused at Luc's comment and stared up through fever-brilliant eyes. She'd murmured something in Huron, then weakly reached out to Luc. He'd recoiled as though from a hot poker, and Andiora had let her hand drop to Marc's shoulder. Half-dreaming, she'd patted him gently.

"And as for the way she touches you, Dupre . . ."

The *shishing* of rattles brought Marc from his memories. He turned.

A man wearing a bearskin lifted the door-hanging, and a gust of wind rushed in, fanning the hearth coals to crimson. Marc went rigid. The bear's ears stood erect on top of his head, while the snout covered most of the man's face. He stared at Marc before adopting a guardian's post at the door.

Six masked dancers entered behind him, disguised as hunchbacks. They walked bent over, swaggering as though from the burden of the huge humps beneath their red shirts. Their masks were carved of wood and brilliant with yellow and white paint; tongues protruded between the wooden lips, sticking out like pointed daggers. Each shook a tortoiseshell rattle. The last man to enter was naked. He'd painted his short, wiry body with streaks of blue and red. Blond hair—blond, Marc thought in surprise—had been fastened to the edges of his mask; it hung in long ringlets about his shoulders. He stopped abruptly when he saw Marc, and glowered through the hammered circles of copper that formed the eyes on his mask.

Marc sat still, uncertain of whether he ought to move or not.

The naked man danced forward, chanting softly, while the other dancers lined up beside Andiora's bed. They shook their rattles and sang with such intensity that people all down the longhouse woke and pulled on their clothes to watch.

The chanting grew to frightful shrieks. The dancers whirled and leaped, some howling like dogs, others spitting like cats. Marc gasped when the naked shaman bent down to the fire and grabbed up one of the red-hot coals that lined the hearth. He pushed it through the hole in his mask and held it between his teeth.

Marc gasped, "Blessed Lord!"

Sparks flew from the coal like wayward fireflies as the shaman approached Andiora. Marc scrambled out of the way. The shaman knelt and began blowing around the searing coals to shower Andiora with sparks. At the same time, he growled in her ear, sounding like one of the wolves that haunted the hills beyond the village.

Marc's heart had started to pound. *The man didn't burn!*

Now people pressed forward, watching and chanting with the masked dancers. Even the exhausted Jatoya had risen to take part in the ceremony. The stamping of dozens of feet made the ground quake.

Marc's eyes widened when the naked shaman leaned toward him and began the blowing ritual again. He lifted a hand to shield his eyes from the heat that rolled off the coals. Sparks coated Marc's hair and beard, but he was too shocked to move. He peered into that grotesque face and prayed heartily to God to defend him against any evil that might lurk there.

The shaman let out a piercing shriek and leaped away to race around the longhouse, blowing into others' faces. The Huron closed their eyes and lifted their chins as if receiving a blessing of the highest magnitude.

Finally the naked shaman trotted through the fires that blazed down the center of the longhouse, scattering sparks as he led the other dancers out into the lavender glow of dawn. Wind blasted the interior of the house. Then everything settled down. People began cooking breakfast and talking.

Blood surged in Marc's ears. He got on his knees again and launched into a fervent recitation of the Lord's Prayer: "'Our Father who art in Heaven, hallowed be thy name . . .'" The sounds of the longhouse—children playing, people talking, dogs barking—faded. Even the roaring of the wind vanished. Only the words of the prayer existed, and they spun a golden veil around him. "'Lead us not into temptation, but deliver us from evil . . .'"

Marc felt suddenly as though his body had lifted off the ground and hovered like a windborne feather over Andiora's bed. A pinpoint of light built behind his closed eyes and rapidly swelled to a torrent so brilliant that his soul could not contain it. Like a dam bursting, the light spilled forth in a blinding flash that made Marc cry out.

He jerked his head up so fast that he toppled sideways, panting. The fire in the hearth behind him flared, casting a strange shadow—like a crouching animal—across the ceiling over Andiora's head. The longhouse went quiet. People were staring at him. All around him he could feel the presence of God. Love pervaded everything. He was possessed by the colors of the bark walls, by the flitting of firelit dust—by more beauty and clarity than he had ever known.

"Marc . . ." a feeble voice whispered.

Andiora's hand crept across the bench toward him. Her eyes opened. Marc reached for her hand and clutched it tightly. Perspiration drenched her face.

"Andiora? How are you? I think your fever has broken."

She blinked wearily at the roof. "I—I had a Dream. Cougar came to me, and he . . ." She seemed to be struggling to find the strength to go on. "He lifted his paws, and they had holes in them. He let the blood from the holes run down over my face. I remember . . . how warm it felt. Warm . . ."

Marc's gaze drifted heavenward, searching. Elation and faith vied with confusion. Was God trying to tell him something about the Lion of God and Andiora's Cougar? He shook his head. Andiora squeezed his hand with as much power as she could muster.

"Marc . . . Cougar told me that you'd been praying to Iouskeha . . . to the sun . . . to make me well. I felt the warmth of the Light."

"Yes," he whispered. "I was praying to the Son."

She shivered and tugged weakly at the heavy moosehide. Marc released her hand and gently pulled the covering up around her throat.

"*Merci*, Marc," she murmured as she drifted back to sleep.

CHAPTER

17

Marc closed his Bible and laid it on the table, his thoughts turning to Andiora while he listened to the rising wind. As afternoon changed to evening, the storm had picked up. Pine needles and old leaves crackled against the walls of the mission. It had been storming for two weeks now, coloring the landscape a ghostly pewter as the trees and brush grew laden with snow. He gazed around the common room at the splashes of purple. They'd celebrated the beginning of Advent yesterday, changing the pale linen on the altar, spreading purple cloths over every table. The paintings of the saints that hung on the walls looked down beatifically.

Jean sat across from Marc, his chair tipped back on two legs, while he worked on translating Father Ledesma's catechism into Huron. His brow had furrowed in thought. The dark giant's graying black hair and beard gleamed in the flickering light of the candle flame.

Phillipe muttered to himself while he dusted the books on the shelves. Smudges of dirt splotched his robe and face. Even his bald head was streaked with a broad band of fine dust. Near the storage room, Luc had been furiously sweeping the same spot on the floor for over an hour, until now there was a shiny depression in the hard-packed soil.

Marc glanced blindly at the candle on the table. He'd had breakfast with Andiora, Jatoya, Maconta and Onrea in their longhouse at dawn—a simple meal of dried fish and corn gruel. He could not keep his thoughts off of Andiora. The way she'd started to treat him left him floundering. She'd begun to touch him gently. A hand on the shoulder as he passed. A squeeze to his arm when he helped her with

† 171 †

dinner. Innocent things. Nothing to include in his confessions. *Then why do I feel guilty?*

For nearly a month, he'd gone to her each morning and evening to pray for her continued recovery. They talked about Huron culture. She taught him the language, and practical skills, like how to weave a fishnet from strips of bark, and how to leach acorns to rid them of bitterness. They laughed a good deal. Nothing more. Yet her beautiful eyes lit up whenever he approached, and the warmth he saw there found an echo deep inside him that his most earnest prayers could not silence.

"When will Mongrave be back?" Marc inquired of no one in particular.

"Hmm?" Jean looked up from his writing, frowning as though he hadn't quite heard. "Oh, Pierre. Today, supposedly. But the storm may have slowed him. Why?"

"I was just wondering. Andiora mentioned that he might be coming in soon." When Mongrave returned, perhaps Marc could stay away from her. Perhaps the hollow longing that tormented him would ease.

Phillipe blurted "Oh!" A loud clatter followed as he stumbled over an irregularity in the dirt floor, crashed into a cot and finally steadied himself. Looking up, he murmured, "I'm sorry."

"It's all right, Phillipe," Jean said with a smile. "That floor has never been—"

"Have you always been so clumsy, Raimont?" Luc asked.

Phillipe's little shoulders hunched. He resembled a small, round-faced owl. "I didn't mean to be clumsy."

Luc shoved his broom against the wall with a loud crack that made Phillipe jump. "You're just addled, aren't you? You can't even concentrate long enough to watch your feet."

Gazing at his writings, Jean said, "Weren't you supposed to gather kindling today, Luc?"

"No. It's Raimont's turn. He promised Onrea he'd take her with him when he went. He never lets that child do anything by herself."

Jean frowned before he carefully laid down his quill. Shadows fell across his patrician face, highlighting his straight nose. "That's smart, Phillipe. It's very dangerous to be out alone these days. In fact, too dangerous for you and Onrea to go out by yourselves this afternoon. Why don't you help them gather kindling, Luc?"

Marc straightened uncomfortably. Jean had said it mildly, but no one could mistake the command in his voice. Jean's dark eyes were riveted on Luc.

Luc's mouth pressed into a hard line. He whirled on his toes and stamped through the storage room, shoving the door wide as he went out into the snow storm. The candle popped wildly, and orange sparks winked as they floated upward.

Philippe grabbed his coat from the peg near the door. "I'll get Onrea and we'll follow Luc's tracks and find him."

"Be careful, Phillipe," Jean warned. "Don't get too far from the village."

"We won't, Father." Phillipe gingerly closed the door behind him.

Jean picked up his quill again and began writing.

Marc glared across the room at the door. The more he thought about Luc, the angrier he became. Luc was unrelentingly distant and sullen. No amount of cajoling lightened his dark moods; if anything, they seemed to be getting worse.

Without glancing up, Jean asked, "Shall I wait for your confession, or should we discuss it now?"

"I . . . I'm sorry, Jean. It's just that Luc seems to hate everything and everyone. Nothing here is what he expected—so he detests it. He acts like a child who wants the moon."

A gust of wind shivered the mission, and snow sifted down through the smoke hole to pirouette around the table. Jean responded, "All the great holy men in history have been little boys who wanted the moon. Their great fortune was that they were willing to chase after it long enough and hard enough that God gave it to them."

Marc leaned forward. "I understand what you're saying, Jean. I know perfection is attainable with the grace of God. But—" in frustration, he clenched his fist "—Luc's blind to our work and our mission!"

Jean caught Marc's fist. "Then we must open his eyes."

As Marc held that strong gaze, he suddenly felt very tired. "Forgive me, Jean. I don't know why I—"

Outside, a musket cracked. Marc froze when another split the air, and then a staccato of shots exploded; they rang like the roll of thunder over the surrounding hills. Jean stood and barked, "Quickly!"

Marc ran for his cot, where his gun was propped. People were racing past the mission, shouting, crying. Marc slung his powder horn over his shoulder and tied the pouch with the balls to the belt of his robe.

The door flew open and slammed back against the wall. Mongrave, Marleaux and redheaded Dafyyd ran into the common room. Their clothing bore spatters of fresh blood. As he stalked forward, Mongrave's brown cloak whipped about him in snapping folds, catching on the bronze hilt of his sword. His black hair had come loose from its tie cord and half cloaked his bearded face.

"Grab what you must and run for it, Jean!"

"Iroquois?"

"Aye, and coming fast. *Go!*" he shouted, waving an arm violently.

"How many Iroquois?"

"Enough! 'Tis a war party of perhaps thirty. Don't make me waste me breath arguing with you!"

Jean lifted his hand and pronounced general absolution over every in the mission. Then he said, "Marc, put your musket down. Come with me. There are Christians here who will need us."

Marc hesitated. He looked from his gun to Jean. "But, Jean. What if—"

"I won't have it said that we're murderers! Hurry."

Marc turned to lay his gun on his bed, but Mongrave came across the floor like a bull ox and jerked it from his hands. His black eyes flamed. "There are people out there more than willing to use this to protect their families, Dupre. Give me your powder and balls, as well."

Marc gave up his powder horn, and had started to untie his ball pouch when shrieks of terror rose outside. Above them, bloodcurdling war whoops eddied through the village, accompanied by the booming of muskets. Mongrave ran for the door, bellowing, "Tristan, Dafyyd, *be fast!*"

*　　*　　*

LUC TRAMPED HEADLONG through the forest. To his irritation, Raimont and that little girl followed in his footsteps. Phillipe kept calling "Father Luc? Father Luc?" and trying to run through the snow to catch up.

Luc walked faster.

His teeth had started to chatter. He'd rushed out of the mission so angrily that he'd forgotten his cape. Now he wished he'd been more prudent; the cold penetrated his robe. Images of France tormented him. Platters of steaming beef, crystal glasses of brandy. Friends in rich brocades. He remembered the admiration in their eyes after he'd been ordained.

"Mother, this is your fault," he muttered under his breath.

By now, his third letter to her should be well on its way. He nodded to himself. Perhaps her social connections would finally be of some use. He had written her in great detail of the demonic methods of Brebeuf, even going so far as to suggest that the Jesuit provincial might have cause to refer the case to the Inquisition. Getting the letter out had taken great cunning. The church ruled that all correspondence must go through Father Paul Lejeune in Quebec, but he'd been clever; he'd paid a wild Huron brave a small copper pot to take it and mail it for him. He'd instructed his mother in how to use the same surreptitious means when responding to him. He'd written:

> *Dear Mother, I'm locked in a dungeon of demons! These savages seek the aid of Satan daily, dancing like devils from the fiery pit to conjure spirits out of the air and water. And Father Brebeuf joins them! He believes in their diabolical rituals and encourages their continuance. It is sorcery, witchcraft more powerful and dangerous than any in Europe!*

French readers would, of course, gasp in horror at the charges.

He didn't relish such methods, but how else could he convey to the proper authorities the sacrilege he had witnessed here? *Someone* had to inform Father Binet, or the situation would never be corrected. His mother would be in her carriage and on her way to the provincial headquarters the instant she read his letter.

Halting by a pine, Luc sharply cracked off several of the dead branches and laid them in the crook of his arm.

"Father Luc?" a high voice echoed through the trees. "Where are you? Father Luc? We're not supposed to go very far!"

He trudged on, keeping ahead of the idiot and the brat. The snow wasn't falling quickly enough to erase his tracks. They'd be able to follow him. He broke into a trot and wove through the trees for almost fifteen minutes before he slowed down and listened for them.

Wind howled, lashing at his face. But no voices carried to him.

Luc smiled. He started to run again, just for good measure . . . but then he stopped abruptly. Dark, roiling clouds were spilling over the crests of the ridges in great amorphous tufts, but . . . he'd never seen these hills before.

He jerked around. Unfamiliar ponds and twisted oaks met his gaze. *No, I can't be lost!*

He raced back the way he'd come, trudging through the snow up over a knoll and down the other side. His tracks grew dimmer as he went.

Panicked, he threw down his branches and ran like a madman. *I could freeze to death out here! Lord, help me!*

He tripped over a snow-covered root and fell face first into the powder. Then he heard voices—Phillipe's voice laughing and talking to Onrea.

"Raimont?" he yelled. "Raimont, I'm over here!" He picked himself up and raced toward them. Suddenly their voices died. Luc slowed down, wondering where they could have gone.

Phillipe's shrill scream made Luc cry out in return. He crouched and begged God to protect him. Another scream erupted. Onrea's? Then Raimont began shrieking, high and breathless screams, so dreadful that visions of the punishments of hell filled Luc's mind.

He got on his knees and sneaked forward to peer through a pile of deadfall into a pine-fringed clearing. There in the center of the meadow, a naked warrior had thrown Onrea on the ground and was raping her. She writhed on the snow, sobbing, "*Teouastato!* No! No! *Teouastato!*"

Two other warriors held Phillipe, while another gripped his chin and forced him to watch. Phillipe's face had gone livid with terror. His green eyes looked as huge as a demented owl's.

Luc's throat tightened. *Oh, Blessed Jesus, save me. I—I've got to get away!*

He scrambled backward, trying not to catch his robe on twigs. Then he got to his feet and ran with all his heart, praying that God would guide him back to the village.

MARC HURRIED OUT of the mission behind Jean, and into the midst of insanity.

Iroquois warriors raced like rabid wolves through Ihonatiria. Some had muskets, but most carried bows and tomahawks. Dozens of women and children darted around the longhouses, trying to reach the safety of the forest, while the Huron warriors hurled themselves at the Iroquois invaders, shooting their arrows and slashing with their iron-studded war clubs. Mongrave had stationed four of his traders at strategic points around the plaza; each had a pistol and musket. The attack had come so quickly that no one had had time to man the empty shooting barricades.

A bloodstained child fled by Marc, screaming, and Jean ran after him. He grabbed the boy, threw him up under his arm and dashed down into the forest.

Mongrave swung around, wild-eyed. "Get down, Dupre! Damn you!" He shoved Marc to the ground with such force that Marc rolled twice before he could stop himself and scramble behind the corner of the mission. A volley of musket fire rained through the cold air.

Four Iroquois braves rushed across the plaza toward them with tomahawks raised. Crimson paint streaked their half-naked bodies. Mongrave fired his pistol into the chest of the lead brave. The warrior toppled sideways and writhed weakly while Mongrave struggled to reload, pouring powder down the barrels of his pistol and Marc's musket and seating the balls in the chambers.

"*Pierre, set!*" Marleaux yelled, and Mongrave hit the ground on his stomach. Marleaux's musket ball caught the next warrior in the throat and dropped him on the spot.

The redheaded Dafyyd stood his ground and aimed, but two warriors leaped on him and knocked him sprawling. His unfired musket flew into the snow a few feet from Marc. The warriors chopped out the back of Dafyyd's head with their tomahawks and careened for Mongrave and Marleaux.

Marc stared unblinking at the red pool that spread through the snow around Dafyyd's mutilated body. Then his eyes fixed on the musket.

I won't have them thinking we're murderers! Obedience. OBEDIENCE!

Mongrave slammed his fist into the attacker's face, then swiftly rolled and blew the man's heart out with his pistol. Getting to his knees, he aimed the musket at the warrior who had straddled Marleaux and was preparing to crush his skull. It seemed to Marc that Mongrave took an eternity to aim and fire the gun. The warrior fell in a bloody heap on top of Marleaux.

Then a flood of Iroquois raced into the plaza, screaming a ululating war cry. In the whirling snowstorm, they seemed ethereal, like apparitions from the mists of France's lowlands. Marc heard the ringing whine of a sword being drawn and watched Mongrave wade into the onslaught swinging his blade. He hacked off one warrior's head and had turned on another before the first's decapitated body even hit the ground.

Across the plaza, Marc saw Jean moving through the distraught Huron, absolving those who lay prostrate and dying, baptizing the wounded, who lifted their hands to him, crying, *"Echon! Echon!"*

A yell erupted as enemy warriors began torching the longhouses. Flames swept up the bark walls, sending black clouds of smoke into the snowy sky.

"Oh, dear God . . ." Marc whispered.

A wounded warrior lay in a pool of blood in the plaza, weeping wretchedly, reaching out to anyone who fled past; an old man with one side of his head bashed in crept out of a longhouse on his stomach, his fingers moving spiderlike in the snow; a woman clutched the dead body of her infant to her breast.

And in that moment, the gentlest of Marc Dupre's dreams withered and died. All of Mendieta's words about purity and innocence melted like snowflakes in hot wind.

How could you have believed? Fool. Damned fool! The voice oozed up through a crack in a wall that Marc had built to last for a thousand years. *There are no virtuous people left in the world! None!* He felt as though he had awakened, and he wanted to weep for the loss of things that had never existed except in his longings.

Andiora ducked out of one of the flaming longhouses, her hair flying about her shoulders. She carried a musket and fired it expertly into a group of three warriors who tried to overtake her, killing one. The other two grabbed her by the arms and forced her to the ground. One put his knee in her chest and drew his knife.

The whole raging world went ghostly quiet around Marc. Snow whirled silently. Traders reloaded weapons, their motions slow, so slow. His eyes saw Andiora on the ground, but his ears heard different sounds . . . *cannons booming in the harbor* . . . *soldiers laughing* . . . *"Marc! Marc, oh God . . . ."*

"No!" Marc lunged, grabbed the musket lying in the snow and ran, shoving aside anyone who blocked his path. Two yards from where Andiora lay, he planted his feet and fired. A puff of blue smoke blinded him. The other warrior struck Marc and slammed him to the ground.

They rolled and kicked, until the brave managed to get on top and lift his knife. Marc twisted, but the Iroquois plunged his blade down. The cold iron struck Marc's hip bone. A roar of fury tore from his throat. He bashed a knee into the man's groin and twisted sideways, throwing his enemy off balance. But the warrior tugged the knife from Marc's hip and raised it again.

Andiora's face appeared at the edge of Marc's vision, her eyes wide with terror. He glimpsed the musket in her hands. She swung it with all the force she could, striking the Iroquois in the back of the skull. Dazed, he slumped sideways, moaning.

"Get back!" Marc shouted at Andiora as he wrenched the knife from the brave's hand, shoved him onto his back and drove the weapon into his chest.

The Iroquois' black eyes met Marc's for a terrible instant before he slowly went limp. Warm blood gushed up around the hilt of the knife and onto Marc's hands. *Thou shalt . . . not . . .*

"Grab the muskets of the fallen!" Mongrave shouted, then repeated the command in Huron and began gesturing toward the guns that lay in the snow around the plaza. Huron warriors sprinted to grab them. "Reload and follow us out to the shooting barricades!"

Dead Iroquois littered the plaza and forest, their open eyes already collecting snow. Unconsciously, Marc ran a count . . . fifteen, as far as he could tell. *Will they fight to the last man? What are they fighting for? What had this village done to them?*

Mongrave, Marleaux and the other traders charged across the plaza, leaping the bodies of the fallen to jump into the barricades. Huron warriors scrambled in beside them and hunkered down, ready to shoot. "Hold your fire until they're on us!"

A brief lull ensued. The ridgepole of a burning longhouse snapped and the roof crashed down in a burst of flame. Someone screamed.

The next wave of Iroquois swarmed out of the trees howling like banshees. Mongrave gave the command, "Now!" A roar of musket blasts thundered. "Reload!"

When Mongrave again shouted "Now!" another roar of musket fire echoed through the forests. The attackers retreated, and Huron cries of joy rent the air. Marc spotted several of the Iroquois fleeing, some of them carrying blankets and pots.

Andiora wrapped her arms around Marc, speaking rapidly in Huron, holding him tightly. He could make out the words "thank you" and "brave."

But Marc barely felt her touch. He wiped the blood on his hands onto his robe. As he stared down into the wide, dead eyes of the warrior, he started to tremble.

"Oh . . . blessed God," he whispered, "forgive me."

Only now did he see that the brave had been very young, maybe sixteen, with most of his hair shaved. A topknot bound in rawhide spiked up from his head. He'd painted his cheeks with red circles.

Marc made a fumbling attempt to cross himself and pray, but the words lodged in his throat, suffocating him. "In the name of . . . the Father . . . and of the Son . . ." He couldn't think, couldn't . . .

Mongrave crouched beside him and put a hand on his shoulder. Snow frosted the trader's black hair and gathered on his crooked nose. His brown cloak was soaked in blood and stank of torn intestines. "That's enough for this one, Dupre. You're bleeding a sight worse than he is."

Marc had forgotten his wound, but when Mongrave gripped him by the arm and hauled him to his feet, he grunted in pain. Blood had drenched the lower half of his robe and pooled in one of his boots.

"Is it over?" he asked, his eyes scanning the snowy forest.

"Aye, for the moment. Though they might be back if they can find more warriors. Andiora," Mongrave ordered, "take Dupre's other side."

She slipped her arm around Marc's waist and helped Mongrave support him across the plaza toward the Jesuit mission.

Three longhouses still blazed. The bark walls had been consumed, revealing the pole frames and charred debris within. Villagers had begun to sneak back from the forest, searching for relatives. The dead lay everywhere, it seemed—some in piles, as though they'd been trying to protect each other when they'd fallen. The coppery scent of blood filled the air. Marc shook his head to stop the images of La Rochelle that snaked out of his memories.

"Seems I owe you twice," Mongrave said, "for saving me Andiora's life."

"You don't owe me."

Mongrave glanced at him. "So, you're bothered by the killing. Aye. You killed. I'd have never thought one of your kind capable of doing a man's work in the din of battle. But you've not forgotten the lessons of La Rochelle, have you, Dupre? When the choice comes down to you and yours or them, you'll make the right decision—no matter that your church will condemn you for it."

Jean dragged a man, one of the traders, through the crumbling doorway of the farthest burning longhouse, and Marc caught some of the words of Extreme Unction. He tried to break loose from Mongrave and Andiora. Jean needed help.

Mongrave tightened his hold, refusing to let go. He said, "The way you're bleeding, I suspect that knife clipped an artery. If we don't get it stopped soon, you'll be hearing Jean say those same words to you. Besides—" his expression tightened "—Draper's dead. Jean's wasting his breath."

Marc closed his eyes for a moment, suddenly queasy and light-headed. "I'm sorry."

"Save your sorrow for the living. They're going to need it."

Marc's gaze drifted over the dead and wounded Huron to the wind-combed hills, where the trees swayed. A sudden tingle climbed his spine. "Mongrave, have you . . . where are Phillipe and Luc? Have you seen them? And Onrea? Has she come back yet?"

"Not that I've seen," Mongrave said. "If they ran into the Iroquois, chances are they're dead or have been taken captive. In either case, they're beyond our help. So settle down. We'll be organizing armed search parties as soon as we've tended the wounded in the village."

Marc made it to the mission door before he had to stop and vomit into the snow.

18

Pierre pushed back his brown cloak and propped his fists on his hips. He'd washed his hands, but blood still crusted his leather shirt and pants. He paced before Brebeuf, speaking softly. "Aye, so your boy killed today. He saved Andiora's life, and probably several more. *That* is what you should be considering."

Jean sat silent at the table, with his chair angled toward the northern wall, where two empty beds stood. His black robe looked as though he had been crawling through a muddy wallow, except that most of the filth was blood. A haze of blue smoke rose from the fire in the hearth to roil above them, waiting for its chance to be sucked out the hole in the roof. Pierre contemplated it briefly, then looked over at Dupre. Marc sat on his bed, his pillow propped behind his back, glaring at his gray blanket and looking as defiant as a Damned soul who has just heard his fate read from the Book of Lives.

A smile touched Pierre's lips. Dupre had iron in his soul. What he was doing in the priesthood was unfathomable.

Andiora hovered around Dupre, bringing him cups of tea and bowls of corn gruel, speaking softly. The sound of her voice soothed Pierre. So much so, in fact, that he almost felt normal again. Were it not for the pungent scent of torn intestines in the air, he suspected that he would have been hungry as a bull.

Pierre bent down to force Jean to look at him. When the priest grudgingly met his eyes, Pierre said, "And as for Raimont, Onrea, and Penchant, you'd best prepare yourself for the worst. You're no stranger in this land, Jean. You know the ways of the Iroquois."

"Was there no trace, Pierre? None at all? Not a scrap of clothing or—"

"Two search parties are still beating the brush, but those that have come in found nothing."

Jean dropped his head. Faintly, he asked, "Did I ever tell you about the dream I had?"

"Not that I recall." Pierre turned when he thought he heard the storeroom door open and close softly.

Jean obviously had not heard it. He said, "I was sick, fevered. I dreamed I heard God calling me. I walked the path to that small pond east of the village." He looked up to see if Pierre knew the pond he meant. When Pierre nodded, he continued. "There was a creature, a woman . . . she rose out of the water and came at me. She told me I was bringing great evil into this world. I called out to God and forced her to retreat, but . . . the mist turned red and formed into a horse."

"So? What's—"

Dupre suddenly sat up straight on his bed and shouted, "Luc! *Where's Phillipe?*"

Penchant had crept in from the storeroom on silent feet. His gray eyes were riveted on Jean; his wet brown hair was matted to the sides of his thin face. "A red horse? The second Horseman! God has sent us a sign that the end is near. Oh, Blessed Jesus, I knew it!"

"Luc," Jean said. He didn't move a muscle, but Penchant squirmed. "Where are Phillipe and Onrea?"

"Raimont? I—I don't know. I never saw him after I left the mission." He veered around Jean and went to his cot to sink down atop the gray blanket.

Pierre stroked his beard. Penchant looked as guilty as Judas, sitting there twisting his hands in his lap. His eyes darted, taking in the fact that Dupre was glowering at Penchant with fiery blue eyes. Penchant shouted, "What are you looking at me like that for? Did my face just turn purple or something?"

Dupre didn't even blink. "Not until I'm well enough to get my hands around your throat. What did you do? Leave Phillipe when—"

"Marc!" Jean snapped as he lurched to his feet. "That's enough!"

Dupre lowered his eyes obediently, but his blond beard vibrated as he ground his teeth. At his bedside, Andiora had begun to weep silently. Tears traced silver lines down her cheeks. Pierre's stomach knotted. No one loved Onrea more than Andiora did. The two were more like sisters than cousins.

"Andiora," he said gently, "I've friends among the Dutch. I'll ask around. Maybe she was taken as a wife. Someone will know."

"Yes," she answered and put a hand over her lips to stop their trembling. When she walked briskly across the room, heading for the door, Pierre started to follow her, but Jean gripped his arm.

"Pierre," he said in a low voice, "I have a favor to ask of you."

The storeroom door thudded shut, and Pierre turned halfway around to face Jean. This close, he could see the specks of blood in the priest's graying black beard. "What is it?"

"How many Iroquois prisoners did the Huron capture?"

Pierre frowned. "One. Why?"

"I want to go to the ceremony. Could you—"

"Good God, Jean!" Pierre spat. "You haven't the sense God gave a goat. His soul's not worth saving. He's a goddamned Iroquois!"

Brebeuf looked up mildly. A log broke in the fire and webbed his face with threads of orange light. "Please. I want to talk with him before . . . before they kill him."

Pierre stalked to the middle of the room. The saintly faces in the paintings seemed hostile. How could Jean even ask? Every time he converted a dying Iroquois, the Huron Christians damn near rioted. They hadn't the slightest desire to share heaven with the men who had killed their families. During the last torture ritual, a genial little fellow named Julop had tried to stab Jean.

"Pierre?"

He threw up his hands. "All right, Jean. I'll ask Taretande. Though the Lord knows why I take such chances for you. One of these days you're going to be baptizing an Iroquois and somebody'll slip a knife between me own ribs in recompense."

PHILLIPE LAY ON his side beneath a maple tree. A few feet away, five Iroquois warriors crouched before a small fire, playing a game. One man shook several painted stones in his hands, threw them out on the frosty ground, then laughed and punched the man closest to him in the shoulder.

Phillipe blinked wearily. He felt dazed and sick. They'd been running for two days, and the Indians wouldn't let them sleep. When they stopped, they bound Phillipe's hands and ankles so tightly that his fingers and toes ached unbearably. And they'd taken his black coat, jerked it off of him while they shoved him between one warrior and another. Phillipe shivered in his thin brown robe.

Onrea lay a few feet away. She whimpered constantly now, saying things that Phillipe didn't understand. A glint of madness had entered her dark eyes. Tonight the Iroquois had stretched her out between three trees. Her hands were bound to one while her spread legs had been bound to the other two. Her dress bore streaks of blood, and her black hair was clotted in tangles around her shoulders. Her eyes had swollen almost shut from the beatings.

The leader of the war party, a big man with a bristly band of hair sticking straight up from his scalp, grunted and slammed a fist into the chest of the warrior who held the painted stones. The man dropped the stones. The leader said something vicious, then took them in his own hands, shook them and tossed them across the ground. "*Da ne ho!*" he said.

A war whoop went up from the men. Two of them jumped up and began howling and leaping around the fire. Their hideously painted faces glowed like the masks of actors Phillipe had seen in Paris theaters.

"*Ka ji, ka ji,*" the leader said as he got to his feet. The other men fell into line behind him and followed him to loom over Onrea. Their shadows wavered against the pewter and ebony background of trees and stars.

The leader unlaced his pants and stepped out of them. His brown body glowed orange in the firelight. Then he crouched and jerked up Onrea's dress. He fell on her like a hungry animal, biting her tiny breasts and thrusting himself inside her.

Onrea sobbed brokenly.

"*No! No!*" Phillipe shouted. He wormed across the frozen ground on his stomach, twigs scratching his face and throat. The two warriors standing behind the leader laughed and pointed at Phillipe, but he kept on moving. When he was close enough, he rolled to his knees and threw himself at the lead warrior, still busy with Onrea. Phillipe slammed the man back against a tree trunk. Angry shouts arose. Phillipe squirmed to cover Onrea with his own body. The first two warriors trotted up, and now all four surrounded him, their faces inscrutable.

Onrea twisted to put her wet cheek against Phillipe's cheek and whisper in his ear, "No, Phillipe. No!" Then she screamed, and Phillipe felt the first blow.

He gasped in agony. In the silver wash of moonlight, Phillipe glimpsed them lifting their war clubs. They slammed into his back. He could barely breathe.

"Oh . . . my Lord . . . Jesus," he whispered. "I commend my Spirit into . . . Your hands."

One warrior leaped away and began singing a shrill war song while he danced. Another stepped back, too, but he did it to give the leader a place to stand. The big man pulled the war club from his subordinate's hand. "*Ot go. Da ne Hob,*" he shouted as he brought the club down on Phillipe's head.

And again.

CHAPTER

19

He (the Iroquois) shrieked like a lost soul, and the whole crowd imitated his shrieks, or rather smothered them with horrible shouts. The whole cabin appeared as if on fire, and athwart the flames and the dense smoke, these barbarians seemed like so many demons who would give no respite to this poor wretch. They often stopped him to break the bones of his hands with sheer force; others pierced his ears with sticks.

FRANCOIS LE MERCIER, S.J.
Ihonatiria, 1636

Jean stood resolutely at the altar, his white alb and red stole catching the tawny brilliance of the candles that had been lit in memory of the dead. A pale, glittering halo played over the chapel walls. Marc sat in the far corner, isolating himself from Luc and the six Huron Christians who listened so attentively to Jean's sermon about the dead and Paradise. The four women and two men had worn their finest clothing to this special evening Mass. Beads of every color shimmered over their breasts, sleeves and moccasins. Long fringes hung from their skirts and pants. Many had cut their hair in mourning.

Marc kept his eyes on the crucifix. Jesus seemed to be peering directly at him, His face agonized.

Forgive me, Lord, forgive me, forgive me . . .

Mass had been filled with tears. One old woman who had lost two sons still wept, but quietly now, her face muffled in her hide sleeve. Marc's heart ached for Phillipe and Onrea. Were they still alive?

When Luc brought out the corporal, purifactor, chalice and missal, then went back for the bread and wine, Marc closed his eyes, unable to watch. He couldn't receive communion until he could approach the altar with a clear conscience, and he'd yet to manage that. He was still reliving the battle, killing again and again in his mind. Incense from the altar wafted down to him, reminding him of his impurity.

He could hear Jean washing his hands before beginning the Eucharistic Prayer.

Marc mouthed the words of the *Sanctus*.

But a different voice intruded: *If you'd disobeyed immediately and taken your musket out, you could certainly have saved Dafyyd's life, and probably several more Huron lives.* Then: *What have you done? You broke your vow of obedience, and you murdered. Murdered! Pray God can forgive you.*

Deep down, he knew he could not have done otherwise. He would prefer the roaring fires of hell to letting Andiora die.

Marc opened his eyes and glared at the floor, barely hearing the rest of Mass. If he had taken his musket and gone with Phillipe and Onrea, they might be here now. His imagination had begun painting horrifying scenes of what must be happening to them.

The bench wobbled as the six Huron Christians shifted to watch Jean take communion and prepare to dispense it to Luc. The church feared apostasy so much that it denied Indian Christians communion until they'd completed a long and arduous training, often lasting for years.

Luc knelt before Jean and received a tiny piece of bread on his tongue. "The Body of Christ," Jean said and reached for the silver chalice. Tipping it to Luc's lips, he murmured, "The Blood of Christ."

Luc responded, "Amen."

With a sharp cry, a young woman threw herself at Jean's feet, weeping and tugging at his vestments. Jean handed the chalice to Luc and knelt to softly console her, stroking her hair as he spoke in Huron. Marc recognized some of the words and knew that Jean was reciting, "'Blessed are the sorrowing, for they shall be consoled. Blessed are they who show mercy; mercy shall be theirs.'"

Marc bowed his head. He thought that when he'd been dead for a hundred years, that gentle voice so filled with forgiveness would still fill his dreams.

The woman kissed Jean's hand and sank back on the dirt floor, laying her head in the lap of the old woman who'd been crying. They whispered to each other. Jean stood. In a low voice, he recited the *Benedicamus Domino*, then dismissed them.

As the Huron began to file out, Mongrave and Marleaux entered. Marleaux knelt and crossed himself, while Mongrave leaned against the door frame. The trader wore a handsome beige shirt and pants today. Green and blue porcelain beads festooned his collar and sleeves. He'd tied his black hair away from his face. When his eyes landed on Marc, he nodded briefly and backed out of the chapel into the common room. Marleaux followed him.

Marc braced his hands on the bench and stood up. Pain lanced his wound. To ease it, he put his hand over the bandage and limped to the door.

The smells of wood smoke, dried corn and musty bark filled the mission. Jean had ground cornmeal that morning, and a full bowl of it sat by the grinder in the southwest corner. Marc's hastily made bed beckoned to him; he'd stumbled out of it just before Mass.

"You're looking better," Mongrave observed from where he stood by Marleaux, his hands extended to the crackling flames in the hearth.

"My body's healing fine," Marc remarked.

"Your soul isn't, I take it? Well, be grateful. 'Tis the lot of living in this unholy land, Dupre. A man's soul trickles out of him at breakneck speed, and if he's a lick of sense, he's mighty glad of it."

"Why's that?" Marc eased down into a chair by the table.

"Because a soul acts like a noose around the neck. The more you twist worrying about it, the more it strangles you." The saffron glow of the fire glinted from Mongrave's teeth as he grinned.

Jean and Luc emerged from the chapel. They slipped off their purple stoles and began helping each other remove their white albs.

"Hello, Pierre," Brebeuf said. "I assume the ceremony is about to start?"

"Aye. The fires are up. People have already started heating iron axes and pokers."

Jean put away his vestments and smoothed down his black robe, then retrieved a small bag from beneath his bed. He tucked a flask of water, a pouch of raisins and one of lemon peel inside. "Will Andiora be available to translate for us?"

"Aye. She's waiting for you."

Luc's eyes darted speculatively between Jean and Mongrave. "What do I need to bring, Father Superior?"

"Nothing. Unless you want to take something for yourself, some private article to give you comfort during the ordeal."

"I have God's Grace," Luc assured him. "It will sustain me."

Jean looked at Marc. "Are you sure you're strong enough, Marc? There's no need for you to go. Luc will be there."

Marc got to his feet and locked his knees. "I want to be there also." He'd witnessed torture during the siege of La Rochelle. It had made him sick to death, but he could stand it. He wasn't sure of how Luc would react. If he ran like a scared cat, Jean would need someone to help him.

They took their capes and followed Mongrave out of the mission into a veil of pale starlight. The trees surrounding the village glowed with a leaden brilliance. Ihonatiria spread before them like a fairy tale carved of ice. The rounded roofs of the twelve remaining longhouses bore a thick glaze; even the charred husks of those destroyed in the attack gleamed with icicles. Marc heard the faint growling of wolves. The people had hacked graves out of the frozen ground for the Huron victims of the battle, but the dead Iroquois had been dragged down the slope and dumped into a pile. All through last night, he had listened to the wild animals fighting over the bodies.

Marc limped along behind Marleaux and Luc as they crossed the windswept plaza. Jean and Mongrave led the way, talking quietly. When they reached Andiora's longhouse, Jean held the door-hanging aside, letting everyone else enter before him. Rich scents of burning hickory and ash wafted out. Their gazes met just before Marc ducked through. So much apprehension brimmed in Jean's eyes that Marc took a deep breath to prepare himself.

*   *   *

ANDIORA SHIFTED, TRYING to avoid Tehoren's anxious stare. He looked smaller and thinner in the long elkhide tunic that hung to his knees. He'd greased his hair into a bun and fastened it with a wooden comb. "Cougar had holes in his paws?" he whispered.

Andiora rubbed her clammy hands on her red dress and nodded. "Yes. I knew the instant my fever broke. It happened when the blood from Cougar's paws ran down over my forehead."

The seven fires in the longhouse burned so hot that everyone had started to sweat. The green stripe of paint across Tehoren's pug nose was melting and running down his cheeks. His dark eyes searched Andiora's face.

"Why didn't you tell me this before?" he asked. "We—"

"I needed time to think about it, Tehoren."

"What else did Cougar tell you? We *all* need his guidance, Andiora. Has he brought you any more Dreams about the blond Black Robe?"

"No. Just—"

"Are you sure this Dupre isn't the one in your Dream?" His tone of voice had grown harsh, demanding.

Andiora folded her arms defensively. "I don't like it when you talk to me that way, Tehoren."

"Well, is he or isn't he?"

"He's not. I'm sure."

She gazed at the naked Iroquois prisoner, who crouched ten hands away in a bed of hot ashes. Tall, with a shaved head and bristly ridge of black hair, he'd painted zigzagging streaks of red and blue across his forehead. In the heat of the fires, the streaks had blurred into a purple splotch. About twenty-five summers old, he had a bulbous nose and small eyes. He gazed arrogantly at the fifty people who filled the longhouse. Everyone had worn their finest clothes. Porcelain and glass beads glittered like a rainbow. Children scurried quietly, shoving iron pokers and ax heads into the flames to heat, while the adults murmured to each other and glared at the captive.

"Andiora," Tehoren pressed, "please. Try to understand. Cougar has guided our people for forty cycles. Your mother never kept any Dreams from us. *You've* never kept any from us, either. Until now. What am I to think? You worry me. Are you well?"

"I'm fine," she answered honestly. Her bleeding had returned to normal and she felt truly healthy for the first time in nine moons. "I just . . . the Dream didn't seem important, Tehoren." A tightness invaded her chest. She'd never lied to him before, either. But she couldn't tell him that Cougar had urged her to listen to Dupre's religious teachings. That would terrify Tehoren. He believed that every word the Black Robes spoke contained evil.

Tehoren sank back against the wall and gripped the medicine pouch tied to his belt. The image of his Spirit Helper, Owl, peered up at her with incredulous eyes. "You didn't think it important?" He gestured his exasperation. "What if Cougar was trying to tell you that the blood of the Black Robes will heal our people? Or—"

"Excuse me, Tehoren," she interrupted him as she rose. She had seen Pierre, Tristan, Marc and the other Black Robes enter the far end of the house.

She made her way around the children who sat on the floor and met the newcomers halfway. Pierre put a heavy arm over her shoulders. He looked apprehensive, and his dark eyes roved the gathering. Sweat had already beaded on his crooked nose.

"Tonner hasn't arrived yet?" he asked.

"He's with Taretande in the council lodge. They'll be here soon."

"Aye, well, we'd best be sitting down, then. Where's your place?"

"Next to Tehoren."

Pierre frowned. He glanced down at her. "'Tis not the best place you could have chosen, darlin'. The instant Jean pulls out his vial of holy water, Tehoren will likely strangle him. Maybe we could—"

Jean edged by them, saying, "To sit with Tehoren will be fine," as he passed. The hem of his black robe swayed as he strode for the Iroquois prisoner. The longhouse quieted. All along the benches, people watched him, wary.

Pierre shook his head. Under his breath, he said, "I don't know how he manages to stay alive."

Tristan leaned close to whisper, "Might be the only true miracle ever to happen in New France." He winked at Andiora before he walked forward. Penchant followed close behind him.

Andiora held her breath.

Marc limped up, his blond hair and beard gleaming like sunlit amber. Their gazes met. Worry shone in his deep-set blue eyes . . .

but not worry about the ceremony. For weeks, warmth had been growing between them, and she knew that he feared it. He nodded politely and moved on.

"About Tehoren," Pierre murmured as he guided her toward the place where Jean knelt beside the prisoner. Penchant stood behind Jean, his mouth pursed distastefully. "I think I'll be sitting next to him, if you don't mind. Just in case he gets a notion."

"I don't mind." It meant that she would have to sit beside Marc. When Marc saw her approaching, his shoulder muscles tensed beneath the fabric of his black robe. Nervously, he rearranged the pile of their black capes that they'd removed and folded on the floor at his feet.

She sat down, her eyes focused on Jean, who had opened his small bag. When he brought his hand out, his palm held several raisins and a lemon peel. He offered them to the Iroquois. The man turned his face away, refusing the only food he'd been offered in two days.

Very softly, and in Huron, Marc asked, "How are you, Andiora?"

"I can't stop thinking of Onrea. I've been trying to keep Jatoya busy so she doesn't think about her, too. But it's difficult."

"I understand. My thoughts have dwelt equally on Phillipe. Do you think they're alive?"

Andiora hesitated. Could she tell him the truth? Should she? The Iroquois might have taken them for no other reason than for sport. In that case, they had already been tortured to death. But Onrea could be alive. Women and girl children captured in raids were often taken to the Iroquois villages to enrich the blood of the clans. But Phillipe? What good would he be to the Iroquois? "I don't know, Marc. I really don't."

Murmurs broke out in the longhouse when Taretande entered and held back the door-hanging for Tonner. The dwarf shaman ducked through, his hunchback appearing even larger beneath the pale gold of his tradecloth shirt. Hundreds of green glass beads draped his neck. His twisted face was stern.

Taretande and Tonner stood on oppposite sides of the Iroquois and gave Jean a resentful look; he picked up his small bag, rose, put a hand on Penchant's shoulder and ushered him to the bench, where they sat down beside Marc. Neither said a word, which was wise given the difficulty Pierre had had in convincing Taretande to let them attend.

Taretande raised his hands to still the noise. Past fifty summers, he had a seamed old face with sunken cheeks and brooding eyes. His tall body had withered to skeletal proportions, leaving him so frail that he looked as though a strong breeze would blow him down. When the voices dwindled, he said, "My people, you know the decrees of Power. Tonight no one may couple with his mate. And you must burn only the prisoner's legs at the beginning." The black porcupine-quill chevrons on his white shirt glimmered as he lowered his hands.

The Iroquois' lips twitched in a smile of contempt.

Taretande continued. "After the sun has taken our enemy up to the sky, Tonner will receive his liver, Andiora his heart, and Mongrave his brain."

Tehoren cast an indignant look at Pierre, but Pierre ignored him, crossing his arms casually as he leaned back against the wall. By all rights, the precious brain should have gone to another clan leader. Taretande was expressing thanks for Pierre's bravery in the battle.

Marc whispered, "What does Taretande mean, that you'll get his heart?"

"We will feast after Iouskeha comes to take the prisoner's Spirit."

"Feast?"

"Yes. We—"

"Andiora?" Jean leaned forward, the gray threads in his black beard shining. "I'll explain it to them later. Could you help me with the prisoner now?"

Taretande fell into a long speech condemning the Iroquois and vowing revenge, but he watched from the corner of his eye as Jean crawled toward the prisoner.

Andiora crawled after him and knelt at the edge of the bed of ashes. "What do you want me to tell him?"

The Iroquois lifted his chin and stared at them with hatred.

Jean said, "Tell him that my heart aches for him and for what he is about to endure. Ask him his name."

Andiroa translated, and the Iroquois' lips curled unpleasantly. "Deskaheh."

"Deskaheh," Brebeuf repeated. "Please translate this, Andiora. I'm sorry, Deskaheh, that you must suffer during the short time left of your life, but if you will listen to me and believe what I tell you, you will have eternal happiness in heaven after you die."

Andiora told Deskaheh. He responded, "Tell the Black Robe that you Huron dogs will keep me very busy amusing you with my cries—but that I will listen to him when I can."

She told Jean, who nodded gratefully and crossed himself. Before Andiora could say anything more, Taretande motioned for Jix and Iman, two great Huron warriors, to come forward. Andiora and Jean crawled back to their places on the bench. She noted how hatefully Penchant peered at her.

Jix and Iman pulled the Iroquois out of the bed of ashes and held him tightly by the arms. Taretande picked up a stick and dragged a "necklace" of glowing metal hatchet heads from the fire. He held it up high for everyone to see. People cooed in awe and approbation, while Jean prayed softly, "*Gloria Patri* . . ." Penchant joined him, and then Marc, their voices mingling into a resonant drone.

Deskaheh stared vacantly as Taretande slipped the necklace over his head. His body struggled vainly, but not a sound came from his mouth. The red-hot metal seared and blackened his neck and chest. Vile-smelling puffs of steam rose to encircle his tormented face like mist. When he could stand it no longer, Deskaheh let out a small cry and his knees buckled. The Huron warriors jerked him to his feet again.

The longhouse burst into a riot of voices and clapping, praising Deskaheh's courage in suppressing his cries for so long. Jean and Penchant had closed their eyes, but Marc had watched. He'd clasped his hands so hard that his fingertips had reddened. Down the length of the longhouse, people moved close to the fires, pulling sticks and iron pokers from the flames.

Tonner brandished a poker over his head. Solemnly, he said, "For the family we buried yesterday," and he jammed the poker into Deskaheh's thigh. The prisoner stumbled sideways, and Taretande shoved him forward through the first fire. People stood to form a barricade on either side, forcing Deskaheh to walk through the fires while they stabbed him with their pokers and sticks. He stumbled and swayed, his feet sizzling.

Andiora searched Marc's face. His eyes had gone hard. "Marc, do you want to know what the ceremony means?"

". . . Yes."

"Fire cleanses evil. Deskaheh murdered many of our people. We—"

Penchant interrupted, whispering, "Murderers . . . I have also told you in time past that they who do such things shall not inherit the kingdom of God, but shall be cast into the fiery pit."

Andiora blinked, not sure that she understood what he meant, then went on, "We are making an offering to Iouskeha, who brought my people fire. We are asking him to protect our warriors the next time they must fight. If our offering satisfies him, he will destroy the power of the Iroquois."

Jean added, "Fire is also a test of bravery. The Huron consider bravery so important that even when there's no danger, their warriors often hold burning sticks against their bodies to reassure themselves and Iouskeha that they have the necessary courage to face their enemies."

The prisoner approached their end of the longhouse, the pungent odors of burning flesh and fear-sweat preceding him. Blood drained from dozens of punctures on Deskaheh's body. Penchant made a deep-throated sound of horror and draped his sleeve over his nose.

Taretande grabbed Deskaheh by the shoulder and shoved him down on the bed of ashes again. He called, "Tehoren? You must take his hands."

Tehoren got to his feet and picked up a large rock from beside the ashes. Jix and Iman came forward and forced Deskaheh to put his right hand on another rock. They held it there while Tehoren lifted his stone and smashed down with all his might. The sound of bones snapping carried over the tumultous cries of approval in the house.

Andiora explained, "A warrior's hands are his salvation. Without them, he cannot steady a bow or wield a knife. If the prisoner were to escape now, he would never be able to lift his hands against another Huron."

"*Escape?*" Penchant whispered hoarsely. "How could he possibly—"

"Oh, it happens. I've seen it myself. While the warrior is running through the fires, he kicks coals out and sets the longhouse on fire. In the confusion that follows, he slips away."

Marc's face slackened as he stared past her, his eyes widening. Andiora turned to see Tonner hobbling toward the Iroquois with a long, red-hot poker. While Jix and Iman held Deskaheh's arms, Tonner stabbed the poker into the warrior's naked groin. Deskaheh shrieked as his penis severed.

People down the length of the house hissed and threw things in disdain. Penchant gasped and started to stand, but Jean grabbed his shoulder and pulled him down to the bench again. "Not now, Luc. You'll forever lose these people's respect. Wait until the first break."

Penchant trembled. "These people are satanic beasts!"

"No," Mongrave whispered. "They're practical. They believe that brave warriors breed brave sons. This one will have no more sons."

Tonner worked his hot poker down into Deskaheh's testicles, and Deskaheh fell backward, unconscious. Jix and Iman took up their guard positions behind him.

People shouted their derision and threw their flaming sticks to the ground. When Tonner and Taretande ducked beneath the door-hanging to go outside for a breath of fresh air, others rose and followed.

Gently, Jean murmured, "Go now, Luc. No one will hold it against you."

Penchant grabbed his cape and fled. Andiora watched him shove people aside to reach the door. When he lifted the hanging, she could see tiny flakes of snow whirling out of the sky. Pierre and Tristan stood, too. Pierre stretched his arms and yawned. "Andiora, we'll return shortly," he said. He and Tristan headed for the door.

Jean picked up his small bag and crawled forward again to sit beside Deskaheh, lying in the bed of ashes. The Iroquois roused slightly at the sound of Jean's voice. "Andiora? Please?"

Deskaheh slitted his eyes when he saw her kneel beside him. Then his gaze went to Jix and Iman, who were watching vigilantly.

"What do you want me to say?" Andiora asked.

"Tell Deskaheh that I want to teach him about He-Who-Made-All. We call him God. God loves all men, the world over. He loves the Iroquois as well as the Huron."

She translated, and Deskaheh whispered something unintelligible. Marc came up beside her, looking at her questioningly. She shook her head. Jean said, "That's all right. Tell him that God loves the captive as well as the free. He loves the poor and the miserable as well as the rich. To win His love, a man must believe in Him and obey His commandments. Deskaheh, will you believe in He-Who-Made-All?"

Deskaheh weakly answered that the Iroquois already believed in the Creator. When she told Jean this, he said, "Ask him if he wants to be happy with the Creator in the place where souls go?"

Andiora did, and Deskaheh let out a breath. Ash flitted up through the firelit air around his face. "Yes," he answered softly.

Jean crossed himself and whispered, "Thank you, Blessed Jesus." He opened his small bag and took out a vial of water and a bark cup. Jix glanced fearfully at Iman when Jean poured the cup half full. "Marc, could you hold up Deskaheh's head?"

"Yes." Marc lifted Deskaheh's limp head, tilting it backward. Jix and Iman muttered scornfully but made no attempt to stop the baptism.

Jean poured water over Deskaheh's forehead, saying, "I baptize you in the name of the Father, and of the Son, and of the Holy Spirit. I give you the Christian name of Joseph."

Deskaheh reached a trembling hand up and jerked the cup from Jean's fingers. He gulped down the remaining water.

"Deskaheh," Jean said, "even in the worst of your suffering, you must say, '*Jesus, taiteur*, Jesus, have pity on me.' Do you understand? If you do, God will hear you and let you die quickly."

At Andiora's translation, Deskaheh squinted, then lost consciousness.

Jean picked up his cup, packed it into his bag, and rose. "Let's get some rest, Marc. We'll teach Joseph more tomorrow."

"*Tomorrow?* Surely this is all of the ritual?" Marc asked. He retrieved their capes, handed Jean his and swung his own around his shoulders.

"No. It will last for days . . . or for as long as Deskaheh lasts," Jean answered.

Andiora walked behind them, out into the falling snow. A few stars still glimmered overhead, but dark clouds were crowding the sky. People had clustered in the plaza, talking, speculating on how long Deskaheh would live. She didn't see Pierre anywhere.

Jean started toward the mission, and Marc said, "I'll be there in a moment."

Jean nodded. "Good night, Andiora. Thank you for your help."

"Good night, Jean."

Marc frowned as he watched the large man go toward the mission. He folded his arms tightly across his chest and inhaled the brittle scent of snow that pervaded the air. The growling of wolves echoed through the trees, and Andiora could see the animals. Their black shapes darted here and there; two were waging a tug-of-war over one of the corpses at the base of the hill. Beyond the trees, a tiny slice of Lake Karegnondi shone, shrouded with starlit mist. As the clouds sailed eastward, casting their long shadows over the water, the mist faded in and out of view.

"Andiora—Phillipe and Onrea—will they be put through something like this?"

"Iroquois rituals are very much like ours. If they're alive . . . probably."

A gust of wind battered them, flapping his black cape and swirling snow around them. Andiora turned her face from the blast. She should have put on her foxhide coat, but she'd expected to be out here only long enough to say good night. Her thin red dress provided scant shield against the cold.

"I have faith that God will protect them," Marc said, but his voice faltered. In the orange glow that seeped from the longhouse, she saw his jaw muscles tense.

"I have faith, too, Marc."

The brass buttons on his cape flashed palely as he turned. "Do you?"

"Yes."

"Even after all the horrors you've witnessed recently? The battle, Onrea's capture—"

"A long time ago Cougar promised me that he would watch over Onrea. If Phillipe is with her, Cougar will protect him, too." After a moment, she mustered enough courage to add, "I believe Cougar. He has told me many important things in my life. When I was sick and you were praying for me, he . . . he told me I needed to listen to you."

"About what?"

"Your religion. He told me to learn as much as I could."

"Why would he tell you that?"

"I don't know for certain. I think he wants me to believe you."

Andiora gazed up into his blue eyes, and the armor he'd worn all night dropped away. He looked vulnerable, and a little frightened. For a time, neither of them moved. He stood so still that a flake of snow in his blond beard held a stray gleam of light, like a tiny star. "Perhaps . . . perhaps Jean could teach you. I'm not sure that I can."

"Why couldn't you?"

Marc gave her a long, desperate look. "You know why."

He backed away. Andiora shivered as she watched him limp awkwardly across the plaza, his cape billowing in the cold wind.

Pierre stepped out of the mission just as Marc arrived. He started to say something, but Marc shook his head and vanished inside. Pierre peered thoughtfully at the door, then turned and examined the throng in the plaza, searching until he saw her.

An odd expression—questioning—came over his face.

She rubbed her arms and headed for her own longhouse, knowing that he would follow, not knowing what she would tell him.

WHITECAPS FROTHED AGAINST the hull of the canoe. For as far as Onrea could see, blue water undulated in the windless twilight. The six Iroquois braves sang and rapped their knuckles against their oars as they rowed; three sat in front of her and three behind. Phillipe hunched beside her. Onrea's chest hurt when she looked at him. He hadn't spoken at all since the beating days ago. His bald head still bore massive lumps and bruises. She sank deeper into the boat. The hull smelled of bird droppings and mildew from having been cached in the damp forest.

"Phillipe?" she whispered.

The little man did not seem to hear. He gazed up at the gulls that soared and dove through the dusk.

"Phillipe? Can you hear me?" she asked anxiously. She moved her foot over to nudge his black boot.

Phillipe frowned at her as though he'd never seen her before. Onrea's throat constricted. Had they hurt him so much? Had his soul severed from his body, leaving an empty shell?

"Phillipe, it's all right," she whispered, knowing that he probably didn't understand the words. "Aataentsic is watching. She will protect us." Onrea pointed to the sky and tried to smile reassuringly.

Phillipe looked up, and his eyes gleamed suddenly. "Roah!" he said. "Roah."

Onrea studied the wheeling birds. Their wings glinted. Roah? The dove that had followed them from Quebec? *Here?* Did Phillipe truly know, or was he raving? Why would Iouskeha send the bird to them? Perhaps Roah was the eyes of the Spirit World? Sent to watch and report back? Hope reared up like Grandfather Brown Bear in her soul. "Phillipe, how do you know it's Roah? How can you tell?"

Tears filled his green eyes. In broken Huron, he responded, "He calls, 'Phillipe, Phillipe, Moriah comes.'"

Onrea frowned, not understanding. She sat up straighter in the canoe and, in the distance, saw columns of smoke spiraling into the darkening sky. The chanting of the Iroquois braves grew to a terrible roar.

20

I n the early morning hours of the third day, Pierre leaned against an oak at the edge of Ihonatiria, his brandy flask clutched to his chest. The cold air rang with the twittering of birds above the quiet murmurs of the people. Almost the entire village had turned out for the last minutes of the ritual. People covered the hillside, their blankets over their shoulders. Andiora and Jean sat on the frosty ground a few feet away, talking in low tones.

Dupre stood off to the side, peering at the mist that twined around the scaffold where Deskaheh had been strung up, his wrists tied to an overarching branch, his feet strapped to the platform. Huron braves had built the scaffold the night before. Seven steps led up to the platform. Tonner climbed them slowly, his malformed legs barely long enough to reach. He'd plaited his gray hair into two short braids that brushed the beadwork on the shoulders of his blue shirt. His deeply wrinkled face shone in the clear purple light of dawn.

Pierre took another swig from his brandy flask, relishing the fiery path it burned down his throat. He'd already drunk half the contents; its glow warmed his body, smoothing the torture's cruelty. *He's just a goddamned Iroquois, Jean!* Michael Jameson's corpse flashed through his memories, and hatred bolstered him.

When Deskaheh saw Tonner walking across the platform toward him, his body sagged and his legs gave way. He broke into a haunting song, begging his Spirit Helper to kill every Huron alive.

People pressed forward, clustering at the base of the scaffold. Among them, four warriors leaped and howled like wolves on a blood trail.

Tonner removed his knife from his belt and lifted it. "It is time! Iouskeha is watching. Bring the instruments of death!"

Jix and Iman ascended the stairs with red-hot, glowing pokers. They stood by while Tonner approached Deskaheh. The Iroquois sang louder, his eyes on the sky. Tonner grunted as he knelt and stabbed his knife into Deskaheh's leg, then carved out a strip of meat. He waved to Jix, who ran forward with the hot poker and shoved it against the wound to stem the flow of blood. Deskaheh screamed, his strength for bravery long vanished.

Dupre limped over to Andiora and Jean. His blond hair and beard blazed against the background of dark trees. When he spoke, his deep voice pleaded not for information, but for solace, "Why is Tonner doing this? Why won't he just let Joseph die?"

Jean tilted his head and answered softly, "If Joseph were to bleed to death before sunrise, Iouskeha would not be able to witness his death and would be insulted. In his anger, he might refuse to accept the sacrifice, and then the ritual would have been for nothing."

"Our warriors would be forced to go into their next battle without his protection," Andiora explained. "This ritual is very important . . ."

She continued, but Pierre turned his attention elsewhere. A single dried leaf flew from the stark branches over his head and danced through the lavender sky. Her voice was so soft now when she spoke to Dupre. Since he'd returned from Fort Orange, she'd been doing a fine job of keeping him at arm's length, talking to him only when someone else was near, steering conversations to trivial things that had nothing to do with him or her. He'd barely touched her since her "cure"—she'd seen to that well enough.

He took another swallow of his brandy, then examined Dupre. *No, don't be a fool. Those thoughts are crazy. He's got nothing to do with it.*

One of the Huron warriors danced up the scaffold's steps with a wooden bucket in his hands. Tonner stepped back. The warrior laughed. "Deskaheh? Are you cold in this morning mist? I'll warm you." He tipped the bucket and poured burning pitch over the Iroquois' legs.

Deskaheh screamed and sobbed, begging them to let him die.

Tonner walked to the edge of the platform and gestured to Jix, who had gone to stand near the central fire below. "Bring me a branch." The tall warrior raced up the stairs and handed Tonner a flaming limb. Tonner scorched Deskaheh's mutilated genitals until they blackened. The crowd cheered.

When sunrise shot golden lances over the horizon, Jean gripped Dupre's arm to help him to the scaffold. Andiora stayed behind. Her foxhide coat moved beneath the caress of the breeze. Pierre let his eyes drift over her long, beautiful hair and the perfection of her heart-shaped face. She was watching Dupre as he worked his way up the steps.

Pierre shifted against the oak, and Andiora's eyes flickered over to him. He saw her tense. Was she afraid he would come to sit by her? What had he done to hurt her so? He listened to the soft whimpering of the wind through the forest and filled his lungs with the smells of pine and smoke. *Maybe 'tis what you've not done.* Marleaux's words about Andiora being an old maid had been echoing in his thoughts for weeks. At last he bravely got up and walked to kneel beside her.

She brought up her knees and hugged them against her chest. "Good morning, Pierre."

"Is it? I'd not noticed."

Tonner sliced off another strip of Deskaheh's leg and handed it to Jix, who forced the prisoner to eat it. The Iroquois choked, retching, blood flowing down his chin. In a throttled voice, Deskaheh shouted, "*Jesus, taiteur! Jesus . . . taiteur!*" Jean and Dupre knelt and began praying for Deskaheh's soul. Their combined voices rose like a thin shadow over the exultation of the Huron.

Pierre saw Andiora's hands tighten as if in Christian prayer. He frowned. What was she doing? She should have been out there shouting and dancing for Iouskeha to take this damned Iroquois to the Village of Souls—not praying for the animal's salvation! He heard her murmur, "In the name of the Father, and of the Son, and of the Holy Spirit." She lifted a hand and crossed herself.

Pierre could not believe it. "You've not gone over to the side of the papists, have you, darlin'?"

"Power lives in special words. I heard Marc use those words when I was sick. They sounded good to my ears."

"Marc, is it?" Her mouth pursed and he could read her thoughts:

Well, you're never here when I need you, Pierre. He took another swallow from his flask, then shoved it into his boot and grabbed her sleeve. "Andiora, I would take it as a great favor if you'd grant me some time alone with you."

She tilted her head reluctantly and he felt as if a hand had closed around his throat and cut off his breath. "Is that too much to ask?"

"No. It's just that . . . when?"

"This afternoon? After the feast?"

"All right."

The sun climbed above the distant hills, flooding Ihonatiria with light. The blanket of snow glistened in a rainbow of colors. When the first golden rays touched the prisoner's face, Tonner lifted the knife and offered a prayer to Iouskeha, then plunged the blade deep into the prisoner's chest and cut out his living heart. He held up the gruesome prize for all to see. People stamped their feet and shrieked in victory. Tonner sliced into Deskaheh's abdomen, pulling out long ropes of intestines. Children gathered beneath the scaffold, their faces glowing, sticks ready. Some jumped excitedly, crying out in joy as the intestines were cut into pieces and dropped from the scaffold into the snow. The children scrambled to gather them and fix them on the ends of their sticks. Then they raced through the village, shouting happily of Deskaheh's death in the name of all Huron warriors.

Jix cut Deskaheh down and dragged the corpse down the stairs of the scaffold and onto the ground where Taretande waited. The leader took his knife and began slicing the body into pieces, creating a great bloody pile of meat in the snow. He gave slabs from the shoulders and hips to the elderly to divide among their families. Whenever a child ran up, Taretande sliced off a thin piece of skin and handed it over for roasting. Jean hastened to lead Dupre away from the scene and back to Andiora and Pierre.

Mockingly, Pierre said, "Huron Eucharist, Jean! Don't tell me you won't be partaking of the blessed sacraments?"

Jean held his gaze with equanimity. "You're drunk, Pierre. Why don't you go somewhere and sleep it off?"

"Can't. I've the honor of eating your 'Joseph's' brain for breakfast."

A dull crack sounded and Jean closed his eyes. Taretande raised the ax again. This time he split Deskaheh's skull, and the brain slid out. Pierre rose and bowed to Jean with exaggerated politeness. "If you'll be excusing me," he said, and swaggered through the snow to accept the bloody gift from Taretande's hands.

TEHOREN'S HEART POUNDED as he watched Andiora, standing with Brebeuf and Dupre. Jix grunted. He'd stripped down to a beaded breechclout, and in the morning chill, bumps speckled his brown skin. His sharp-nosed oval face was tense. "Why does she soil herself with the Black Robes?" he demanded.

"She says they're her friends."

"Friends? She acts like she has no relatives."

Cook fires already blazed in the longhouses. The scent of roasting human flesh hung greasy and sweet in the air. The door hangings had been pulled back and draped on pegs. Tehoren could see the children inside crouching eagerly before the fires, holding out long sticks impaled with chunks of sizzling skin or meat.

"Do you know what I heard yesterday?" Jix asked. "Raca said that maybe Andiora knows this blond priest is the one in her Dream and doesn't care anymore."

"Foolishness. She would never disobey her Spirit Helper . . . or hurt us."

"Raca said this Black Robe has cast a spell on her to make her love him and that she doesn't know what she is doing."

Tehoren fumbled uncomfortably with the fringe on his sleeve. He'd known Andiora all of his life, and he had to admit that it did seem she loved Dupre. Not so long ago he'd seen that same soft look in her eyes when Mongrave was close. Had this Black Robe bewitched her? Certainly Brebeuf was a sorcerer of the highest order; perhaps he commanded this underling.

"No" Tehoren responded. "I don't believe she's under a spell. I spoke with her yesterday about the sick in the village, and she agreed to Dance in the next curing ritual. Andiora is still on our side."

Two small boys emerged from the longhouse and raced across the plaza. Jana, the one in front, held a juicy piece of meat high as he ran. He giggled wildly when his friend, Wagoh, tackled him and wrestled him to the ground. Wagoh snatched the meat from Jana's greasy fingers and shoved it in his mouth before dashing away. Jana shrieked in anger, the game suddenly no longer fun. He scrambled to his feet and sprinted after Wagoh.

Jix shifted to watch the people filing into their longhouses to share the meat. "We'll see," he said ominously as he headed for his own longhouse.

Tehoren stood alone in the plaza. Dupre broke away from Andiora and Brebeuf, walking with his eyes focused on the snowy ground. His blond hair shone like the sun itself. Behind him, the pale lavender of dawn had changed to a bright glowing pink. The trees transformed themselves from black rustling giants to frail bark and sap again.

When Dupre neared him, Tehoren wiped sweaty hands on his buckskin pants. "You're Dupre, aren't you?"

The blond priest stopped, surprised. He seemed to understand the Huron words. He responded "Yes, Tehoren."

"Let me see your hands." When Dupre didn't instantly comply, Tehoren grabbed his forearms.

"What? I don't understand."

"I want to look at your hands! Let me see them now!" Tehoren shouted threateningly.

As though he'd caught some of the words, the Black Robe opened his hands wide, lifting them for inspection. Tehoren turned them over twice before shoving them away. No holes pierced the flesh, but that didn't mean they wouldn't be there sometime in the future.

"Why don't you go home to France?" he snarled. "You're not welcome here."

"Please . . . sorry," Dupre said in poor Huron. "I don't understand. Come with me to Jean." He tried to lead Tehoren to Brebeuf.

Tehoren turned and strode for his longhouse. Laughter and songs were rising there.

PHILLIPE STUMBLED OUT of the longhouse at sunrise. His brown robe hung in tatters. The warriors had been toying with him for eight hours with their knives. The morning breeze seeped into his cuts like a river of fire. Three of the fingers on his left hand had been sliced off knuckle by knuckle.

Phillipe's mind didn't work very well anymore. He kept forgetting where he was. At times, like now, he vaguely remembered hearing the screams from the battle at Ihonatiria and the nightmare journey across the lake.

Oaks surrounded the village. Their bare branches waved gently in a cool, rose-hued blanket of mist. Birds sang to the dawn, hopping from branch to branch.

Phillipe took a weak step, then another. From behind, a warrior shoved him face first into the snow.

"I'm sorry," he murmured, "I—I'm sorry."

Phillipe's head throbbed sickeningly. He thought he recalled beatings.

A crowd had gathered, lining the plaza in two rows. There must have been over two hundred people leering at him, their brightly colored trade blankets snugged over their shoulders.

"Get up!" someone shouted in French. "Get up or, by God, I'll give them my own knife to use on you!"

Phillipe struggled to pull his knees under him, but the action only forced his chin deeper into the snow. He gasped and rolled to his side.

"Who spoke?" he begged. "Who speaks French? Help me talk to these people! Where's Onrea?"

A stocky warrior came forward. Hatred twisted his face.

Phillipe propped himself up on one elbow. "Please," he begged, "don't hurt me any more."

The warrior raised his hand and slapped Phillipe across the face, knocking him back to the snow. Phillipe cried, "Please, please . . ."

The snow no longer felt pleasantly cool; now it wounded him with its icy touch. Again he struggled to stand, but his legs would not hold him. The warrior kicked him hard in the side, and Phillipe cried out in pain.

A strong hand twined in Phillipe's torn collar. The warrior hauled him to his feet, then roughly shoved him forward.

Phillipe stumbled toward the rising sun. All night his body had been aching to die, and now it appeared that the Dark Angel stood only feet away. He thanked God.

Two warriors flanked him and forced him to walk down the plaza between the rows of people. An old woman with a sharp stick stood at the head of one line. She stabbed her weapon into his stomach. Phillipe gagged and vomited into the snow. People began to push him back and forth, laughing, some of them stabbing him, others pelting him with rocks. Children giggled as he passed. The young Iroquois women who lounged near the longhouses stretched on tiptoes to see, trembling with excitement and cold.

Off to one side was a man dressed in a green velvet coat and black trousers of Dutch styling. A trader? Phillipe stumbled toward him, calling weakly, "Help! Help me, Monsieur. Please, I beg you!"

"You're a goddamned papist," the man growled in French, and Phillipe realized that it was he who'd spoken earlier. "They've promised me your heart, little Brother. Think on that for the rest of your short life. A Protestant is going to feast on your black heart!"

Three women whirled Phillipe around and shoved him toward a longhouse. Pale light gleamed from the icicles fringing the roof. Six dogs romped along in front, their tongues dangling. Perhaps the Iroquois would let him pet them before he died. Phillipe reached out to them.

He tripped over a rock hidden beneath the snow and landed hard on the ground. Tears blurred his vision, but he wept soundlessly and reached out to the closest dog again. "Come. Come."

A club bashed into Phillipe's skull and he clawed at the snow, trying to drag himself away. The club came down again, landing this time on his spine and legs.

A gray haze fluttered around the edges of his mind, then flowed inward like a rushing wall of smoke.

21

Pierre stepped out of the longhouse and held the door-hanging aside for Andiora. She ducked under and glanced at him briefly, then lowered her eyes. The collar and hem of her red tradecloth dress showed beneath her foxhide coat. He let the hanging drop, shoved his hands into the pockets of his brown cloak, and followed her. She took the closest path into the forest.

The noon sun fell through a wispy layer of clouds, piercing the trees with pale lances. Pierre watched Andiora push back an overhanging branch. Every move she made, every wave of her hand, every tilt of her head, the way her lips teased when she smiled, went straight to the vulnerabilities in a man.

She led him into a small meadow. As she stopped to look around, sunlight drenched the blackness of her hair and shimmered in her fur coat. She found a tip-tilted log in the center of the meadow and brushed the snow off of it before sitting down.

The damp scents of melting snow and rotting wood stung his nostrils as he stood in front of her. She looked up at him expectantly. As reasonably as he could, he said, "I love you."

She stared at him with those huge midnight eyes, and Pierre threw up his hands. "Andiora, I'm not blind! I've been noticing for some time the way you look at Dupre. I haven't said anything, because the man's a *priest* and I figured you knew what that meant. He's told you of his vows, hasn't he?"

She nodded. "Yes."

"Well, then . . . you're not doing something foolish, are you?"

She tucked her fingers beneath her arms and shivered. "What would I be doing if I were being foolish?"

"You'd be falling in love with a man who can give you nothing, darlin'. That's what. And doing it, I might add, before the very eyes of one who loves you more than he can ever tell you."

Pierre cracked off one of the branches on the log, then drove it into the snow and leaned on it like a walking stick.

"Is that what you wanted to say to me, Pierre?" She gazed at him forlornly, her head cocked.

"No, not completely. I—I'm trying, Andiora, to tell you that I want you to . . . that . . . that . . . you are throwing happiness away with both hands and I'll not stand by and idly watch you do it!"

A small smile touched her lips when he almost said "I want you to marry me." She seemed to hear the words even though they were unspoken . . . the same words he'd tried on several other occasions to say but could never quite manage. She frowned up at the sunlit clouds. "Pierre, there's something I've been wanting to tell you for a long time. But I couldn't. I was too afraid of losing you."

"Tell me. What is it?"

"When you left for France, I had not had my bleeding for two moons, but I wasn't sure of the baby, and so I didn't—"

"*Baby?*" A cold pit expanded in his gut. He stared down into her calm eyes and whispered, "Andiora, are you telling me that you are pregnant with our child?"

"No." The pain in her voice tugged at his heart. "Evil entered my womb and the baby died, and I . . . I got sick."

Slowly, Pierre sank to the log beside her and ran a hand through his black hair. "Andiora, if I had known . . . I've sea salt in me veins, but I wouldn't have left you to face it alone. You must know that."

"I needed you, Pierre."

"I know, darlin'. I'm so sorry." He lifted his arms to embrace her, then hesitated . . . she hadn't let him touch her for so long. His arms hovered uncertainly. She searched his face for a moment, then slipped her arms around his waist and hugged him tightly.

"Andiora?" He nerved himself by stroking her silken hair. "Will you marry me? I won't be a good husband. I'll be gone for half the year and maybe a little more. But when I'm here, I'll love you with all the heart I've got in me."

She stayed quiet for so long that he couldn't breathe.

"Andiora?"

"I'll never stop loving you, Pierre. I've loved you since I was a child. But you're already wedded to your boats and to the sea. They're your family. I wouldn't be happy married to you."

The cool breeze droned through the trees around him, and he thought he could hear it laughing at his foolishness. He'd always been certain that if he ever gathered the courage to ask, she'd say "Yes." Hurt blended with anger to form a sour brew in his belly.

"Tell me why," he demanded

"I just did, Pierre, I can't share you with—"

"I want the truth, damn it!" He lurched to his feet so violently that he almost pulled her off the log, then stood panting, staring down at her. "You've laid your hopes on Dupre, haven't you? For the sake of God, Andiora! Even if he would cast aside his vows for you, he'd never be free. Those vows are for life. If he gave himself to you, the guilt would suffocate him. You'd kill his soul, darlin'!"

She gazed at him steadily, but a shimmer of tears glazed her eyes.

Pierre knelt before her. "I'm not saying it to be cruel, Andiora. 'Tis just the truth. You'd not want him to hate you, would you?"

"No."

"Then you must see—"

"I do see. I'd never do that to him . . . or to you, Pierre." She put a hand affectionately on his shoulder, rose and headed back across the snowy meadow toward the village.

He watched her disappear amid the twining shadows of the forest and fought with himself. He wanted to stop her, to force her to listen until she agreed with him. *But you don't need to be a bigger fool than you already are. Let her go.*

He shook his head and glared at the sunlight's lemon patchwork on the meadow.

CHAPTER

2 2

Phillipe gathered up handfuls of ash from the floor and tossed them into the air. People laughed. The ash fluttered like snow in the firelight. He squealed in delight and pointed at them. "See, Onrea? *Look!*"

She didn't answer. Her face was hidden in her hands. Her long, tangled black hair cloaked most of her naked body. They sat in a big bed of ashes in a strange room in the cathedral that Phillipe had not seen before. He wondered why Father Uriah had never taken him here. Father Uriah had taken him everywhere else in the cathedral, even down to the old rooms that held the precious church treasures. And Phillipe had seen the secret catacombs where some of the saints were buried. It perplexed him that Father Uriah had never brought him here.

He looked sideways at Onrea. She was older than he, and very pretty. He'd been trying to teach her French. She hadn't learned very much, but he didn't care; he'd never had friends to play with in Notre Dame.

Phillipe lifted his head and whistled, two long and two short, and waited. "Henri? Henri, where are you?" Where could he have gone? Henri was always close by at dinner time. And it must be dinner time by now. Phillipe was starving.

He shivered suddenly and turned to look at the door. Wind swept beneath it. He scowled. It was made of bark and hung on leather hinges. He'd never before seen one like it in the cathedral. A thick pole barred it shut. Two very tall men wearing leather skirts stood on either side with their arms crossed. They looked like guards.

He frowned at them. Lots of things were strange today.

Ten fires blazed down the length of this room, and not one of them was in a fireplace; they were in pits on the dirt floor. Their flames cast the shadows of the people like giants on the ceiling. Men, women and children sat on wooden platforms that lined the walls. All of them had black hair and wore it greased into buns and braids. They were dressed in fringed clothing made from bright cloths. Some had beads on their sleeves. Tiny bells tinkled on a few of the shoes. People had shoved iron pokers into the fires. They smiled at Phillipe. He smiled back and threw more ash into the air to make them laugh. The children giggled and pointed.

A big man with long black hair entered the room at the opposite end and strode toward him. Phillipe blinked. The crowd cheered and clapped. The man wore a beautiful shirt and pants. Beads shimmered everywhere, covering his chest and sleeves and hanging from the fringes on his pants. Phillipe smiled at the way the red and blue beads sparkled, like the rose window. Every afternoon Phillipe waited until the sun streamed through the window. Then he'd jump from one red triangle on the floor to a blue one, and so on until he made his way all around the colorful circle. Henri even got to play sometimes, when Father Uriah let him.

Where *was* Henri? He glanced around, under the platforms, behind legs. Henri always barked and jumped on him. Where could he be? He'd have to ask Father Bre . . . Father . . . *Father . . . ?*

Phillipe gasped suddenly and bent forward. Terrible images flashed through his mind. He saw people running and screaming, and felt himself being beaten with fists and clubs. He thought he recalled riding on a big boat and watching the birds soar and dive around the masts. He saw faces. One, a tall blond man with a beard, filled Phillipe's dreams. When he saw that man's face, his stomach hurt, because a faint voice in his head told him that he belonged with him—with him and—and with who else? He couldn't remember. He had a bad headache all the time now, and it made it hard to think. Besides, he was happy here in the cathedral with Henri and Father Uriah and Onrea. He was afraid to think about the blond man.

"Phillipe? *Oh, Phillipe,*" Onrea whispered. She gripped his hand and held it tightly as she watched the big man in the pretty shirt.

Phillipe patted her hand. "Pretty beads," he said and pointed. "See the pretty beads, Onrea?"

The man circled the fire in front of Phillipe and stopped next to him. Phillipe shyly reached out and touched the twinkling beads on the man's pants. The man didn't seem to notice. He stood waving his arms and talking loudly in a language Phillipe didn't understand. People in the room laughed and pounded the bark walls until the sound was like thunder.

Onrea started to cry. She squeezed Phillipe's hand so hard that it ached. He tried to tug his fingers away. "That hurts, Onrea. Don't!"

The two men by the door came up behind Phillipe and Onrea and dragged them to their feet. Gray ash covered Phillipe's bare legs and streaked his hands. He craned his neck to gaze up at the men questioningly. "What's wrong?"

The beaded man used a stick to pick up a necklace of glowing ax heads from the fire. Onrea fought, but her guard dragged her forward and held her while the ax heads were draped around her neck.

She screamed as steam boiled up around her face and her chest blackened. Phillipe stumbled backward and began yelping like a wounded animal. The smell of cooking flesh made sickness rise into his throat.

"Why are you hurting her?" he shrieked. "She hasn't done anything bad!"

Onrea dropped to her knees and writhed in the bed of ashes, wailing and reaching out to him. "Phillipe, run!" she cried in French. "Run! Run!"

His heartbeat boomed in his ears. Bits of memories flashed: Snow . . . forest . . . have to follow Luc. See his footsteps . . . there! Let's hurry! Trees. Bare-branched in the wind. Onrea? Did you hear that? Maybe that's Luc. Brush catching on his brown robe. Who . . . Onrea, who are they? Iroquois! Run, Phillipe! Run! . . . Have to get to Father Brebeuf . . . Marc? Where's Marc . . . Marc? MARC!

Phillipe looked around, and terror gurgled in his throat. Where were Marc and Father Brebeuf?

People threw more wood into the fires to build up the flames. The guards laughed as the beaded man picked up a glowing poker and came at Phillipe.

Phillipe shrank back. "Don't. No, please!"

The man seized Phillipe's arm, then flung him in a headlong stumble into the first fire. Phillipe staggered over the roasting coals, while people stabbed him with flaming sticks and pokers, trying to force him into the next fire. "*No!*"

As though God had touched him and frozen his mind, he became so confused that he didn't know which way to turn. He screamed and screamed. Flames shot up around him, licking greedily at his arms and chest. Blisters rose and popped so fast, his flesh seemed to boil. The laughter of the people echoed in his ears.

"Forgive them, Father!" he shrieked. "Forgive them. They do not know You! *Oh, Lord Jesus—*"

Something massive struck the barred door at the end of the longhouse, shaking it with earthquake force, sending copper pots bouncing from the walls. They crashed on the benches before tumbling to the floor. People quieted in shock, their eyes riveted to the door.

A deep-throated growl rose, low, terrifying.

The beaded man's black eyes widened. "*Genonskwa?*" His shirt shimmered brilliantly as he backed away.

Phillipe staggered out of the fire and hobbled toward Onrea, moaning. The toes of his left foot had been seared off, and his entire body blazed with agony.

The growl exploded into a shriek. Then long yellow claws edged beneath the door, raking the dirt.

People rose in a shoving swarm. One man tripped and stumbled into the fire. He wailed like a demon as he dragged his roasted hands out.

Four warriors shouldered through the chaos to stand by the beaded man, arrows nocked in their bows. Their faces glowed crimson in the light of the fires.

The door rattled under the hideous scratching.

And something else moved out there, above, like outspread wings battering the roof.

Onrea ran to Phillipe, weeping while her eyes tried to follow the movements of the wings as they circled the house. "It's all right," he whispered. "Today we will be with the Savior in heaven." He patted her cheek with his mutilated hand. The fire had charred away his bonds. "Pray with me? Can you? Say, 'I believe in God, the Father Almighty, Creator of heaven and earth. I . . .'"

The terrible sounds stopped.

The beaded man glared wild-eyed. He whispered, "*Wiyohene! Oneh ne ho!*" and gestured for Phillipe to continue speaking.

Phillipe stuttered, "I—I believe in Jesus Christ, His only Son, our Lord. He was conceived by the Power of the Holy Spirit and born of the Virgin Mary. He suffered under Pontius Pilate, was crucified, died and was buried. He descended to the dead. On the third day He rose again. He ascended into heaven, and is seated at the right hand of the Father. He will come again to judge . . ."

Outside, an ear-piercing screech erupted as something slammed the door. Onrea screamed and clung to Phillipe. Fragments of bark showered them as the bar snapped in two and cartwheeled across the floor.

The leather hinges on the door groaned, and a gray bird fluttered through the crack, its wings flashing golden in the firelight. The longhouse went deathly silent.

"*Otgo*" the beaded man whispered. He raised a hand and sliced the air, shouting at the warriors, "*Deswa sa ye!*"

Men lifted their bows just as the bird tucked its wings and soared down the length of the longhouse. People fell to their knees, terrified. Some scurried beneath the benches, clutching their children to them.

The bird turned and flew back, swooping low over the fires so that its feathers sparkled as though aflame. It pulled up over Phillipe and Onrea and softly fluttered in the air before landing on Phillipe's naked shoulder. The dove cooed to him, and Phillipe murmured, "Roah?"

The door whined again. Onrea's mouth fell open, but she couldn't seem to scream. Phillipe turned and looked into glowing eyes—eerie eyes—shining like black pearls that had been frozen in amber for a thousand years.

The cougar took a step, shouldered the door aside and peered in. Its tan coat glistened like a luminous haze as it stalked closer to the fire and lifted its nose to scent the longhouse. Scarlet flashes rimmed its nostrils and whiskers.

The Iroquois broke into a frenzied wailing, fighting to get away.

Warriors threw down their bows in panic and ran. People flooded out the door at the other end of the longhouse.

Phillipe just stared, too terrified to move. The cat stood so close that he could see the muscles ripple on its shoulders and haunches. Though every nerve in Phillipe's wounded body screamed for him to flee, he only held Onrea tighter and prayed.

The cougar seemed to hear those silent sacred words, for it cocked its massive head and looked at Phillipe. They held each other's gaze for a minute, then two, and a sound made its way to Phillipe's ears, a sound almost too beautiful to be borne. As if the dance of the firelit dust and the flickers of light emitted music, the notes wove a radiant web around and through him, tingling in the marrow of his bones.

Roah spread his wings suddenly and flew through the door. The cougar backed out and loped away into the night.

"Hurry, Phillipe!" Onrea raced around the longhouse, grabbed several abandoned blankets, and a knife, then came back and tugged Phillipe's hand. "Phillipe, come on! Cougar wants us to follow him."

She dragged Phillipe out into the magnificient starlight.

A gust of wind whistled through the cracks around the two windows in the common room. Marc pulled his coarse wool blanket up around the shoulders. The gold embossing on the spines of the books lining the shelves glimmered dimly in the light of the red hearth coals. He could make out the hourglass silhouette of the grinding mill in the corner, and the doorway to the storage room. Luc snored to his left and next to Luc, Jean slept soundly. Phillipe's bed on Marc's right stood empty. Marc's eyes kept straying to the door, waiting, waiting . . .

Where are You, God? Why didn't You protect him?

He couldn't sleep. Every time he closed his eyes, he heard Phillipe calling his name. And it felt as though his soul knew something his body and mind didn't. *Phillipe needed him.* For two weeks he'd gone through the motions of his daily offices—preparing Mass, listening to the confessions of the few Huron Christians—and all the while he longed to grab his musket and run down the trails, searching for Phillipe.

Marc laced his fingers behind his head and watched a slate-colored band of starglow pool on the table and spill over across the floor. To make matters worse, Andiora had been treating him like a stranger. He wanted her to be his friend, just not . . . *yes, deny it, and keep on denying it.* Whenever he visited her longhouse, she left. And when they met by accident walking across the plaza or in the woods beyond the village, she acted as if he stared at her over the sights of a musket. The world always seemed to suck in a breath and hold it, waiting for the muzzle blast . . . or for the faint trumpets of Judgment Day.

Something glinted at the corner of his eye. He turned; a light flashed against the frosted windows. It winked again, and he threw off his blanket and started to rise, praying that no fire had taken hold of a longhouse.

Jean sat bolt upright in bed, his dark eyes wide. Sweat coated his bearded face. He wiped a trembling hand across his forehead.

"Did you see that, Jean?" Marc asked.

"W-what?"

Marc pointed. "The light. There was a light outside. It flashed three times."

Jean crossed himself, whispering, "Father, Son, Holy Spirit." Then got to his feet to slip his black robe on.

Marc frowned. "If you didn't see the lights, why did you awaken?"

Jean crossed the room and pulled his cape from its peg. As he put his arms through it he said, "They're alive, Marc. They're coming home to us."

Marc rose and threw on his own robe. "How do you know?" he asked as he tugged on his boots.

Jean's eyes glowed like black pits in the semidarkness. "God told me."

"Did he tell you what trails they're following? Perhaps we could go meet them, or get word to Mongrave. He's traveling the major roads to Fort Orange. If he and his armed party could intercept Phillipe's path—"

"No, Marc. It's too dangerous," Jean said, as he walked through the storage room and opened the outer door. Glacial wind blasted their faces. Beyond, longhouses sat silhouetted like long furry worms against the ice-bitten trees and midnight skies. "Phillipe and Onrea have the Holy Spirit to guide them. We'd be of little use."

As he started out, Marc caught hold of his sleeve. "Where are you going? Can I go with you?"

Jean shook his head. "God and I must face each other alone. But I thank you for offering. Go back to sleep. I've a feeling that the next few weeks are going to be long indeed."

Jean clamped his hand briefly over Marc's, then strode out into the dark plaza, his robe swaying around his long legs. From the hills, the howls of wolves rose forlornly. Marc stood for a moment, listening to

222 † KATHLEEN O'NEAL GEAR

them, then quietly closed the door. He turned to the stack of split wood in the corner of the storage room and filled his arms. Going to the hearth, he made a pyramid over the warm coals then blew on the embers until the wood caught and flared. Gradually he added more wood. When the fire crackled warmly, he extended his cold hands to the flames.

"Dupre?" Luc called. He had propped himself up in bed on his elbows. His brown hair straggled over his forehead.

"What is it, Luc?"

"What was that sound?"

"Just the wind. We may have another storm coming in. The temperature is dropping."

Luc ran a hand through his hair and gazed around. "Where's Brebeuf?"

"I think he went walking in the forest. He told me that Phillippe and Onrea are coming home to us."

Luc stiffened. "How does he know that?"

"He said God told him."

Luc sank back into his gray blankets. "Well, thank the Lord," he whispered, but if he'd blurted, "How dare they?" it would have sounded the same.

Marc went to the shelves to pick up their copper tea kettle. He sloshed it to see how much water it held: half full. "Some day, Luc, you're going to have to confess that sin," he remarked as he brought the kettle back and set it on the coals.

"What sin?"

"Is it that difficult to single one out? I was thinking specifically about how you abandoned Phillipe to the Iroquois."

"God will punish you for making false accusations, Dupre. And, anyway, I'd be worried about my own soul if I were you. My Huron is getting better every day."

"What does that mean?"

Luc arranged his pillow behind him and sat up, clasping his hands over his stomach. The fire flared and threw a shaft of light over his smug face, outlining the hooked arch of his nose. "That satanic shaman, Tehoren, has been asking around about you."

"Why?"

"He thinks you're a witch and that you've cast a spell on Andiora. Apparently," he said as he smiled, "she's in love with you, and Tehoren doesn't think it's *natural*."

Marc's heart slammed sickeningly against his ribs. For a moment, he couldn't move. He had to force himself to rise and go back to the shelf for the tea. Starlight sheathed the copper tea box with a layer of silver. When he reached for it, he clumsily knocked it over, and his attempt to catch it sent it clattering across the dirt floor.

"Shall I hear your confession, Dupre?"

Marc retrieved the box and took a bark cup off the shelf.

"Thanks. No."

"Are you saying you never encouraged her? Never tempted her?"

Marc took the lid off the kettle, then sprinkled tea into the water. A wreath of steam glistened around his face. "I'm saying Tehoren is mistaken." *Please, God, let him be mistaken.*

Smoke wafted like a transparent silken veil between himself and Luc, but he could see Luc's face twist with amusement.

"Indeed?" Luc folded his arms. "A lot of people seem to believe it. I heard old Jatoya whispering about it with Maconta. If I were you, Dupre, I'd go to the village council and inform them—"

"I don't need your advice, Luc."

Soft footfalls thudded outside, coming closer. Marc rose as the storeroom door opened and a gust of frigid air made the fire dance. Jean took off his cape and hung it back on its peg, then came into the common room, his eyes downcast, his thinning hair windblown. He walked into the light of the fire and gazed absently at the flames. He had a preoccupied expression.

"Jean," Marc said softly, "that must have been a cold walk. May I pour you a cup of tea?"

"No." Jean shook his head. "No, but . . . tell me . . ." He paused and looked up. "Tell me what you recall from Revelation. About the sequence of the events at the End of Time."

"Armageddon?" Luc asked. "Why do you want to know about that?" He grabbed for his robe and hurriedly dressed.

Marc frowned. Jean's dark eyes look troubled. "Chapter five is where the sequence of events is described."

"Yes, five," Luc said while he jammed on his boots. "The Victor appears. Though our Lord came first as the Lamb, He returns as the Lion, but He bears the marks of the Lamb's slaughter upon Him. He is the only One in heaven worthy to unroll the seven-sealed scroll."

Blood drained from Marc's head. *A lion with the marks of slaughter on him?* Andiora's feeble voice echoed in his memories: "Cougar came to me and he . . . he lifted his paws and they had holes in them. He let the blood from the holes run down over my face . . . ."

Luc came to stand by the fire, his gray eyes wide. "Each time our Lord breaks a seal, one of the Horseman of the Apocalypse appears. First, the white horse, *war*, Then the red horse, the black horse and the pale horse: civil strife, famine, plagues. The fourth Horseman's name will be Death. He will kill by famine, pestilence and wild beasts."

Jean smoothed a hand over his graying beard. "And the fifth seal reveals the altar of souls who were slaughtered for the Word of God."

"Yes!" Luc agreed. "Our Lord tells them to rest a little longer, until the last martyr joins them. Then—after the death of the last martyr—our Lord breaks open the sixth seal and there are earthquakes, the moon turns to blood, and the sun becomes as black as sackcloth. The great day of God's vengeance has come, and the angels stationed at the four corners of the earth will unleash the winds of justice. And then—"

"—and then," Marc said, noticing that Jean had closed his eyes as though against the telling, "scourges—locusts and dragons—strike the earth. A third of mankind is slaughtered, but the suffering is still not at an end. The wicked will try to destroy all the witnesses while Satan is trying to kill the child who is destined to rule over the earth."

In an imploring whisper, Jean asked, *"What child, Lord?* Which one am I supposed to protect?"

Neither Marc nor Luc said a word.

Jean opened his eyes. Reflected flickers of the fire danced in their dark depths. "I don't understand. Who is the child?"

"The Savior!" Luc blurted.

"Yes, but . . ." Jean's voice faded until it was barely audible. *"Who?"*

"What do you mean, 'who?'" Luc asked. "It's our Lord! He comes to battle Satan. One Peter, chapter five, verse eight, says that Satan will appear as a roaring lion. And Revelation tells us that he will mimic the works of our Lord by performing miracles, calling fire down from the sky, healing the sick, raising—"

"*Healing?*" Marc felt as though an iron maiden had closed around him. He hesitated, then said, "Jean, I must tell you about a dream Andiora had. I haven't told you before because it didn't seem important. But I think now . . . I think it is important."

He related the details of Andiora's dream, and Luc sank unsteadily onto one of the chairs around the table. "I told you, Dupre," he rasped, "she's wicked. If the Antichrist came to her, she must be the harlot in Revelation."

Jean shifted, his eyes lifting to the windows, where the white disk of the moon shone through the dark branches. As the wind blew the trees, the moon seemed to waver, like a waterborne reflection of itself. "We don't have enough information to make judgments. When the Lord decides to reveal Himself to us, then we'll know who the Antichrist is."

"When the last martyr dies. That's when He'll do it." Luc nodded. "I pray God grants me the privilege of being that martyr, so I can stare our Lord in the face before I die."

Pewter moonlight streamed through the windows, landing like a pale cerecloth across the table. Marc studied the way it shadowed the irregularities in the rough-hewn wood.

"I'm glad you're not afraid of martyrdom, Luc," Jean said softly. "This afternoon I heard that sickness has struck the village of Ossossane. Four people have died. Seventeen are ill. I must go to them. I was thinking about taking you with me."

"Of course, Father."

He turned to Marc. "That means you'll be alone here, Marc. Will you be all right?"

"I'll be fine, Jean."

"If you need help, ask Andiora. She's been indispensable to me in the past."

Luc glanced knowingly at Marc, and Marc's chest began to sting as if tiny teeth were eating him from the inside out. "Yes, Jean. I will."

He concentrated on the popping and hissing of the fire.

CHAPTER

24

It is the Black Robes who make us die by their spells; listen to me, I prove it by the reasons you are going to recognize as true. They lodged in a certain village where everyone was well; as soon as they established themselves there, everyone died except for three or four persons. They changed location and the same thing happened. They went to visit the cabins of the other villages, and only those where they did not enter were exempted from mortality and sickness. Do you not see that when they move their lips, what they call prayers, those are so many spells that come forth from their mouths? It is the same when they read their books. . . . In their cabins they have large pieces of wood—they are guns—with which they make noise and spread their magic everywhere. If they are not promptly put to death, they will complete their ruin of the country.

HURON WOMAN, 1640

What does *he* want?" Jatoya whispered as she washed the face of a sick child. The little boy's fever had risen so high that he didn't even know she stood there. All through the house, the sick moaned and thrashed.

"Who?" Andiora asked.

Jatoya pointed, and she turned. Tehoren strode purposefully toward her. He wore ceremonial clothes; a pale buckskin shirt and pants, covered with shell beads. His Owl medicine pouch hung from his belt. He'd left his long hair loose so that it framed his pug nose and dark eyes. Two red lines of paint streaked his cheeks. Andiora stopped stirring the kettle of fish soup that hung on the tripod. "I don't know."

Seven fires glowed down the length of the house, their heat battling the freezing wind that seeped around the door-hangings and through the smoke holes. Snow had started whirling out of the leaden sky at dawn, and two hands' worth coated the plaza already.

Tehoren looked up and down the benches, noting each sick person, then came to Andiora and said, "I must speak with you. At noon a runner came in from the Montagnais villages."

"What did he say?"

"Come outside and I'll tell you."

"In the snow?" Tehoren nodded firmly, and she reluctantly hung her stirring spoon on the tripod. "All right. Let me get my coat."

When Andiora passed Jatoya, the old woman put a hand on her arm. "I'll need you back soon. Someone has to feed the sick while Maconta and I clean up after them."

Andiora patted her hand. "I won't be long." The number of blankets and hides soiled from body wastes grew each day. They had few to begin with, and in winter the washing and drying of them took a great deal of effort. "Is there anything I can get when I am out?"

"Bring back some fir needles for tea."

She nodded and walked to her place on the bench, where her foxhide coat lay. Putting it on, she asked, "Is it so bad, Tehoren?"

"When we get outside," he answered stiffly.

He lifted the hanging and she followed him out into the falling snow.

He led her into the forest. Snowflakes glistened on his loose hair like a net of wispy cattail seeds.

Andiora dogged his footsteps, ducking beneath overhanging branches and around gnarled brush. Wind gusted, whimpering in the tongues of the lost *oki* who haunted these woods.

Tehoren stopped beside a cluster of four pines grown so closely together that their limbs wove like fabric. He ducked beneath the branches and disappeared into the shadows. Andiora bent low and followed. She found him sitting on a dry bed of needles, leaning against a tree. The snow-free space stretched about twelve hands square and ten hands high.

"All right, Tehoren." She sat down across from him. "What terrible news did the Montagnais runner bring?"

He looked thin and small against the massive, smoke-colored trunk of the pine. "This illness has spread over the whole country. Everyone has been struck, from the Montagnais in the north to the Iroquois in the east, the Neutral in the South and the Tinnontate in the west." His words came short and fearful: "And there are stories, Andiora."

"About?"

"People are saying the sickness rides on the shoulders of the Christians. It began the instant those new Black Robes arrived in Quebec."

Andiora stared into Tehoren's eyes. "He's not the blond in my Dream, Tehoren. I told you."

"But how can you be sure?" Tehoren reached out pleadingly to her. "So much has happened since he came. The Iroquois attack, the sickness. Your Dream is coming true!"

"Tehoren, Dupre is *not* the one."

He drew his hand back to his lap. "All right. I—I believe you. There are other possibilities." He frowned at the brittle bed of pine needles. Their tangy scent filled the small shelter.

"What?"

"Aenons, the chief of Wenrio, says the Black Robes keep the corpse of Jesus in their house. He says they eat it and that it causes the disease."

Andiora shook her head. "Aenons has not seen their ritual. They say the food is the body and blood of Jesus, but it's just bread and wine. Pierre brings them the wheat and wine from Quebec. There's no corpse. Ask the Christians in the village. They will tell you the same."

"I *have* talked to the Christians. They say that the priests say magic words over that bread and wine and it changes into flesh and blood."

"I have seen it, Tehoren! There is no corpse." She shook her fists in frustration. "This is nonsense. Do you think Pierre would bring it to them if it caused deaths among our people?"

Tehoren put a hand on his medicine pouch to stroke the face of Owl. "I don't know what to think."

"What else have you heard?"

"Many things. Tsonda says they spread the disease through those lemons and raisins they feed the sick. But Gewona, at Ossossane, says the sickness lives in a book they keep hidden in their house. Maybe they pass it by all of these means."

"Tehoren, I have seen three members of my longhouse die. *I* want to find the cause of this sickness, too, so we can stop it! But I can't believe it's Christian witchcraft."

Tehoren cocked his head. "You always defend them."

"I don't think they're guilty."

"And why is that?"

"There's no proof!"

"I think you defend them for another reason, Andiora." He lowered a hand and began drawing magical signs over the pine needles, as though sealing the two of them from the ears of any evil Spirits that might be lurking in the trees or stones. "I want to Sing for you and make you a charm."

Her frown deepened. "What is it you think I need protection from?"

"*Everyone! Everything!*" he shouted suddenly, and his face flushed. "Andiora, last week your curing society, the Atirenda, Danced. You said you would go. You didn't. Why?"

"Linnal begged me to attend the baptism of her daughter. She was terribly frightened, and I—"

"You went to a Christian ritual rather than helping to heal your own sick? Do you love the Black Robes more than you do us?"

"Oh, Tehoren, please!"

A gull screeched and Tehoren's eyes darted up to the dense tangle of limbs above their heads. Andiora saw shadows moving over the snow outside as the flock soared to land in the pines.

"Every time we talk about the Black Robes," Tehoren whispered ominously, "the birds come. Have you noticed?"

She blinked, trying to think back. "No."

He bent forward, and his long hair swung over his chest. "I want you to tell me the truth."

"About what?"

"Do you . . . some people are saying that you love this Black Robe."

The shelter felt suddenly colder, as if Iouskeha had breathed the deepest of winter over it. She hugged herself. "He's cast no spell on me, Tehoren. Is that what you think?"

"That's not an answer."

"Tehoren," she pleaded softly. The discussion made her ache. She'd been desperately trying to put Marc from her mind. She reached out to touch this old friend, but he pulled away and glared.

"Answer me!"

"I would never hurt my people, Tehoren. You *know* that."

When he didn't respond, she murmured, "I must be getting back. Jatoya needs me."

Andiora crawled out of the shelter and stood up. Clouds rolled over the hills, dropping snow in ivory veils. She walked aimlessly through the deepening snow. She felt numb, like a warrior who has been bashed in the head and can no longer tell night from day. Since she'd met Marc, a chasm had opened in her soul. What had she done to herself? How could she have slipped so easily into this abyss of longing and despair?

Pierre, how could I do this to you?

But she knew how. Since she had lost the baby, her feelings for Pierre had been changing. She'd felt so alone when she'd looked upon that tiny blue fetus in the pool of blood that she had begged Aataentsic to dry up her womb so she would never have to go through that again. She'd needed a friend to hold her, not a lover.

Perhaps that's why . . . Marc.

She'd opened her soul to him, knowing that he wasn't interested in her body. That was how it had begun. Why had she let it continue? Why had she let him sit beside her around the fire, talking for whole days, laughing? The glint in his blue eyes had warmed something inside her that she'd never known was cold. He'd been there the day she'd fallen into the river, and every day since when she needed someone. And now . . . Her throat tightened with tears.

You know why . . .

You'll kill his soul, darlin'.

The wind buffeted her, whipping her hair around her face.

You don't need this, Andiora. So just stop it. Taking a deep breath of the cold air, she tramped through the snow, angry with herself. But as she headed for the fir tree she had spotted in the distance, intending to gather needles, grief mixed so powerfully with the anger that she felt sick to her stomach.

DAWN'S PEARLESCENT RAYS touched the gray world, lighting the narrow path that Onrea and Phillipe followed through the forest. In the deep stillness, Onrea could hear the murmur of the lake just over the next rise. The lonesome honks of geese echoed in the air.

"There!" Phillipe said in Huron, and pointed.

Onrea nodded, seeing the fox tracks in the snow. On the trail ahead, alert ears and a bushy tail glinted, before the Spirit animal disappeared around the bend. He'd been leading them north for two days, stopping to wait when they had to slow down because of Phillipe's injured feet.

Onrea glanced down at Phillipe's moccasins. She had made an awl from the leg bone of one of the rabbits they'd snared, then sewn the rabbit skins together with dried sinew. The soft fur cushioned their feet, while the rabbit fat kept their burns moist. But she knew from the way that Phillipe walked, taking one agonized step at a time, that his pain must still be unbearable. "How are your feet, Phillipe?"

He cocked his head and frowned. She pointed to his feet, and he said, "Oh! Fine."

Onrea patted his blanketed shoulder. She'd cut holes in the blankets for their heads and arms, then woven strips of bark together for belts. They'd each put on three blankets and kept fairly warm during the day, but at night the cold was bitter. And her own burns had festered, making it impossible for her to sleep.

Phillipe smiled and said, "Look, Onrea." He picked a leaf out of the trail and showed her the different splotches of color.

"It's pretty, Phillipe."

Since he'd stared into the eyes of Cougar, he'd grown serene. He made her stop frequently during the day just to study the patterns of ice crystals on fallen logs or to appreciate the sweep and soar of birds. She kept trying to tell him that they had to hurry or the Iroquois would catch them again, but he didn't seem to care.

Fox let out a sharp bark, and Onrea jumped. "I wonder what that meant?"

Phillipe shook his head.

She took a wary step forward and peered through a tangle of dead vines. The musty scent of autumn still clung to them. Beyond, the lake glimmered and sparkled, only a hundred hands away. Fox yipped again. There! He was digging at something and growling. As she watched, he tugged a clump of brush away with his teeth and dragged it down onto the path.

"Come on," Onrea said. "Let's see what he's found."

As they rounded the bend, Fox let out a howl and bounded away through the forest. Onrea edged forward, then gasped. "Phillipe! Fox has found us a canoe!"

The boat lay upside down and was covered with two frozen moosehides. "Thank you, Fox. I pray Aataentsic takes good care of your soul. Phillipe? Can you help me pull it out?"

Together they dragged it into the pink dawn. A small canoe, only ten feet long, it carried four oars. Onrea shook out the musty-smelling moosehides. "It will still be a very cold trip, Phillipe. But these will cut some of the wind."

He smiled. "We will sleep warm."

"Maybe. We should gather food, then rest today to build up our strength. The voyage takes at least four days if the weather stays good. Pray no storm comes up. If one did we'd go faster, but we wouldn't be able to take turns sleeping; it would be too dangerous. Both of us would have to paddle to keep the canoe from swamping in a wind."

Phillipe put his mutilated hand against her hair. "God loves us, Onrea."

"I hope so, Phillipe. We need the magic of all of our gods to stay alive for the next week."

She straightened to stretch her aching back and unwittingly frightened a flock of loons. Twelve of them raced over the lake, squealing, splashing in their half-flying runs to lift into the air. They curved up and around, heading toward home. Their winged shapes reflected so perfectly in the mirrorlike surface of the lake that for a moment Onrea thought she saw two flocks instead of one. *Going home. Home.*

Her heart ached with longing. Was her village still there? Or had the Iroquois burned Ihonatiria to the ground and murdered all her people? She'd seen the billowing smoke on the terrible day she and Phillipe had been captured.

Don't think of that she told herself. *You'll go crazy if you do.*

She walked down to the edge of the ice and stamped on it until water gurgled up. Clams glistened, half-buried in the mud.

"Phillipe? Why don't you rest? I'm going to get us some food."

He shook his head and hobbled forward to crouch and look through the hole. "I'll help."

They spent until noon scooping up clams and piling them in the bottom of the canoe. After they'd eaten their fill of the raw juicy delicacies, they wrapped themselves in the moldy moosehides and slept deeply.

Nicholas Barrow leaned across the table and hissed, "'Tis the strangest story I've ever heard in this barbarous land." The ugly little Englishman wore a grimy leather shirt and pants, heavily beaded. He had a wary face, with a lumpy nose and chill, pale blue eyes that never stopped roving the shadowed corners of the Ale House at Fort Orange.

Pierre took a sip of stout from his pewter mug and sank back into the booth. A dank, windowless structure, the tavern smelled of dried spices and unwashed bodies. The candles on the tables cast long shadows over the ceiling. Two dozen men crowded the place, some lounging against the rough-hewn bar, others hunched in the booths that lined the walls.

Tristan sat beside Pierre, drinking a mug of amber ale. His pointed face bore lines of sleeplessness. Purple bags had grown beneath his eyes. He wore his old elkhide coat, black with soot and grease from hundreds of camp fires. "So the Iroquois did capture them?"

"Aye," Barrow answered.

Tristan braced his elbows on the table. The fringes of his coat sleeves shone like spiders' legs in the brassy glow of the candle. "What have you heard? Did they kill 'em right off, or force 'em to hang on for days?"

"'Tis said they're alive. And thereby hangs the tale."

"*What?*" Tristan asked in awe.

Pierre rubbed the beads of water that had formed on his cold pewter mug. He ought to be listening to this discussion, he knew that, but his thoughts lay elsewhere. Somewhere dark and painful.

Over the past week he'd been mourning the loss of a child who had never really been at all—but something within Pierre had given the dead baby life. He didn't even know whether it had been a male or a female, but his mind had been weaving images of a laughing, black-haired boy. In his dreams, Pierre took the boy sailing and taught him about knots and rigging and how to climb the shrouds so he wouldn't fall to his death. He sat on the deck at night, holding *Matthew* in his arms as he pointed out the constellations and talked about their names and stories.

In his dreams . . . he'd loved that boy.

Barrow chuckled. "Oh, me friend, you're going to be liking this tale, yes, indeed. Not many traders are brave enough to speak of it, for fear that the Indian ha'nts will come looking for 'em next time they're alone in the dark of the woods."

Pierre knew that Barrow was telling the truth. Tristan and he had been roaming the fort for two days, trying to convince men to tell them the whole story, but they could get only pieces of it. Frightened gibberish about Spirit cats and evil *okis* in the form of birds, from drunken traders too witless to care what flowed from their mouths.

Tristan said, "Don't you know that Montmagny would pay a pretty sum to the man who rescued Raimont? The new governor's a Catholic-lover."

Barrow glanced around the room before leaning across the table. Pierre's hand instinctively dropped to his holstered pistol.

"Aye, sure," Barrow scoffed, "but what man would have it said that he'd rescued a Catholic? Why, the poor imbecile would not be living more than a day in New Netherland after such news became known."

Tristan's lips pressed into a tight white line, as though he were about to say something unseemly. Pierre spoke quickly. "So, give us the story, Barrow. 'Twas a long, hard journey across Lake Ontario, and we're of a mind to be entertained."

Barrow looked at his empty mug, and Pierre cursed silently before he lifted a hand to the bartender. After three pitchers already, Barrow ought to be feeling right talkative. "Ho! Charles! We'll be having another two pitchers here. A stout and an amber."

"Aye, Pierre! On their way," Charles shouted over the patrons' laughter and raucous voices. A towheaded kid, with a turned-up nose, he looked barely fifteen. He grabbed two pitchers and began filling them from the oak kegs behind the bar.

"Why don't you start, Barrow?" Pierre prompted. "The ale's on its way."

Barrow's eyes took in the room again, lingering for some time on the dark corners. "'Twas like this, so the story goes. The Catholic and the little Huron girl were taken from Ihonatiria during a raid and forced to the Iroquois village." He bared broken yellow teeth in a grin. "I've heard tell that the Seneca braves had quite a sweet time with that little girl. They took turns every night, climbing atop her and pumping her full." He laughed. "The Catholic screamed and cried like a madman, they say, begging God to *forgive* the Iroquois! Can you imagine? Why, it's pure insane, if you're asking me. Had I been there, I'd have been calling for God to throw fire from heaven and burn the filthy Seneca to ashes. I'd have—"

"What happened in the Seneca village, Barrow?" Pierre pressed him.

"Oh, well, mostly the usual . . . 'til the very end. They tortured them for two days. Then, on the third day . . ."

Charles set the two pitchers on the table. "There you go, gents."

Pierre tossed him a coin. "Keep the extra, Charles."

"Thank you, sir." The youth backed away smiling and returned to the bar.

"So," Pierre poured Barrow's mug full of ale. "You were speaking about the third day."

Barrow clasped his mug in both hands and took a long drink. "Why, sure. The third day. Well, 'tis said that night had come and the Catholic had lost his mind. He'd been acting like a babe, playing with the children in the longhouse, giggling and wrestling with the dogs . . . but you're knowing how it works. The night before the headmen think you're going to breathe your last, why, they stoke up the fires and get set to make you scream 'til your throat bleeds and swells itself closed."

Pierre saw Tristan's hand clench into a fist before he tucked it under the table. "Sure," Pierre said matter-of-factly. "So they stoked up the fires and heated every scrap of iron in the village. Then what?"

Barrow wiped his mouth on his filthy sleeve. "'Tis crazy, this part, but 'tis said that they'd put the glowing ax heads 'round the girl's neck and then shoved the Catholic down the fire line, when, of a sudden, something threw itself against the longhouse door and let out a shriek like the Damned in hell." Barrow glanced around the ale house again. "Why, that creature bashed down the door, and a bird flew in." He lifted his hand and swooped it over the tabletop. "It soared over them all, peeping and carrying on 'til it found that Catholic and lighted on his shoulder. But the best part's this—after the bird lighted, a cougar slammed the door back and growled like a demon at the Iroquois, driving them all out of the longhouse."

Tristan softly asked, "And then?"

"Why, then that cougar took that little Huron girl and that Catholic and led them away through the woods like the children of Israel leaving Pharaoh's cruelty." Barrow lifted a shoulder. "Aye, 'tis the strangest story I've ever heard in this barbarous land."

"Aye. Strange, indeed," Pierre said and rose to his feet. "'Tis a grand storyteller you are, Barrow. Here's a coin for your trouble."

Pierre threw a copper on the table. He and Tristan picked up their mugs and shouldered through the crowd out into the cold afternoon light. A stiff wind blew up from the south, flailing at the few trees that shaded the trading plaza. Pierre frowned up at the clouds. Odd. Winter storms almost never gusted from the south, and this wind had the strength of the northerlies.

The plaza bustled with people. The Dutch had palisaded the fort, as would any half-wit who had to deal with the Iroquois. The defensive walls rose twelve feet high. Short, stocky buildings clustered along the inner walls, forming a rough square. Fox, beaver and otter furs lay bound and stacked in piles around the edges of the buildings, where Dutch and English traders haggled with Indians over fair prices.

Tristan strode across the open area beside Pierre, not saying a word.

"What are you thinking, Tristan?"

"Hmm? Oh, that Christmas is only nine days away."

"Christmas?"

"Aye." Tristan squinted. "The season of miracles."

Near the north wall, four men in fine European clothing sat at a rough-hewn table. Two at one end, two at the other. Their fine velvet coats marked them as newcomers. Pierre eyed them distastefully, but this was the least crowded area in the plaza. He went to stand six feet away from them, beneath a towering spruce.

Propping an arm on the lowest limb, he sucked foam off his ale. "So you believe Barrow? You think they're alive?"

In the mottled shadows, Tristan's nose seemed even longer and more pointed than ever. "Maybe. If the Lord has taken them in His hands."

At the table, a tall, dark-haired man dressed all in black slapped a palm on the wood and peered menacingly at his redheaded friend—wearing a mauve velvet jacket, of all things. "Damn the Iroquois! They're always complaining we don't pay as much as the French and charge too much for trade goods! They forget we're two hundred goddamned miles closer to their villages! We ought to wipe out every Iroquois in New Netherland. That way—"

Tristan choked on a gulp of ale and coughed it out in a crude spray. Pierre chuckled.

"What are you laughing at?" the man called angrily.

"Your foolishness," Pierre replied, still chuckling. "You're new to this part of the world, or you'd know that the Dutch survive purely at the whim of the Iroquois."

The man straightened. "Do you *know* who you're talking to?"

"Take some advice," Pierre said amiably. "Don't try that tone on any of the other seasoned traders here. They're liable to slit your throat four times before you hit the ground."

The Dutchman snarled, "Seasoned? Is that what you call it? I call it coarse and brutish!"

Pierre took a sip of his stout. "Mister, if you'd been worth the time it would have taken to kill you, I'd be stepping over you by now. You're not a trader, are you?"

"I'm a political official of His Royal—"

"A politician. God help us. I could be taking a liking to the Iroquois after all. Come on, Tristan. The trails to Ihonatiria are looking better all the time."

Pierre had taken three steps away when Mauve Velvet shouted, "*Ihonatiria?* Is that where you're headed?"

Pierre swung around. In the noon light, Mauve Velvet's hair gleamed like tarnished copper. His flat nose and beady eyes did not help his priggish image. "What's it to you?"

"Well, I'm Daniel Kirke, just in from Holland on special business. I need to get to Ihonatiria, too."

"*You?* Why?"

"I need to see one of the priests there."

Pierre strolled back to loom like a burly avenging angel over Kirke. "*Which* priest?" Dupre had been filling his thoughts. He'd already decided he'd be having a talk with the boy when he got back.

Kirke grimaced and pulled a rose-scented handkerchief from the pocket of his velvet jacket. He held it to his nose. "All I need to know from you is how to get there."

Pierre, amusement in his eyes, lifted his arms and smelled himself. What *man* found a little sweat offensive? He lowered his arms. "Well, Kirke, you could take either a northerly trail or a southerly one. Do you prefer to be killed by the Mohawk or the Cayuga?"

"Don't jest with me."

Pierre propped a boot on the bench beside Kirke and smiled down unpleasantly. An Indian whooped in the background, and others began chanting. A couple of traders shouted. "I've better things to do than jest with the likes of you, Kirke. Just what are you so interested in the priests at Ihonatiria for?"

"I've a letter to deliver to one of them. Nothing important, just—"

"Nothing important? I take it you're not aware that all mail for Jesuits has to go through Father Paul Lejeune in Quebec."

"I was paid handsomely to deliver this letter directly." Kirke cast a wary look at the tall man beside him, lowering his voice. "How many men will I have to hire to get me to Ihonatiria?"

"Seven or eight with muskets, pistols, and half their weight in powder and lead. And that's if they're *good* men."

"That's a lot of money."

"Aye."

Kirke seemed to be reassessing his situation. "You say you know the village. How much would you charge to deliver the letter for me?"

"What kind of deal did you make?"

Kirke waved a hand impatiently. "I told the priest's mother I'd deliver it personally . . . so no one would know."

"Who is this woman?"

Kirke scowled. "How much to deliver it?"

"Depends on who the priest is."

"You charge more for some than others?"

"Aye. I do. What's his name?"

Kirke reluctantly unbuttoned his velvet coat and pulled out the letter. "Penchant. He's under the charge of a Father Jean de Brebeuf."

Tristan cursed and Pierre's brows drew together. "I've a mind to let you face the Iroquois by yourself."

"Why? What—"

Pierre leaned close, tormenting Kirke with his smell. Kirke turned away to breathe through his handkerchief. "You'd better have a lot of money, me friend."

CHAPTER

26

O my God, why are You not known? Why is this barbarous
country not all converted to You? Why is not sin abolished from it?
Why are You not loved? Yes, my God, if all the torments which the
captives can endure here in the cruelty of the tortures were to fall
on me, I offer myself thereto with all my heart, and I alone will
suffer them.

JEAN DE BREBEUF, S.J.
Ste. Marie, 1644

Andiora wiped her brow with her hand and went back to stirring
the huge kettle of cornmeal gruel over the fire at the north end
of the house. Steam had soaked her blue tradecloth dress
until it hung in limp folds about her. One third of the longhouse lay
ill. Four had died so far, and fear had risen so dramatically among
the people that fights had begun to break out. Her cousin Yled had
passed to the Spirit World that morning. Andiora's heart still ached
for him. She'd shorn her long hair in mourning, cutting it until it
hung even with her shoulders. Copper combs pinned it over her ears,
but straggles kept falling into her eyes whenever she bent over. The
longhouse air shuddered with moans and fevered cries.

She leaned the spoon against the side of the kettle and gazed at
Jatoya. The old woman had fallen sick yesterday, and by this
afternoon, red pustules had begun to cover her body. Damp wisps of
her yellow-white hair made a spiky halo around her withered face.
Her five children knelt beside the bench where she lay. Ranging in
age from three to ten, their eyes were swollen with tears. They were

too young to understand. They knew only that their relatives kept dying so quickly that they had almost no time to mourn one before another passed away.

Jatoya groaned suddenly and called, "Onrea? Onrea, where are you? Where is my baby? Have you seen her?"

Andiora went to kneel beside Jatoya. The old woman's pregnant belly made a huge lump beneath the elkhide robe. Tears traced glistening silver lines down her cheeks. "Onrea?"

"No, Jatoya. It's Andiora." She dipped a cloth in the gourd of water by the bed and mopped Jatoya's brow. "Don't cry. I'm here. I've been here all along."

Jatoya's face twisted as though against some horror. "But where's Onrea? Where is my little girl?" She gazed wide-eyed at her other children. "I see Vernay, Dalbeau, Atsina, Begourat, and . . . Oute." She smiled lovingly at her three-year-old, and the little boy rose to bury his face in his mother's arms, sobbing.

Jatoya weakly tilted her chin to kiss Oute's forehead. "Mama is all right, Oute," she assured. "You be a good boy. Mind your older sisters."

Oute wrapped his arms around Jatoya's neck, and Andiora reached over to stroke his dark hair. "Oute? You should be sleeping. It's very late." She pointed at the stars visible through the smoke holes in the roof. "Bring your blanket, and you can lie here on the floor beside your mother."

Oute's mouth puckered miserably, but he went and dragged his blanket off the bench, then raced back and stretched out on the floor with his head in Dalbeau's lap. Dalbeau, ten summers old, patted her little brother's back tenderly to help him go to sleep.

Andiora smiled at Dalbeau and reached for the cold bowl of soup made from corn, dried pumpkin and roots. She'd tried to feed Jatoya earlier, without success. A few ashes from the fires dusted the top; she stirred them in for flavor. Slipping an arm behind Jatoya's neck, she gently lifted her. "Try to eat, Jatoya. You must eat to get back your strength."

Andiora tipped the horn spoon to Jatoya's lips, and the old woman ate a little. "Good. Try some more." Andiora stirred the soup again and held the spoon to Jatoya's mouth.

At the other end of the house, Tehoren began a deep, melodic chant. He sprinkled a sick boy's face with water from a kettle, then fanned him with a turkey wing.

"What's happening?" Jatoya asked.

"Tehoren. The Lake Spirit came to him, teaching him a new baptism to cure our people."

Jatoya grunted. "The fool . . . still pretending he has Power. He lost it all . . . long ago."

Something metallic clashed at that end of the house. The clatter intensified, accompanied by shouts and pleas. Meiach, a slump-shouldered little man with a bulbous nose, grabbed Tehoren's kettle and bashed it against the wall, screaming, "No! You're a false shaman!"

Water splashed half a dozen people, including Tehoren, who stood rigid, his nostrils quivering with rage and embarrassment.

Meiach's wife, Carigo, a short woman with shorn hair, shrieked, "Leave Tehoren alone! I don't care what your priests tell you, Meiach! Since Brebeuf told us to pray to his God, what's happened? Where are your relatives? Where are mine? Most of them are dead! This is no longer a time to believe in the white man's god, Meiach!"

Meiach's black braids swung back and forth as he shook his head. He knelt and clasped his hands in prayer, as Brebeuf had taught him to do. "Forget about Tehoren! He is a false shaman. We must pray to God to heal our sons."

Andiora ached for both of them. Meiach was a recent convert to Christianity, and he truly believed everything that Brebeuf had taught him about heaven and Jesus.

Carigo shook a fist at her husband. "Have you lost your senses to this wicked Jehovah? Will that god send my babies to burn in hell if I do not let them be baptized with Brebeuf's water? What kind of a god is that? What kind of god would send my babies to *hell*?"

"Carigo," he implored, "I know only what I have been taught. I want you and my children in heaven with me! I do not want you tainted by this . . ." he gestured contemptuously at Tehoren ". . . this pretender!"

Tehoren backed away and strode out of the longhouse. People

watched him pass and shook their heads. Everyone knew that the look on his face meant trouble. In his entire life, Tehoren had never been able to accept rejection or criticism—now least of all, when he believed the entire village needed him and his Powers.

Carigo leaned over Meiach. "I do not want to go to heaven. I want to be with my ancestors in the Village of Souls! I am content to be damned by your god!"

"The priests," Meiach pleaded. "They are good men. They want to save us, to—"

"They are not men. They are demons who destroy us! Ask Tehoren." Carigo pointed at the swaying door-curtain.

"No, my wife. You do not understand."

"And you, *you* refuse to participate in your own curing society. What's the matter with you? Look!" Carigo stabbed a hand at the moaning and fevered child that Tehoren had been "baptizing," and the sick boy next to him. "Yours sons are dying, and you keep away from our Dances." A sob caught in her throat and she clamped a hand over her mouth. "You fool. Can you not make a truce with the old ways for a day and Dance? Why do you refuse to have our children treated by our own shamans? Do this small kindness for me." She held out her hands.

Meiach bowed his head. "Our rituals are bad, Carigo. Father Penchant told me that if I take part in any heathen ceremonies, Jehovah will send me to hell and all my family will die. I cannot—"

"It's the Christians who are killing us!" his wife shouted. She glared at every convert in the room. "Look around you! You who have converted refuse to help the rest of us. You are all killing us . . . killing your own families!" She knelt beside Meiach. "Come . . . come and Dance tomorrow. Just for a day. Then you can go back to the faith of Jehovah."

Meiach looked up at her. Pain twisted his face. "No. Not even for a day. God would abandon me. And you will see, Jehovah will make our sons well. *I believe.*"

Carigo burst into tears.

Across the room, Sebi, a toothless old man, rose. His gray hair hung in greasy strands around his face. He pointed a finger and slurred, "There is nothing I would not do to protect my family. We were never sick like this before the priests came. And it seems that wherever they set foot, death and disease follow. If I had to Dance all day and all night, decrepit as I am, I would do it to save lives. And if my god did not understand, I would spit on him!" He glared at Meiach, then hobbled out the door.

Andiora forced her gaze back to Jatoya and lifted another spoonful of soup. "You must eat more, Jatoya. Here, please?"

She pressed the spoon to Jatoya's slack lips, but Jatoya didn't react. Andiora frowned and looked up. Jatoya's faded brown eyes had gone wide. She stared breathlessly at the firelit dust flitting through the air. She nodded feebly. "Yes," Jatoya whispered. "I see the light. It's very beautiful."

Andiora turned to follow Jatoya's gaze, but saw nothing. "Who are you talking to, aunt?"

Jatoya pointed with her chin. "That man . . . that beautiful man."

"Jatoya," Andiora whispered, "there's no one there. Just some smoke from the fire."

"No, no," Jatoya insisted. "I see him there. And I know from his face that he comes to help me die well."

Dalbeau cried out and dove for her mother. The other children, who'd been dozing, woke and grabbed onto Jatoya, hugging an arm, a leg, a hand. Andiora stepped back, giving the children more room.

But Jatoya kept her eyes focused on nothing. Occasionally she would nod and smile. After several seconds, she turned. "Andiora, I must speak to Father Dupre. Could you get him for me?"

"Yes. I—I'll go now."

She raced down the length of the longhouse, past the other sick, and threw aside the hanging. Emerging into the moonlight, she sprinted across the snowy plaza, fear rising with each heartbeat. Strong winds blasted the forest. Where had this southern gale come from at this time of year? Brebeuf and Penchant had left yesterday morning, and Marc had been working tirelessly in the longhouses. He'd kept his distance from her, being polite when they crossed paths, never speaking more than was necessary. Andiora had thanked Aataentsic for the kindness.

She ran up to the Jesuit mission and pounded on the door. "Marc? Marc, please come! It's Andiora. Jatoya needs you!"

She heard movements in the dark longhouse and waited. The wind sucked every ounce of warmth from her damp blue dress until it stuck to her like a blanket of frost. In a few seconds, Marc opened the door and looked at her worriedly. He carried a small bag in his hand. His blond hair and beard were like mussed gold around his handsome face. His black robe had so many wrinkles that he must have slept in it. He'd probably fallen wearily into bed the instant he'd arrived back at the mission.

"What's wrong, Andiora? Is Jatoya—"

"I don't know," she said. "Hurry. You must hurry."

She turned and ran. His steps crunched the snow behind her. She threw back the door-hanging and raced down the length of the house to Jatoya. Dalbeau and the other children still lay across their mother, covering her from throat to toe, while Jatoya stared unblinkingly at nothing.

Andiora knelt and brushed yellow-white strands from Jatoya's burning forehead. "Jatoya? I've brought Father Dupre." She nodded to Marc and he crouched beside her.

"Jatoya," Marc said in his warm, deep voice, "it's Marc. How are you?"

Jatoya blinked tiredly. "Do you see him?" she asked.

Andiora translated and turned to Marc imploringly.

He frowned and glanced uneasily around the longhouse. "Who?"

"That beautiful man. He told me to ask for you. I've never seen a Man of Light."

When Andiora told him what Jatoya had said, Marc's face slackened. This time when he followed Jatoya's gaze, reverence glistened in his eyes, as though he did perceive some faint shimmer in the smoke. "My Lord never abandons those who have faith in Him. Is that why Jatoya called for me?"

Without waiting for the translation, Jatoya nodded heartily. "I need you to pour some of that water over my head."

When Andiora told him, Marc crossed himself and murmured a soft prayer, then opened his small bag. He pulled out a vial of water and uncorked it. "Jatoya, I know you're a good woman. Do you repent of having sinned?"

Andiora started to translate, but Jatoya answered "Yes" before she could finish.

Marc did not seem surprised that the old woman understood him. He looked at Jatoya with so much love and hope in his eyes that Andiora twisted her hands in confusion. "Do you want to go to heaven, Jatoya?"

"Yes," she answered softly.

Marc held the vial over Jatoya's forehead and lifted her shoulders slightly. "Are you ready?"

"I am." Jatoya took a deep breath and closed her eyes.

Marc poured a little of the water over her brow and murmured, "I baptize you in the name of the Father, and of the Son, and of the Holy Spirit."

Jatoya smiled, but then she grimaced. And shivered. The tremors came feebly at first, increasing until her body convulsed.

"What's happening?" Andiora shouted. She grabbed Jatoya's right arm. "Dalbeau, help me hold her down!"

Dalbeau raced around her younger sisters and gripped Jatoya's shoulders to press her hard against the bench. "Mama!" Dalbeau cried.

Jatoya's eyes rolled up in her head. Moments later she fell back against the drenched blankets, her muscles slack.

Dalbeau looked into Jatoya's wide eyes and whispered, "Mama?" She shook her gently. "Mama!" Dalbeau screamed and threw herself across Jatoya's chest. The other children joined her, crying and clawing at their mother's body.

Andiora couldn't breathe.

She stared at Jatoya's unblinking eyes.

Marc crossed himself. "Andiora, I . . ." He recorked his vial with a trembling hand. "She's with God now. He'll take good care of her."

Andiora opened her mouth, but she couldn't force her lips to speak. The wailing of Jatoya's children wounded her soul. She turned one way, then another, not knowing where to run. Finally she hurried toward her place on the bench, grabbed her foxhide coat, and ran out into the night.

She had to run, to run hard and fast from all this suffering and death! Her moccasins squealed on snow as she raced along the same path she'd taken when Pierre had asked her to marry him. She thrust branches out of her way haphazardly, so that many slapped her in the face or the back as she rushed by.

"Aataentsic!" she wept. "What have we done to anger you so? Where are you? I have been praying and praying, and you never answer!"

She thought she heard faint footfalls behind her, but she kept on running. An owl hooted overhead and she looked up to see wide amber eyes blinking ominously. The owl let out a screech, and Andiora ran faster, thrashing out into the meadow.

She slogged through the deep snow, past the log where not so long ago she had given up the only thing she'd ever really wanted in her life. And her steps faltered as memories rushed up. *I love you, Andiora . . .*

Her heart pounded agonizingly. She bent double. *Pierre, what happened to us?*

All the pain and fears she'd been forcing away so she could cook food, clean blankets, tend the sick, came crashing down on her.

Her knees buckled and she fell. The wind howled through the elms and birches, sending a shower of old autumn leaves and glittering snow whirling down over her.

Andiora heard his boots on the snow. He stopped at the edge of the meadow, but for only a moment. Then he ran toward her.

"Andiora?" Marc slipped his arms around her shoulders and pulled her to her feet. "Please, you mustn't do this to yourself."

She buried her face in his black robe, and he clutched her tightly against himself. She felt his breath warm on her cheek and tried to memorize the feel of his body against hers, the tug of his beard tangling in her hair, the strength of his arms enfolding her.

"I know how much it hurts to lose someone you love," he said softly. "But God is here with us. Can't you feel His presence?"

She stretched out with her soul, seeking, and she did feel something . . . like Cougar, but different, more silver than gold. "Yes," she answered, "I do, Marc."

His heart pounded as rapidly as a bird's as he brushed snow from her hair. He hugged her again before gently pushing away and resting his hands on her shoulders.

"Are you all right?"

She nodded. "Yes. It's . . . it's just so hard. More die every day."

"I know."

Andiora looked up at him. His gaze caressed her disheveled hair and traced the line of her jaw before coming back to her eyes. Longing and bewilderment tightened his face. She could see the muscles of his arms contract, swelling against the fabric of his black robe. The forest-scented winds swept the meadow, tousling his blond hair, and blood began to surge deafeningly in Andiora's ears. The longer they looked at each other, the more he seemed to be fighting with himself. In a halting motion, as though against his will, he released her shoulders and turned his back to her.

"Forgive me," he said, "I shouldn't have touched you."

"You were kind to come after me. Thank you, Marc."

He looked at her over his shoulder, a warm, worried expression on his face. His eyes gleamed silver-blue in the moonlight. After a long interval, he said, "Let me walk you back to your house."

They crossed the meadow together, his black sleeves and hem dancing in the wind.

ONREA FOUGHT TO stay awake. They had been on the lake for two days, unable to sleep, and still they could see no land . . . only the vast expanse of black, undulating water. The moon had gone down long ago, and utter darkness had gripped the lake like a monster. Onrea guided them by the stars, knowing almost without looking in which direction lay home. But in all her thirteen years of life, she'd never seen the waves this high.

What could Iouskeha be thinking? He must have sent the wind to get them home quickly, even though he knew they would have to fight for their lives in the process.

Spray splashed up over the bow of the canoe and froze on the lip of the boat in a shimmering silver shroud. Onrea shivered and pulled the moldy moosehide more closely around her throat. If dawn didn't come soon to warm them, their lives would be truly in danger. The blasting wind drove the boat home like an arrow, but it also twined into their very bones to eat their meager warmth.

The canoe soared down into a valley and rode up on the crest of a swell, then listed sideways. The south side, heavy-laden with ice, dipped toward the water.

Onrea screamed and threw herself to the opposite side, paddling with all her might to keep the boat upright. Froth splashed into the canoe. "Phillipe?" she shouted over the wind and waves. "Phillipe, what's the matter?"

She whirled to look back at him and saw that he was leaning sideways, *asleep!* Onrea bashed him in the leg with her paddle and he jerked awake.

"I . . . I was listening to the angels!" He pointed to the dark, star-studded sky.

"Phillipe! *Hurry!* The ice! Take your paddle and break it off the canoe or we are going to roll over and sink!"

She began pounding the ice and he followed, slamming at the shimmering crust, cracking it loose and sending it tinkling into the water, or into the bottom of the boat, where it glistened like crystal tears. Onrea's soul cried out for him. He was so tired and so hurt that he could barely lift his paddle—but he had to stay awake!

A fierce gust of wind shoved Onrea into the bottom of the canoe, and she grabbed on to the slick sides to pull herself back up again. "We have to keep paddling, Phillipe. Both of us. If either one of us falls asleep, we both die!"

CHAPTER

2 7

s they neared the western shore of Lake Ontario, Pierre leaped out of the boat into the shallow water and guided the canoe up on top of the sheath of ice that made a blue ridge along the shore. The six other men jumped out and began pushing and tugging. Whitecapped waves, pushed by the incessant wind, lapped over their dirty hide pants.

As soon as the canoe was ashore, Pierre grabbed his musket out of the bow and looked to the west. Sunset shot purple filaments of fire through the wispy clouds, but smoke marred the distance. The fierceness of the gale had dragged it over the hills in a black smear. Tristan joined him, shielding his eyes.

"Could be a forest fire, Pierre."

"This time of year, with the amount of snow on the ground?" He turned and shouted, "James? Yona? Cache the boat and follow us up the trail. We'll be going on ahead to see what's become of the village."

Yona waved a hand. "Aye, we'll meet you." The men began to pull the six-hundred-pound canoe over the sand to dense brush, all the while murmuring and squinting at the smoke.

Pierre pulled his pistol from its holster and tucked it into his belt, closer to hand if need be. Gripping his musket, he trudged through the wet sand up onto the snow and into the shadows of the forest. Tristan followed close behind him. Their soaked boots squished and squealed on the cold snow as they made their way up the drifted trail.

At the first sight of the village, Pierre threw out a hand for Tristan to stop. Charred roof timbers creaked mournfully against fire-gutted walls. Bodies lay strewn in the plaza, mutilated, the hearts cut out. Pierre edged forward cautiously, scanning the trees and the husks of longhouses for movement.

"Take a look at the fletching on those arrows," he said.

Tristan ground his teeth as he surveyed the corpses. "Iroquois. Seneca, if I'm not mistaken."

Pierre clutched his musket tighter. "Keep your wits about you."

He picked his way through the carnage. The fires had been hot enough to roast the nearby trees to blackened spears. The villagers must have had a feast going on when the Iroquois struck. The scorched remains of cook pots and bowls lay scattered in the plaza.

The other members of his trading party entered the village cautiously, muskets and pistols ready, eyes darting like captive eagles'. Heavy packs made each resemble a hunchback. Yona carried Pierre and Tristan's packs, as well as his own.

"Be taking your packs, gents," Yona urged. "I'll feel better when I've a hand free for me pistol."

Pierre took his pack and put it on the ground to dig out his brown cloak, which he fastened at his throat. Then he bent and shrugged on his pack.

"Let's be moving along," he said. "We've got to find a place to camp where we can watch the trails."

"THIS IS NEKOUBA's longhouse, Luc," Jean said as they approached the doorway. Wind flapped the hem of his black cape. "He's a powerful man. Be careful of what you say and do."

The village of Ossossane spread around them, larger than Ihonatiria, with the longhouses arranged in an irregular pattern. A stockade wall of upright poles, fifteen feet high had been erected. Towering oaks were visible over the top.

"I'm always careful," Luc insisted. "Have I ever—"

"I didn't mean to imply you weren't, Luc." Jean stopped outside the door and reeled slightly before he caught himself. He hadn't slept in forty-eight hours, though he'd insisted that Luc get at least six hours of rest a night. He turned. The firelight streaming around the edges of the door-hanging outlined Luc with a glittering halo. He appeared skinnier, the cheekbones of his thin face sharp. "It's just that Nekouba is very important to us. Many of the people in this longhouse are Christians because he converted. We can't risk alienating him."

"I understand fully well."

Jean gave him an uncertain glance. Luc had been acting like a pouting child, but he was hungry and tired—just as Jean was. "All right."

Jean led the way into the house, and a variety of stenches met them: sweat, urine, feces and vomit. Luc draped his black sleeve over his nose to filter it.

"Good Lord," Luc whispered. "How can we stand this?"

Jean didn't answer. He strode forward to greet the little man with shaggy gray hair and impish face who was bent over a woman lying on the bench.

"Nekouba, how are you?" he asked, concern in his voice.

Nekouba turned and shook his head sadly. "Bad. Very bad, Father."

"How many have fallen ill?"

"Twenty in this longhouse. Fifty total in the village."

Jean's gaze took in the house. Everywhere, people lay prostrate on the benches, delirious with fever, while others tended them. Enormous copper kettles boiled over the fires, all of them filled with soiled blankets.

Houses here had a different design from those in Ihonatiria. A hundred feet long by thirty feet wide, floor-to-ceiling racks stood about midway down their length, filled with clay pots, ironware and clothing. Beads glimmered on the folded dresses and shirts. Children's cornhusk dolls and toy muskets carved of wood stacked the lowest rack. Raised benches, four feet off the ground, lined both long walls.

"And your own family, Nekouba?" Jean asked.

"Little James is the worst," he said and pointed.

Jean studied the five-year-old child, who was waving his arms weakly. Dirty black hair straggled around his ears. A pile of striped blankets covered him on the bench. Jean nodded. "Why don't you go back to tending your wife, Nekouba? We'll talk more later."

Nekouba put a hand on Jean's forearm, gripping it in gratitude. "Perhaps, if you have time, you will take dinner with me? I made the corn soup myself."

"We'd be honored. Thank you." But Jean frowned, knowing that men never cooked in Huron society unless there were no women to do it.

Nekouba's hand slid down Jean's arm before he went back to his wife.

"Luc," Jean said. When he extended his hand to point to James, it shook from exhaustion. "This is Nekouba's son. Please tend to him while I check on the other Christians here."

"But, Father, we've been at this for fifteen hours straight. I'm starving. When will we eat?"

"As soon as we finish this house. I promise. Nekouba offered to share his cornmeal soup with us, and—"

"Again? Don't these people eat anything but corn?"

"I know you're weary, Luc. But, please, try to be kind."

"Oh, very well." Luc knelt and began roughly washing the little boy's pustule-covered arm with a wet rag that had been soaking in a gourd by the bed.

James screamed, and Jean said, "*Gently*, Luc. Gently."

"Yes, Father."

Jean walked away. He'd heard God calling for over an hour. The pain had grown so severe that each step he took struck him like a physical blow. God had not called him this strongly since that night months ago when the woman demon had risen up from the pond and reached for him. He would have to go outside and talk to his Lord soon or his heart would burst.

The moans of the ill and the cries of the bereaved rose in intensity, echoing inside Jean's head like hammerfalls.

He knelt quietly at Atondo's bedside. A beautiful girl with an oval face and full lips, she'd converted two years ago and had been living a model Christian life. Her virtue and kindness were renowned in all the nearer villages. Her cheeks had grown gaunt since he'd seen her three months ago, and she'd shorn her hair in mourning. It draped raggedly around her face.

She smiled at him, and Jean smiled back. "Hello, Atondo," he said. "How are you?"

She murmured something breathy that he didn't understand, but when she lifted a weak hand to cross herself, Jean recognized the words, "Father, Son, Holy Spirit." He moved closer and took her hand in his. Her flesh seemed boiling hot. The presence of God magnified around him, prickling painfully over his skin.

Please, Lord. Just give me a few more minutes.

Atondo struggled to focus her eyes on him. "Father . . . I have sinned."

"God understands all things, Atondo. Have confidence in Him. What have you to confess?"

She creased her blanket with shaking fingers. "Forgive me, Father. I—I lied to Khotoa. She has been very sick, and she asked about her brother, Ehwae. He died . . . three days ago. But I told her he was all right. I told her he had gone out to hunt. I did not mean to lie, Father. I just could not . . . tell her . . . the truth."

Brebeuf squeezed her hand soothingly. The lie must have heartened Khotoa and given her strength to battle the disease. "I saw Khotoa. She is well and working very hard to heal the others in her longhouse. God forgives you for lying to her, Atondo. He knows that you were just trying to ease her pain. What else have you to confess?"

Atondo took a tired breath. Jean touched her cheek tenderly. "Do you want to sleep, Atondo? I can finish hearing your confession later."

She shook her head limply. "Father, my little girl, Chelaga, she came to me and wanted to sleep with me—she was distressed. I was afraid. I shoved her away and shouted at her to leave me and not come back until I was well." Atondo started sobbing miserably, but the sounds came so softly that Jean could barely hear them. "She ran away crying. I made my baby cry!"

"But you didn't do it to be unkind. God knows that, Atondo. You just didn't want Chelaga to get sick, too. What else?"

"Nothing, Father."

"When you feel well enough, I want you to pray the rosary five times."

"I am sorry I offended God," she wept. "I didn't mean to. I just . . . I'll try harder to be good, Father."

Jean placed his hands on her head and prayed, "God, the Father of mercies, through the death and Resurrection of His Son has reconciled the world to Himself and sent the Holy Spirit among us for the forgiveness of sins; through the ministry of the church may God give you pardon and peace, and I absolve you from your sins in the name of the Father, and of the Son, and of the Holy Spirit. Give thanks to God, Atondo, for He is good."

"And merciful. Amen."

"The Lord has freed you from your sins. *Live* in peace. God doesn't need you in heaven just yet. We want you to get well."

She lifted her arms, and Jean bent over to hug her. His whole body ached with the need to talk to God, ached so violently that he had to force himself not to throw off Atondo's weak arms and race outside. But so many of these people still needed him. Old Matabach, lying next on the bench, reached out a withered hand to him. He winked at her.

Atondo whispered, "Father, when can I receive communion?"

"I'll be coming back in an hour. You try to sleep until then."

"Will you wake me?" she asked anxiously.

"Yes, of course."

She kissed Jean's hand and pressed it to her cheek, then closed her eyes and gradually let her grip loosen. Jean slipped his hand away and rearranged her blankets, making sure that her arms and feet were covered.

When he straightened up, God no longer requested consultation, He *demanded* it. Jean's bones felt on the verge of snapping into a thousand pieces.

He hurried to Matabach. The old woman's wide eyes were riveted on him. Her withered lips hung open; pustules covered her square face like beads of honey. At the end of the house, young Gewona glared at him. Her long hair hung in damp strands over her dark eyes. The village gossip, she hated Christianity, and she blamed the Christians for every evil that befell Ossossane. She was one of the few non-Christians in this longhouse.

Jean knelt at Matabach's side. "When Nekouba told me you were sick, I told him I didn't believe it. I told him that no disease would have the courage to get you. I guess it must have sneaked up when you weren't looking."

Matabach smiled. Wispy straggles of gray hair glued themselves to her forehead. "I've been waiting for you. Atondo told me you were coming."

Jean glanced back at Atondo. He'd told no one he was coming— but perhaps the Lord had told her. Jean nodded at Matabach. "I think God talks to her more than He does to me."

As soon as he'd said the words, his stomach cramped and he hunched over Matabach. God swelled like an incoming tide in his chest, filling him until he couldn't bear it.

LUC FINISHED WASHING James's face and arms and rose to his feet. The stench of these people was suffocating. It affected his empty stomach like a poison, making him want to retch. To make matters worse, a thick haze of smoke filled the house. He could barely see Brebeuf where he knelt by an old woman. Quickly, Luc strode down the length of the house, not even looking at the people. When he reached Brebeuf, he impatiently pulled out his breviary and began reading.

Brebeuf said, "Matabach . . . forgive me. I . . ." He groaned.

Luc lowered his breviary and looked up in time to see Brebeuf clutch his stomach.

Matabach cried out jaggedly and pointed. "Atondo, look!"

The younger woman rose up on her elbows and stared at the billows of smoke eddying along the ceiling. "Mother Mary! Mother Mary!" she cried.

Brebeuf wobbled and fell backward, crossing himself. In a barely audible voice, he said, "Hail, Holy Queen, Mother of Mer-Mercy . . ." His voice faltered.

Luc stared openmouthed. What were these people doing? He squinted at the smoke. It billowed and fluttered in the breeze that blew down the smoke holes, but that was all.

"Yes, Mother," Brebeuf answered softly. Tears filled his eyes. "Please give me the strength."

Atondo weakly pulled herself into a sitting position and began stroking the air, as though touching the hem of a garment. A beatific expression came over her pustule-ridden face.

"Father," Luc asked irritably, "what is happening?"

Brebeuf sat unmoving while tears traced lines down his cheeks. At last he nodded. "I pray I am worthy, Mother."

Luc stared. The longhouse had gone silent. The wails of the bereaved had stopped. The sick no longer cried out. Atondo smiled joyously at Luc. He scowled at her, disgruntled.

Then he noticed that the pustules on Atondo's face had vanished.

Fear gripped him. "What . . ."

Brebeuf grabbed the edge of the bench to get to his feet, then ran down the longhouse, checking each sick bed, finding the afflicted hugging their families or sleeping calmly. Luc shoved his breviary into his pocket and ran after Brebeuf, calling, "Father? Father, what are you doing? *What did you see?*"

When he reached the end door, Brebeuf sagged against the wall. Luc strode swiftly to him. "Let's go outside, Father," he said and grasped Brebeuf's arm to lead him into the chill wind. The snow beneath their boots glimmered in the dim yellow light streaming from the longhouse. He guided Brebeuf out into the center of the plaza.

The gale howled. Brebeuf lifted his arms to the squalling wind and let it shake him with its fury.

"Father," Luc demanded, "what—"

"Didn't you see her?" Brebeuf asked hoarsely, his eyes on the stars as though entranced by their crystalline beauty.

"No, I saw only the smoke billowing. Was it the Blessed Virgin?"

Brebeuf lowered his arms and hugged himself, nodding. "Yes." He filled his lungs with the scents of the night, wild and wet, redolent of ponds and burning hickory logs.

"What did she say to you?" Luc asked. Why would the Virgin appear to a bunch of sick savages and not to him, a man of God?

Brebeuf looked at him radiantly. "She told me to remember her torment and said I must be submissive to the will of God for the sake of the newborn Son of Man. Then she told me to beware of the deceptions of the Serpent."

Luc blinked. "The greatest deception of Satan in the last days,

Father, is the false prophet, who mimics the works of our Lord. To him Satan gives the power that he offered to Christ during the Temptation in the Wilderness."

Brebeuf pulled his collar closed. He frowned at the moccasin prints lining the trail through Ossossane. "We must head home tomorrow, Luc. I feel that something terrible is about to happen there."

28

While he was in prayer, God detached him from all his senses and
united him to Himself; again, that he was enraptured in God, and
fervently embraced him. . . . Often he felt this love as a fire which,
having inflamed itself in his heart, kept increasing day to day, and
consuming in him the impurity of nature.

FATHER PAUL RAGUENEAU, S.J.
Writing about Jean de Brebeuf, 1645

Marc's eyes fluttered open. He knelt in the chapel before the
crucifix, his head bowed, his hands clasped and pressed to
his lips. He'd been praying for so long that the candles on
the altar had melted and guttered out. He blinked and tried to
reestablish contact with his flesh. His body had vanished in the past
eight or nine hours.

His soul had been resting in the deep Silence of God.

When he had come into the chapel, he'd cried out desperately for
God's guidance. He had begun praying as he always did, searching
for the wellspring of love in his heart, gathering every ounce and
offering it to God. But tonight something else had happened. Marc
had given himself up completely.

And God had come to him as He never had done before.

A blinding flood of pure light had swept Marc up and away. He'd
been afraid at first, but God's love had melted his fears. All of Marc's
agonies of sin and exile, all of his self-doubts, had disappeared.

For the first time in his spiritual life, Marc realized that God had long been calling and calling to him, and he'd been so ensnarled in the names and games of his religious life that he had not been able to hear that divine voice.

Marc forced his lungs to take a deep breath. With an effort, he convinced the muscles of his shoulders and neck to lift his head so he could look his Savior fully in the face. Words had vanished from his mind. He and God no longer needed them. The pale glow of the rising moon that filtered through the windows in the common room penetrated into the chapel. Soft, luminous light flowed into the wooden crevices of Jesus' face, making the lines of agony as deep as gullies washed by centuries of tears.

Marc numbly crossed himself and placed a hand on the bench behind him. He rose to his feet slowly. Everything in the chapel struck him as though for the first time. The simple wooden altar with its three carved crosses radiated beauty beyond his imagining. Even the patch of moonlight stretching across the dirt floor brought tears to his eyes.

"*Gloria Patri*," he whispered. His vocal chords didn't want to work. "Thank You, Lord."

Marc felt as though his feet barely touched the floor as he walked into the common room. Through the windows he could see tatters of cloud hanging over the silver-tipped branches of the maples next to the mission.

He knew what he had to do now, and it was a duty he no longer dreaded. He only regretted the late hour and the fact that she would probably be asleep.

He walked to the outer door. The moonlight that streamed over him when he opened it made him stand still for a moment. The beauty of God drowned him; it radiated from the moon, from the bare whispers of wind in the forest, from the brittle scents of snow and pine.

He started through the snow for her longhouse.

ANDIORA LIFTED HER head when the wind stopped. She had been drifting in and out of sleep. An eerie silence fell over the world, as though Iouskeha had been startled into holding his glacial breath. The wolves and owls had quieted. It was after midnight; the fires in the dark tunnel of the longhouse had burned down to crimson coals. They threw a faint glow over the rounded roof and glimmered from the copper pots hanging on the walls.

Andiora rubbed her eyes. They had tacked the door-hanging to the bark wall to keep it from sailing away in the windstorm. Now it didn't even sway.

Carigo mumbled feverishly. She'd taken sick that afternoon, just after one of her sons had died. Meiach spoke to her consolingly.

"No. No!" Carigo raised her voice. "They're witches. They killed my baby. You saw it, Meiach. That blond Black Robe poured water over Niwo's head, and Niwo died! He did the same thing to Jatoya! Oh, Aataentsic, what have we done? Meiach . . ." She lowered her voice to a whisper.

Andiora strained to hear, but the voices were too low now. If the epidemic didn't end soon, the charges of witchcraft would sweep the country like wildfire in a dry year. First the shamans would scour the villages, looking for Huron witches. Then they would "question" the Black Robes. Anxiety gnawed at her.

She pulled the softness of her blanket up over her bare shoulders. Her Dreams had been disjointed and strange: walking on the moon as it turned to blood, and reaching for a garment of light when the whole world went dark. Things she did not understand.

And Cougar had not been to see her in weeks. That, above all things, terrified her. *Where are you, Cougar? Have I angered you, too?*

Secretly, she doubted that anyone's Spirit Helper had appeared since the epidemic started. But she dared not voice such a fear—for if it were true, it would mean that the Huron had been abandoned by the Spirit World.

Dalbeau started weeping softly. The little girl had moved her blankets next to Andiora's. She slept with Oute cradled in her arms like a dark-haired doll. All through the house, people tossed and turned beneath their mounded blankets.

Could no one sleep?

Wolves, howling and snarling, had encircled the hills around the village earlier this night. The disease had begun taking people so quickly that the living had been forced to pile the dead on the frozen ground outside Ihonatiria, where the wolves had found them.

Andiora had prayed that Pierre was safe in the storm.

She'd seen Marc once today, but for only a few minutes, when he'd come into the longhouse to baptize Meiach's dying boy. Carigo's screams of rage had driven him out immediately afterward. Even so, Andiora didn't think that Marc would have stayed to see her. She told herself that he'd left so abruptly because the other longhouses had ill people who needed his attention. As the epidemic worsened, more of the Huron coverted and Marc's responsibilities increased. Many Christians now flocked to his daily Masses.

Andiora sat up to check on Dalbeau, who slept at her feet. Tears marked the girl's face. Andiora reached out to touch and comfort her, but stopped when steps crunched in the snow outside the door, then halted.

Andiora studied the door-hanging. Snow squealed as the walker shifted his weight from foot to foot, as if trying to decide whether to call out or not. Who would be coming at this time of night?

The steps retreated.

She rose and slipped on her red tradecloth dress, tied her moccasins and tiptoed over to pull out the pegs that tacked the hanging to the wall. Pulling the curtain aside, she peered out. The crescent moon hid behind dark tree limbs, but its glow burnished every undulation in the snow. Boot prints shone darkly.

They led her eyes to Marc. He stood with his back to her, staring up at the white cross on top of the mission. His blond hair was pale blue by the moonlight. He remained motionless for a few more seconds, then walked to the mission door. It closed behind him.

He came to talk to you.

Andiora took a deep breath and strode after him. Since they'd stood in the meadow two days ago, she'd been afraid to approach him. She ran her fingers through her black hair before knocking on the mission door.

She heard steps inside, and then the door opened. Marc gazed down at her calmly. Dirt clung to the knees and hem of his black robe.

"Come in, Andiora." He opened the door and moved aside so she could enter. "I'm sorry I woke you. I should have waited until morning."

His voice was deeper, more serene, than she'd ever heard it. "It's better for us to talk now, Marc, when no one can bother us."

Andiora stepped into the storage room. The sweet scent of dried corn permeated the air; in the dim light, she could see whole ears tied to the ridgepole. Marc stood so close that she was acutely aware of his masculine scent. She tucked her icy fingers into her red sleeves.

"Let's sit at the table," he said. "I'll make a new fire."

He knelt by the woodpile in the corner and took a load of split hickory, then edged by her into the common room. She followed. The fire in the hearth had dwindled to cooling embers, leaving the room chilly and dark. Marc laid down his wood and said, "Please, sit down."

Andiora sat and watched quietly as Marc dug out the few warm coals from the ashes in the stone-lined pit, then arranged the wood over them and blew. He moved with such grace tonight, as though everything around him had grown a heart and soul and he was taking care not to harm them.

Fire licked up around the hickory. Sparks danced toward the ceiling. Andiora rubbed her cold arms.

"It is freezing in here, Marc."

"I'm sorry. I didn't notice that it was cold. Let me get you a blanket."

He rose and walked to the six beds along the north wall. Each had its gray blanket tucked under the cornshuck mattress and a small pillow placed neatly on top; she noted that he hadn't slept. He pulled the blanket off the second bed from the left, then came back and draped it around her shoulders.

"You haven't been to bed?"

"No," he responded softly.

Going to the shelves, he removed a single candle and secured it in the brass holder on the table. When he lit it, the tiny flame filled the room, its light a pale flaxen shawl over the table and chairs.

Marc sat in the chair farthest away from her, his straight nose and forehead golden in the candlelight. For a time, he stared at his hands, saying nothing, then he leaned forward and braced his arms on the table. "I've been praying," he said. "About you."

Those words were softly spoken, but they affected Andiora like a shout. "Why?"

"I've been troubled." He tilted his head, and the candle flame reflected in his eyes. "My heart has been drifting more toward you . . . and away from God."

Andiora bowed her head. She could hear the buried desperation in his voice. "I'm sorry."

"It's not your fault. It's mine. I . . . I lost my way . . . for a time. Tonight, God showed me the path again."

She lifted her gaze to meet his. "What did He tell you?"

Marc moved slightly, and the crucifix around his neck flared as though molten. "He told me there was no shame in loving you."

"Did He?"

"Yes." He nodded solemnly. "But He asked me to make a decision. A great saint in my religion put it this way. He said that 'either we pray always and are virgins, or we serve in marriage and lose the liberty to pray.'" Marc paused. "Andiora, no matter how I feel about you, I cannot give up my liberty to pray. I wouldn't be any good to you if I did."

Andiora's heart pounded. Pierre's words returned to her: *If he gave himself to you, the guilt would suffocate him.* In what she hoped was a matter-of-fact tone, she said, "Our religions are different. In mine, a holy person can love and pray at the same time."

"Not in mine."

A cloud darkened the moon. The tiny flickers of the hearth and the candle seemed suddenly very weak to stave off this night.

"I love you, Marc."

He brought up his hands and clasped them tightly, pressing them over his lips. "Please don't, Andiora. I can't return it in the way you'll need me to."

She looked away. "I remember the first time I heard about the vows you take. Brebeuf explained them at a village meeting long ago when Maconta was trying to marry him off to her niece. And then I heard you talk about them again the night . . ." Grief struck her anew. ". . . the night after you pulled me from the river."

"Andiora, how could you fall in love with me knowing that I could never—"

"Because." She put a hand over her heart. "You gave me part of your warmth. A very precious gift. It came to live inside me."

"Part of you came to live inside me, too, Andiora." A fleeting smile crossed his face. "I don't suppose you know how I could give it back to you?"

She smiled. "No, I wish I did. I've had the same problem with Pierre the past few moons. Not knowing how to carve him out of my heart."

"He loves you very much."

"Yes . . . as much as he can."

"You don't love him?"

Andiora pulled Marc's blanket more snugly around her shoulders. "Not the way I used to. Some time in the last year, I grew into a woman." *When my baby died.* "Pierre is still a little boy. And happy. As he should be. I think I would wound that in him . . . and he would never forgive me for it." Despite the fire, the cold had started to seep into her bones. She'd be shivering soon. Why hadn't she thought to grab her coat? Damp wood smells rose with the chill that breathed from the floor and walls. She added bravely, "Just as you would never forgive me for taking you away from your god."

He leaned back in his chair. "I would forgive you, Andiora. I'd never forgive myself. It's the hour of the Garden and the Night. I know you don't understand, but what I mean is that God needs me."

"And He's enough for you?"

"It's sufficient for me to know that I'm carrying on His work, even though my labors are infinitesimally small. I *know* I am in the place where God needs me most. And I can't let Him down."

Andiora gazed at Marc. She felt nothing but a terrible emptiness. Every day it was harder to be in the same village with him, but she had nowhere else to go. The chasm in her soul yawned wider, threatening to swallow her up. "Then you must do His work."

Marc rose and stood before the crackling fire. His blond hair and the dirt on his robe glittered with a coppery sheen. "Andiora, I need to stay away from you for a while. I know we'll see each other every day, but I can't . . ." He shifted awkwardly. "I can't let myself be alone with you. Do you understand?"

She smiled gently. "Yes. Better than you know."

She rose and stood beside him. He looked down at her with pain in his eyes. Oh, how she longed to touch him, but she simply drew his blanket from her shoulders and handed it to him.

"Thank you, Marc," she said, "for being honest with me. It's much easier when a woman knows what's in a man's soul. Good night."

"Good night," he answered softly.

She turned for the door.

The tears didn't come until she'd made it halfway across the plaza.

CLOUDS CREPT ACROSS the dark sky like skeins of goslin down, wispy and gray. Tehoren turned up the collar of his bearhide coat to protect his ears. The night smelled of smoke and frozen corpses. From where he stood, just outside the village, he could see the bodies of those who had succumbed to the illness lying in rows beneath the trees. And there would be more to come. Thin cries from the longhouses seeped through the darkness like the whimpers of people caught in nightmares.

Tehoren watched Andiora cross the plaza and duck into her house, then glanced at Jix, who was leaning against a poplar. The tall warrior wore a moosehide coat with the hood pulled up. In the moonlight, his sharp nose and thick braids had a dim blue patina.

Jix's lip curled in disdain. "That priest pumped her full of his semen quickly." His breath hovered around them in a silver wreath.

"She would not have surrendered her soul willingly. Carigo is right. The Christians are demons who come to destroy us. I think they bewitched Andiora because she was the only one who could recognize them. Their spells have blinded her eyes to reality."

"But Dupre is the only blond, and he has no holes in his hands."

"I know," Tehoren said irritably. He'd thought about that long and hard. "But maybe he will some day in the future . . . and . . . and maybe that little bald priest who got stolen with Onrea had blond hair once. I don't know."

Jix frowned. "None of the priests are sick, and you heard what Gewona said about Ossossane. Brebeuf conjured a demon and healed that woman in Nekouba's longhouse." Jix shoved his fists into his coat pockets. "How do they do it, Tehoren? What magic do they use?"

Tehoren shook his head. For weeks a hunger had been rising in him, the same hunger that had stalked him all his life. Power whispered in his Dreams, but he couldn't get a grip on it. It slithered out of his grasping hands like a wet snake, leaving him impotent and helpless against Brebeuf's might. "I think it's the water they use, Jix. You saw. When Dupre poured that water on Jatoya's head, she died."

"The same thing happened with Meiach's son, Niwo. Not more than an hour after Dupre poured the water on him. And Meiach is a Christian. Why would Dupre have killed his son?"

"Perhaps to punish Carigo for her disbelief."

Jix's eyes narrowed. "It may be poisoned water. But I'm not so sure. Gewona believes that they use a book to spread the disease. She said that just before the demon appeared in Nekouba's longhouse, Penchant took out his book."

A nighthawk swooped over the trees, its wings glowing in the moonlight, and lit in the poplar above them. It did not cry out, but cocked its head as if listening.

Tehoren made a magical sign in the air to ward off the evil creature's spells. "The birds always come when we talk about the Black Robes," he whispered.

Jix swiveled his head to look up. The hawk's eyes gleamed like fire.

"No!" Tehoren ordered. "Don't look into its eyes. Never look an *oki* in the eye."

Fear made his blood surge. It was not simply that *okis* could overhear your conversations and report back to their masters. They could also snag your soul and tear it from your body. And even if you managed to escape them, part of your Spirit remained locked forever in the shining depths of their eyes.

Jix swallowed convulsively. "Then let us speak of this later, Tehoren. But soon. We must do something before they kill all of us and take our country as their own."

"Talk with your most loyal warriors, Jix. Then we'll discuss what we should do next."

Tehoren led the way back toward their longhouse.

29

Snowflakes fell from the cloudy sky, lighting softly on the trees and the bark longhouses in Onnentisati. The songs of shamans wove through the village. Pierre shifted the weight of his pack and studied Bekon. The chief was a medium-sized man with jaggedly shorn black hair and a broad, flat nose. His shirt and pants were grease-splotched. People peered through the doorhangings of every longhouse, watching them.

"How long ago, Bekon?" Pierre asked.

The chief shrugged. "They set out just before you arrived. You should be able to catch them. They are traveling the main trail back to Ihonatiria."

Pierre slapped the chief on the shoulder. "We're obliged. Take care of yourself and your family."

Bekon lifted a hand in farewell as Pierre and his trading party headed down the trail at a trot. Cold wind whipped through the trees lining the path. It had howled in off the Atlantic, jangling the brass and copper pots his party carried in their packs.

Tristan trotted alongside Pierre in silence, but the men behind them whispered excitedly to each other. Pierre cursed himself for not speaking to Bekon alone. But who could have guessed the sort of story the chief would be telling about Brebeuf? Now his men would be skittish enough to shoot each other at the first fright. And Pierre didn't feel so sane himself. Some slithering creature had grown in his gut, where it was scratching and chewing, trying to get out.

Pierre looked at Tristan. "If I hear one more word of visions or Spirit animals, I'll pack me things and head back to the ocean, where all I've to worry about is sea monsters and ghost galleons. I'm half scared that we'll get to Ihonatiria and hear that Christ rode down on a white horse with an army of angels on His heels."

Tree shadows played over Tristan's thin face. He watched his footing as they ran up a hill. "I wish we'd had the time to see the woman who was healed in Ossossane."

From behind him, someone said, "Aye, me, too. I'm wondering if maybe the End has not truly come at last."

Tristan crossed himself and muttered, "Amen."

As they crested the hilltop, Pierre saw the two Black Robes climbing on the next hill. "Ho! Brebeuf! *Jean!*"

Jean turned, shielding his eyes against the glare of the snow. "Pierre?"

"Aye, hold up! We've news for you." Sure, news. A mighty peculiar thing to be calling the tales they'd heard whispered around the camp fires of a dozen villages—stories that made a man's skin creep.

Jean waited beneath the arching limbs of a huge oak. Penchant stood beside him.

Pierre panted as he sprinted up to them. "You're not an easy man to catch, Jean. The whole of this week we've been dogging your path through the Huron villages."

Jean smiled. "You're safe. I thank God." He extended his hand.

Pierre shook it. Jean had a radiant look on his face that caught Pierre's eyes and held them. "You're looking well, Jean. We've been hearing much of your exploits."

"Indeed?"

"Aye." Pierre gestured at Tristan, whispering, "Could you keep the men back a few paces, so I can speak to Jean in private?"

"Aye, Pierre." Tristan trotted back down to stall the rest of the party.

Jean cocked his head. "What don't you want your men to overhear?"

Pierre led the way farther along the path. Jean's black cape fluttered around his broad shoulders as he followed, with Penchant behind him. Freezing wind gusted around them, swirling snow and singing through the boulders that studded the forest. A vista of gently rolling hills lay before them.

"Is there truth in the rumors that you healed a woman in Ossossane?" Pierre asked as the path flattened out and Jean came up beside him.

"I healed no one, Pierre. She was healed, yes. But Mother Mary did that."

Pierre shook his head. "That's not good news, Jean. Do you know that the healing looks sinister to the other villages?"

"Why?"

"Because apparently you have the power to heal this sickness that's ravaging the country, but you won't use it . . . with the exception of one Christian woman in Ossossane. Every shaman for miles is laying curses on your name and making charms for his people to protect themselves from your witchcraft."

Penchant blurted, "That's ridiculous! We've done nothing evil!"

Pierre gave Penchant a look that would have melted iron. The letter in his cloak pocket seemed to grow heavier every day.

Jean glanced at Pierre questioningly. "What else have you heard?"

They tramped through a low spot where the snow lay a foot deep and trudged up the other side, passing a cluster of fragrant pines.

"Before I get to the hard part, you should know that the Christians at Arontaen have fallen very ill. They've heard the stories about the Blessed Virgin appearing in Ossossane and have been calling for you like you were God Himself."

The lines in Brebeuf's forehead deepened. "I'll go to them as soon as—"

"I wouldn't if I were you."

"Why not?"

"Your conversion rate in Ihonatiria is about to soar, and I suspect that the new Christians will be demanding every ounce of strength you've got."

"You mean because of—"

"No. I mean because *he's* coming."

"Who?"

"Raimont."

272 † KATHLEEN O'NEAL GEAR

Jean stopped dead in his tracks. Snow frosted his hair and black cape. "When? Where is he?"

"Close. He and Onrea made the village of Teanaostaiae a week ago."

"Are they all right?"

"No one is all right after they've been captured by the Iroquois, Jean. But they're well enough to know in which direction home lies—though I can't tell you when they'll arrive."

Pierre squinted up at the tumbling clouds that rushed over the trees. His stomach had begun to roil just as violently. Stories of haunts and witchcraft always did that to him. Probably because he half-believed them. From the first day he'd set foot in the New World, he'd had the feeling that unseen things lurked in these wild lands, watching from behind brush and fallen logs. Andiora had told him so many tales of ghosts, rock ogres, and shamans who could send their souls flying to do evil deeds, that he never felt quite at ease—especially at night, which was closing fast.

Pierre took a breath. "Here's the part of the story that will set your hair on end, Jean. The story's spreading like wildfire. The Iroquois are spouting gibberish about a Spirit Cougar. They say the creature broke down the door of the longhouse where they were torturing Raimont and Onrea and led the two of them away into the forest. The Neutral reported seeing them winding through the hills with a fox leading them. Every village is adding tales to what Raimont and his Spirit Helpers did as they passed by. Already the story is a legend."

"Spirit Helpers?"

"Demons!" Penchant hissed next to Pierre's ear, so close that Pierre could feel warm breath on the back of his neck. "In these Last Days, demons will rise up from the very earth and go about deceiving people."

Pierre glanced back. Penchant had a wild look about him. Unkempt hair straggled into his gray eyes. "I'm no expert on the Last Days, but I'll tell you this: the Iroquois tried to track Raimont and Onrea. They scouted every trail, trails they know better than the inside of their longhouses, and they could not find a single print in the fresh snow." Pierre narrowed his eyes. "Are you grasping what I'm saying, Jean?"

Jean nodded soberly. "Yes."

"The healing in Ossossane aroused suspicion, but what with the stories of Raimont and Onrea, why, you've set up to be the most powerful shamans in the Huron country. People will be flocking to you. The sick and the lame and the dying. You'd best decide what you're going to say to those you can't heal." A suave brutality tinged his voice. "For they'll be wanting your blood."

Jean bowed his head. "I pray God will heal them all."

"Aye. Sure." Pierre made an extravagant gesture. "And perhaps the sun won't rise tomorrow, just because you're of a mind to ask God for it."

Penchant, his mouth open in outrage, stamped away down the trail, leaving Jean and Pierre alone.

Jean gave Pierre a disheartened smile. "You're a blasphemous rogue, Pierre."

"Aye."

"I'll try to think of something to tell them."

"Good."

Jean stroked his beard. "And I must send someone to Arontaen. The sick will need to be baptized, and the dying will need final absolution."

"It's dangerous, Jean." Pierre ran a hand through his tangled hair. "But if you're set on sending someone out with the Iroquois, who are prowling like wolves, make it Dupre. He's good with a musket, and he's not yet been tainted by the 'miracles.' Hopefully, they won't expect him to wave his hand and heal the whole lot of them." *And it'll get him out of me way—so I can talk sense to Andiora.*

CHAPTER

30

Onrea's breathing quickened as she and Phillipe worked their way up the trail toward Ihonatiria. Enormous white pines clustered on the shores of the ponds they passed, spiking up into the clear blue sky. Human and rabbit tracks marked the melting snow. The sun had come out bright and warm this morning, and Onrea felt certain that Iouskeha shone just for them. Every breath she took brought her the sweet scents of the warming forest.

"Just one more hill," she said.

Phillipe's round face glowed with happiness. The red and green stripes on his blanket-robe had turned brown with dirt and the smoke of dozens of camp fires. "Marc, Father Brebeuf and Luc will be there."

"Yes," she answered. But fear knotted in her belly. For twelve days her fear had been growing. Would they crest this last hill and find nothing but the ashes of burned longhouses? Ten paces ahead stood the alder tree where she'd hidden once to escape the wrath of her mother after she'd pinched her cousin Pewti and made a huge welt rise on her arm. And over there, in that tiny pond, she'd spent hours in the autumn weighting unshucked ears of corn so they would ferment beneath the cool green water and provide the winter delicacy her people loved so much. She craved her mother and her family more than she had ever wanted anything in her life.

Onrea reached out and patted Phillipe's shoulder, comforting him in advance for whatever they might find.

Phillipe smiled, but then he hadn't stopped smiling since they'd escaped the Iroquois. Only, sometimes he smiled a little more or a little less. Everything seemed a wonder to him. Once, days ago, they'd broken out of a dense section of woods and glimpsed a lake in the basin below. Phillipe had cried out and run headlong down the trail . . . just to watch the noon light swirl in golden rings on the surface of the water. His Power seemed to be growing like moss in the spring rains. She'd seen it happen before in people who had given part of their souls in exchange for help from their Spirit Helpers, or from the *oki* that inhabited the land, and she wondered what sort of shaman this little bald Black Robe was becoming.

Onrea took Phillipe's good hand and half-dragged him up the last rise. "Not much farther," she said. "Just a few more steps."

As though in warning, the scabs covering the burns on her chest and back began to ache. The edges of the scabs had been catching on her blue blanket-robe for a week now, spilling pus on the coarse woolen fabric. Yellow splotches made a hideous scallop around her shoulders. Phillipe's burns had been healing less well. The constant pressure of walking on his feet kept them raw. But he seemed oblivious to the agony.

They crested the hill, and she saw Ihonatiria. The longhouses still formed the square she knew so well, and the white cross still rose above the Catholic mission house. Onrea let out a cry of joy and relief. A few of the houses had been burned. But not her house. It still stood!

But why was no one in the plaza?

Where were the children? Totiri and Dalbeau always played outside on sunny days like this. And Maconta, and her mother? They should have been grinding corn or gossiping by the longhouse. An eerie stillness possessed the village. The closer Onrea went, the more her knees shook.

She dropped Phillipe's hand and ran down the hill and up the trail that led into the village. A woman emerged from her longhouse wearing a plain tradecloth dress with fringes on the tan sleeves; her hair lay in a stubby braid. She carried a copper pail of water, which she emptied over the snow.

"Andiora?" Onrea cried and raced forward.

But her feet faltered when her cousin looked up. Andiora's black eyes were haunted, empty.

"It's me, Andiora. I'm home!"

Andiora dropped the copper pail and put a hand to her lips. She took an uncertain step forward. *"Onrea?"*

"Yes, we're home!" Onrea threw herself into Andiora's arms, kissing her cousin's hair and face. "Oh, Andiora, it was terrible, but we escaped. Cougar came and rescued us." Onrea laughed. "Where's Mother? Where are Dalbeau and Oute?" She gazed eagerly over Andiora's shoulder to the longhouse. "What . . ."

Her questions dried up at the look on Andiora's face. Only then did the faint moans and cries coming from the longhouses reach her.

Andiora stroked Onrea's hair. "Onrea, there is sickness in the village. Your . . . your mother died two weeks ago. But your sisters and brothers are fine. They—"

Onrea broke free from Andiora's grip. She choked, "No. No, not Mama. I've been wanting her so badly." She started to sob uncontrollably.

Andiora enfolded the girl in her arms. "It happened very quickly. None of us had time to prepare. Your family will need you even more now. You will have to be the mother to your younger brothers and sisters."

Onrea saw Maconta peek through the door-hanging. Her grandmother cried out in surprise and ran forward on wobbly legs. "It's Onrea! She's home!" A few people emerged from the other houses and gathered around them. Voices rose in joy, and some in weeping.

Father Dupre opened the door of the mission. He glanced at Onrea, his blue eyes widening. He looked down the trail, then dashed toward it, his black robe flying about his legs. "Phillipe?" he called. "Phillipe!"

Phillipe was coming slowly, as though each step hurt. His sunken eyes were ringed with purple, but a broad, angelic smile lit his face. He wore a frayed dirty blanket with holes cut in it for the head and arms. A braided bark belt encircled his waist. Marc broke into a run when he noticed the splotches of dried blood on Phillipe's makeshift robe. And Phillipe's feet . . . swollen flesh bulged over the wisps of rabbit fur that edged the moccasin tops.

"Phillipe, let me help you." He slid an arm around Phillipe's shoulders to help him up the trail.

"Marc," Phillipe murmured lovingly. His eyes shone like luminous green jewels. "Marc, I missed you."

Marc was so worried that he barely noticed the malignant looks Tehoren gave them as they entered the plaza. The shaman stood at the edge of the small crowd milling about Onrea. Jix was beside him, whispering.

Marc carefully skirted the edge of the throng and shoved the mission door open with his boot, led Phillipe through the corn-scented storage room and sat him down on his bed. Phillipe's sunburned face seemed to glow as he looked around at the purple Advent decorations.

"Jean said you were coming home, Phillipe. I prayed and prayed for you. How did you get away?"

"Our Lord came, Marc. He came and set me free. Me and Onrea."

Marc's brows lowered. "Our Lord? What do you mean?"

Phillipe stared absently, as though looking into a strange and wonderful world that no one else would ever see. A monstrous thought rose in Marc, almost too monstrous to be borne. Phillipe was such a gentle, innocent man: had the torture taken his mind?

He put a hand tenderly on Phillipe's shoulder. "You must be hungry." He plumped Phillipe's pillow and helped him to lie down. "There's a pot of stew still warm on the fire." Then he turned away, but Phillipe caught him by the sleeve. "What is it, Phillipe?"

Marc lowered himself to sit on the edge of the bed. Phillipe frowned at him in a dazed way, as if not quite sure he was real. Then he worked a finger into Marc's sleeve to feel for his arm, and Marc saw that Phillipe had only one finger and the thumb left on that hand.

"I . . . I love you, Marc. I missed you."

"Oh, Phillipe, I'm so glad you're home." He leaned forward and hugged the little Brother.

"Is there . . . some water?"

"Yes, of course."

Marc rose and took a wooden cup from the shelf, filled it from the copper kettle and took it back to Phillipe, who drank greedily. Water poured down his chin and drenched the front of his robe. Marc studied him while he drank. Even beneath the blankets he wore, it was easy to tell that he'd lost weight. His plump face had slimmed, his belly vanished. Phillipe drained the last of the water and let his head fall forward. His chin sank into the loose skin of his throat.

Marc took the cup and went to the fire. As he lifted the lid off the pot, the robust fragrance of beaver encircled his head. He filled the cup, grabbed a spoon from the shelf and went back to sit on the edge of Phillipe's bed.

"They hurt us, Marc," Phillipe whispered.

"I know they did."

"They put burning axheads around Onrea's neck, and they made me walk through fiery coals."

"If I'd known where you were, Phillipe, I'd have come to get you. I don't care what it would have taken, I'd have never let you—"

"Onrea took care of me," he said lovingly. "She made a paste of rabbit fat and put it on my feet, and we ate clams and caught fish. Once Onrea snared a baby deer. And a fox found a canoe for us. All the animals helped."

"I thank God," Marc murmured, his eyes riveted on Phillipe's detached stare. *A fox found a canoe?* "Phillipe, would you mind if I look at your wounds?"

Phillipe raised his cup of stew and began eating ravenously. Marc went to the foot of the bed and untied Phillipe's rabbitskin moccasins. He slipped off the left one and almost dropped it. Revulsion rose in him. The toes had been seared from Phillipe's foot. Only blackened stubs remained. Scabs marked the swollen flesh, torn loose in places where the oozing infection had glued them to the fur. *Blessed Lord, how did he walk at all?*

Around a mouthful of stew, Phillipe mumbled, "Marc? I had no one to say confession to."

"I'll hear your confession. Let me tend your wounds, and I'll—"

"And I couldn't celebrate Mass, or receive communion. I felt very alone. Until our Lord came." He dropped his spoon in his empty cup and lifted his mutilated hand to gesture in the firelit air. "Sometimes He swooped down as an eagle, and other times He appeared as a bear, and when He saved Onrea and me, He came as a lion." Phillipe tipped his cup and licked the last drops of stew from it.

Marc's chest tingled. "A lion?"

"Yes."

The fire in the hearth crackled and spewed sparks across the dirt floor. Marc whirled to make certain they'd landed nowhere near the wooden table or chairs. He turned back, his heart pounding.

"Phillipe, what did the lion look like? Andiora . . . when she was ill, she had a dream where she saw a cougar with the marks of our Lord's passion on him. Did the cougar that rescued you—"

"God talks to her. He told me."

Marc crushed Phillipe's moccasin in his hands. Thoughts raced through his mind so quickly that he couldn't make them connect. "He told you?"

"Yes, God needs her."

"Why?"

Phillipe smiled.

"Did God tell you why?"

Phillipe didn't answer.

Marc rose and fetched a large bark bowl, which he filled with warm water, then threw a cotton cloth and a piece of soap in it to soak. He knelt by Phillipe again. "I'm going to pull your foot over the edge of the bed so we don't get your blanket wet, Phillipe."

The stench of the infection almost made Marc vomit. He lathered the wet cloth with soap and very gently began washing Phillipe's foot. The paste came off first. Beneath it, soft scabs shone. Marc tenderly prodded them to see if he could identify the boundaries of the infection. It seemed isolated around the heel.

Phillipe watched him with glistening eyes. "God told me He'd talked to you, too, Marc."

Marc glanced up. "Yes. . . . He did."

"Were you confused?"

"I was, Phillipe. I felt empty, and . . . I couldn't seem to find my way."

"Sometimes we have to leave the way to find God, Marc."

Marc dipped the cloth in the water and wrung it out. "We have to leave the way?"

"Yes. God does that to people." Phillipe sighed. "He causes us to lose our way so that He can guide us to Him. Then He makes us empty, so He can fill us with his Light. It hurts—but only in the beginning." Phillipe leaned forward and patted Marc's shoulder.

Voices penetrated the bark wall, and Marc turned as the outer door opened and Jean, Luc, Mongrave and his entire trading party tramped into the storage room, batting dirt from their clothing and talking. Jean entered the common room, and his eyes widened.

"*Phillipe!*"

PIERRE, WHO WAS right behind Jean, stared at Raimont in wonder, then shifted his gaze to Dupre. The youth stood tall, his blond hair and beard gleaming with a muted orange glow in the firelight. Pierre's gut tightened in anticipation of the discussion he'd been rehearsing for two weeks.

Tristan looked up at Pierre. "Best be getting the business over with, Pierre. Me and the boys'll head over to Maconta's longhouse, then we'll set up the tents on the lee side of the hill."

Pierre swept his brown cape back and put his hands on his hips. "Aye, Tristan. I'll be over in a short while."

Tristan nodded and backed out, taking the other traders with him.

Pierre gritted his teeth. Penchant had entered the room, walked over to the table and slumped down in a chair, all the while casting furtive glances at Raimont. "Father Penchant," Pierre said, "would you be gracing me with a moment of your time?"

Penchant looked up as if Pierre had slapped him. "Why?"

"I've a private matter I'd like to discuss with you."

"I have things to tend to here, Mongrave. I can't be running off—"

"Jean," Pierre called gruffly, "tell your little boy to join me outside. I promise not to hurt him."

Jean didn't even take his eyes from Raimont's face. "Pierre is a man of his word, Luc. Please go with him."

Penchant hesitated, peering suspiciously at Pierre, but then he lifted his pointed chin and headed for the mission door. Pierre followed and closed the door firmly behind him.

"What do you want?" Penchant demanded as he folded his arms across his chest. The slant of the sun heightened the hawkish angularity of his face and glinted in his gray eyes.

"I've brought you a gift."

"A what?"

Pierre reached into his pocket and pulled out the letter. "I'd the misfortune to meet up with a priggish Dutch messenger boy at Fort Orange—just the sort I'd expect your family to hire." He shoved the missive roughly at Penchant's chest.

Luc gripped the letter as he would a life raft in a turbulent ocean. "From my family?"

"Aye, from your mother." Pierre stepped so close that Penchant leaned backward. "Listen, boy. Part of me bargain with the Dutchman was that I wouldn't mention this delivery to anyone. But . . ." He lowered his voice threateningly. "If I ever discover that bad comes of it, I'll break that promise and take me revenge on your hide. You understand?"

"I don't know what you're talking about!" Penchant declared indignantly.

"I think you do. For you must've instructed your mother to send messages avoiding Quebec's oversight. I don't take kindly to such underhanded means from anybody, let alone from one of Jean's priests. If I find out you've used it to hurt him . . . Well, you remember me warning."

Pierre straightened, and Penchant backed toward the mission door, then turned and slipped inside. Pierre stood silent for a moment, listening to the weak cries coming from the longhouses. Were so many down?

Stop delaying, he chastised himself and walked back into the mission. Penchant had disappeared, but Dupre stood next to the fire, a curious expression on his handsome face as he listened to Jean's conversation with Raimont.

"Dupre?" Pierre called. "Might I be talking with you next?"

Dupre came across and into the storeroom. "What is it, Mongrave?"

Pierre kept his voice low, for Dupre's ears alone. "How are things in the village?"

"Very bad. The illness has spread dramatically."

"And Andiora?"

"So far she's escaped, but her family has been hit hard. Jatoya died. I'm not sure how many more cousins—"

"That's not what I meant," Pierre said candidly and spread his legs as though getting set for a fight.

Dupre stared at him. "Forgive me. What did you mean?"

In the background, Raimont giggled in that childish way of his.

"I'm asking about you and Andiora, Dupre. I'd like you to be giving me the truth straight. Are you in love with her?"

Dupre's blue eyes tightened as he straightened up. "I don't know where you could have gotten such an idea—"

"Because I know her feelings for you—and I can't see her getting so deep with no encouragement. Have you talked to her about it?" When Dupre hesitated, Pierre said, "I'm asking you man to man, Dupre. And just in case you're worrying, I've said nothing to any of your brethren concerning this matter. Nor will I."

"Andiora—" the name came as though torn from Dupre against his will "—understands my vows."

Pierre stroked his beard and eyed the priest. "Aye, that's fine . . . *and do you?*"

Dupre lifted his chin. When the youth wanted, he could level a look as deadly as any battle-weary soldier's. "That was uncalled for, Mongrave."

Pierre smiled faintly. "Aye, 'twas. But you answered me question, and I appreciate it, Dupre. If you'll be excusing me, I'll be going now."

He turned in a whirl of brown cape and shoved open the mission door. His steps felt lighter as he headed for Andiora's longhouse.

LUC SAT IN a corner of the chapel, his letter clutched to his bosom. Three candles gleamed on the altar, throwing a golden halo over the crucifix and benches. Scenes of Paris—blessed, civilized Paris—welled so strongly in his mind that he felt faint. Memories of the rich architecture, of the sweet pastries sold on the streets, filled him.

With shaking fingers, he tore the wax seal to read his mother's almost illegible scrawl.

Dear Luc,

I've received three of your letters now and am attempting to bear your sniveling with good grace. When will you learn that a grown man must accept responsibility and carry out his duties obediently?

You were always a weak-minded child, but I'd hoped that when you entered the priesthood, you'd gain strength.

I had a long talk with Reverend Father Binet about you, and we both agreed that perhaps you simply are not suited to minister to the savages of the New World. He's looking into the possibility of calling you back to France, but I warn you, my son, once you are home, I will not tolerate any further whining. I told you to join the Dominicans, and you wouldn't listen. . . .

Luc crumpled the letter into a ball in his fist. *Mother, I hate you. Oh, what had he done?*

Brebeuf's vision of Mary at Ossossane surely meant that the New Israel *would* be established in this barbarous land. The Blessed Virgin's words—submissive to the will of God for the sake of the newborn Son of Man—rang like thunder in his mind. The End was certainly coming, and Luc wanted to be a part of making straight the way for the Lord's triumphant return!

He dropped his head in his hands. This proposed recall home couldn't be taken seriously. Not now.

Raimont's laughter penetrated the chapel, and Luc heard him telling Brebeuf of the beautiful lion that had saved him from the Iroquois. *A demon. Or perhaps even the Antichrist!*

Surely the Lord didn't want him to go home now! Could this be part of some satanic plan? Had the Prince of Darkness seen into his heart, seen his zeal to destroy the devil's wicked manifestations in the New World, and decided to eliminate him?

Luc blinked at the amber-tinged darkness of the chapel and thought he could sense a presence swelling, black and malignant, growing into an amorphous monster. He shivered.

"It won't work," he whispered. "I'll fight you, Satan! You can't frighten me away from here. I won't go. You'll have to kill me to get rid of me!"

Violently, he threw his crumpled letter across the chapel and fell on his knees to pray.

CHAPTER

3 1

The Hurons observed with some sort of reason that those who had been nearest to us, happened to be the most ruined by the disease. Whole villages of those who had first received us, now were utterly exterminated. It has happened very often and has been remarked a hundred times, that where we were most welcome, where we baptized more people, there it was, in fact, where they died the most. . . . in the cabins to which we were denied entry, although they were sick to extremity, at the end of a few days, one would see every person happily cured.

JEROME LALEMANT, S.J.
Ossossane, 1640

Pierre ducked into Andiora's longhouse. A riot of noise filled the place. People had gathered in the center around Onrea, listening raptly to her tales of the Iroquois. The long benches running the length of the house held at least sixty people, most of them in their twenties and thirties, because the old and the children had been struck hardest by the disease. Pierre could see that the ill had been moved to one side of the house. Eight lay sleeping there, and even through the excited conversation circling Onrea, he could hear their whimpers.

Onrea told about crossing the river with the Iroquois braves. Pierre's jaw clamped at her vivid description of their rape and brutality. His eyes searched for Andiora. Finally he spotted her, sitting on the floor by herself. Her hair was pulled back from her heart-shaped face and braided into a short plait. Her large midnight eyes seemed chiseled from stone. She wore a white-cotton dress that clung to every curve. He'd brought her that dress from France. It was beautiful, with tiny bands of lace around the neck and hem. She prized it, and wore it only for special occasions.

He worked his way toward her, stepping around people, pausing to talk to those who called friendly greetings. When Andiora saw him, she gazed at him tiredly.

He sat down beside her. "How are you, darlin'?" he asked.

"As well as I can be, Pierre. The village has been hit very hard by the sickness."

"I know. I heard about Jatoya. I'm sorry. I'll miss her."

"So will I."

Andiora propped her chin on her drawn-up knees. She looked so slender, so frail, it touched something deep within him, some consuming need to protect and pet her. Brashly, he reached out and put an arm around her shoulders, then drew her against him. She tensed but made no move to escape. He kissed her forehead and stroked her hair.

"The winter's been a hard one, and only half through. I was thinking of leaving early this year. Of going back to England . . . and taking you with me."

She lifted her eyes to his. "Pierre, please don't—"

"Think about it for a time, would you? I'd like to show you some of the world." Having to ask embarrassed him. He fumbled with the lace on her collar. "'Twas wrong of me not to have invited you aboard the *Soleil* long before now."

"It doesn't matter anymore, Pierre." The misery in her voice wounded him.

"Darlin', listen to me. I—"

"Pierre, don't do this. To you or to me. What we had is *finished*. Let it rest."

He sat stunned, not knowing what to say. Tears welled in her eyes. Andiora tenderly pulled him against her and stroked his back, as though in apology. It drove him mad. He knew she still loved him. Love couldn't die so easily!

"Andiora," he said, "I've been a fool these past five years, thinking I could have both you and the freedom of the sea. All I'm asking—"

She released her hold on him and looked up. "No. You've never been foolish, Pierre. You gave me as much of you as you could without losing yourself. I won't be the cause of that." She touched his bearded cheek gently. "Let me back away. It's as hard for me as it is for you. But we both know that the freedom of the sea is what makes you happiest."

"Andiora, I—"

"No, Pierre. *Please*," she said doggedly.

She started to rise, but he gripped her arm and pulled her back to the floor. Andiora gazed at him through tears.

"I want you to know," he announced sternly, "that I have talked to Dupre. He's told me that he does not love you."

"You talked to Marc? Oh, Pierre!" Andiora wrenched free of him and lunged to her feet. Her breast heaved beneath her white dress. "Pierre, if you cannot be my *friend*, please, leave me alone!"

She hastened past the sick and ducked through the door-hanging into the bright afternoon.

Pierre gritted his teeth. His soul seemed to twist up around his throat like a noose. The people had gone silent listening to Onrea:

"And on the third day Brother Phillipe started praying to call the animals to come." She made a swooping motion with her hand. "A bird fluttered into the longhouse and soared down over all the people, making them dive for the floor to hide beneath the benches . . ."

Pierre noticed absently that Tehoren had perked up at the mention of birds. The shaman's pug nose flared, and he glanced at Jix and several of the other warriors; they seemed to be making some sort of silent communication. Tehoren's red-quilled shirt glimmered in the light of the fire as he leaned sideways to speak in Jix's ear. When Jix nodded fervently, Tehoren called out, "And what did the bird do after it frightened the Iroquois?"

Onrea answered, "It flew down the center of the house and landed on Phillipe's shoulder. Then Cougar pushed open the door and came in and all the Iroquois ran." She laughed triumphantly. "Phillipe and I, we—"

"And what did the bird do?" Tehoren pressed. "Did it fly away when Cougar entered?"

Onrea blinked thoughtfully. "Yes. But only after—"

"So!" Jix interjected as he got to his feet. "Maybe Cougar came in to drive the evil *oki* away so he could save *you*, Onrea."

She frowned. "The bird didn't feel evil. It felt good."

"An *oki* can make you feel anything it wants to," Tehoren said ominously. "I think . . ."

Pierre rose and headed for the door. Surely Andiora would come to her senses. He could not believe that she would throw away his love so cavalierly. *You cannot give up. Not until you've tried every way you know to bind the wounds.*

Olive-colored shadows stretched like tentacles across the plaza. Sunlight cast a veil of gold across the drifting clouds.

Andiora was standing in front of the mission house, talking to Jean. He towered over her. Her white dress stood out like a splash of cream against Brebeuf's black robe. Determined, Pierre strode toward them. Andiora ignored him, keeping her gaze riveted on Jean.

"No, Jean," Andiora was saying. "I don't think I should leave my family right now. Many are ill."

"But it won't take more than three days," Jean assured her. "And Marc truly needs you. So do the Huron Christians in Arontaen. I'll watch over your family while you're away."

Pierre put a hand on his holstered pistol. "Andiora's needed here, Jean. Find someone else."

"Who else is there, Pierre? Andiora is the only—"

"I said, *find someone else*, Jean. I won't have Andiora traipsing over the country with no better than Dupre to defend her. Besides . . . she and I have business to discuss."

Andiora stared at him, and he felt it like the clash of swords. "I've changed my mind," she said. "I will go, Jean. Perhaps I need to get away from the village, after all."

Jean glanced back and forth between them, then said, "Thank you, Andiora."

"When will Marc and I be leaving?"

"As soon as possible. Tomorrow? I'd like to have Marc back by Christmas, next week."

"That's fine. Maybe I can talk Maconta into coming with me. She has relatives in Arontaen who are ill. I think she would like to see them just in case . . . she would like to see them," she finished.

Jean nodded. "I'm sure that Marc would be very happy to travel with both you and Maconta. I'll see to it that he's prepared to leave at dawn."

Andiora folded her arms and rubbed them briskly to fight off the chill in the air. "I'll fix my pack this afternoon." She turned and brushed by Pierre without a glance.

Pierre headed after her, desperate to make her listen to him.

"*Pierre?*" Jean called quietly.

He stopped and grudgingly demanded, "What?"

Jean ambled forward—slowly—and it seemed for all the world that he took just the amount of time necessary for Andiora to duck into her longhouse.

Jean eyed Pierre in a kindly way. "May I give you some advice?"

Pierre growled, "So long as you're not expecting that I'll take it, go ahead."

"'The way of a fool is right in his own eyes, but he that harkeneth unto counsel is wise.'"

"So you've stooped to throwing tidbits from Proverbs at me? I should be running before I get more. Speak your mind, Jean."

Jean took a moment to appreciate the sunlight glinting off the snow that rimmed the roofs of the longhouses. "I don't know what's gone on between you and Andiora, Pierre. But it's easy to see that you're both hurting. She's trying to step away and you're working as hard as you can to keep her close. Can't you grant her enough time that she can think things through?"

Pierre balled his fists. "And how much is enough, Jean?"

"Only she can decide that. She has a lot to think about besides you. The fear of Iroquois attacks, combined with this illness—"

"That's not the half of what she's worried about. If you would only open your eyes, you'd—" His mouth hung open, but he couldn't force any more words out. "Forget it. I'm dim-witted, but not yet a scoundrel."

"What are you talking about?"

Pierre shook his head and sighed. "I thank you for your advice. But I need to go find Tristan to talk with him about the trip to Arontaen. Since Andiora's set on getting away from me, I want somebody with her who can shoot straight. I'll speak with you later, Jean."

He left Jean standing to muse alone in the sunny plaza.

CHAPTER

32

Do you wish to serve this Great Spirit and save yourselves from the pestilence that afflicts you? First, you must give up your belief in the power of dreams. Secondly, when you marry, you must bind yourselves to one woman for life. . . . Thirdly, you must not indulge in vomiting feasts, since God forbids such gluttony . . . you must not eat human flesh, even though it be that of your enemies.

JEAN DE BREBEUF, 1636

Echon, my brother, I must speak to you very frankly: I believe that your proposition is impossible. I cannot be a hypocrite. I express my thoughts honestly. I judge that what you propose will prove to be only a stumbling block. We have our own ways of doing things, you have yours and other nations have theirs. When you speak to us about obeying and acknowledging Him as our master, Who, you say, has made heaven and earth, you are talking of turning the country upside-down. Your ancestors assembled in earlier times and held a council. They resolved to take as their God the one whom you honor, and they commanded all the ceremonies that you observe. We have learned differently from our ancestors.

AENONS, CHIEF
Village of Wenrio, 1636

The people of Ossossane take God for their Lord and Master . . . they renounce all their errors . . . do not believe in dreams . . . no vomit feasts . . . keep the same wife . . . not eat human meat . . . build a cabin to God in the spring . . . provided He stops the progess of the disease.

OKHIARENTA, SHAMAN
Village of Ossossane, 1636

O ld Maconta led the way on her spindly legs; her gray hair flew around her shoulders like frosty grass. Marc walked at the rear of the line, behind Tristan Marleaux and Andiora. Their small packs were filled with enough food and clothing to last for three or four days. Marleaux's musket hung securely over the shoulder of his grease-stained hide coat. He'd been laughing a good deal, speaking with Andiora about the winter and the Iroquois and Onrea's escape.

Andiora looked especially beautiful this morning. She wore her red tradecloth dress beneath her foxhide coat. The fringes on the hem brushed her moccasin tops. She'd braided her hair, then secured it against the back of her head with a large copper comb. She talked about everything but Mongrave. He'd come out briefly at dawn to say good-bye, but Andiora had avoided him. The closer they came to Arontaen and the farther they left Ihonatiria behind, the more she seemed to relax.

"I'm sure glad that Onrea and little Phillipe made it home alive. If ever a miracle occurred in this vast land, 'twas that."

"Yes," Andiora said. "Iouskeha protected them."

"And that cougar of yours," Marleaux added, as though he didn't quite believe the story but was afraid to say so. Marc's ears perked up to listen. He'd heard Phillipe's telling, but he longed to hear Onrea's as well.

"If it *was* my Spirit Helper, yes," Andiora responded. "Cougar was gone during that time, but I don't know if the Helper who rescued Onrea and Phillipe was mine."

Marleaux's gray eyes narrowed. "And what are you thinking about the bird that flew down the center of the longhouse before Cougar came in?"

"I'm not sure, Tristan. Tehoren thinks the bird was an evil *oki*, one of the Forest Spirits that live in rocky places. My Spirit Helper has never traveled with a bird before—at least not that I've seen. But perhaps the bird was—" she glanced back at Marc "—Phillipe's guardian angel."

"Aye, might a been," Tristan sighed. "Birds are big in our religion. Aren't they, Father Dupre?"

"Yes," Marc answered. "The Holy Spirit often takes the form of the bird, as it did on the day of our Lord's baptism."

"Aye, I remember. I wonder how Tehoren could be thinking the bird wicked. It helped save Onrea and Phillipe."

Andiora shrugged. "*Okis* sometimes do things that seem good but bring about evil in the end. They're very clever."

Marleaux rubbed his pointed chin as he thought. "Is it in the Book of Matthew, Father, where our Lord cures the blind boy and the Pharisees go to saying that He did it by the power of Beelzebub?"

"Chapter twelve of Matthew, yes. Jesus denies it, of course, then counters, 'But if it is by the Spirit of God that I drive out the devils, then be sure the kingdom of God has already come upon you. He who is not with me is against me.'"

They started climbing a steep slope, slogging through the melting snow. The hills around them were dotted with upthrust rocks that glinted blue beneath crusts of ice. Quaking aspens dotted the spaces between the pines. A few brown leaves still clung to their bare branches and rattled in the wind.

Marleaux asked, "If the bird was the Holy Spirit and frightened away the demon Iroquois, do you think that maybe the kingdom of God has come? Just as our Lord said?" He turned halfway around to gaze questioningly at Marc.

"I pray it is so," Marc responded.

Had the Third Age of the Holy Ghost begun? Marc wished he could believe it. But his faith had been shaken by the Iroquois attack and the brutal torture of Phillipe and Onrea. He found himself debating the same questions as Tehoren: Which is good? Which evil? He'd found no answers. Jean's description of Mother Mary in Ossossane and Her words about the *newborn Son of Man* had left Marc torn betwixt hope and dread. What with Phillipe's identification of the lion and Jesus, a strange, haunting picture emerged. Marc had always assumed that the descriptions of Lion and Lamb were allegorical. But what form would the Lord take were He to make His triumphant return to the New World? Would it be an Indian spiritual form? Like a cougar?

He lifted his eyes to Andiora as she gripped Maconta's arm and struggled up the last few paces of the slope, her foxhide coat glittering in the brilliant sunlight. When she reached the crest, she stopped and stood as still as a painting. Old Maconta grumbled about the melting snow and mud that clung to her moccasins, but Andiora didn't seem to hear. Marc moved beside her. Her black eyes were focused on the drainages that flowed into Lake Karegnondi. Blue shadows crept among the trees that whiskered the slopes. And in the distance, the lake shimmered with flecks of gold. Andiora smiled.

Marc turned away. Why couldn't he put her out of his mind? Since the night of his long prayer vigil, when he had made his decision to "pray always," he'd barely been able to pray at all. He'd been obsessed with thoughts of Andiora, reliving their quiet talk a thousand times. Even in his dreams, he heard the intimate sound of her voice when she'd said she loved him, saw the tears in her eyes when he'd told her, "Don't."

Old Maconta tipped her face to the warm sunlight and declared, "Snow coming. Can you smell it?"

Marc inhaled, but only the pleasant earthiness of the forest met his nostrils. The trail had begun to melt out, sending rivulets of water trickling down the right side of the path.

"Bad storm," Maconta said. She added something else, so rapidly that Marc couldn't decipher it, then pointed to the northwest and began hobbling down the trail as fast as her ancient legs would carry her.

Andiora studied the northern sky. "Maconta says we had better get to Arontaen quickly, before the storm rolls over those hills."

Marleaux lifted his long nose and sniffed, then squinted up at the brilliant ball of sun that hung over the treetops. "Well, I'll take her word for it."

"So will I. I've never known her to be wrong." Andiora adjusted her sagging pack and trotted down the hill after Maconta.

Marc and Marleaux brought up the rear, their boots slipping on the patches of ice that crusted the way.

"WHAT'S HIS NAME?" Marc asked Andiora as he worked down Jemos's longhouse. The cries of the sick rang in his ears. In his left hand he carried his bag, which contained a vial of holy water, consecrated wine and bread, oil for extreme unction, lemon peel and raisins.

"Rumet. He is my second cousin. Thirteen. Maconta says he has been sick for four days. The woman on the bench beside him is his sister, Lopos. She's sixteen."

Lopos gazed hollowly at Marc as he approached; she looked as though every ounce of her faith had fled. Marc stepped over the extended legs of a woman dozing half beneath the bench. She had one hand twined weakly in the yellow blanket of a little girl maybe three years old. This longhouse brimmed with relatives and refugees from villages that had been raided by the Iroquois. Everywhere, people with bandaged arms and heads tried to sleep, moaning and calling the names of those who, Marc assumed, would never answer again. Despair rode the sickly sweet air like the hooded specter of death.

They had arrived in Arontaen eight hours ago and had been baptizing and tending the sick ever since. The illness here was far worse than anything he'd seen at Ihonatiria. Marc's nerves felt strung as tight as a violin. Already four of those he'd baptized had died.

"When did Rumet convert?" he asked.

"A year ago. With his whole family. But Brebeuf would not baptize any of them. I don't know why."

Marc did. Jean feared apostasy in converts almost as much as he feared the fires of hell. He reserved baptism only for those who had proven their faith by extensive efforts, or for those near death.

Marc crouched next to Rumet. Andiora knelt beside him, her beautiful face tense, her black eyes as wide and luminous as a night owl's. She had worked tirelessly at his side, translating and comforting the sick. Sometimes he caught her Huron words, telling a frightened victim that Marc had great Power and wanted to help.

He would have been lost without her. Several times he had stopped himself from reaching out to touch her in gratitude. She seemed to understand, for each time she smiled patiently and moved on to the next sick person.

Marc gently brushed wet hair out of Rumet's glazed eyes. Short black locks framed the boy's face. He wore a cross, roughly carved from ash wood, around his throat. A filthy brown blanket lay rumpled around him.

"Hello, Rumet." Marc smiled. "How are you feeling?"

The boy made a breathy, incomprehensible response, but Andiora understood. Her chin trembled. "He asks that you beg God to take him away. He says that his mother and brothers are dead and he wants to go to heaven to be with them."

"No, no, Rumet," Marc said in a soothing voice. "We want you to get well. Your village needs you. Your sister Lopos needs you."

When Andiora translated, Rumet's gaunt face twisted with tears. He reached out for Lopos, who smiled wearily and murmured something tender, but was too ill to reach back. Andiora gripped Rumet's hand. She kissed his burning palm and held it against her cheek while she spoke. Marc understood almost none of her words, but he saw Rumet smile feebly and pat Andiora's face. When the boy looked back at Marc, he seemed calm. And this time Marc understood his request: "Father, forgive me. Please hear my confession." Rumet drew his hand up to his chest and made a very small cross over his heart.

Marc crossed himself and bowed his head. "God understands all things, Rumet. He is listening." And Marc listened, to the sins that were so devastating in the eyes of the young boy: desires for a girl in the village who had died shortly after a passionate dream of Rumet's, unkind words uttered in a moment of fear . . . doubts about God's goodness when he'd watched his last brother die.

Marc shifted.

Shamefully, he himself had felt similar doubts.

Mother Mary had come to heal a woman ill at Ossossane. Why hadn't God seen fit to heal the fatally ill at Arontaen? So many Christians here had perished. Was it because Marc administered the sacraments, not Jean? What had he done that God would abandon these good people because of *his* inadequacies?

A voice in his mind hissed, *It's because you're a failure. You've always been a failure. You failed Marie. You failed Phillipe . . . and you've failed God. You've* never *been what He needed you to be.* With all his will, Marc had striven to empty himself of himself so that God might fill him. But he had succeeded only in emptying God from his soul. Where had the sweetness of the divine presence gone? Just when he had seemed on the verge of true spiritual illumination, God had flown from him like a bird from his hand. Dread had taken His place, glutting Marc with such darkness that he wanted to scream in angry despair, demanding why God had forsaken him to this inner hell. *In inferno sumus, sed misericordiae, non irae; in caelo erimus*, he recited mechanically to himself: a hell of mercy, not of wrath.

Rumet's dark eyes closed suddenly. His head lolled to the side.

"No . . ." Marc grabbed the boy's hand from Andiora and checked his pulse.

Lopos cried, "No! No! Not my brother!"

Rumet's pulse was so faint that Marc could barely sense it. He threw open his bag. Grabbing out his vial of holy water, he tipped Rumet's head back and, in panic, sloshed the holy water over the boy's face and hair.

"I baptize you in the—the name of the Father, and of the Son, and of the Holy Spirit."

He gently laid Rumet's head back down. The boy's mouth fell open. After a few seconds, a terrible last gush of breath puffed from Rumet's slack lips. Andiora knelt to embrace Lopos. They wept together. It sounded like the mewing of kittens.

Marc clasped his hands in prayer and began the *De Profundis*. But his voice fell silent. *Where are You, God? Where are You . . . where are You?*

LUC, WADING THROUGH the sick and injured crowding the mission, was headed toward the box of tea on the shelf. If he didn't have something warm to drink soon, he would perish. Through the windows he saw the pink echoes of sunset dancing amid the drifting clouds. And still a dozen Indians huddled in the cold outside, waiting their turn. They'd started trickling into Ihonatiria that morning, coming from all over the Huron territory. Many were so sick they could barely stand. Others had arrow and musket wounds and were lucky to have escaped their Iroquois attackers with their lives. Stories of burned and looted villages had become commonplace. Father Brebeuf had placed the ill in rows on woven mats along the east wall of the common room. Nineteen in all so far, with another twenty loitering around the room. Their stench filled the mission like rotting meat, and their fevered shrieks affected Luc like a plague of stinging flies.

He reached the tea, threw a pinch into his bark cup and shouldered through the crowd of savages to the kettle at the edge of the fire. "Excuse me. *Excuse me!* Yes, you. Please move," he said in Huron. The old man with scraggly gray braids blinked his fever-glazed eyes and tottered out of the way. Luc picked up the kettle and slammed it down when he found it empty.

"Raimont?" he called. The ugly little Brother looked up; he'd been washing the leg wound of a two-year-old boy. His round face had flushed crimson with the effort. "Why is this kettle empty? You were assigned water duty."

Raimont stared as though he hadn't heard. Luc gritted his teeth. Raimont's eyes had had an unearthly glow ever since he'd returned from the Iroquois. Angrily, Luc demanded, "Well?"

Phillipe pointed to the pan of dirty water sitting on the floor next to the injured boy. "I needed it, Luc."

"The rest of us need some, too, you know!"

Raimont rose and limped across the room on his heavily bandaged feet to grab a five-gallon pail. "I'll go and get more from the pond."

Brebeuf straightened from where he'd been kneeling, administering extreme unction to a dying old woman. His gray-streaked black hair hung damply around his pale face. "Phillipe? Wait, please." He turned. "Luc, get a pail and help your brother. We'll be needing a great deal of water before this night is over."

Luc started to object, to tell Brebeuf that it was Gaudette, the third Sunday of Advent, and they hadn't even changed the altar linen from violet to rose! That he'd been laboring since dawn and needed to rest! But Brebeuf's expression was such that he thought better of it. He gruffly shoved through the crowd and collected a pail. He saw Raimont slip the bale of his bucket over his arm because he hadn't enough fingers to hold it. Luc made his way out the door, Raimont hobbling slowly behind.

The wretched scent of unwashed and festering bodies clung to the air of the plaza. People swarmed around Luc and Phillipe, begging for help and for food. Most of them were starving. Since their villages had been attacked, they'd been living off of bark, rodents and roots. Some just wanted to touch their robes. Luc backed away and turned to Raimont. "You can't keep up with me. I'll meet you at the pond."

"All right, Luc." Phillipe took a step at a time, stopping frequently to pat a child on the head or to soothe one of the sick.

Luc held his breath until he reached the edge of the plaza and felt it safe to inhale. He headed east. The day had been so warm that the snow in the trail had melted, except in heavily shaded areas. The sun had sunk below the horizon. Dusk lay over the woods in a smoky blanket of the deepest lavender.

Luc glanced over his shoulder for Raimont. The path was empty. Raimont had undoubtedly been caught up with the Indians. *Good.* Luc swung his pail carelessly as he walked, thinking about Raimont. The fool had grown so queer and silent that Luc loathed being in his presence. He'd stayed awake most of last night watching Phillipe sitting up in bed staring at nothing, calling "Henri? Henri?" Luc felt certain that Satan had possessed the man's soul.

He crested a hill and plunged down the path toward the heart-shaped pond below. The weak, inverted images of trees spread spidery arms across the mirrorlike surface. A squirrel hunched on the bare branches of a birch, quiet, as unmoving as though a hawk's shadow had just darkened the skies. Curious. No birds twittered, either.

Luc squatted by the pond and shoved his pail into the icy water to let it fill. There was a soft rustling in the woods, but he paid it no attention. He wanted only to get back to the warmth of the mission house.

Luc jerked when Raimont grabbed him by the shoulder with such strength that his fingers bit through Luc's black robe. "Raimont! What are you—"

"Look, Father Luc. It's our Lord." Raimont gazed breathlessly into the forest.

Luc whirled and peered into a dark cluster of firs. Amber eyes glowed in the shadows. They grew into brilliant flames as the cougar stalked forward. The creature moved with such lithe strength that it seemed to float across the patches of snow glittering beneath the trees. It made no sound. *Dear God. Look at the size of it!*

Luc's whole body prickled with fear. He dropped his pail, letting it sink into the pond.

Raimont limped around the edge of the pond toward the beast. The cougar stopped, and its eyes narrowed as though to attack. With a demented smile on his face, Raimont fell to his kness in the dead grass three feet from the animal and clasped his hands in prayer. "Behold, my beloved and good Jesus, I cast myself upon my knees in your sight, and with the fervent desire of my soul, I pray . . ."

Luc swallowed convulsively. Brebeuf's voice whispered from the depths of his mind: *She told me to beware the deceptions of the Serpent.*

Luc started to tremble. *The False Prophet! The evil one, who will mimic the works of Jesus!*

Another sound began, rhythmic, rasping, like the breath of an animal forced to run long beyond its endurance. The sound grew louder, coming closer. *Or was it just his heart? No! It was the thudding of hooves.* Luc caught sight of something dark rushing through the trees.

Terror smothered him.

He screamed and ran.

Hooves slammed on the trail behind him, shaking the frozen ground like an earthquake. Luc raced wildly through the mud. The demon thundered up almost on top of him. Its hot breath ruffled Luc's hair.

A garbled cry of horror caught in his throat. "Help!" he shrieked insanely. "Help me! Father Brebeuf? Please, *anybody!*"

The beast would surely crush him beneath its hooves if he didn't get out of the way. Luc dove headfirst off the path into a tangle of dead vines. The briers scratched his face until blood flooded hotly down his cheeks. He rolled onto his back, looking frantically at the trail. There was nothing there.

Voices rose in the village; people were calling out and running.

"Luc?" Brebeuf yelled. "Luc, where are you?"

"Here! I'm here."

Brebeuf dashed over the hill with a dozen savages behind him. When he spied Luc in the bristly vines, he leaped off the trail, jerked the briers out of the way, then gripped Luc's arm to help him crawl out.

"Are you all right, Luc? What happened?"

"A horse! It chased me. It was as black as night."

"A black horse . . ." Brebeuf's breathing stilled.

Before Luc could say another word, Raimont came ambling up the path, softly singing a hymn to himself. His mad eyes glowed like green moons.

Luc slid backward. "A demon came for him! I think it was the *Antichrist*!"

The savages screamed and began shoving each other in their haste to get away, and Luc turned to see what frightened them so. The cougar bounded up the trail. Luc shrieked. Brebeuf slowly got to his feet and went to stand beside Raimont.

The slate-blue light of dusk shimmered in the lion's fur. It lifted a paw and tilted its head at Brebeuf, who crossed himself. Then the cougar let out a soft, mournful whine and trotted silently into the shadows of the trees.

33

Marc rolled onto his back and rubbed his eyes. He, Andiora, Marleaux and Maconta lay on woven mats around a flickering fire at the north end of Jemos's longhouse. Marc faced the door-curtain. It swayed gently in the silent wind of deep night. Occasionally a flake of snow would penetrate around the hanging and flutter to its death in the hot house. Though it had to be two hours before sunrise, brilliant fires crackled, keeping the chill at bay to ease the torment of the sick. Of the forty-five people in this house, thirty-three moaned feverishly.

They'd been in Arontaen for two days now, and in that time Marc had barely had five hours of sleep. He'd prayed, baptized, used his lancet to puncture veins and bleed away fever, and cared for the souls of the dying. At dusk Andiora had forced him to eat. Without her he would have gone hungry and not even noticed. Andiora spent her time translating for him while they tended the sick. Her voice never lost its gentleness.

Marc had been hovering on the edge of slumber for hours, listening to the soft words Andiora murmured in her troubled sleep. She lay so close that he had only to extend his hand to touch her beautiful face. In the orange gleam of the fire, her black hair had a coppery sheen. Sweat beaded on her small nose. Her voice was so breathy, he could only make out certain phrases: *a baby . . . when? . . . oh, please . . . why me? No. Pierre?*

It made Marc almost ill, hearing the pain in her voice and unable to let himself touch her, to waken her, to comfort her. A part of him wanted to run long and hard, to a time before Father Burel . . .

Andiora shifted in her sleep, pushing her blanket down to her waist. Her red dress glimmered with an amber tinge. Tears had made glistening lines down her cheeks.

Marleaux, who slept across the fire from Marc, roused to look at Andiora, and pity creased his face. He patted her foot. She woke with a tiny sound and rolled over to look at him. His head was propped on his worn boots; his long nose caught the light.

"You were talking in your sleep. Are you all right?" Marleaux whispered.

"I had a Dream . . . odd."

"Well, with the war and the disease, 'tis no wonder you're having nightmares." He paused, then added, "You called out Pierre's name."

"Did I?"

"Aye."

There was a silence, broken only with the crackling of the fires and the soft moans of the sick. Andiora's eyes drifted over the soot-coated ridgepole, and Marleaux fumbled uneasily with the hem of his blanket.

"Pierre says we're to be leaving for England in less than two months and that he's asked you along. Will you be coming?" Marleaux asked.

"No, Tristan." Her voice sounded forlorn.

Marleaux sighed. "I feared you wouldn't. Pierre'll probably hang himself over it. Or worse, he'll drive the crew so mad, they'll hang him in self-defense. He needs you more than he'd ever admit—even to himself."

The door-curtain flapped and a cool flood of air rushed in. A few wayward flakes of snow melted before they struck the floor. Somewhere near the longhouse, a stick cracked, as though a heavy hoof had stepped on it. Marc cocked his head but heard no more sounds. A moose, probably.

"Pierre and I . . ." Andiora said, "well, things have changed between us."

"Are you saying that you don't need him anymore?"

Andiora folded her arms to tuck her fingers into her red sleeves. "He's never *let* me need him. I remember once when Maconta was very sick. I was so worried, I could barely think. Pierre had planned to leave for the trade fair in Quebec, and I asked him to stay with me for another week—just to be close by, maybe to hold me when I got frightened. Do you know what he told me?"

"Something dim-witted, no doubt. 'Tis his way when he goes to thinking he's being caged."

"He told me that a trader from Spain had brought in some bolts of fabric so gold they would 'put the sun to shame.' And he had to be there early or they'd all be gone before he had the chance to buy them. Bolts of cloth were more important to him than me and my fears, Tristan."

"I recall that trip. Three years ago, wasn't it?"

"Yes."

The door-curtain swayed again. Marc heard wind sweep the forest, but for a moment it sounded like a moccasin crunching on snow. He strained his ears. The howls of wolves eddied over the hills.

Marleaux continued "Well, I can tell you this: Pierre worried about you that whole trip. Why, he couldn't talk of nothing but Maconta being sick and you taking care of her. I'd never thought about it before, but guilt must've been eating on him pretty bad."

"But not bad enough to make him stay with me."

"'Tis just his way, Andiora. The man would stand up and die for you—but he can't bear to have anyone depend on him. He looks on each instance as if it were a brick being laid to jail his soul. I'm not defending his peculiar way of thinking, just wishing you could forgive him for it. He loves you as much as a man can."

Andiora rubbed her forearms unhappily. "I've spent much of my life forgiving him for one thing or another, telling myself he didn't mean to hurt me, that he had business to do. Telling myself not to be such a child, wanting him close. I'm tired of hurting, Tristan. I can't—" She bolted up suddenly, her dark eyes wide. "What's that?"

Maconta screamed "Look!" as the roof burst into flame. Fire greedily spread across the creosote-soaked bark.

Muskets thundered as war cries erupted outside. The longhouse seethed with people running to arm themselves. The sick who could walk stumbled to their feet, while the healthy dragged delirious family members from their blankets and prepared to flee.

Andiora threw Marc's musket into his hands. "Get ready!" she ordered as she slipped on her foxhide coat and jerked her pistol and powder horn from her pack. "The Iroquois set fire to the houses at night because it gives them light to shoot by when we have to run. But we won't be able to see them! They'll be hiding in the darkness."

Marc scrambled to his feet, shrugged on his pack and tied his blanket around his waist. As the flames grew to a deafening roar, thick smoke billowed down the length of the house. "Where can we run to?"

Andiora shook her head. "I . . . I don't know. Into the forest."

All around them, people shoved and cried like scared animals, everyone afraid to be the first through the end doors.

"Follow me!" Marleaux yelled. He grabbed a hand ax and ran to the middle of the longhouse, where he began chopping a third exit. Marc slung his musket over his shoulder and went to help, kicking out sections of wall as Marleaux weakened them. People, well and sick, crowded around them. Children shrieked, while the ill watched with panic in their glazed eyes. By the time they'd hacked a large enough hole, the heat of the flames was suffocating.

"Hurry! Run! Go on!" Marc shouted to the screaming horde.

As the people rushed the exit, Marc and Marleaux were shoved against the wall, then swept outside in the flood. Marc stumbled out of the torrent and stood watching for Andiora and Maconta in the continuing stream of people. The eerie orange glow bleached the life from their horrified faces as they raced for the trees.

A segment of roof wrenched free of the ridgepole and swung downward like a blazing fist to bash the floor. An explosion of flame and dust gushed into the forest.

"Andiora?" Marc shouted. He lunged toward the opening in the fiery inferno.

"*Marc?*" Andiora screamed. "Marc!"

The musket blasts seemed to come from nowhere, from everywhere at once. Screams filled the world, screams and the roaring fire and the shrieks of people still inside the flaming house. He saw Lopos go down, a wound in her stomach. Marleaux whirled and fired his musket into an oncoming wave of Iroquois warriors, then fell backward, grabbing at his right leg.

Marc ducked through the opening and met a blinding wall of smoke. "Andiora! Where are you?"

"Here!"

He fell to the floor on his stomach and scrambled toward the sound of her voice. He found her huddling at the edge of the fallen roof. "This way!" he shouted as he reached out and grabbed the sleeve of her coat, brutally dragging her away. "Get on your stomach!"

"No, no, Marc! Maconta is trapped!" She jerked free of his grip. "Help me get this off of her!"

Through the smoke, he saw the old woman. She was lying on her back, her left side pinned beneath the debris. Already her gray hair had singed. Marc gripped the edge of the heavy slab of bark and shoved with all his strength while Andiora tugged Maconta free. Then they crawled for the door.

"Hurry!" Maconta kept saying. "Hurry, hurry, hurry."

They emerged into chaos. People fled by them, some of them wounded, some dragging children by the hand. A musket ball exploded to Marc's right, kicking snow and dirt into his face.

"Run!" he ordered as a hail of arrows *thwonged* against the wall at his back, followed by more gunfire.

Andiora shrieked, "No!" and Marc spun to see Maconta sprawled on the ground, the hole in her chest draining blood onto the firelit snow.

"Leave . . . me," Maconta whispered.

"I'll *never* leave you!" Andiora gripped Maconta by the arm and struggled to drag her to the darkness of the woods.

Two men sprinted from the shadows, yelling war cries. Marc aimed his musket and fired. The flash of powder half-blinded him, but he saw the lead warrior stagger. Marc was turning toward the other man before the first even toppled to the ground. He swung his empty gun like a club, smashing the man across the temple and sending him sliding through the snow. Then he sprinted after Andiora.

She knelt beneath the spreading limbs of an oak, looking down on Maconta. The old woman's dead eyes stared back, her mouth agape.

Barely breaking stride, Marc took Andiora's hand in a hard grip and pulled her to her feet. "This way. We have to go, *now*!"

The pungent scents of blood and shredded intestines rode the wind as they ran.

BY DAWN, A broad patch of clear sky had appeared in the clouds. Andiora followed behind Marc as he led the way along a game trail just below the crest of a snowy ridge. To the west, Lake Karegnondi shimmered cold and blue. Behind them, hills humped like dark turtles.

Andiora stopped near a boulder and braced a hand against it to catch her breath. Marc turned. His eyes scanned the lightening world. "Do you have to stop? They might be tracking us."

"I just need a moment."

Behind them, the haze of smoke rising from Arontaen billowed like the storm clouds themselves. But through the haze, the moon shone full and bright. Now, as the sun edged above the horizon, spikes of gaudy light pierced the smoky veil, and the higher the sun rose, the redder the moon turned, until it seemed glutted with blood.

Marc leaned back against the boulder, his eyes glued to the moon. "No, it can't . . . can't be."

She frowned at him. "What's wrong?"

"Andiora, wh-what's today? Isn't it Christmas?"

"I don't know."

In a deep, frightened voice, he said, "'And the moon became like blood.'"

"It's just the light through the smoke, Marc. I've seen it before, during forest fires."

He swallowed and pulled his eyes away to look at her. "Perhaps, but . . ." He paused. "Would you let me baptize you?"

"Why?"

"*Please.*" He straightened and took a step toward her. "Please. Do this for me?"

"But, Marc, I believe in Aataentsic and Iouskeha and my Spirit Guardian, Cougar."

"But can't you believe in Jesus, too? Just have faith that my Lord is also your Savior. He *is*, Andiora. I promise you."

The pleading in his blue eyes touched her. She longed to bury her face in the folds of his robe and weep in confusion, as she had on that night after Jatoya's death. But she only lowered her eyes.

Below, the small ponds that dotted the land glistened like drops of tears. What difference did it make if she called Iouskeha by the name "Jesus"? She'd been thinking about converting for several weeks . . . since the blood from Cougar's paws had run warm in her hair. Jatoya had converted, and Onrea said that she was going to. That meant that most of Andiora's family would not be going to the Village of Souls anyway. She didn't want to be separated from them.

"Will you be in heaven, Marc?" she asked.

"Yes. I—I think so."

Andiora nodded. "Baptize me, then. I will learn your ways."

He briefly closed his eyes and crossed himself, then softly murmured a prayer in Latin. When he had finished, a glow had entered his eyes. "Come," he said. "We need water."

He walked down the trail and Andiora followed. At the base of the ridge, a series of small caves pocked the stone. Andiora studied them as Marc tramped out across the snow to the closest pond. He used his boot to bash a hole in the ice, then knelt and extended a hand to her. "Sit beside me. Let me open the door to heaven for you."

Andiora walked up to him and crouched. He took her hand. The feel of his large fingers entwined with hers was soothing.

"This will feel strange, but it's the Water of Life. I'm going to tip you backward. Don't be afraid." Marc gently turned her around and slid his strong arm beneath her shoulders. "Lean against my arm. Let your head fall."

She did as he told her, and he lowered her toward the pond. Dipping his fingers beneath the surface, he poured a handful of water over her forehead and let it trickle through her black hair. It was so cold that it stung. In a startlingly beautiful voice, he said, "I baptize you in the name of the Father, and of the Son, and of the Holy Spirit." The moon seemed to grow even redder, turning a dark maroon.

Marc lifted her and hugged her tightly against his breast. "Thank you, Andiora. Now I know that if the End is here, you'll be safe."

"Safe?" She blinked back tears. Maconta's dead eyes stared out at her from the depths of her soul. The stench of smoke and blood still clung to the back of her throat. "We'll never be safe, Marc. Not ever again." She pushed out of his arms and stood, her knees shaky. "We—we must find shelter. Now that it's light, the Iroquois will be looking for us."

She trudged back through the snow toward the caves. She had to get down and crawl through the largest opening, but once inside, she could tell that the cave spread at least ten feet in front of her. She put her hand over her head. The ceiling was low, maybe five feet high. Crawling to the back, she sat down near a pack-rat midden of sticks and dead pine boughs. The musty scents of rat droppings and mildew filled the air.

Marc's form darkened the entrance as he crawled inside. He hesitated, frowning at the darkness. "Andiora?"

"I'm here. In the back."

He unslung his musket and pack and braced them against the wall, then untied the blanket from around his waist, before he carefully crawled across the floor. His leg touched hers as he sat down beside her and draped the blanket over her shoulders. In the dimness, his blond hair gleamed like moonlit snow. Why had he sat so close? Didn't he realize what it did to her? Her confusion and despair magnified a thousandfold. She began to tremble.

Several moments passed before Marc moved. But when he did, he slipped an arm around her shoulders and gently drew her against him. His blond beard tangled in her hair. "What is it?"

"I'm frightened, Marc. Everything I love is dying. My family, my people . . . everything."

Softly, he said, "And maybe even the world."

She looked up at him dumbly, like a wounded animal too exhausted to move away from the hunter on its track. Tears welled in her eyes. She murmured, "I don't want the world to die."

Marc touched her wet hair, and it seemed that neither of them breathed. The calls of ducks on the ponds came to her through the cave entrance. Marc sat so still that the crucifix around his throat caught and held the light like a wet shell.

Suddenly she tipped her face up and pressed her lips to his. He didn't pull away. Her fears faded. If only for this moment, she forgot about the Iroquois, the disease, and Maconta's eyes. After several seconds, Marc kissed her back, gently at first, then strongly. His arms tightened powerfully around her.

A warm dizziness swept her. She leaned backward, pulling him to the floor with her, and they lay facing each other, the hard muscles of his thighs pressing against her. Marc touched her face and throat, and his hand traveled lower, to the collar of her coat.

Andiora opened the coat and slipped her arms out of the sleeves, leaving it beneath her to buffer the cold stone. Then she smoothed her fingers down his chest . . . and every muscle in his body tensed.

"Marc—"

"No, don't say anything. *Nothing.*"

He kissed her so desperately that a fire built in her veins. When he rolled on top of her, Andiora opened herself to him.

And he stopped suddenly, tearing his mouth from hers to stare down in terror. He tried to speak, but no words came.

Then, in a bare whisper, he said, "Oh, God. Forgive me."

CHAPTER

34

Pierre slumped back against the bench and watched a half-dozen people file into Andiora's longhouse, joining the twenty already present. He took a long drink from his brandy flask. He was already plenty drunk, and planned to be drunker still before the night was through. Snow fell so heavily that it penetrated the smoke holes in the roof, rushing inside to sparkle like a shower of crushed diamonds before melting in the rising heat. The sick had been moved from the northern longhouses and the Jesuit mission to two houses at the southern edge of Ihonatiria. With two-thirds of the village dead, many houses now sat empty.

"Looks to be a big gathering," Tristan whispered. He sat beside Pierre with his broken right leg extended out in front of him. His brown deerhide shirt had smudges of soot across the front. He'd cut his hair, which accentuated the thinness of his face and the length of his nose. "And not a Christian among them."

"Tehoren's got the whole lot scared silly, what with his talk of witches and spells."

Tristan rubbed his leg and nodded. "Aye." The bone had begun to heal, despite the fact that he'd hobbled on it for twelve days after the attack on Arontaen, managing somehow to return to Ihonatiria in the blizzard.

One of the worst storms I've ever witnessed in the New World. 'Tis as though Iouskeha's trying to keep me here so I can't go searching for Andiora.

Pierre listened morosely to Tehoren's lecture on *okis*. The little pug-nosed shaman paced angrily at the far end of the longhouse, talking to a rapt audience. His white, heavily beaded shirt glittered as he moved.

Pierre took another sip of brandy, trying to drive out the despair and guilt that tortured him. Refugees from destroyed villages had been flooding in for days—but not Andiora, not Dupre. Before Tristan had left Arontaen, he'd found old Maconta's body, torn and mutilated. And he'd searched diligently for Andiora, but without success. He'd last seen her inside the flaming longhouse.

Pierre stroked the brass image of a sailing ship that embossed his flask. More than likely one of the charred corpses Tristan had seen had been hers.

His fingers tightened around the flask.

Why didn't you go with her? If you'd been there, you might have been able to save her.

Andiora's things surrounded him. Her neatly folded blankets lay atop the bench; beneath it, a beautifully carved cherrywood box could be seen, filled with jewelry and trinkets: Delft thimbles, and silk handkerchiefs from China. He knew, for he'd brought them to her over the years. *Aye, a fine set of pretty apologies.* They'd been his way of saying "Forgive me, darlin', for never letting you get too close to me. But you know I have to have me freedom."

Tehoren shouted, "Before Sebi died, he told me his illness was caused by Christian witchcraft." Tehoren reached into his pocket and pulled out a lead pellet. "He vomited this up three days ago."

Frightened gasps sounded. People fumbled anxiously with magical objects, calling on their Spirit Guardians for protection. Tehoren turned the pellet over and over. "The only people in Ihonatiria who own such bullets are the Black Robes. They rub their charms with the skin of their serpent, Satan, and then shoot them into people's bodies to kill them."

Tristan's gray eyes narrowed and his mouth opened. Before he could speak, Pierre kicked him. "'Tis not our battle."

"But, Pierre, we can't sit by and let Tehoren spout such nonsense. You know what they'll do to the priests if they judge them guilty of witchcraft!"

Pierre took another swallow of brandy. His head had started to feel pleasantly light. "I do." The Huron believed there were three types of illness. One, caused by natural things, could be cured with roots, herbs and poultices. Another was caused by unfulfilled desires of the soul. The last came from witchcraft. "But they'll be trying to scare the priests into stopping their sorcery first."

"Aye. Sure. Then, if the sickness doesn't end, they'll kill them!"

Tehoren raised his voice until it echoed down the longhouse. "Who wants to speak?"

Enda leaned forward to rub his hands over the fire. His short black braids glistened. He had a crooked nose and tiny porcine eyes. "I'm convinced it's *Huron* witchcraft. You all knew Aouandoie. Remember how rich he was? Just before the dying started, he packed everything he owned and left Ihonatiria, moving to Arente. I think we should make him come back and answer some questions. Like why he was scared to death to stay here. He might be our witch."

One by one, people elbowed each other and pointed at Tonner, who sat on the bench behind Tehoren smoking a long pipe. A wreath of blue tobacco smoke swirled around his malformed face.

"What is it, Tonner?" Tehoren asked reverently.

The elderly dwarf gestured with his pipe. "Last week an Arendar-honon brave came back from the dead. He said he met two women from England in the other world. These women told him that the Christians were evil. That they would not go home until every Huron had died."

Firelight limned the taut faces, shadowing hollow cheeks and dark, frightened eyes.

Gewona lifted a hand and waved, trying to get Tehoren's attention. No one looked her way. Pierre smirked. She'd come over from Ossossane a few days ago and had been doing nothing but causing trouble ever since. Gewona cleared her throat.

Enda ignored her and fixed Tonner with a harsh look. "I say it is our own people. Why would the Christians want to kill us?"

Tonner lifted a shoulder. "Maybe it's Champlain's death. The Algonkin say that just before Champlain died last year, he told a Montagnais headman that if he died, he would carry off the Huron with him."

"Foolishness," Enda pronounced. "Champlain liked us."

"The Nipissing," little Achio from Contarea interjected, "think it is that other Frenchman we killed, Brule. They robbed him of over two thousand wampum beads once. They think that the French are punishing all of us for it. They are going to give that many beads back to the priests if they'll take away the disease."

"They already tried that," Tonner said. "The priests would not accept them."

Tehoren's brows lowered. "Brebeuf would never accept them because he doesn't want to stop murdering us. He wants us all dead."

Enda shrugged. "Well, if Brebeuf is the witch, we have to know how he is killing our people before we can stop him. Tonner, do you think Tehoren is right about the snakeskin and the charms?"

"It may also be their baptism," Tonner said. "We have all seen it. They wash people's faces with water and they die."

"It is the book!" Gewona yelled, lifting a hand again to draw attention to herself.

Tonner turned toward her. "What book?"

She said eagerly, "Penchant has it. Just before Brebeuf called his demon in Ossossane, Penchant took out his book. I think that demon, that Mother Mary, brings the sickness, and Penchant keeps her locked in his book."

Marleaux's eyes widened in outrage. He struggled to get to his feet, and Pierre put a hard hand on his shoulder to keep him down. Harshly, he whispered, "Leave it be."

Marleaux cursed under his breath.

"Listen!" Tehoren shouted. "Nearly every story blames the Christians for this sickness. Remember Andiora's Dream of the blond man with the holes in his hands? I think that little bald priest may be the one! He might have had blond hair once. And you have all heard Onrea talk about the *oki* in the form of a bird that came to Raimont's call in the Iroquois longhouse!"

The hushed murmuring rose to a din. Tehoren lifted his arms high. "If I were the headman of this village, I would slay every Black Robe. *Then* the disease would stop!"

Pierre couldn't help it. He laughed out loud at Tehoren's suggestion. People swung around. Hot eyes pinned him. Tristan stiffened, and Pierre saw his hand drop surreptitiously to his holstered pistol.

Tehoren yelled, "What are you laughing at, Mongrave?"

"*You.*" Pierre raised his voice for all to hear. "I'll tell you the truth, and you'd best listen. Touch one hair on the priests' heads and you will all *certainly* die."

"What do you mean?" Tonner demanded.

"When Governor Montmagny hears that you've slit a Jesuit's throat, he'll stop all trade with the Huron. And if you're unable to trade for just two years—two!—why, you'll be lucky to beg enough food from the Algonkin to stay alive."

"Traitor!" Tehoren spat angrily, and Pierre's blood started to rush. "You pretend to be our friend, but you just want to protect the priests to enrich yourself! You don't care how many of our people die so long as you keep getting more of our furs!"

Warriors began to glance boldly at their sheathed knives.

Tristan whispered, "Thought you said 'twasn't our battle?"

Pierre grunted and got to his feet. "And I think, Tehoren, that Brebeuf has shamed you so often that you've a personal grudge against him. Eh? Maybe you'd see him dead even if it meant all of the Huron would starve."

Tehoren started forward, hatred in his eyes, but Jix caught him around the waist and swung him about. "Not now," Jix ordered gruffly.

Pierre glowered at the villagers and murmured, "I'm heading out, Tristan. You coming with me?"

"Aye, of course. What sort of fool do you take me for?"

Pierre threw a final challenging look at Tehoren, grabbed his brown cape from the bench and flung it around his shoulders. The entire longhouse watched as he and Tristan ducked beneath the door-curtain into the storm.

Snow fell around them in thick, icy veils. Pierre could barely make out the shape of the Jesuit mission across the plaza. A dull orange glow poured from the windows.

"I'm going out to the tent camp," Tristan said. "Being around men with muskets will make me feel a sight safer tonight."

"I'll be there soon enough," Pierre said as he watched Tristan disappear into the haze of white.

* * *

JEAN LAY IN bed staring at the soot-stained ceiling. The fire near the table flickered feebly, throwing a pale yellow glow across the common room. Luc snored in his bed, and on the other side of him, Phillipe slept soundly. Jean had been trying to talk to God, but no one in heaven seemed to be listening. He reached out with his soul . . . and met only emptiness. *Emptiness, emptiness, all is emptiness . . .*

"What have I done, Lord, that You won't talk to me?" he muttered.

He pulled his blanket up over his chest and fumbled with the collar of his white nightshirt. Something deep in his soul had started to ache, like a dagger wound in the heat of battle. His soul seemed to be bleeding away . . . vanishing into a dark pit that he didn't understand.

But he knew that it had to do with Marc.

A small part of Jean had died when he'd learned of the attack on Arontaen. He felt almost certain that Marc had been killed.

In the two weeks since the news had come, Jean had tended the sick and tried to find time to sort through all the biblical passages that discussed demons and angels—lions and birds. He raised his head to look at Phillipe. His round face had an angelic serenity even in sleep. The little Brother had curled onto his side to free his bandaged feet from his gray blanket; they hung over the edge of the bed.

What is the nature of the cougar, Lord? A demon? Perhaps even the Antichrist, as Luc thinks? Or have You sent us an angelic messenger in a form strange to us, but perfectly normal for our Indian converts?

Jean shook his head wearily. Snow scalloped the edges of the windows. Outside, boots squealed on snow, and the mission door opened very quietly.

Jean sat up in bed. *Oh, Lord, let it be Marc.*

But Pierre walked into the common room, his brown cape glimmering with snow. His bushy beard and shoulder-length hair blended with the darkness.

"What's wrong, Pierre?" Jean whispered, trying not to wake Luc or Phillipe.

Pierre brushed off his cloak, picked up a chair and carried it over to set it next to Jean's bed. He sank down clumsily, then pulled a flask from his boot. "You're in a sight of trouble, Jean."

"Why?"

"I was over listening to Tehoren's tirade 'bout witches and such . . . ."

He paused to drink from his flask and scowled when Luc sucked in a soft breath. Though he continued to feign sleep, Luc's shoulder muscles bulged beneath his nightshirt. "Sebi's dead, and folks are pointing the finger at you and yours, speaking of how powerful your sorcery is. You've got to march over there and tell 'em they're fools."

Jean sighed. "I've told them that until my throat is raw, Pierre."

"Those people are passing judgment on your life right now. Don't you want to have some say in the final decision?"

"Pierre, you know as well as I that once they've made up their minds—"

"You're *going*," Pierre said with polite brutality. "You'll go if I have to drag you every step of the way by your crucifix."

In the soft light, a bleary glitter shone in Pierre's eyes. He leaned close to Jean's face. "You know what's wrong with you, Brebeuf?"

"I don't suppose I can escape having you tell me."

"You're not priestly material." Pierre swayed as he sat back. "I mean, look at you."

Jean folded his hands over his stomach. "Be specific, Pierre."

"'Tis obvious as the nose on me face. Good God, Jean, you're a son of Norman aristocracy, weak-spirited and tenderhearted to a fault. You've got no business out here trying to save souls. Go home. Go home and do something you're fit for, like ruling peasants and sleeping late." Pierre gave him a sidelong look. "If you stay, you'll regret it. Before this is through, Jean, they'll murder you . . . if for no reason other than your annoying persistence, preaching Jesus-this and Jesus-that."

"If God chooses martyrdom for me, then I will have died well, Pierre."

Pierre scowled. "You're a bigger fool than I thought. . . . And now get up. It's time we—"

"I'm not going, Pierre. There's no point in repeating myself for the thousandth time. Especially not with Tehoren."

Pierre rose, picked up Jean's robe from the foot of his bed and threw it at him. "Get dressed. I'll escort you."

Jean caught the garment. "Why are you so adamant about this? I don't understand—"

Pierre ruthlessly grabbed him by the arm and jerked him out of his blankets. Jean stood in his white nightshirt, getting a little angry.

When Pierre saw the hot glint in Jean's eyes, he grinned. "Aye, 'tis adamant I am. 'Cause if you don't go now, you'll never have another chance to save yourself and the Huron missions. If you can just get two elders on your side—"

"I thought you told me to go home and sleep late. When did you start caring about the Huron missions?"

Pierre staggered sideways. "'Tis a good question, and one I'd not be asking again if I were you, not until we're through with this. I might come to me senses."

Jean combed his disheveled hair with his fingers. "All right. Let's hurry and get it over with." He slipped his robe on over his nightshirt.

In the dark plaza, night-scented winds brushed them, flapping their sleeves. Faint moonlight silvered the edges of the clouds. Perhaps the storm was finally breaking?

"Now think, Jean," Pierre warned. "If you go in acting as righteous and stubborn as you usually do, they're liable to kill you on the spot."

"Since when did I need your advice?"

"All along, I suspect. But I had the wits not to offer it before."

They stopped outside the longhouse door and Pierre tipped up his flask, draining it and wiping his mouth on his sleeve. Then his hard black eyes fixed on Jean. "Ready?"

"Of course." Jean stepped for the door, but Pierre's hand stopped him, pressing firmly against his chest.

"Remember, sorcerers fear death."

"I'm familiar with their religion, Pierre. Thank you." Jean pulled the hanging aside and stepped into the longhouse. Mongrave followed on his heels.

Over twenty people sat around the fires. Murmurs broke out at the sight of the two. Pierre peered around and demanded, "Where are Achio and Enda?"

"Gone," Tehoren responded coldly. He stood small and rigid before the largest fire, his eyes narrowed. His beaded shirt glittered like a bed of emeralds and rubies.

Pierre leaned sideways to whisper, "They were the only ones who were grantin' you might not be the witch responsible for the sickness."

Jean's stomach muscles tightened. It was the Huron way. His defenders had been asked to leave, so that the decision might be unanimous.

Jean walked toward Tehoren. People moved back, as far away from him as they could. Tonner sat on the bench behind Tehoren. The little dwarf was the most powerful shaman in the Huron confederacy. If Jean could gain a stay of execution from Tonner, he . . . Tonner's face contorted at Jean's look. He made a magical sign of protection in the air before him, then covered his face with his hands.

Jean glanced back at Tehoren. "There are rumors that you think we Christians are responsible for this terrible disease. I've come to tell you that that is a lie. None of us would lift a hand against a Huron. We've . . ."

His voice dried up. One by one, people bowed their heads, *judging him*. Some stared into the fire, others at the floor. Futility swept Jean. What would his sentence be? Death? Probably.

"Damn you, Tehoren!" Pierre shouted. "He's come to tell you the truth!"

Tehoren glared defiantly.

"My Brothers and I are innocent," Jean said.

Still, no one met his eyes.

"My friends," Jean said amiably, "in four days, at dawn, I will give an *athatoaion*, a Death Feast. Everyone in the village is invited."

Pierre looked as stunned as if the devil had just appeared out of a ball of fire and demanded his soul. When understanding dawned, his face twisted into begrudging admiration. The announcement would force Jean's accusers to either carry out their "sentence" or drop the charges. And giving a Death Feast would convince some that he did not fear death as a sorcerer would.

"Good night," Jean said. He exited into the snow again. A sliver of moon glowed in the sky. He gazed at it longingly. If Marc and Andiora had taken shelter somewhere, they might come home now. He crossed himself and offered a silent prayer.

Feet pounded behind, running to catch up with him. Pierre said, "So you threw down the gauntlet. 'Twas brave of you."

"Brave?" Jean scoffed. "Hardly. I was desperate."

"Brave acts are always the bastard children of desperation."

"Well, please keep that to yourself when people are eulogizing me at my funeral."

"I don't think you're going to die. Not yet, anyway. But if it turns out I'm wrong, I think I'll give one of the grave-side speeches. I can lie as well as anyone in your church. In fact—"

"I know that, Pierre. I've known you for years, after all." Jean opened the mission door and stepped into the storage room. The scent of hickory rose strongly from the woodpile. "You know, I've never been certain that I actually like you, Pierre."

"Good. It would worry me if you were."

"By the way, do you have a place to sleep? You made a good number of enemies tonight. You're welcome to stay here if you or your men need to."

Pierre slumped against the door frame and frowned. He stood silently for a moment, then heaved a ragged sigh. "We'll be fine. But . . . I've a favor to ask you, Jean."

"What is it?"

The crow's feet around Pierre's black eyes drew together. He stammered, "Could—could you pray for Andiora for me? I'm . . . not so good at it." Then he turned and careened out into the snow, as though embarrassed that he'd asked.

Jean called, "I've been praying for her all along, Pierre."

He started to close the mission door, but a trail in the snow caught his eye. He stepped out to get a better look; the prints were deep, and narrower than a man's gait. As he knelt to examine them, a prickle went up his spine. His gaze darted through the trees around the longhouses.

Cougar tracks.

The animal had stalked up and down this side of the mission, like a beast in a cage waiting for someone, anyone, to open the door a slit, waiting to pounce.

Jean stared at the long mission wall. Through the windows, he saw candlelight and a small shadow moving over the ceiling.

And he wondered how long Phillipe had been up.

*   *   *

MARC WALKED OUT of the forest, his arms loaded with wood, and paused in a shaft of bright sunlight. It felt blessedly warm on his face, too warm for January. Clouds fringed the sky, but a broad halo of turquoise encircled the sun. Snow had started to melt from the trees and softly pattered to the ground. Across the rolling hills, the blanket of white glimmered and sparkled.

Silence had possessed the world. Not a breath of wind stirred Andiora's hair where she knelt by the pond in front of their cave. In the flight from Arontaen, she had forgotten her pack. Marc had loaned her one of his robes to wear while she washed and dried her red dress. She'd rolled up the sleeves and knotted the long hem to shorten it to the right length. Her eyes were closed. She'd tipped her heart-shaped face to the sunshine, letting the glory of the day pour life into her body. The image of her sitting there, so slender, so beautiful, made his heart ache with longing.

Snow crunched as Marc started across the meadow toward her. Above him, birds sailed on the air currents, their caws melodic in the stillness.

"Andiora?"

She took a deep breath, then opened her eyes and smiled at him. When she rose, Marc laid his wood into the furrow of the packed trail and walked to meet her. As easily as if they'd been lovers for years, not mere weeks, she slipped into his arms. He held her tightly.

"I was talking to the Pond Spirit," she said, "asking him to send fish into the net we made yesterday."

Marc stroked the silken web of hair that fell down her back. A squirrel boldly ran across the rock outcrop above their cave, knocking off clumps of snow that shimmered like wreaths of gold dust as they fell. "Did you catch any?"

"I haven't checked it yet. Want to help me pull it in?"

"Yes."

She took his hand and they walked back to the edge of the pond where she had staked the edges of the net on the ice. The rest of the net she had tucked into the cold water through a hole in the ice.

"You take one side of the net and I'll take the other," she instructed. "But we have to pull it up fast."

Marc slipped the right-hand edge over the stakes and twined his fingers into the cottonwood-bark mesh. "You tell me when."

Andiora nodded absently as she took her side of the net and peered down through the hole in the ice, as though searching for dark, gliding shapes. Her graceful brows had drawn together in concentration.

A smile curled Marc's lips. He'd discovered that Andiora was an expert hunter. She could throw a rock as accurately as he could aim a musket. Many a grouse had fallen to her wiles. She'd shown him how to strip the stringy inner bark from cottonwoods and pines, then weave it into nets, or make braids for snares. They'd been afraid to use their guns for hunting, fearing that enemy warriors would hear the sound and find them. But they'd never gone hungry. The forest abounded with small game. Chipmunks, rabbits, pack-rats, fowl, squirrels and fish provided them with a daily banquet.

She whispered, "Are you ready, Marc?"

He nodded and waited for her signal. When she said "Now!" they jerked the net and hauled three flopping fish out onto the ice.

"Oh, quick! Catch them before they get back into the water!" Andiora yelled as she threw the net over the two closest and dragged them onto land.

Marc tried to grab the last fish, but it slipped out of his hands and shot away across the ice.

"I can't go out there. I don't know how thick it is," he protested.

"Try using a branch to get it to shore!"

Marc ran to get one of the branches from the wood he'd gathered, but by the time he returned, the fish had managed to flop its way across the ice and slither through the hole.

"Sorry," he said sheepishly.

Andiora laughed at the dejected look on his face. "It's all right. Two will be enough. I'll clean these if you'll start a fire in the cave."

"That I can do." Marc shrugged and went to gather up his armload of wood.

The bed of coals from their morning fire still glowed faintly. He dropped his wood in the corner and pulled twigs from the pack rat's nest in the back of the cave. When he laid these in the center of the coals and blew on them, they flared and crackled. He added larger twigs and, finally, branches. By the time Andiora crawled through the entry with the fish, the fire was blazing warmly. Orange flickers danced across the ceiling, lighting up his blanket and Andiora's foxhide coat atop it against the rear wall.

They skewered their fish on long sticks, which they propped over the flames to roast. Then Andiora slipped her arm around his waist and leaned her head against his shoulder. Strands of her hair fell over the front of his robe. Marc traced the smooth line of her cheek with his fingers. Her skin was as soft as an infant's. He felt oddly as though his soul *remembered* that softness from a time long before birth. Perhaps the eiderdown of angels' wings felt like this . . .

Dear God, even if You damn me for all eternity, I wouldn't give up the joy of the past four weeks.

Through the cave entrance, he watched the snow resume its lazy dance. Another brief flurry. They'd had one after another all morning. The flakes glittered in the sunlight.

"Marc." Andiora turned their skewered fish so they'd cook on the other side. "I've been wondering about something."

"What is it?"

"You told me that the world is going to end. But I don't understand why. Why would Jehovah destroy such a beautiful place?"

"Because He's angry at man's wickedness. And His wrath cannot be stemmed. When the last martyr—the last innocent person—dies, the Lion of God will break open the sixth seal. The sun will turn black. And a child will be born who will rule over the world."

"But there are many good things in the world, too." She tipped her chin to kiss him tenderly. "I don't want the world to end."

"I don't either, Andiora. But it's God's decision. Only He knows the appointed time."

She tilted her head and blinked at the fire. Quietly she said, "The storm has broken."

"I know."

"It . . . it could be the end of the world . . . for us. Couldn't it? Do you want to go home?"

A cold pain entered Marc's heart. "No."

"Marc, I have relatives in the Montagnais villages. We could go there. They would accept us, and then we could—"

"Andiora, please," he whispered. "Not now. Let's not discuss it yet. Give me a few more days."

He thought of Jean. What would he tell him? The very question made Marc's breathing go shallow with sick dread.

Andiora shifted to look up at him. In the fireglow, her beautiful face looked as wistful and delicate as a Renaissance madonna's. The warmth in her eyes filled a hole in his soul that he'd thought would remain empty forever. He felt truly happy for the first time since Marie's death.

"Marc, if we did go back to Ihonatiria, no one need ever know about us. We could keep seeing each other secretly, and you could keep on being a priest. Jean doesn't have to—"

"No." He let out a bitter breath. "I couldn't do that."

Andiora brushed her hair behind one ear and peered unblinking into the flames.

God might forgive him for a lapse into carnal lust, but his love for Andiora would be there always, tempting him away from prayer. And he could no more force her into such a charade than he could himself.

Yet . . .

If he continued to love Andiora, every day he would betray his vows and his Savior. With every tender look she gave him, every intimate touch, the hair shirt of shame would chafe him. It would take a miracle of divine grace to cleanse that guilt away.

Could he survive the guilt—and not blame Andiora? Was he strong enough?

An insidious voice whispered: *Why don't you just forget the past month? You could go back to your priestly duties. Confess your sins, do penance, and Jean will allow it. Of course he will. You could even request reassignment to another village. That way, you'll never have to see her again.*

Marc crushed Andiora to his chest in a grip that must have hurt her. His arms had begun to tremble. "I love you, Andiora. Please, I don't want to think about it yet. Let's stay here for a few more days. Then we'll decide."

CHAPTER

35

And when the soul is indeed assailed by this Divine light, its pain, which results from its impurity, is immense; because, when this pure light assails the soul, in order to expel its impurity, the soul feels itself to be so impure and miserable that it believes God to be against it, and thinks that it has set itself up against God. This causes it so much grief and pain (because it now believes that God has cast it away) that one of the greatest trials which Job felt when God sent him this experience, was as follows, when he said: Why have you set me against you, so that I am grievous and burdensome to myself?

ST. JOHN OF THE CROSS
Dark Night of the Soul, II, V, 5.

Andiora slipped her foxhide coat on over her red dress and glanced at Marc. He'd awakened remote, quiet. He went about putting his pack together like an angry sleepwalker, hastily stuffing things in, jerking the straps tight, muttering crossly when something wouldn't fit just right.

Andiora knelt near the entry of the cave, waiting for him. She'd washed and braided her hair, and it gleamed in the sunlight that filtered in. Cool puffs of wind scattered the ashes from their morning fire, playing with the charred fishbones they'd thrown there after breakfast.

A strange, haunted light had entered Marc's eyes—as though he expected his God to rise up and strike him dead at any moment.

Would Jehovah do that to him? For loving her? What kind of God was He? Wrathful, Marc had said, and loving. She thought that perhaps He was more of the former than the latter. Wasn't Jesus more forgiving? Like Iouskeha? Wouldn't Jesus plead for Marc before Jehovah?

Marc lifted his eyes to her, and Andiora ached for him. Pain and longing stirred in those blue depths.

"May I help you do something, Marc?"

He shook his head. "No. Thank you. We should be leaving if we're going to make it back by nightfall." He slung his pack over his broad shoulders and crawled outside.

Andiora followed him. They stood in the warm sunlight, listening to the hissing and creaking of snow melting around them. Spears of fir and spruce had emerged from the white blanket that covered the hills. The pungent scents of soaked willow and chestnut caressed her face.

"Let me lead, Marc," she said. "I don't think we should take the main trails back. It will take us a little longer, but we'll be safer if we follow the animal trails."

He gestured for her to go in front of him, and when she passed, he gripped her arm and looked down at her with love and sorrow in his eyes.

She'd seen that look before . . . every time Pierre told her he was going away. It tore her heart.

"You know I love you," Marc said.

"Yes. I know."

She managed to smile at him. He touched her cheek gently.

They walked in silence for about an hour, until they entered a thick stand of birches and oaks, where the twining branches created a dense canopy over their heads. Cool shadows cloaked them.

Andiora gathered her courage. "Marc, could we talk about the last few weeks?"

His steps faltered. "Yes," he answered softly.

Andiora grabbed a branch to steady herself as she went around a curve in the frozen path. "What we did—loving each other—it's wrong in the eyes of your church, isn't it?"

"Yes."

"I don't understand this part of your . . . our . . . religion. Who says it's bad?"

"Saint Paul maintained that we should hold ourselves aloof from all that might interrupt our prayer. He told us above all to avoid marriage, not because it was condemned in and of itself, but because it was an obstacle to the perfect continuity of the Christian life. Paul wrote: 'He who is unmarried is concerned with God's claim, asking how he is to please God; whereas the married man is concerned with the world's claim, asking how he is to please his wife; and thus he is at issue with himself.'"

"I would never interrupt your prayer, Marc." She edged down a slick slope and passed a clump of willow iced in silver. As she went by an upthrust rock, she looked back at Marc. He had an agonized expression on his handsome face.

"You already have," he replied faintly. "Paul said that the very essence of an intimate relationship between a man and a woman was against prayer, because it necessitated the loss of personal liberty. The man could not belong to himself, nor the woman to herself. They belonged to each other. 'Let every man give his wife what is her due, and every woman do the same by her husband; he, not she, claims the right over her body, as she, not he, claims the right over his.' My church has for centuries held that it is the duty of a priest not to turn over such rights to anyone. I must be free to pray always." Red crept into his cheeks. "I've begun to think about you far more than I do about God, Andiora."

She tilted her head apologetically, for she understood that it pained him that he loved her, that he believed it would be better if he didn't. Sunlight broke through the trees ahead, darting the snow and melting it into puddles. She skirted around them.

And wondered about the future.

For four days she had felt sick to her stomach in the mornings. Her back hurt constantly, and by noon she felt so weary that she had to take a nap.

She knew what the signs meant. Her bleeding was only a week late, but she felt almost certain that a child stirred in her womb. "What will happen, Marc, when we get back to Ihonatiria?"

Squinting at the sky, he said, "I don't know. Really . . . I can't tell you."

"What will you say to Jean?"

He tilted his head reluctantly, and her throat constricted. She understood without his having to say it: he just wanted his old life back.

"You are not my husband, Marc," she said stiffly, her heart breaking. "I don't even know that I would want you to be. You owe me nothing."

He gazed at her as though she'd just offered him salvation. Then he looked away for a long moment. "Let me talk to Jean. I'm not seeing very clearly."

THREE HUGE COOK pots steamed over a large fire in the center of the plaza. Every Christian for miles around had been bringing in food. Phillipe had snared some rabbits, and Meiach had netted five geese to add to the stews. Even Pierre had shot a deer to contribute to the Death Feast. The sweet scent of meat filled the air. They would let the pots simmer all night.

Ironically, Jean felt good, standing there with Phillipe and Luc. The Huron might kill them tomorrow, but at least the village would eat well while they did.

All day the brilliant sun had been chasing the snow from the plaza. Now a gooey mixture of mud and pine needles covered the ground. People clustered outside the longhouses, talking quietly in the fading sunset that laced the clouds with lavender and pink.

Ihonatiria was no longer the raucous, happy place he had first entered twelve years ago. The somber shroud of death had glazed everyone's eyes. Faces were pinched and worn.

Only Pierre's traders seemed untouched by the anguish. Sharp laughter rang out from where they lounged beneath a spruce tree at the northern edge of the village. A runner had come in from Quebec less than an hour ago with a half-dozen bottles of liquor and, Jean suspected, lots of news. Pierre had immediately uncorked three of the bottles and passed them around to the six men. They drank as though they would never get enough.

"Father Jean?" Phillipe said.

Jean looked down. Phillipe's brown robe had mud on the hem. He stood with his hands behind his back, rocking back and forth on his healing feet. Phillipe had told him they'd started to itch like the devil's own. A strange, faraway look possessed his green eyes.

"What is it, Phillipe?"

"I . . . God says . . ." He paused, as though listening to a voice no one else could hear. Birds sang suddenly in the trees, lilting and beautiful. Two gulls hopped from branch to branch, cocking their heads to study Phillipe.

Luc stiffened, glared at the birds, and stepped quickly away toward the mission.

Jean watched him go. "What does God say, Phillipe?"

"He wants you to think about Golgotha."

"The mount where our Lord was crucified? Why?"

Phillipe blinked owlishly. "I don't know, except that He says Mary Magdalene would have rather climbed it a thousand times herself than let our Lord climb it once."

Jean frowned. "Yes, I'm sure that's true, though our Lord had to climb it Himself to save the world, Phillipe."

"But the Magdalene's sacrifice would have been important."

"Oh, yes, as a gesture of love. But her sacrifice would have redeemed no one, especially not our Lord. She would have taken His whole reason for being in the world away from Him."

"Yes," Phillipe said, so softly that Jean had trouble hearing him. "His whole reason. Great souls are sometimes promoted to great suffering. But . . ." Phillipe stopped, as though he'd forgotten what he was saying. He ambled off through the village, playing games with his own footprints.

Jean used a long stick to lift a lid and stir the venison stew. He slid the heavy lid back on and cast a curious eye heavenward. *What was all that about, Lord?*

At times like this, when Phillipe used words and phrases that seemed to be none of his own, Jean felt the hand of God at work, but often he couldn't decipher the Lord's message.

A burst of laughter rose from the traders. Pierre stood and left the gathering. He swaggered through the mud, cocking a brow at Phillipe as he passed him. Dressed in a clean yellow shirt and brown pants, he looked the epitome of a sea captain, but not much of a New World trader. The heat of the day had forced everyone out of their winter clothing.

Pierre cursed blasphemously as he scraped mud from his right boot onto one of the hearthstones. "Here." Paper rattled. "Karo, the messenger who arrived an hour ago, brought this."

Jean took the letter. "What is it?"

"I'm not the sort to be reading another man's mail."

"Well, who's it from?"

"Lejeune. He wants you to send Penchant home. Binet has ordered it."

Jean had been about to remind Pierre that he didn't "read another man's mail," but was so startled that he simply ripped open the letter. As he did so, Phillipe let out a shrill cry, and a roar of surprise went up from the Huron. People began running headlong toward the southern trail head, their arms raised high, some with brimming eyes.

Pierre shouted, "Oh, thank God!" And sprinted after them.

Jean turned. Marc and Andiora were walking tiredly up the path. A mob encircled them, jumping and shouting with excitement. Phillipe embraced Marc as Pierre shouldered his way through the swarm to Andiora; he lifted her off her feet and kissed her madly.

"Thank you, Lord," Jean murmured. He tucked the letter from Lejeune into his pocket, promising himself he would read it as soon as he could, then trotted to the edge of the crowd. When Marc saw Jean, his face tightened and he swallowed hard. Jean blinked. Marc almost looked . . . frightened.

Gently, Marc disentangled Phillipe's arms and walked toward Jean. His blond hair was clean; it shone like gold in the sunset light.

"Marc, I was so worried," Jean said as he embraced him. "What happened? We knew about the attack, but—"

"Father Superior . . . please. May I offer you my confession?"

Jean examined Marc's tormented face. "Yes, of course. But don't you want to eat first?"

"No. No, I beg you. Let me do it now."

Uneasiness squirmed in Jean's stomach. He glanced at Andiora. She was gazing forlornly at Marc, as though sharing some hidden pain with him. Jean put a hand on Marc's shoulder. "Come. We'll go into the chapel."

They made it halfway across the muddy plaza before Phillipe caught up to Marc and gripped his hand, smiling radiantly.

"I love you, Marc. God loves you."

"I love you, too, Phillipe. I missed you."

"I was worried . . . until our Lord came to tell me you were all right."

Marc stopped dead. His black hem waffled around his legs. "Came?"

Phillipe held Marc's hand to his breast. Behind him, sunset flamed through the clouds. Joyously, he said, "Oh, yes. He's here. He's come back to us."

Marc frowned questioningly at Jean, and Jean said, "It's a long story. A huge cougar has been stalking around Ihonatiria. It circled the mission several nights ago. We saw its tracks in the snow."

Marc's face slackened. "*A cougar?*"

"Yes," Phillipe said. "The Lion of God."

The elation in that childlike voice clutched at Jean's heart. He patted Phillipe's shoulder. "Brother? It's been a long time since Marc has had communion or been able to go to confession. He'd like to do that."

"Oh, of course. I understand." Phillipe hurried to the mission and opened the door for them.

When they entered, Marc headed for the chapel with the deliberateness of a man facing a firing squad, apparently just wanting it over with. He barely greeted Luc, who sat openmouthed on his bed, his breviary on his lap.

Jean stopped for a moment in the common room and murmured to Phillipe, "Could you help Luc prepare Mass, Brother? Marc and I won't be long."

"Yes, Father. But the things are in the chapel. May I get them?"

"Yes, Phillipe. Luc?" he called. "You don't mind preparing Mass, do you?"

"No, Father." Luc closed his breviary and rose. He threw a speculative look at the chapel.

The letter in Jean's pocket seemed to grow warmer, demanding to be read . . . but it would have to wait. "Thank you. I should be out to help you in a few minutes."

Jean and Phillipe entered the chapel and found Marc on his knees before the crucifix. His head was bowed and a sheaf of blond hair hid most of his face, but Jean could see the tears that formed a spatter of amber diamonds in his beard. Phillipe's mouth puckered with misery. Jean stepped around Marc and went to draw the sacraments from the tabernacle on the altar; he handed them to Phillipe, who tiptoed by Marc as he left.

Jean sat at the far end of the second bench, the most private place in the mission, and waited. Seven candles glowed on the altar. Their warm light flickered over the bark ceiling and walls like windblown gold. A wavering halo enfolded the body of Jesus. Jean tried to suppress his worry for Marc so he could open himself to God. He closed his eyes and cleared his mind of thoughts, praying without words for God to come and fill him.

The scents of the mission sharpened: hickory smoke and cornmeal, the lingering fragrance of precious imported incense, melting tallow. Whispers came from Luc and Phillipe in the next room, and the occasional clink of silver. Serenity touched the edges of Jean's soul. He concentrated on it, abandoning himself to God, and peace seemed to seep in from the air itself. It flowed like a sweet torrent. Jean let himself drift on the waves of this tranquil ocean . . .

MARC CROSSED HIMSELF and rose. His heart had started to thunder sickeningly in his breast. He took a moment to brush at the dust clinging to the knees of his clean robe. *Stop delaying! Coward . . . coward . . .* He turned. Jean was sitting in the corner with his eyes closed. Candlelight fluttered over his balding crown and black beard. He was such a big man, and yet he seemed small sitting there with his head bowed and his fingers laced in his lap.

Marc filled his lungs and went to sit beside Jean. He whispered, "Bless me, Father, for I have sinned. It has been seven weeks since my last confession."

Gently, Jean said, "Have confidence in God, Marc. His love is everlasting and He is merciful."

"Amen." Marc crossed himself.

"What have you to confess?"

"Father, I . . . I have broken my vow of chastity."

Jean turned sharply, his face like stone. "*What?*"

Marc fumbled for a moment. "Forgive me. I . . . Father, for months my love for Andiora has been growing, until . . . when we were alone in the woods, I loved her. As a man loves a woman. But it is more than just the lust of the body, Father. My soul aches for her."

Jean closed his eyes. "Oh, my son. How could you abandon God?" He dropped his head in his hands.

Marc sought the gaze of his crucified Savior. So much courage and love poured from Jesus' anguished face that it soothed Marc. *God, please . . . forgive me.*

Jean softly murmured, "Golgotha. Yes," as though the words tore his soul. "We must all carry the cross with Him, Marc. That is our whole reason for being and for taking our vows. But none of us is as perfect as He. We are frail flesh and blood. God understands that."

"I'm confused, Father. I don't know what to think or do."

"Yes, you do, Marc. You must purge her from your heart."

"But I *love* her."

Jean gripped his crucifix in both hands, and an ache built below Marc's heart. "I could send you to Quebec, Marc, or to another village. I could even send you home, if you need me to—to help you get her out of your mind."

Marc shook his head wearily, feeling as though he were in some dim nightmare country where time had ceased and he stood on the edge of a precipice, always about to fall, never able to.

The mission door opened and closed, and several loud Huron voices spoke in the common room. Luc hushed them, asked the visitors to be seated and told them that Mass would be ready soon.

Jean lifted his chin. Marc met those dark, tormented eyes. Jean said, "Father Daniel is in the Neutral villages in the south. In penance, I want you to go there, Marc. Fast, pray day and night. Engage yourself for thirty days in the spiritual exercises of Saint Ignatius. I know you hunger for a clearer understanding of what God wants of you. If, by the time you return here, you are still confused . . . well, we'll discuss it more then."

Marc rubbed his throbbing temples.

When he did not respond, Jean said, "Marc, do you repent of having sinned?"

"Yes, Father." The words of contrition came automatically to his lips: "'Oh, my God, I am heartily sorry for having offended You, who are all good and deserving of all my . . . my love. I firmly resolve . . .'" He almost couldn't finish "'. . . with the help of Your Grace, to sin no more and to avoid the near occasions of sin.'"

Jean put a hand on Marc's head. "God, the Father of Mercies, through the death and Resurrection of His Son, has reconciled the world to Himself and sent the Holy Spirit among us for the forgiveness of sins; through the ministry of the church, may God give you pardon and peace. *Ego te absolvo. In nomini patris, et filii, et spiritus sancti.*"

Marc answered, "His mercy endures forever and ever. Amen."

"The Lord has freed you from your sins. *Pax vobiscum.*"

Perhaps the separation and constant prayer would kill the ache for Andiora that tortured him. A momentary relief spread through Marc—then the pain came again. *A month or a year, it won't make any difference. You know it.* He fought that voice, silently shouting it down. "When should I leave, Father?"

"Day after tomorrow. I'm giving a Death Feast in the morning. I'd like you to be there just in case I—"

"A *Death* Feast?"

Jean shrugged. "It's a Huron ritual. Men dress for burial and give a farewell feast to show that they don't fear death. Tehoren and a group of prominent warriors have labeled us witches and, I think, condemned us—or at least me—to death. They're blaming us for the disease."

"But we have nothing to do with it!"

"No, of course not, but they've convinced themselves we do. The only way to bring the thing to a conclusion is to challenge them. Thus the Death Feast."

"Jean, I don't think I'll be able to stand by and watch them murder you."

"I don't expect to just stand there and let it happen myself. Don't worry. I've made plans." Jean looked up at the crucifix, and tears filled his eyes. He wiped them away and exhaled a deep breath. "Marc . . . promise me. Promise me you'll search your soul carefully. You've been my hope. You're the best priest I have in the New World. You seem to have an instinctive understanding of the people. They like and respect you."

The unspoken words, *Please, don't do this to me—or to God—and most of all, don't damn yourself*, hung like the sword of Damocles over Marc. He nodded. "I promise, Father."

Jean's robe rustled as he rose. "Well, let's tend to our Christian brethren. I think they're more frightened about tomorrow than I am."

CHAPTER

36

A ndiora cried out when Pierre picked her up and began kissing her. The smell of rum encircled him like a foul mist, blotting out the fragrances of venison and rabbit that hung heavily in the air. Villagers crowded around, smiling, weeping, reaching out to touch her as though she were a Power totem. The familiar faces and bark longhouses would have made her weep with joy . . . were it not for the fear on Marc's face as he walked across the plaza with Jean.

"Oh, darlin'," Pierre said, "I was half crazy with worry. What happened to you? Tristan said he searched all of Arontaen, looking for you."

He tightened his hold to a crushing grip that sent darts of pain through her. Her womb cramped so badly that it made her gasp. *No, not the baby. Not* this *baby!* She put her hands in the middle of his chest and tried to push him back. "Please, Pierre, let me go. You're hurting me!"

His muscles went rigid for a moment, then he released her. He looked as though she'd just stabbed him in the heart. People shoved by Pierre to hug her, and Andiora hugged them back, laughing, telling them that she was all right, that she and Marc had hidden in a cave after the attack on Arontaen and then they'd had to wait until the storm passed. Pierre watched her fiercely, as if he could tell just from the way she said "Marc" what had happened in that cave. He put his hands on his hips. The creases in his yellow shirt caught the lavender rays of sunset and sparkled as though pools of amethyst had flowed in to fill them.

Tehoren came through the crowd and threw a look of pure hatred at Pierre. Andiora stiffened. Pierre glowered back menacingly. Tehoren embraced her and whispered in her ear, "Much has happened. Onrea is ill, but she is getting better. We accused Brebeuf of witchcraft. The sentence of death was unanimous. He is giving a Death Feast tomorrow."

Andiora wrenched out of his grip. "No! Tehoren, tell me this is not true. Jean would never—"

"It is done!" He lifted a clenched fist, and people went silent. Tehoren's voice rang out: "Jix and his group of warriors are already preparing their bows, breathing Spirit into them so that Brebeuf's Power cannot turn their arrows."

"And Taretande approved this? I cannot believe it!" Andiora protested.

Tehoren's lips pursed. "Taretande is dead, along with his whole family. *Two-thirds* of the village has been carried away by this disease! It is time to end it before the rest of us die!"

"What has Tonner said? Where is he?"

"At the death council, Brebeuf came in and cast a spell on Tonner. The next morning Tonner took the trails back to Onnentisati. He had an accident, and they say he's dying."

Grief welled in her. "Who told you this?"

"His sister sent a runner this morning." Tehoren threw back his head and let out a chilling war cry, then stalked away across the muddy plaza. A few more war yells went up.

The crowd began to disperse, some following Tehoren, devotion in their eyes. Andiora frowned. She would have to do something— *and quickly, or Jean will be dead, and his priests with him, most likely. Oh, not Marc. Dear Jesus, I offer You my first prayer. Do not let this happen!*

Andiora ran for the mission, but just as she passed the cook pots, Pierre roughly grabbed her foxhide coat.

"Slow down, darlin'," he ordered.

She struggled to break his grip. "Pierre, I must see Jean. We'll have time to talk to each other later."

"We're going to talk *now*."

He jerked her backward so hard that she stumbled into him. Angry, she slammed a fist into his chest. "Let me go! Jean is in trouble. I must see him before—"

"*Jean* is it? I think not."

Pierre swung her up in his arms and carried her unsteadily to the closest longhouse, the one next to the mission. She flailed and kicked, but he was drunk, and deaf to anyone's needs other than his own. Around the side of the longhouse, he set her on her feet, then put his hands on either side of her shoulders, trapping her against the wall. He stood huge, silhouetted against orange and lavender clouds, a venomous hurt in his eyes. He swayed on his feet.

"'Tis time you were listening to me, Andiora. Me patience has run thin. I want to know about you and Dupre, and this instant, by God, or I will—"

"Pierre, you are drunk! You don't know what you're saying. Let me go!"

Andiora tried to duck beneath his arms, but he grabbed her shoulders and pinned her to the wall. "You're not leaving, darlin', not 'til I say so." A pathetic softness pinched his face. He lifted a hand and tenderly ran a finger along her cheek. "Andiora, I've told you how much I love you. What are you hurting me for?"

"Pierre, it does no good to talk to you when you are like this. You never listen, you just—"

"I'm listening! Talk to me! I want to hear you say it. Tell me you don't love me."

Tristan edged around the rear of the longhouse to peer at them, but when he saw what was happening, he retreated. Andiora desperately hoped he hadn't gone far. Tristan would intervene if Pierre went out of control.

"You're my friend, Pierre. I *do* love you—*as my friend*. But I . . ." Her voice quaked. "I do not love you as I used to."

He grimaced sourly. "And why not, darlin'? I'm not to blame for your losing our baby. You're the one who got sick."

Softly, imploringly, she said, "Don't say such things, Pierre. You're acting like a man I don't know." His fingers dug into her shoulders like claws. She squirmed, trying to make him let go. "Pierre, stop this! Please!"

"What were you a-doing out there in that cave, Andiora? Seducing him? Or did he, in his *goddamned blessedness*, seduce you?"

She slapped him with all the force she could muster. He turned away with a small grunt. Blood trickled from the corner of his mouth.

"Sure," he said in a cutting voice. "I'll bet he threw you down, forced you, isn't that right? He'd have been in a hurry, trying to get his pleasure before his God laid eyes on what he was up to."

Pierre tore open her coat and ran a hand over her breasts and down her waist. She grabbed his fingers and tried to shove them away, but he fought to keep them there. "Dupre didn't touch you like this, did he? No. His sort don't have much experience with bodies, leastwise not with women's bodies."

"Pierre, you're making a fool of yourself. Stop—"

"Here I've been saving meself, trying not to eye the women that smile at me, and you've been out bedding a holy priest like a gutter whore in Paris."

A sob worked its way up her throat. To hear such words from him left her speechless. He was drunk. She knew that, but he had sundered her heart. She had never thought him capable of such low cruelty.

"Pierre, you have just killed the love I had left for you. I thank you for that. We have nothing more to say to each other. I'm going!"

She kicked him hard in the shin and dropped like a rock when his grip loosened, crawling away as fast as she could.

"I'm not done yet, Andiora!"

He dove after her, crushed her into the mud and pinned her arms over her head. Andiora pleaded, "Stop this, Pierre. Stop it!" If she screamed, she knew what the result would be. Her village would come to her rescue, and they would kill Pierre for doing this to her.

She squirmed violently and managed to slip partway out from under him. He threw a knee up, into her abdomen. Andiora gasped and screamed, "No, Pierre! Not my stomach. I am pregnant! Do you hear me? *Pregnant!*" She pushed at his knee, forcing it down.

From behind the house, Tristan hurried forward on his splinted leg. He gripped Pierre by the shoulders and jerked him backward. "You drunken idiot! Leave this be now, or I'll call Andiora's relatives and help them chop you into little pieces!"

Pierre backhanded Tristan, knocking him into the wall. The brutal act seemed to clear some of the stupor from Pierre's brain. His mouth fell open when Tristan stumbled and crashed to the ground on his injured leg.

Pierre cried, "Tristan? Oh, blessed Lord, I—" He slid off of Andiora and crawled to help Tristan sit up.

Andiora rolled to her side and held her stomach. Nausea swept her. The world swam in a blur of color. She shook her head, fighting not to vomit.

Tristan shook off Pierre's hand. "Get out of here, Pierre," he growled. "Take the men and light out for Quebec, before anybody hears what you've done."

Pierre's gaze had riveted on Andiora. Hot. Malignant. He got to his feet and walked over to her. "So tell me . . . *darlin'*. Is it me child, or Dupre's?"

When she didn't answer, an eerie light entered his eyes. He broke into an unsteady run, swerving around the longhouse.

"Oh, dear Lord," Tristan moaned. "No telling what he'll do." He rose, wincing in pain, and gritted his teeth as he followed in Pierre's footsteps.

Andiora lay with her cheek in the cool mud and prayed to Iouskeha . . . and Jesus . . . to keep her baby safe.

MARC KNELT IN prayer while Jean and Luc administered the Holy Eucharist to each other, offered the benediction, and blessed the Huron Christians who filed by the altar. One young woman, wearing a brown tradecloth dress, knelt before Jean and kissed his palm. "Father, my little girl, Gotim, fell into a deep sleep this morning. Please come and make her well. Her body has turned purple . . ." Her voice faltered. "I need God to come and heal her. Tonight, Father, please?" She sobbed quietly.

"I'll come, Mibdo," Jean answered. "After dinner. We'll pray together. I'm sure God will hear us."

"Thank you, Father." Mibdo rose and wiped her eyes on her sleeve as she left the chapel.

Phillipe slid closer and put his shoulder firmly against Marc's. He was endeavoring to keep his eyes reverently closed while leaving one half open to peer at Marc. "I'm glad you're home, Marc," Phillipe whispered.

"I missed you, Phillipe. I'm sure that if I'd had you with me, I wouldn't be in so much trouble right now."

"Sometimes God needs us to be in trouble, Marc." Phillipe continued very softly, "'And there appeared a great wonder in heaven—a woman clothed with the sun, and she brought forth a male child who was to rule all nations with a rod of iron.'"

Marc frowned. "Revelation? What does that have to do with the trouble I'm—"

A cold laugh filled the chapel. Marc turned to see Mongrave slouching against the door frame. A hateful grin curled his lips. His black hair and beard were muddy, and his yellow shirt and brown pants looked as though he'd been wallowing in a bog. He steadied himself with a hand against the wall and glared drunkenly at Marc.

Jean stepped down from the altar and amiably inquired, "Is there something we could do for you, Pierre?"

"Aye. I would be speaking to Dupre, if I might."

Marc got to his feet, nodded, and walked into the common room. Phillipe hurried along, hanging on to Marc's sleeve. Marc's stomach churned. Had Andiora told Mongrave what had happened?

Jean came out of the chapel, removed his sacramental garb and stepped between Marc and Pierre. "What do you want, Pierre?"

"Get out of me way, Brebeuf. I've no quarrel with you." He pushed by Jean.

Jean stepped between them again and put a restraining hand in the middle of Mongrave's chest. Marc could feel Phillipe's good hand still twined tightly, protectively, in his sleeve.

Marleaux hobbled stiffly into the mission, breathing hard. Jean glanced at him, then his calm gaze came back to Mongrave. "Marc is going away, Pierre. There's no need to—"

"Hiding behind Jean's skirts, are you, Dupre? Face me like a man!"

"Monsieur," Marc said cautiously, "I don't know what's wrong, but—"

"Don't you?" Mongrave wiped at his bloody lip and glared. "Have you forgotten me Andiora's charms so soon?" He shoved Jean's hand away from his chest.

Luc's mouth dropped open and his gray eyes narrowed. "What does he mean?" he demanded.

Blood began to pound in Marc's ears.

Mongrave staggered as he turned. "I mean," he shouted, "that your brother here has taken a liking to the flesh of women. Andiora's the only one I'm sure of, but I'd not doubt there've been others. What do you think about that, Jean?"

Jean responded mildly, "That all men are sinners, Pierre. That's all. God's heart is large enough to forgive almost anything."

"Aye, good for Him." Mongrave balled his fists and stepped forward, only inches from Marc. "But I am not God."

Marc said, "It wasn't her fault, Mongrave. It was mine."

"I figured as much. So why did you lie to me, Dupre? If you'd told me your feelings when I first asked, I could at least have prepared meself—" He stopped as the mission door opened and soft footfalls entered the storage room.

Marc's heartache eased. When the fires of hell roasted his soul, he would draw up those featherlight steps from the depths of his memories and be able to endure. He turned and gazed at Andiora with his whole heart in his eyes.

"Marc?"

Mud coated her red dress and hair. Marc glanced back at Mongrave's muddy clothes—and anger rose in him. They'd fought . . .

As she walked forward, she said, "Pierre, please. Marc knows nothing of what I told you."

Mongrave squinted, a fire in his black eyes. "You haven't told him?"

"No."

"Good God Amighty, Andiora!" he yelled. "Don't you think he *deserves* to know? I'm getting meself set to kill him for touching you, but before I do, you ought to be gracing him with the knowledge that you are carrying his child!"

Marc's blood turned cold. "What?"

"Aye, Dupre," Mongrave said, and swung his right fist with all his might. Marc ducked, and Mongrave's own motion sent him tumbling into the table.

"No!" Andiora screamed.

Mongrave scrambled up and lunged again. Marc ducked a clumsy left and responded instinctively, landing a hard fist in Mongrave's ribs. Mongrave doubled over, gasping for breath. Marc spread his legs, getting set . . . but then he saw Andiora standing by the table. She had a hand pressed over her lips. The pain on her beautiful face shredded his soul.

Like a raging bull, Mongrave charged, grabbed Marc around the waist and knocked him to the dirt floor. They rolled, Mongrave yelling, trying to connect with punches while Marc fought to escape his iron grip.

"I'm going to kill you, Dupre!"

In self-defense, Marc landed a knee in Mongrave's chest, then brought his clenched fists down on that thick skull. When Mongrave groaned and released him, Marc twisted and sprang to his feet, panting.

"What are you stopping for, Dupre?" Mongrave demanded. He tried futilely to rise, but fell back onto the dirt. Finally getting his feet under him, he staggered up against the wall. Marleaux went over and pulled one of Mongrave's arms over his shoulders to support him.

"You're finished fighting, Pierre," Marleaux said. "I'm taking you to your blankets. After you've had some rest, then you can think about what a dim-witted ass you are."

Marleaux turned the stumbling Mongrave around and managed to head him for the door, but Mongrave gripped the door frame and held it fast. He squinted over his shoulder, watching as Marc went to stand in front of Andiora.

She looked up at Marc with sad eyes, and he reached out and gently drew her against him, holding her fast. "Is it true?" he murmured.

"Yes . . . I'm sorry."

Jean crossed himself and bowed his head. Luc stood like a paralyzed scarecrow, his gray eyes wide. "Pregnant?" he muttered. "That woman is pregnant?"

Phillipe smiled like a wistful angel.

Marc kissed Andiora's temple. The feel of her arms around his waist, the steady beating of her heart, calmed him. He stroked her hair. "Don't be sorry," he whispered.

Jean eased down onto a chair by the table. "Blessed Lord, please tell me what to do now?"

CHAPTER

37

Phillipe stood in the corner of the common room, grinding corn. His robe and face bore a dusting of meal. He had a big wooden bowl of dried kernels wedged between his stomach and the machine. Another bowl sat beneath the spout on the opposite side to catch the yellow meal that came sliding out. He threw a handful of corn into the grinder and cranked the handle. It clicked and clacked as it crushed the fragrant kernels.

Phillipe blinked somberly at the fire in the hearth. The flames fluttered as though alive. Marc had left the mission with Andiora right after the fight with Mongrave—but that had been hours ago, and he was worried.

Sometimes God had to make people suffer, but Phillipe didn't really understand why. Some nights he lay awake, fiddling with the stubs that had been the fingers of his left hand, and wondered. He knew only that God could see farther ahead than he could and that He was working very hard to bring about the deliverance of Creation.

That was enough to sustain Phillipe.

That, and seeing the footprints of his Lord in the forest every day. He went searching for them whenever he could, looking beneath the brush or in lingering patches of snow.

He always found them.

Jesus is just waiting to reveal Himself. It won't be long. He smiled in delight.

Flickers of gold candlelight illuminated the part of the chapel visible through the door. The long shadows of Father Jean and Luc stretched across the bark wall. Luc's harsh voice said, "But, Father

Superior, this is Satan's work! I can't leave now!" Then the shadow of his hand flashed. Phillipe trained his ears on the hushed murmurs.

"I don't have any choice, Luc," Father Jean said firmly. "I can't disobey orders from Reverend Father Binet. You should have thought of that before you wrote those letters."

Luc hurried out of the chapel into the common room, a hand over his quaking mouth. He stopped and clenched his fists. "I won't go!"

Father Jean came into the door frame and massaged his forehead. God had lain so much on him so quickly. Phillipe tossed another handful of corn into the grinder and cranked it as quietly as he could, though the machine squeaked and rattled anyway.

Luc extended his hands pleadingly to Father Jean. "Don't you understand? I've seen Satan in this New World! Now I know the meaning of the dream I had so long ago, when angels thrust a flaming sword into my hand!" He took a step toward Jean. "God sent me here for a reason, Father! *I* am to be the last martyr! I've felt the truth growing in me for months. The End is only a breath away. Can't you feel it?"

Jean studied Luc intently. "I believe that. But—"

"Then surely you see that I must stay in the New World! You need me!" Luc dropped to his knees before Father Jean and began weeping. "Please, Father, I want to be here when the sun goes black. Don't deny me the gift of looking my Savior in the eyes before I'm put to death!" Luc tugged at Jean's hem. "Father, I beg you!"

Father Jean studied the foamy patterns of smoke undulating near the smoke hole. "The decision is out of my hands, Luc. I'm sorry."

Luc hunched forward until his forehead touched the floor. He slammed a fist into the dirt, shouting, "No! No! I won't go home!"

Tears welled in Phillipe's eyes. How bewildering God's will could sometimes seem! It tore at his heart to see Luc so distraught. He put down his bowl, wiped his hands on his sleeves and hurried across the floor to kneel beside his brother. Phillipe looked up at Father Jean, then put his mutilated hand on Luc's shoulder and closed his eyes, praying, "Dear God, don't make Luc go home. He wants to stay here to do Your work. Please hear him. I ask in the name of—"

A hard hand slapped Phillipe's face. He opened his eyes, startled.

"*Luc!*" Father Jean shouted as he grabbed Luc's upraised hand. "How could you *do* such a thing?"

"He touched me! I don't like to be touched! Especially not by a demon incarnate!" Luc shrilled. He scooted back against the wall, his breast heaving while he glared fearfully at Phillipe. "Look at him! You can see Satan in his eyes. I'm sure that beast he calls is the Antichrist! And he talks to the devil's own familiars that fill this land! Birds and foxes—"

Confused, Phillipe stammered, "Wh-what familiars? I've only seen God." His cheek stung. He rubbed it and blinked back the tears that blurred his eyes. He didn't know why Luc didn't like him. He'd tried very hard to love Luc.

Father Jean took Phillipe's arm and helped him to his feet. "It's all right, Phillipe. All of us wish we could see God the way you do." He pulled out a chair for Phillipe. "Why don't you rest here while Luc and I finish our discussion."

"Yes, I—I will."

Father Jean went back and offered a hand to Luc to help him up, but Luc only sobbed and shook his head. Jean knelt and extended his hand. "Luc, come. Let me help you. We must talk."

Angry voices split the air outside, and Jean rose to his feet as the mission door slammed back. Five men entered, wearing cornhusk masks. Each carried a war club. The lead man's eyes drifted warily over the common room, checking every shadowed corner as though for lurking demons. He motioned for his accomplices to fan out. They formed a rough semicircle around the table and hearth. In the flickering light, their shadows jumped over the floor and walls.

Phillipe held his breath. The masks fascinated him. The Huron called them "bushy-head" masks. They were formed of coiled strips of corn husks. Lolling tongues or conical, whistling mouths were the main features. Through the eyeholes, black eyes glistened. Phillipe twisted his hands. He had heard Onrea say that the masks often spoke to their owners about God and bad Spirits. The leading shaman had painted red circles around the holes in his mask. A small man, he wore fawnskin pants and a shirt with blue porcupine quills woven across the chest.

"Brebeuf," the shaman called gruffly, and Phillipe stiffened when he recognized the voice. "We've come for the book. Where is it?"

Father Jean shook his head. "What book, Tehoren?"

Tehoren lifted his war club threateningly. "The one you carry the sickness in! Penchant has it. Give it to us!"

Luc had gone very still, staring wide-eyed. He whispered, "What's he talking about?"

Tehoren waved two of the maskers forward. Cautiously, they edged around the table and headed for Luc. Phillipe wanted to touch their costumes as they passed, but he dared not. Father Jean backed up to stand before Luc like a tall, dark fortress. Luc huddled on the floor, his eyes glazed with fear.

"Give it to us!" Tehoren shouted. "The book you keep that Mother Mary in. We want it now!"

Luc's mouth gaped. "Does the beast mean my breviary?" He flung an arm out at the maskers, and shrieked in heavily accented Huron, "Begone, you demons! All of you! Before I beg my God to send you to the fiery pit!"

The maskers gasped. The two men with Tehoren crouched, ready to attack, but the other two backed toward the door.

Sensing that he had them on the run, Luc howled the Our Father prayer in Latin and drew a huge cross in the air.

"*No, Luc!*" Jean whispered. "Don't! Don't make them think we're using magic against them."

One of the men walked forward bravely, his war club held high. Luc rose to his feet and glowered. "Begone, you devil!"

A frightened youth's voice quavered, "Tehoren says we have to get that book or my sick mother will die from your witchcraft."

"Tehoren is an ignorant savage," Luc said. "He knows nothing of—"

The man slammed his club into Luc's shoulder. Luc yelped and dodged the second blow. "God will curse you all! He'll damn you to eternal torture in hell. If you think the Iroquois know how to torture—"

"*Hush*, Luc!" Jean ordered. He shoved Luc behind him, trying to force him to back up into the chapel, but Luc rebelled. He edged away and walked forward.

"These barbaric beasts deserve to hear the truth," Luc said defiantly. "If you don't leave us alone, our God will kill all of you! I am *oki*," Luc shouted, jabbing a finger at his own chest. "You hear? *Oki!*"

The masker nodded in fear, tears blurring his eyes. "I know."

"*No! No!*" Jean shouted. "Father Penchant doesn't understand what he's saying!"

Tehoren let out an earsplitting war cry and waved his accomplices toward the door. "Don't move, Brebeuf! We can't kill you tonight, or we'd break our promises to Power, but we can kill Raimont!" He swung around and pointed at Phillipe.

Phillipe bit his lip.

The other two maskers crept catlike to Phillipe. Father Jean lifted his arms slowly and backed away to stand against the wall. "Luc," he commanded quietly, "give Tehoren your breviary."

"No! It's mine!"

"Do it!"

The young masker pleaded, "Please, *oki*, stop hurting my mother!"

"You fool!" Luc spat. "Your mother is sick because she's wicked. I'm not hurting her! My book has no demons in it!"

The youth shook his head. "You lie. You all lie. Our grandfathers have told us the truth." He raised his club menacingly and eased forward to search Luc's pockets until he found the breviary. He handled it as though it might strike him like a snake. "Here," he said, handing it to Tehoren. "Kill it!"

Tehoren snatched the book and tossed it into the fire. The pages curled and blackened, sending a cloud of dark smoke billowing toward the ceiling. Luc put a trembling hand to his lips.

The maskers retreated, filing out the door. Before he left, Tehoren promised, "Tomorrow, Brebeuf, you die for your crimes against our people!" He slammed the door, and piercing wails rose outside, cries of triumph.

Phillipe rubbed his forehead. Words drifted through his mind, and he repeated them without thinking: "Behold, with a great plague will the Lord smite thy people, and thy children and thy wives, and all thy goods."

"Goods?" Jean's chest rose and fell swiftly. "The Lord will smite 'goods' with plague? Where is that from, Phillipe?"

He pointed to his head. "An angel just whispered it in my ear."

Jean stood unmoving for a time, then he asked, "Luc, when did you get that breviary?"

His eyes still on the charring pages, Luc said hoarsely, "My mother gave it to me when I was ill, several years ago. And it's never been out of my hands since then."

"Never? Did you have it with you when you were ministering to the smallpox victims in France just before you left?"

"Yes, of course. I even passed it amongst those who could read Latin—so that the words of our Lord might comfort them."

The voices in Phillipe's head grew stronger. There were several angels now, their voices weaving into a beautiful song:

Worthy is the Lamb . . . behold, He comes quickly . . . quickly!

Father Jean's eyes narrowed as he stared at the book. "I wonder if we haven't been carrying the disease with us all along."

CHAPTER

38

God flies from them and abandons them to see whether they seek
Him or not. There are some who, when the Spirit had fled from
them, and abandoned them, remain heavy and without movement
in this torpor. They do not pray God to lift this weight off them
and to send them the joy and sweetness they knew before . . . they
become strangers to the sweetness of God. . . . If God sees that
they implore Him with sincerity and with their whole heart, and if
He sees that they really deny their own will, He gives them a
greater joy than they had before.

ST. AMMONAS
Fourth-century monk

Luc paced up and down the common room, his stomach tying
itself in knots. An hour before dawn, darkness still held the
world outside. The room seemed frustratingly narrow this
morning; he kept bumping into the beds at one end and the door to
the storage room at the other. Only two candles and the fire burned,
casting a muted radiance over the table and chairs. Luc had dressed
in a clean robe and had combed his hair back from his thin face.

Brebeuf had risen very early to stoke up the fires beneath the cook
pots, readying them for the dawn Death Feast. Dupre sat on his bed,
staring vacantly, while Raimont stood grinding corn in the far corner.

Luc hadn't slept at all last night. He'd been wrestling with himself,
reliving every wretched moment of yesterday. When would Brebeuf
send him back to France? He'd said "as soon as possible." The very
idea of facing his mother left Luc's knees knocking. Far worse, he
knew that God had ordained a special role for him in the final

moments of the End, the *Parousia*. How could God let this happen to him now? After all the sacrifices Luc had made, humbly accepting the squalor of the New World and the hostility of its savage peoples.

It made no sense! He felt as if some malignant force had intervened and hurled the world into a chaos so black and spinning that not even God could penetrate it.

Luc stopped pacing. Satan had done that frequently in the course of history, spun so much hatred and darkness that God couldn't stop the wickedness.

The fire in the hearth crackled. The corn mill squeaked and grated. Luc eyed at Phillipe. The ugly little Brother methodically scooped up another handful of kernels and tossed it into the grinder. Brebeuf had said they'd need another ten pounds to be added to the cook pots, for thickening the stews. Raimont had been cranking that blasted squealing device for over half an hour. *Phillipe, yes, he's certainly possessed by the devil, if not willingly Satan's servant. Perhaps he's the reason I've been condemned to ignominy.*

But Dupre and his consort, the witch Andiora, couldn't be ruled out.

Dupre hadn't moved in hours. His elbows were propped on his drawn-up knees, and his fingers steepled over his bearded chin. He looked deep in thought in the dim, flickering light. Luc sniffed in disgust. Dupre hadn't returned to the mission until three hours ago and when he had, he'd simply said, "Andiora and I were talking."

"Talking," Luc whispered now. *"Really?"*

Dupre barely stirred. "What did you say?"

The corn grinder ceased its irritating squeaks. Luc saw Raimont looking at him. Sternly, he demanded, "What are you looking at?"

Raimont wet his lips nervously. "I was watching you, Luc. You look sad and worried."

Luc blurted, "How could I not be worried? I'm locked in this insane asylum with a possessed oaf—that's you, Raimont—and a . . ." he pointed at Dupre, "depraved priest who's no better than the savages he fornicates with!"

Dupre ignored him, as though he had concerns far more important than Luc's accusation.

Luc took three long steps to stand between Dupre and Raimont and shouted, "I'm the only one in this New World worthy of helping Father Brebeuf ring in the Apocalypse, and he's sending me *home!*" He threw up his hands and burst into angry sobs.

Raimont dropped his bowl of corn kernels and rushed across the room, extending his meal-covered hands to Luc. "Oh, Father, don't cry. I've been praying so hard for God to let you stay. I'm sure He's heard and will—"

Luc balled a fist to ward off those demonic hands, but Dupre suddenly sat forward on his bed, a murderous glimmer in his eyes that Luc had never seen before. Luc's fist hovered uncertainly.

"Put down your fist, Luc," Dupre ordered in a cold, clear voice.

"I'll put it down when I please!"

Dupre got to his feet.

Raimont glanced at Dupre, then at Luc's fist. "I'm sorry. I—I forgot you don't like to be touched, Luc. Forgive me." He backed away and anxiously clasped his maimed hands behind his back.

Dupre glowered at Luc. "It's time to help Father Brebeuf with the feast, Phillipe. Let me help you carry the cornmeal outside."

Raimont and Dupre divided the meal into three equal portions, one bowl for each stew pot.

Luc could barely keep from screaming.

PIERRE WOKE, QUEASY, and rolled onto his side, resting his cheek in the frosty duff. Spruce needles tickled his black beard and pricked at his skin, but he had neither the strength nor the will to move. He sprawled limply in his blankets, breathing in the dawn scents of the forest. Darkness still shrouded the hills, but somewhere in the back of his splitting head he had the impression that he'd been awakened by voices.

Then he heard Tristan say, "'Tis a meteor shower. We see them often at sea, but I've never witnessed the likes of this one."

Pierre judiciously slitted one eye to gaze up at the night sky. Meteors streaked the heavens like hoarfrost, some so huge that he could see them tumbling in splashes of pale green and red.

"Odd for this time of the year to be having such a good show."

Jean responded, "They're beautiful, aren't they?"

At the sound of that deep voice, Pierre winced. He raised on his elbows to see several people standing around the cook pots in the center of the plaza. They'd stoked the fires beneath them, getting ready for the feast. Memories of yesterday flooded back to him. Well, he'd made a fine fool of himself this time. He wondered how he'd ever make amends . . . especially to Andiora.

"Damn you," he cursed himself.

Suddenly his heart throbbed. He slipped a cold hand under his tangle of black hair and massaged the base of his skull. His own words came back to him, jumbled: ". . . I'm not to blame for your losing the baby . . .' twas your fault for getting sick, darlin' . . . bedding a holy priest like a gutter whore."

He'd have to face her today, this morning, in all his shame. He prayed she'd greet him with that glittering, stubborn look in her eyes that he knew so well—anything but hurt. *Blessed God, don't let her look at me with hurt in her eyes.* Still he could not bear the thought that she might hate him for what he'd done and said. He'd not been himself, surely she knew that. But would that—and the trifling fact that he still loved her—matter to her when she carried another man's child?

In his befuddled sleep last night, he'd been dreaming about that baby. There didn't seem to be any way around it. In England there were things that could be done, though no woman went into those dirty chambers lightly. Pierre had seen more than one girl die from the procedure, bleeding her life away. . . . But here, in New France, nothing could be done. If God willed the child to be born, it would be. But what would Dupre do? Did the priest have the courage to be acting like a husband and father, or would he turn tail and run as hard as he could, back to France and the blasted citadel walls of his holy church? Well, if he left, it would be all the better for Pierre. He'd only to convince Andiora of that.

Pierre reached for his boots, but his shaking fingers knocked them over. He cursed himself and reached again, this time with success. He shook them out to make certain nothing had crawled in during the night, then tugged them onto his feet.

He rolled up his blankets and swung his brown cape around his shoulders. Standing was misery. The longhouses had begun to awaken. Voices rose, sleepy, hushed. Pierre's eyes drifted to Andiora's longhouse, expecting to see her slender form emerge, dreading what he'd do when he saw her. If he could just put off having to confront her for another day, why, he'd think up some excuse for himself that would tear at her heart and make her forgive him.

But he knew he didn't have another day. He'd have to be accounting for his actions soon, and he figured that Andiora would give him one chance only.

Tehoren and five warriors leaned against Andiora's longhouse, whispering behind their hands. Pierre could sense from their manner that they were on the edge of violence. Was it just the Death Feast? Or had Andiora told Tehoren of how roughly he'd treated her?

"Well, you deserve whatever Tehoren gives you," he muttered as he reached down and grabbed his sword belt. He buckled it around his waist, then shoved his pistol into it. Almost as an afterthought, he took a bottle of rum from his pack and refilled his flask, which he then slipped into his right boot. He took a breath to clear some of the fog from his aching brain and headed for the cook fires.

"So," Tristan said as Pierre joined the circle around the largest fire. His long nose was pink with cold, and he wore his fringed elkhide coat with the collar turned up to keep his ears warm. "You're alive."

"You're an optimist," Pierre responded, and a low ripple of laughter went through the gathering. "Me body's being a sight stubborn is all."

Tristan squeezed Pierre's shoulder affectionately, and Pierre threw him a look of gratitude. When the rest of the world had abandoned him for his wild ways, he knew that Tristan would still be there.

Tristan spread his legs and took a sip from a steaming cup. "How's your stomach? Could you hold some coffee?"

"Aye, sounds good."

Tristan picked up a bark cup from near the copper coffeepot sitting at the edge of the glowing coals, slapped out the dirt on his pants leg and poured the cup full. Pierre took it and smelled the rich aroma before sipping the strong brew. Steam whirled around his head in a glistening amber-tinted wreath. Normal conversation picked up around the fire again, and Pierre breathed easier. He took another long sip, not minding at all that the hot liquid scorched the hide off the back of his throat. The coffee seemed to ease the threatening gurgles in his stomach.

Jean barely looked at Pierre. He slid his pot lid sideways and dipped a long stirring stick into the venison stew. An explosion of steam hissed into the chill air, obscuring Jean's face. Pierre walked over to stand at the priest's right. Behind them, the eastern sky turned a slate blue and the stars began to fade, although the meteor shower still streaked the sky.

Pierre glanced sideways at Jean, who was stirring with unnatural diligence this morning. He'd dressed in a fresh black robe and polished his silver crucifix; it glimmered in the middle of his chest. His lips were pinched together tightly.

"Are you speaking to me?" Pierre inquired.

"Doesn't look like I have any choice."

Pierre shoved his hands into his cape pockets. "No, you don't, since I'm of a mind to be speaking to you. You're looking uncommonly well. At least for the moment."

"Try not to sound so eager, Pierre. What did you want to talk about?"

"I'll be leaving for France at the end of next month. Do you want me to take Penchant home?"

"Yes, I'd appreciate that. I need him here, but . . ." As though in response, the first wails and moans of the sick rose from the southern longhouses. A baby coughed and then cried. Jean lowered his eyes to the fire. ". . . But Father Binet's orders were clear."

Pierre wiggled his fingers in his pockets. The trees had started to emerge from the cloak of night; dark limbs stood out against the lightening sky. "Well, 'tis probably for the best. The tribes never liked him to begin with."

"But he was growing, Pierre. I think that in a few months he might have become a true asset to the Huron missions. Now . . . well, we'll never know. I wish—"

"And what of Dupre?"

Jean pulled the stirring stick out and slid the pot lid back on. A faint spiral of steam rose from the stick. At the other side of the circle, Tristan laughed heartily. People had begun to emerge from the longhouses, taking care of morning duties. Pierre's eyes strayed to Andiora's door.

"You're really worried about Marc, aren't you, Pierre? Well, so am I."

Pierre shrugged. "I was hoping you might want me to take him home, too."

"As I tried to explain to you yesterday, I've ordered Marc to go south, to work with Antoine in the Neutral villages . . . and to spend a month engaged in spiritual exercises."

"So, you won't know what's to be done with Dupre until just before I'm to leave?"

"That's right."

"Well, I could be convinced to wait a few days, then."

Jean turned to face Pierre squarely. His black eyes shone with reflections of the flames. "I may not be here to make that decision, Pierre. I am, as you pointed out, giving a Death Feast today."

Pierre saw Andiora duck beneath the door-curtain of her longhouse. Her hair was pulled away from her face and pinned with copper combs that glowed as though afire in the light from the longhouse. She wore a blue tradecloth dress beneath her fox coat.

Pierre took two long strides toward her, but Jean caught his cape and pulled him backward. "Let go of me, Brebeuf!"

"Wait!" Jean said sternly as he released the cape. "I want you to keep something in mind. She and Marc spent most of the night talking. I don't know what they discussed, but I'm sure she's still as wounded and uncertain as Marc is. All you ever do is bull your way through life. Try not to do so today. If you truly care about Andiora, don't push her."

Pierre hesitated, then nodded before slowly crossing the plaza.

When Andiora saw him coming, she stood as still as stone. Her family, including a weak and thin Onrea, paused by her, speaking quietly. The dog Suma edged out from beneath the hanging, a ghostly white form that wagged its bushy tail at the sight of Pierre.

He knelt and scratched the dog's pointed ears. "Good boy, Suma. See, I told you Onrea would get well." He smiled at the girl. "You're looking prettier than ever, Onrea. How are you feeling?"

"I'm much better, Mongrave." Her eyes drifted through the growing crowd. "Is Phillipe up yet?"

"I've not seen him, but I'd wager he is. Why don't you go to the mission and see?"

"Yes, I will. Thank you." She walked slowly across the plaza with Suma at her heels.

Pierre stood, pushed back his cape, and propped his hands on his hips. The bronze hilt of his sword flashed in the dawn light. When he mustered the courage to look Andiora in the eyes, he saw nothing there—not rage, nor hurt, nor anything else. Her soul seemed to have emptied itself overnight, leaving nothing but a hollow shell.

"Andiora," he said softly, "I don't remember much of what happened yesterday. But I know I hurt you badly." He reached out to her. "Would you grant me a few moments? I'd like to speak with you. About the baby . . . and Dupre."

She tucked her fingers beneath her arms, as though erecting a barricade over her heart. "I don't want to be alone with you, Pierre. You frightened me last night."

It was like a stiletto between his ribs. "I understand. How about if we sit at the edge of the cook circle? We'll be in sight of a dozen or more, but far enough away to have a private talk."

Andiora led the way. Pale beams of morning light lanced through the branches, striking the earth in a lacy patchwork of blue and black. A chill wind swept the land, teasing wisps of Andiora's dark hair loose from their combs to dance around her face. She heard Pierre's heavy, sluggish steps behind her and knew that he must be suffering, both for what he'd done to her and what he'd done to himself.

She sat down on a dry patch of ground twenty feet from where Jean stirred his pots. He turned briefly and gave her a supportive smile. Unconsciously, her gaze searched the crowd for Marc. But he wasn't there. Unhappily, she lowered her eyes and rubbed the soft fur of her sleeve, remembering how he'd held her last night while they talked, held her tightly. He'd poured out his heart, telling of how much he loved his church and his God, and of how lost he would be without them; telling her that in a few months, if he gave them up, she would not love him anymore. For he would hate himself. Andiora had listened patiently and assured him that her culture was different from his, that she did not need him. She could and would raise the child alone, if Aataentsic granted her such a gift.

But she did need him. Not for the child, but for herself. *I love Marc more desperately than I've loved any man. I won't be able to stand it if he goes away.*

Pierre grunted as he lowered himself to the ground beside her. His crooked nose and bushy beard made him look reckless, but his dark eyes seemed contrite. They'd lost their usual fire.

He pushed his cape back and drew up his knees to prop his elbows on them. "I feel like a puppet, Andiora."

"Puppet? I don't know that word."

"It's an empty-headed wooden doll, darlin'." He kicked at a beetle that scuddled across the cold ground. It darted away. "Every time I try to get close to you, I find I'm being pushed farther away, as if God were twisting us up and around for His own purposes. I . . ."

Andiora's stomach lurched; Marc had stepped out of the mission, carrying a bowl. He walked to the last pot and dumped his cornmeal in. Dark patches stained the skin beneath his eyes. Hadn't he slept either? Phillipe and Onrea came out behind him, each with a bowl.

Marc headed toward Jean, but his steps faltered when his eyes met Andiora's. His gaze took in Pierre's haggard face, then lingered for another moment on Andiora before he strode forward again. He said something softly to Jean.

A crowd had gathered in the plaza, waiting for the first glimpse of Iouskeha's face on the horizon, knowing that was when the feast would begin. The refugees who'd streamed into Ihonatiria were weak from starvation. Their tattered clothing hung loosely about them, accentuating their gaunt cheeks and frightened eyes. When they'd fled their burning villages, they'd left with nothing, not even a spare set of moccasins. They sniffed the air hungrily now, as if the fragrances of venison, rabbit and fowl could heal their wounds by themselves.

Tehoren, smug and defiant, leaned against Andiora's longhouse. Four warriors stood around him: Jix, Iman, Anenki and Calo. Bows hung from their belts, quivers of arrows from their shoulders. Each wore his best beaded shirt. Diamonds of red, blue and white glimmered across their chests.

Andiora suddenly felt very tired.

"Andiora? Andiora, are you listening to me?" Pierre asked.

"I am sorry, Pierre. What did you say?"

He thrust his chin forward pugnaciously and looked hotly at Marc, then lowered his eyes, dropped a finger to the dirt and drew a series of interlocking circles. "I was asking, Andiora, what your intentions are . . . with Dupre. Do you want to marry him?"

"No, Pierre. He needs his God."

"He's told you this?" Pierre asked, too eagerly. Seeing the hurt on her face, he gently added, "When I was speaking to Jean, he said that Dupre would be going south to the Neutral villages for a month or so, and that he wouldn't know Dupre's decision 'til that time was up. Has Dupre already told you for certain that he's chosen his God over you and your child?"

Andiora studied the indigo shadows of the forest. A cold waste expanded in her soul, threatening to gobble up her life. "No, he has not told me for certain, Pierre. He asked me to wait." She twined her fingers in her lap. "But I think I know his soul."

The lines around Pierre's eyes deepened. "Are you just preparing yourself for the worst?"

She shrugged.

Conversations had risen around them like the tides of the sea; voices rolled over them in waves. Hesitantly, Pierre reached over and took Andiora's right hand and tenderly kissed her fingers.

"Well, Andiora, if Dupre's fool enough to let you go, I'm still here. and I'm . . ." He let out a sharp breath. "I'm more than willing to be raising his child as me own. Think about that—in case things don't work out the way you want them to."

Pierre's voice was so gentle and soothing that it did not seem his at all. Some of the old love she used to feel for him surfaced. "Thank you, Pierre."

He squinted out at the eastern horizon, where the pink rays of the sun impaled the drifting clouds. Birds chirped and twittered in the trees, and the laughter that spread through the hundred people who had gathered in the plaza almost obscured the moans issuing from the sickhouse.

Andiora put a hand on her queasy stomach and took several deep breaths. The morning sickness would pass, she knew, in another moon.

Pierre watched her intently. "Could I fetch you a cup of coffee? You're looking near as bad as I feel."

"I would like some coffee. Thank you, Pierre."

He rose, walked wide around Marc, and went to kneel beside Tristan. He chatted while he filled two cups, then stood and brought them back and handed her one. "This should ease some of the sickness."

"If anything can." She took a tiny sip of the brew and felt better when it warmed her stomach.

A crescent of gold edged over the hills and shone blindingly through the tangle of trees. The sky seemed to expand, shimmering with an opalescent purple fire. The roar of voices died down. People pointed and looked expectantly at Jean.

"Come," Jean called, waving his hands. "Come and fill your bowls!"

People gathered into a pushing, whispering wave, their bowls clutched to their chests. Jean, Marc and Phillipe slid the lids off the huge pots and gestured for people to help themselves. Penchant edged out of the mission to sniff at the rich scents of meat that mixed pleasantly with the damp smells of the forest.

Pierre sipped his coffee and watched Andiora. She was making a deliberate attempt not to follow Dupre with her eyes. He set his cup down and fiddled with it, idly shoving it around the dirt in an irregular square. "I think I'll get us some food, if you could stand some?"

"Yes, thank you."

He went to his pack to pull out two bowls and spoons, then shouldered his way through the milling, laughing crowd to the far pot. Dipping up the ladle, he saw that it was rabbit stew. He dished out two healthy servings. Dupre stood ten feet away, but refused to meet Pierre's gaze. He was speaking quietly to Raimont and Onrea. Disgruntled, Pierre went back to Andiora. "Here you go, darlin'."

Her hand trembled when she took the bowl, and Pierre frowned. Did the pregnancy make her so weak? Or was it just the strain of tending the sick and the lack of sleep? He sat down and began shoveling meat into his mouth, looking at her from the corner of his eye.

From the closest longhouse, four elders filed out. Tehoren and his group of warriors met them and led them to the feast pots. Dressed in fine, pale leathers, they looked like royalty. A hush fell over the plaza. Everyone waited to see what they would do. But as Enda stepped up to fill his bowl, they all knew. He did not look at Jean. Not a single elder graced him with a glance.

"Fools!" Pierre spat. "I still can't believe they'll go through with it."

Andiora put her bowl down. "I don't know. Tehoren has been crazy with grief and hatred."

Jean spoke quietly to Dupre, then put a hand on Raimont's shoulder before striding into the midst of the gathering. He lifted his arms high. "Blessed be the sun," he announced. "Blessed be the Son."

The crowd echoed the blessing, "Praise be to Iouskeha, son of Aataentsic!"

Jean smiled. "My friends," he shouted, "there are those amongst us who have called me a witch and a liar." He spread his arms wide. "You know who these people are. And you know me. All of you. We've worked and lived together for years. You, Antaoin." Jean singled out one of the tribal elders, a withered old man with a stooped back. "Remember when your father died and I came to grieve with you? He was such a good and generous man. He never cared a moment for himself, always thinking only of others. We wept for three days, you and I. Wept and prayed to God, begging that your wife and children would be left unharmed by the disease. I see them sitting beside you there." Jean bowed his head. "Praise be to God."

People around the plaza stared at Antaoin. The man clamped his jaw tight and looked at the ground, refusing to meet anyone's eyes.

Jean addressed another elder, a woman with thin gray braids, one of the female powers of the tribe. "And you, Dyslanta. Remember when we treated your granddaughter's sickness? Everyone thought she was dying, and no one would come close to her for fear that the evil Spirits that had possessed her would hurt them." His voice lowered when he saw tears well in the old woman's eyes. "Remember how I carried her from Ossossane to Ihonatiria, bringing her home to her family?"

The old woman nodded.

"She wasn't so very heavy. God gave me the strength."

Jean's eyes came to rest on a very old shaman, undoubtedly one of his accusers. The man squirmed uncomfortably. "And you, Tenosheaton? Remember when you wanted a pair of boots like mine so badly that you couldn't sleep for a week?" He laughed affectionately. "I see you still have the ones I took off my own feet that day. I'm glad. It made me happy to give them to you."

Jean's smile faded. "I'm no witch. Nor are any of my brothers witches. You all *know* that. Those who accuse us are desperate men trying to find a cause for the terrible sickness that's killing our people. They're not bad men—just men worried so terribly that they aren't thinking right. I know that."

Pierre found himself waiting breathlessly. All around the plaza, faces had gone slack, eyes wide. No one moved.

"I'm not the cause of the disease. I wish I were. That way we could end the epidemic today, with my death." He took a deep breath. "I'm not afraid to die. I know my path leads to heaven. And yours, Thinosta and Rylao, and yours, Ocanta and Mylasa. And all the other Christians here. I will see you there. If God will let me, I will welcome each of you at the gates of Paradise."

He turned to the elders standing by Tehoren's group of warriors, and faced them directly, studying their downcast faces. "Enda? Tehoren?" Neither raised his head. "I'll be waiting for you at the edge of the village. Be merciful. Come quickly." Jean turned and walked slowly through the crowd, touching people tenderly as he passed, speaking a few final words to those who met his eyes. Then he vanished among the trees beyond the plaza.

Pierre whispered to Andiora, "The man's been wielding words for so long he's become eloquent."

Andiora ignored him. She got to her feet and lifted her hands high. All eyes turned toward her. Silence gripped the plaza. She stood tall, slender, her hair blowing in the chill morning breeze. Behind her, the sun blazed like a golden torch.

"My people," Andiora said in a ringing voice, "we have all lost family in this sickness. We have wept together often in these past weeks. You know my love for you. But today I am ashamed. *Ashamed!* You accuse innocent men of sorcery!" She shifted to glare at Tehoren. The pug-nosed shaman stiffened. His warriors crowded closer around him. "If you do this thing, I want it known now that I will leave this village and never return!"

Andiora walked across the plaza like a pale ghost and ducked into her longhouse.

People shouted and wrung their hands. Onrea wept. She ran for the longhouse behind Andiora. Tehoren slammed a fist into the longhouse wall. Pierre grinned. Andiora was a respected woman. She had shamed Tehoren, made him look petty and vengeful. But would it force Tehoren to back off his charges? Or just make him all the more want to take his frustrations out on Jean?

Pierre rose and shouted. "I want to speak!" An ominous buzz filled the plaza. "I've already told Tehoren what will happen if you kill any of the Black Robes. He doesn't care. But maybe some of the rest of you will. Montmagny will stop trading with you. Are you yearning so much to see your people poor?" He waved an arm at the crowd. "What will you do when you can't get more blankets or iron axes, arrowheads or pots? No more dried peas. Worse, Montmagny will threaten all the surrounding tribes. He'll tell them that if they're trading with you, the French won't buy from them either. Think! You ran out of beaver a year ago. You have to trade for most of your furs. Where will you get plews if no other tribe will deal with you?"

"We'll take otter to the Dutch," Tehoren declared hotly.

Mongrave laughed. "Will you now? And how do you plan on getting there? Will you just prance through the middle of Mohawk territory? You *are* brave—or a fool."

Rage twisted Tehoren's face, but he stayed still, as though riveted to the dirt.

"Eh?" Mongrave yelled. "Without trade, you'll starve. The Iroquois have already taken to the warpath. When you're starving and poor, they'll steal your women and kill your warriors. Do you want that?"

No one answered, but people began exchanging knowing looks and soft, anxious mutters. He waited, letting the tension build.

"You want the Huron dead, Tehoren? Enda? Well, then, go ahead. Kill Brebeuf!"

Pierre strode to the trees, grabbed his rolled blanket and walked down the path Jean had taken.

Gulls wheeled, squawking, over the treetops. In the northern distance, snow fell in a gray sheet, obscuring the tops of hills. A roiling bank of blue-black clouds edged closer by the second. Pierre found Jean kneeling beneath a maple: far enough away that he could barely hear the noise in the plaza, but close enough that he could still see the goings-on. His eyes were cast heavenward.

Pierre halted and asked, "I assume you'll be sitting here until they come?"

"Can't you see that I'm talking to God, Pierre?"

"Well, forget it. He hasn't helped you so far, has He?" Pierre gruffly threw his blanket at Jean's feet. "There's a storm coming in. The blanket should keep you warm enough."

Then Pierre sank to the ground beside Jean, bracing his back against the maple. He pulled his boot flask out, took a long swig and handed it to Jean. "Drink some of this. It'll calm you."

Jean sighed in exasperation. "Being able to talk to God—alone— would calm me a lot more." He squinted at the flask. "Besides, I don't drink anything that hasn't been blessed."

"Well, say some mumbo jumbo over it and let's get on with it."

"Are you planning on waiting with me? It's too dangerous."

Pierre worked his shoulders against the tree and gazed upward. In the sky, hawks dove, chasing each other, playing, ignoring the nearby gulls. He lifted his flask to the rising sun, swirled the contents and took a sip. His stomach knotted—and so he took another to ease it.

Jean grudgingly rose from his knees, sat down next to Pierre and extended his long legs in front of him. He looked old beyond his years; his hair seemed suddenly thinner, his skin more deeply wrinkled. "I don't want you to stay with me, Pierre. I left the plaza specifically to give Tehoren an opportunity to kill me—and me alone."

Pierre tipped the flask to his lips again. The rum burned its way down his throat, lighting a fire in his belly. "Just the same, I'm staying."

"You're being foolish."

"Aye, well, 'tis nothing new." Pierre frowned at the plaza. "You know," he said, "if you happen to live through this, you could make a good living back in France as a *colporteur*. You know, selling religious books and such. Why, with your knowledge of the church—"

"I prefer to die here, thank you."

"Be realistic. You've been selling sin for years. You ought to be able to sell anything."

"I've been selling redemption!"

"You think people come to you because they want to be saved? Bah. They come to you out of guilt, hoping you'll tell them it's all right that they're fools and cowards."

Jean fumbled with his crucifix. "No one should have to face guilt alone, Pierre. Not even you, or me."

Pierre saw Jean's expression change, and sighed knowingly. "Confession time? Well, I'll listen." He took another healthy swig of rum to prepare himself. "Go on. Tell me."

Jean arched a brow. "I hardly think you're qualified."

"I've been baptized!"

"But the Lord revoked it years ago."

Pierre scratched his beard and grinned. "Let me guess. You ravished young women before taking your vows?" When Jean merely scowled, Pierre pressed, "Oh, tell me, will you? I've always hoped that beneath all that righteousness lay a man."

"Shall I lift my robe and prove it to you?"

"God forbid." Mongrave squinted with mock disgust and crossed himself. "Well, then you murdered someone."

Jean closed his eyes.

"Did you?" Pierre asked. "They probably deserved it, so stop worrying about it."

Jean opened one eye. "Why, thank you, Father Mongrave."

Pierre laughed and lifted his flask again, then halted. "Are you sure you won't have some of this? It'll take the edge off your fears."

Jean pushed the flask away. "Only God can do that, Pierre. But it looks like I'm stuck with you. Well, it's probably penance I need. Go ahead. Keep talking to me."

Pierre opened his mouth, but a curse came out as icy drops of rain began to spot his leather shirt and sparkle like diamonds in Jean's beard and hair. The wall of indigo clouds had reached the edge of the village, though the sun still sat bright and gaudy on the eastern horizon.

"For the sake of God, Jean!" Pierre growled. "Couldn't you have chosen another day for your Death Feast? We're going to get soaked out here!"

Thunder rolled over the hills like the quaking fist of God. Then, as if disembodied Spirits rode the shoulders of the storm, a low keening began, mournful, angry. The wind rifled through the forest like a hungry beast. The leading edge of the storm struck. It raged across Lake Karegnondi, battering the trees and longhouses, kicking up plumes of dust in the plaza. People shouted as they ran for shelter. Pierre covered his head.

Jean gasped and bent forward, as though pierced in the breast. He folded his arms and hugged himself. "Oh . . . Lord, no. Not now."

Pierre grabbed his arm. "What's wrong?"

Jean shook his head violently. "Don't you *feel* Him?"

39

Phillipe ate another spoonful of venison and watched the huge drops of rain splat on the dirt. He turned to smile at Marc and Luc, who were eating stew on either side of him. They sat with their backs against the front of the mission. The long shadow thrown by the white cross stretched across the plaza, landing like a dark scarf over the faces of the Indians sheltering in the lee of a longhouse.

Marc had barely touched his food. He looked unhappy and confused. Phillipe reached out and touched his forearm gently. "I love you."

Marc looked up. For a moment his blue eyes seemed to blaze; then he blinked the harshness away. "I love you, too, Phillipe. You're my best friend."

"No," Phillipe corrected. "Our Lord is. He loves you very much, Marc." He took another bite of stew, filling his mouth so full that he couldn't quite close it. A trickle of juice ran down his chin and he tipped his head back to keep the rest inside while he chewed.

Marc shook his head. "Here, let me help you, Brother." He mopped Phillipe's chin with the sleeve of his black robe.

Phillipe's jaw suddenly went slack as the world spun out of control for a moment. He reached for Marc's shoulder. The spoon fell out of his hand into the dirt.

Marc grabbed his hand. "Phillipe? Are you all right?"

Phillipe cocked his head. Clouds tumbled over the land, so low that they scraped the hilltops. The gale blasted the village, and Phillipe let out a small cry and threw up his arm to shield his eyes.

Ashes scattered from the fire and blew this way and that over the ground. The pots hanging on their tripods swung and clanked . . .

And Phillipe knew.

God came with the storm. From nowhere, everywhere, Phillipe heard angels singing. Their melody swam in the gale, high and sweet. He heard them in the clattering of the tree branches and felt their gentle hands in the fingers of wind that whistled around the mission. But he couldn't make out what they were saying to him.

"*What?*" he called. "I can't hear you!"

Luc struggled to stand, but the force of the wind shoved him back down. "Good heavens!" he yelled. "Where did this come from?"

"God!" Phillipe said certainly. "It's God's storm!"

"Come on!" Marc urged. "We must get inside."

He grabbed Phillipe's arm and pulled him to his feet. Marc stood like a fortress against the storm, bracing a hand against the wall as he shoved Phillipe ahead of him toward the mission door. Luc crawled on his knees and groped for the latch, his eyes half-closed against the stinging windborne grit.

Father Jean and Monsieur Mongrave stumbled across the far end of the plaza toward the mission. And Phillipe saw Tehoren, too, hunched beneath a tree near Andiora's longhouse. Almost everyone else had taken shelter. Tehoren's four warriors stood in a semicircle around him, holding on to branches to keep standing. As Father Jean neared them, Tehoren lifted a fist and sliced the air. A horrifying war cry rent the day, ululating over the plaza. Jix fell to his knees and drew his bow.

Phillipe's heart froze. A scream of "*No!*" tore from his throat.

He broke free from Marc's grip and ran out into the plaza, staggering in the wind, trying to reach Tehoren to stop him.

"Phillipe?" Father Jean shouted. "No, go back!"

Mongrave shoved Father Jean to the ground and jerked out his pistol . . . and Phillipe thought he heard Marc screaming at him . . . but the singing of the angels grew louder, so loud that Phillipe could feel their voices throbbing in his chest. The hand of God lifted his chin and forced him to gaze out into the forest.

Rapture filled Phillipe, wonderful and terrible. He lifted his arms and turned around and around, letting God flow into him like a great torrent. Every nerve in Phillipe's body sizzled with God.

And from far away he heard a faint voice calling, *Phillipe, Phillipe?*

"Roah? Roah, where are you?" he yelled and searched the roiling heavens. "Roah, I'm here! Over here!"

A growl echoed through the village.

Phillipe turned. His Lord came loping through the forest, His golden coat gleaming with beads of rain. "You've come! You've *come!*" Phillipe wept and held out his hands.

Luc shouted, "Oh, dear God, there it is! Tehoren, you fool! If there's an *oki*, it's that animal. Kill it!"

Tehoren and his warriors stood paralyzed at the sight of the cougar, their bows lowered.

Suddenly Tehoren shrieked, "He's called his demon to help him!"

The warriors let fly. Arrows sailed toward the cougar, their beautiful feather fletchings gleaming. They landed, and Phillipe's Lord fell sideways, snarling and kicking.

Three of the warriors nocked arrows and rushed to stand over the cougar.

Jix yelled, "Hurry! We must kill the *oki* to take Raimont's Power!"

Phillipe ran so hard that he thought his heart would burst. "Don't hurt him!" he cried. "He's come to save the world! He never hurt anyone! Please, *please*, don't hurt him!"

Father Jean shouted, "Phillipe, stop! Don't go any closer!" Then, in Huron, he screamed at Tehoren, "Don't shoot! He doesn't know what he's doing!" and, "Marc! Stay back. *Obey me!*"

From the corner of his eye, Phillipe saw Marc hesitate, then charge forward, screaming, "Tehoren, don't!"

The cougar squirmed to look at Phillipe, its huge paws clawing at the earth. A deep-throated groan rent the air. His Lord was pleading with him for help!

"No! Tehoren, stop! *Please, please* . . ."

Tehoren raised a fist, his eyes wide and haunted. "Get away!"

"Leave him alone. He won't hurt you!"

Jix shouted, "Kill it. Hurry!" In a swift motion Jix jerked his knife from his belt and plunged it into the cougar's neck. The animal struggled violently and turned toward Phillipe.

Again and again Jix stabbed until the cougar ceased to writhe and its golden head thudded dully on the ground. Phillipe ran forward, screaming incoherently . . .

. . . and he felt the moment his Lord's Passion poured into him. It entered his veins in a divine flood of light. Phillipe staggered when blood spurted from his hands and feet and rushed in a hot river down his side.

Tehoren's face contorted. "It's *him*! I knew it! The one in Andiora's dream!" His upraised fist wavered, trembling, before it slashed down.

Jix let his arrow fly into Phillipe's chest. Arching forward, Phillipe tumbled atop the dying Lion of God. The cougar's blood smeared his robe as he clutched the golden fur and laid his cheek against his Savior's.

"Witch!" Jix shrieked. He sent another arrow, this one into Phillipe's side. "You killed my children!"

Wonderingly, Phillipe brushed at the bright feathers. Another *thock-hiss* sounded as the third arrow pierced his stomach. The sharp stone point sliced through him, and he writhed in pain. The force of the shot made him roll sideways, off of the Lion of God.

Phillipe blinked at Tehoren. The shaman's eyes gleamed with hatred and fear. "It's all right," Phillipe said thickly. Blood bubbled up in his throat. "God knows . . . you didn't mean . . ."

Darkness swallowed the edges of Phillipe's vision. How would he find his Lord in the coming night? Frantically, he patted the ground for the cougar's paw, and clutched it tightly.

Peace filled him. He felt no pain, only a tightness in his chest and a sensation of floating. Phillipe let himself go, willing his soul to God . . .

. . . and he found himself back in the Cathedral of Notre Dame. Afternoon light streamed through the rose window, splashing the floor with red and blue geometric designs. The rich smell of incense wafted on the warm air. Joy touched him; he turned and saw Henri. The old dog had his ears pricked, his gray head cocked, and was wagging his tail happily. Then he barked and bounded forward. Phillipe sat down on the cool stone floor and hugged Henri to his chest, kissing that old gray muzzle desperately . . .

"Oh, dear God," Marc cried as his steps faltered. He fell on his knees beside Phillipe and gathered the little Brother in his arms. Wind blasted him, shoving him sideways.

Tehoren wet his lips and backed away into the trees. "It's finished now," he said. "The sickness will end."

"No it won't!" Marc yelled. "It won't stop. Phillipe wasn't to blame!"

"You Black Robes all lie! We know—" Tehoren paled when flutters of white began coming down from the clouds, falling all around him. "What—"

Birds! Hundreds of them. Flying in with the storm.

Tehoren gaped at the flock as they swarmed through the plaza, tumbling in the wind, trying to find a place to land. Then Tehoren screamed, "*Okis!* Hundreds of them!"

He grabbed Jix's bow and let fly with an arrow. The other warriors began firing. A bird shrieked in pain and thumped the ground, flopping, one wing pierced by an arrow. Two more birds fell to the earth at Phillipe's feet.

"You fools!" Mongrave shouted. "The birds get caught up in the winds and carried for miles! I've seen it a dozen times at sea. There's nothing supernatural about it!"

His chest heaving, Tehoren scanned the billowing clouds, then eyed Mongrave and Jean as they ran across the plaza. "It is *finished*!" Tehoren repeated. He backed away uneasily and strode for the nearest longhouse. His warriors followed at a trot.

Wounded birds fluttered helplessly across the plaza, their wings beating the ground.

One by one, Marc broke the arrow shafts from Phillipe's body. With each crack of the wood, madness grew in him. Madness so dark he could barely see a pinpoint of light. He rocked Phillipe in his arms. Memories flashed . . . of Marie . . . of carrying her through the streets of La Rochelle praying for God to help them. Running for hours. *No, no, she needs me. I—*

The wind died and trees stopped flailing. The birds in the trees began to preen themselves, and Marc lifted his head.

On the horizon, the black clouds parted. The crimson ball of sun glowed eerily as a sliver of black crept across its face like a thief in the night. The blackness spread. A smoky blue haze fell over the world.

Luc screamed, "Oh, Blessed Jesus! It's happening! The End has come! *The End has come!*"

"'Tis an eclipse!" Mongrave shouted. "I've had it on me ship's calendar for months!"

"No! No, it's the Apocalypse. It's here!"

Mongrave knelt beside Marc and put a hand on Phillipe's neck, testing for a pulse. But Marc knew that Phillipe was gone. Mongrave's fingers slipped down and he bowed his head, heaving a tired, tired breath. Rising without a word, he walked away.

The Huron began coming out of their longhouses. They gasped when they saw the sun.

Behind him, Marc could hear Andiora's muffled sobs. Then Jean crouched beside him, putting an arm around his shoulders. "Marc, let's take him back to the mission."

"No, no, I . . . we . . . we have to stay here with the cougar. We can't . . . Phillipe wouldn't want to leave him. I—"

Softly, Jean said, "There's nothing you could have done, Marc. You helped him in every way you could. God—"

"*God!*" Marc shouted. He glared into Jean's worried eyes and loneliness replaced his rage, loneliness so terrible he could barely stand it. In a tortured voice, he murmured, "God? Where has God been these past few months when people have been dying by the hundreds? Where . . . *where has he been?*" Agony rose to choke him. "Go away, Jean. Leave us alone."

Jean touched Marc's shoulder, rose and walked a short distance away. He spoke softly to Mongrave, but Marc could hear the fear in his voice as more Huron flocked out to gape at the vanishing face of Iouskeha.

Marc stroked Phillipe's bald head and reached down to touch the holes in his palms and side. The blood still felt warm. In Phillipe's wide, dead eyes, only love shone. No fear. No hatred.

"Marc?" Andiora knelt beside him.

"Oh, Andiora. Hold me." He turned to bury his face in her hair and weep.

*   *   *

LUC HAD RUN to the edge of the village. The sun was *turning as black as sackcloth*! His heart thundered. He could almost hear the Lamb cracking open the sixth seal. He braced himself, waiting for the earthquake and for the moon to turn to blood. Huron gathered around him, shoving him, staring at the miracle on the horizon.

"*Get back!*" he shouted at them. "The great day of the Lord's wrath has come! Do you hear me, you filthy demon worshipers? None of you will be able to stand. He's come, and you'll all be damned to hell!"

Luc drew himself up and spread wide his arms to heaven. He stood rigid, his robe flapping around his legs, until the sun vanished and a midnight hole gouged the sky. The forest went quiet. Not a breath of wind stirred through the branches.

The Indians screamed and covered their faces. Some ran away to hide in the longhouses. But Luc boldly stared into the last moments of Creation. Righteousness filled him to bursting. He started praying at the top of his lungs; "Our Father who art in heaven, hallowed be thy name, thy Kingdom come.. . .."

Luc blinked.

A crescent of gold emerged from the other side of the sun. The black shroud slipped away, crossing the face of the orb like the wave of a dark hand. Luc's arms started to shake.

"No. No, Lord! Why aren't You rolling up the heavens like a scroll? What's happening? Where are You, Lord!"

On the other side of the plaza, he could hear Dupre's strained voice echoing his own, "*Where are you, Lord? Where are you . . .*"

CHAPTER

40

P ierre stood outside Andiora's longhouse watching her grind corn. The kernels nestled in the base of a hollowed-out log. Andiora pounded them with a long, thick stick. The *thunk! thunk!* of her labor resonated through the village. Two old women sat drying fish in the shade of a nearby spruce. Onrea and three other children played dice with painted stones in the center of the plaza. Their bright giggles eased Pierre's anxiety. Of a village that had numbered one hundred and twenty only months ago, forty people remained.

Andiora tossed another handful of corn into her log. Sweat stood out on her brow and small nose. She wore the new yellow tradecloth dress that Pierre had brought her from Fort Orange. Her belly had started to protrude slightly. Her hair had filled out in the past six weeks and lay in a luxurious blue-black wave down her back. Her dark eyes kept straying to the path that led south.

Pierre turned his untouched cup of spruce tea in his hands. "He's coming, darlin'. Don't be fretting."

Andiora gave him a warm look, but he could see how tight the lines around her mouth had drawn. Tristan had come in that morning from a short trading jaunt south and said that he'd passed Dupre and Antoine Daniel just outside of Ossossane. Unless something terrible befell them, they would arrive by nightfall.

Pierre sipped his tea, relishing the pungent, citrusy flavor. He and Andiora had made their peace, uneasy though it might be. For he still loved her, and his heart was having a hard time believing that he could never have her. But his head believed it. Andiora had pounded it into him just as ferociously as she now pounded the corn.

† 373 †

"Do you fear he'll have found his God in those spiritual exercises and forgotten you, darlin'?"

"I'll live with whatever his decision is, Pierre." Her rhythm faltered for a moment before she picked it up again. "I just want Marc to be happy."

"You're not an easy woman to forget. Keep that in mind."

The love in her voice when she spoke of Dupre hurt Pierre deep down. He remembered too well when she'd spoken his name that way, when she'd looked at him with those luminous eyes. He drew a design on his cup with his thumb. His white sleeves glistened in the sunlight. Well, he'd made his bed, he might as well learn to sleep in it. He still had the sea and the *Soleil*. God knew, not many men could claim such glorious freedom . . . nor could they face the loneliness of the long, dark nights when the winds did not blow and the crew went mad from boredom.

It was age setting in. No doubt about it. The loneliness had never struck him before. But since losing Andiora, some of the glitter had gone out of the sea. It was almost as though he'd been seeing life through a gilded veil and someone had torn it from his eyes, forcing him to see things rightly for the first time. He'd begun to long for roots that sank deep into the soil, no longer floating like the waving tendrils of jellyfish. He yearned for the laughter of children and the gentle touch of a woman who loved him—the very things he'd taken lightly all his damnable life.

Penchant walked out of the mission and slammed the door. His arms were loaded with belongings. He stalked to the edge of the plaza and dropped them next to the traders' mound, already three feet high. The packs had been ready for two days. Pierre was only waiting on Dupre.

Andiora eyed Penchant grimly. "Has he spoken to you?"

"Not a word. And I've thanked the Lord for the favor. Since his little-boy visions of martyrdom and the End of the World failed to come true, he's not been much of a talker."

Andiora gazed out across the almost empty plaza and murmured, "Wasn't it the End, Pierre?"

She had the same look in her eyes that he'd seen on that cold day when he'd asked her to marry him: the sad resignation of one seeing that endless winter has covered the world and realizing that she will never be warm again.

Her eyes rested on certain places—the front door of her longhouse, the clump of trees to the north, the path that led down to Lake Karegnondi—and Pierre knew that she was seeing Jatoya and Maconta, and the rest of her family who were gone. He felt almost as though he, too, heard Jatoya's brittle cackle on the wind.

Andiora's eyes came back to him, empty and aching. "Many fields will lie fallow this summer because there are not enough hands to tend them. Our best hunters are dead." She shook her head. "This is a widowed land, Pierre. I'm terrified about next winter."

Pierre could find no words with which to answer her.

Rumors had it that only ten thousand Huron had survived the diseases. And if it were so, God, oh God, he knew what the Iroquois would do when they heard. He could imagine them mounting an army of a thousand to attack the scattered villages and wipe the last Huron from earth.

Onrea stood up suddenly in the center of the plaza. "Andiora! He's coming!" she cried as she started running down the trail. The other children followed her.

Andiora didn't move. She stared unblinking after Onrea. Pierre had never seen such fear in her eyes. He extended a hand to her. "Your standing here won't change a thing, darlin'. Best to get it over with."

Andiora wiped trembling hands on her yellow skirt and quietly laid her stick aside. With a deep breath, she took his hand.

They walked in silence to the trail head. The oaks had started to bud out, painting the hills with a faint wash of green. Scents of newborn grass and warming wood filled the forest. Spirals of steam rose from rotting logs where the sunstruck moldy decay.

Pierre let go of her hand and put his arm around her slim shoulders, holding her the way he used to, pretending for a brief instant that nothing had changed between them.

They looked down the trail. Dupre and Antoine Daniel walked up the slope, Dupre a head taller than Antoine; his blond hair contrasted sharply with Antoine's wavy black. Onrea and the other children danced around them, asking questions, laughing.

Antoine lifted a hand and shouted, "Pierre! You haven't changed. You still look like a scoundrel."

"Aye, and I'm planning on staying that way!" he announced.

Dupre's blue eyes found Andiora and never left her. He hiked purposefully up the hill, his black robe billowing out behind him in the spring sunshine. Pierre felt Andiora's shoulder muscles bunch beneath his arm. As Dupre neared, Pierre reluctantly stepped aside.

Andiora stood unmoving. Her chest barely rose and fell. But her black eyes shone like the darkest of jewels. "Hello, Marc."

Dupre stopped in front of her. His gaze went over her beautiful face for several moments before he opened his arms. Andiora stepped into the circle of his warmth and held him.

"I love you," he said softly as he caressed her black hair. "If you still want me—"

"*I want you*," she responded, and clung to him as though he had saved her from oblivion.

Pierre greeted Antoine with a hearty handshake. "You're looking well, Father. How are things to the south?"

Antoine glanced at Dupre and lowered his eyes. "Not well. The sickness this year took a heavy toll. Where's Jean? Is he here? Marc . . . and I . . . need to talk to him."

"Aye. Why don't you and Dupre stow your packs in the mission? I'll go fetch Jean."

JEAN STOOD WITH an arm braced against a maple branch, looking at Phillipe's grave, his chest prickling. A huge cougar lay atop the mound of earth. It's head rested on its crossed paws, and its yellow eyes riveted unblinkingly on Jean. Its golden fur rippled in the warm breeze. A flock of gulls strutted fearlessly through the tender grass around the cougar, fluttering their wings while they searched for insects. And a dove—a single dove, with lavender feathers—cooed mournfully as it wandered among the gulls.

"What are you, Cougar?" he whispered.

The lion merely gazed at him.

In the distance, Lake Karegnondi shimmered blue and vast. He could hear the noise of the waves lapping the beach.

He'd drifted like a sleepwalker through this past month and a half. Days had slipped by when he couldn't even remember waking. He missed Phillipe. Sometimes he swore he could hear the little Brother late at night, padding around the mission, grinding corn, dusting the books.

The twittering of the birds comforted Jean . . . as they must have comforted Phillipe. He lowered his forehead against his arm. So many things had happened, he barely grasped them all. In the depths of his soul, he wondered if the Third Age had not indeed arrived. Somehow, the world had changed with Phillipe's death. Jean's dreams had been violent and strange. In them he heard a child calling his name, over and over. It sounded like a frail little boy's voice, filled with tears.

He almost didn't hear the feet crunching on dry twigs behind him.

Pierre called, "Jean? They're here. Dupre's—" He stopped suddenly when he saw the lion. His hand dropped to his holstered pistol. "What's it doing here?"

Jean gazed into the animal's alert eyes and responded, "Guarding. Protecting. There's no need to be afraid. I've been standing here for two hours and it's made no moves toward me."

Pierre swallowed convulsively. "Aye, well . . . Dupre's waiting for you in the mission. He told Andiora—"

"I know. I think . . . I think I've known all along. I just didn't want to believe it."

Jean turned, briefly met Pierre's black eyes and walked around him, heading down the trail for the village. Pierre's boots pounded along behind him until he caught up and threw Jean a speculative glance.

"Don't be taking it so hard, Brebeuf. 'Tis not as though you failed him. He just found something more important to him than the church."

Jean studied the autumn leaves that still lay clustered, brown and rotting, under the bushes. The songbirds had returned from their long journey south. A symphony filled the trees. "It's not that easy, Pierre."

"You mean because his loving Andiora damns him? It does, doesn't it? In the eyes of your church."

"God can forgive anything, Pierre. But it has always been a difficulty. Pope Gregory the Seventh forbade married men to be ordained and, if ordained, forbade them to exercise their priestly functions. The Council of Trent made it clear that if clerics in sacred orders married, the marriage was invalid."

"So, every day he'll be committing the sin of fornication. He won't be able to receive communion again—not ever."

"Unless he repents and reconciles himself to God. And I believe he will—someday." Jean stopped and looked down over Ihonatiria. "It's the time in between that frightens me."

Children raced through the plaza, dogs nipping at their heels. Marc stood in front of the mission with his arms around Andiora as though he would never let her go. Her pregnancy was obvious now. She'd been attending Mass faithfully, and her confessions brimmed with fears for Marc and what her love might do to him.

"What do you mean? The time in between?" Pierre pressed.

"How does a man . . ." Jean gazed heavenward. The presence of God filled the day, flowing through the air, riding the light, like the blood of the world. The sky had been swept clean of all but a few puffs of clouds. They glowed with the palest of golds as they sailed lazily westward. "It's hard to explain." Jean bowed his head. "Marc has parted the darkness with his hands . . . he's looked nakedly upon the brilliant eye of God. I fear he'll spend the rest of his life fighting to forget what that felt like."

Pierre looked at him pensively, his face dark and inscrutable. His white shirt reflected the sunlight with blinding intensity. "Are you all right, Jean?"

Jean shrugged. "I haven't been sleeping well. I just need some rest."

"You ought to be getting out of this priesting business, too, Jean. I'm planning on offering Dupre a job in me company—as a regional trader. I might have a place for you, if you decide you want to work for a living."

"As a *colporteur*?" Jean asked sharply.

Pierre grinned. "I was thinking more on the lines of a bookkeeper, or—"

"No. But thanks anyway."

"Well, think about it. I'll leave the offer open."

Jean smiled. Above them, a hawk cried and they both looked up to watch it dive over the trees. "You know, Pierre, I have the uncomfortable feeling that I may like you after all."

Without waiting for a response, Jean started down the trail. Sunlight falling through the trees wove a golden spiderweb across the hills around him.

HISTORICAL AFTERWORD

Most of the major characters in this story are fictional: Marc Dupre, Luc Penchant, Phillipe Raimont, Pierre Mongrave. But several of them are real, or are based on real people.

Andiora was the sister of the powerful leader of the village of Teanaostaiae, Tsondakwa. Her family always opened their house to the Jesuits, even in the worst of the epidemics, sheltering and defending them against charges of witchcraft.

Tehorenhaegnon and Tonneraouanont, who, for the readers' sanity I have called Tehoren and Tonner, were two of the greatest shamans of the Huron confederacy. Tehorenhaegnon considered Brebeuf his archenemy. During the devastating epidemic of 1636–37, he accused Brebeuf of witchcraft and sought divine help on the shores of Nottawasaga Bay. After he spent twelve days of fasting and crying for a vision, the Lake Spirit appeared to him and revealed a cure for the sick: a ritual that involved fanning his patients with a turkey wing and sprinkling them with water. The ritual was performed in one form or another through 1639. Many claimed to have been cured by it.

Tonneraouanont, the dwarf, hunch-backed shaman, died in 1637 after suffering a mysterious accident. He maintained until his death that the Jesuits were sorcerers of the highest order.

Taretande was one of the headmen of Ihonatiria. Fathers Antoine Daniel and Ambrose Davost served in Huron country in 1633–48 and 1633–36 respectively.

Father Jean de Brebeuf is also, of course, historical. A deeply spiritual man, he was graced with visions the entire time he labored in New France. He claimed that Mother Mary came to him in 1640. She appeared with three swords piercing her breast and urged him to be submissive to the will of God. Brebeuf also had frequent visions of Christ and angels, as well as several of the saints. Demons occasionally tormented him. In August of 1637, he reported, ". . . during evening examen of conscience and the litany of the Blessed Virgin, by an actual or an imaginary vision, I seemed to see a vast throng of demons coming toward me in order to devour me . . ."

The priests who braved New France suffered both verbal and physical abuse at the hands of the Huron, who charged that wherever the Black Robes traveled, they carried the disease to "purify the faith" of those they sought to convert. These men were often beaten until near death. They endured, for they believed that saving souls was worth whatever sufferings might be inflicted upon them.

Jean de Brebeuf suffered greatly. On March 15, 1649, he and newly arrived Father Gabriel Lalemant were at the village of St. Louis when the cry of "The enemy! The Iroquois!" rang through the longhouses. Etienne Annaotaha, a famous Huron Christian warrior, pleaded with Brebeuf and Lalemant to leave. "My brothers, save yourselves! Go now, while there is time."

Brebeuf told Annaotaha that those fighting would need him and Lalemant. The Huron warriors took their places atop the palisade walls that surrounded the village and prepared themselves for the attack. It came like the roar of thunder. The Iroquois burst from the forests, shrieking and firing their bows and muskets. Brebeuf and Lalemant rushed through the village baptizing and absolving.

The Huron fended off the first attack, and drove the Iroquois back into the cover of the trees. When one Huron brave suggested to Annaotaha that they flee, he said, "What do you mean? Do you ask us to save our lives and abandon the Black Robes? They were not afraid to sacrifice their lives for us. Their love for us will cause their death. We might escape, but there is no time left for them to flee across the snow. Let us die with them. Let us go in company with them to heaven."

The Huron repulsed the second assault, but the third penetrated the palisades and the Iroquois raced through the village, killing the old and the sick. They captured sixty, Brebeuf and Lalemant among them. After running with the other captives for three miles, Brebeuf and Lalemant were stripped naked and fed to build up their strength. They lifted their hands to absolve each other, for they knew what was coming.

The Iroquois forced Brebeuf and Lalemant to run the fiery gauntlet through the longhouse, then broke their hands and held them in the fire. As Brebeuf and Lalemant watched, the Iroquois ate the cooked flesh from their fingers.

Brebeuf did not move or cry out.

The Iroquois tied them to posts and built fires at their feet. Brebeuf said only, "*Jesus, taiteur!*" Jesus, have mercy. When his tormentors draped six fiery hatchet heads around his neck, Brebeuf pulled himself up and gazed at Lalemant and the Huron captives. "My sons, my brothers, let us lift up our eyes to heaven in our afflictions," he called. "Let us remember that God is the witness of our sufferings, that very soon He will be our exceedingly great reward. Let us die in our Faith. . . . Bear up with courage under the few remaining torments. The sufferings will end with our lives. The grandeur which follows them will never have an end."

The Iroquois heated pots of boiling water that they poured over Brebeuf in a blasphemous mockery of baptism while shouting, "*Echon, we baptize you so that you may be happy in heaven. You know that you cannot be saved by your god without proper baptism.*"

They cut out his tongue and blinded him. Then, finally, when he could no longer stand, they dragged him outside into the light of the sun. While he was still alive, they began dividing his body for their feast. One brave hacked off Brebeuf's charred feet. Another scalped him. Finally, while the Iroquois danced and sang, one of the chiefs thrust his knife into Brebeuf's chest and tore out his living heart.

Pope Pius XI canonized Jean de Brebeuf in 1930.

SELECTED BIBLIOGRAPHY

Barthel, Manfred. *The Jesuits. History and Legend of the Society of Jesus*. New York: William Morrow, 1984.

Baudet, Henri. *Paradise on Earth. Some Thoughts on European Images of Non–European Man*. Middletown, Conn.: Wesleyan University Press, 1988.

Cohn, Norman. *The Pursuit of the Millennium*. Oxford: Oxford University Press, 1970.

Columbus, Christopher. *The Libros de las Profecias*. Gainesville: University of Florida Press, 1992.

Eccles, William J. *The Canadian Frontier, 1534–1760*. New York: Holt, Rinehart and Winston, 1969.

Eliot, J.H. *The Old World and the New, 1492–1650*. Cambridge: Cambridge University Press, 1988.

Hardon, John A. *The Catholic Catechism. A Contemporary Catechism of the Teachings of the Catholic Church*. New York: Doubleday, 1975.

Jacobs, Wilbur R. *Dispossessing the American Indian. Indians and Whites on the Colonial Frontier*. Norman: University of Oklahoma Press, 1972.

Jane, Cecil, tr. *The Journal of Christopher Columbus*. London: The Hakluyt Society, 1960.

Jennings, Francis. *The Invasion of America. Indians, Colonialism, and the Cant of Conquest*. New York: W.W. Norton, 1976.

Lescarbot, Marc. *The History of New France*. Toronto: The Champlain Society, 1907. Vols. 1–3.

Moore, James T. *Indian and Jesuit. A Seventeenth Century Encounter*. Chicago: Loyola University Press, 1982.

Ott, Ludwig. *Fundamentals of Catholic Dogma*. Rockford, Ill.: TAN Books and Publishers, 1974.

Phelan, John Leddy. *The Millennial Kingdom of the Franciscans in the New World*. Los Angeles: University of California Press, 1970.

Reeves, Marjorie, and Gould, Warwick. *Joachim of Fiore and the Myth of the Eternal Evangel*. Oxford: Clarendon Press, 1987.

Sale, Kirkpatrick. *The Conquest of Paradise. Christopher Columbus and the Columbian Legacy*. New York: Penguin Books, 1991.

Talbot, Francis Xavier, S.J. *Saint Among the Hurons. The Life of Jean de Brebeuf*. New York: Harper & Bros., 1949.

Trigger, Bruce G. *The Children of Aataentsic. A History of the Huron People to 1660*. Montreal: McGill-Queen's University Press, 1987.